P9-DLO-964

WINTER WOOD

You have been granted three wishes.
The Various was but the first,
Celandine the second.
Now, all will be fulfilled as you enter
Winter Wood . . .

Also available by Steve Augarde:

THE VARIOUS
Winner of the Smarties Bronze Award

'A children's classic'
Sunday Telegraph

'The narrative pace never falters, the writer so
confident and respectful of his creation that the
reader is drawn gladly into the enchantment'
Guardian

CELANDINE

'A wonderful tale about coming of age . . .
Steve Augarde lures the reader right in, making
it impossible to read without empathising with
the main character'
Writeaway!

WINTER WOOD

Steve Augarde

David Fickling Books

OXFORD · NEW YORK

A DAVID FICKLING BOOK

This is a work of fiction. Names, characters, places, and incidents either are the product of the author's imagination or are used fictitiously. Any resemblance to actual persons, living or dead, events, or locales is entirely coincidental.

Copyright © 2008 by Steve Augarde

All rights reserved. Published in the United States by David Fickling Books, an imprint of Random House Children's Books, a division of Random House, Inc., New York.

Originally published in hardcover in Great Britain by David Fickling Books, an imprint of Random House Children's Books, a division of the Random House Group Ltd., in 2008.

David Fickling Books and the colophon are trademarks of David Fickling.

Visit us on the Web! www.randomhouse.com/kids

Educators and librarians, for a variety of teaching tools, visit us at www.randomhouse.com/teachers

Library of Congress Cataloging-in-Publication Data

Augarde, Steve.
Winter wood / Steve Augarde.—1st American ed.
p. cm.
Summary: In Somerset, England, on her family's farm, Midge has the duty of finding a lost artifact that will help the warring tribes of the Various—little people that only Midge can see—return to their homeland, but in order to accomplish this, she must first find her great-great-aunt Celandine, who also spent time with the Various as a child.

ISBN 978-0-385-75074-5 (trade) ISBN 978-0-385-75075-2 (lib. bdg.)
ISBN 978-0-375-85357-9 (e-book)

[1. Fairies—Fiction. 2. Supernatural—Fiction. 3. Great-aunts—Fiction. 4. Farm life—England—Somerset—Fiction. 5. Somerset (England)—Fiction. 6. England—Fiction.] I. Title.

PZ7.A9125Wi 2009
[Fic]—dc22
2008018428

Printed in the United States of America

May 2009

10 9 8 7 6 5 4 3 2 1

First American Edition

Random House Children's Books supports the First Amendment and celebrates the right to read.

To Bella and David, with thanks.
And relief.

Howard Family Tree

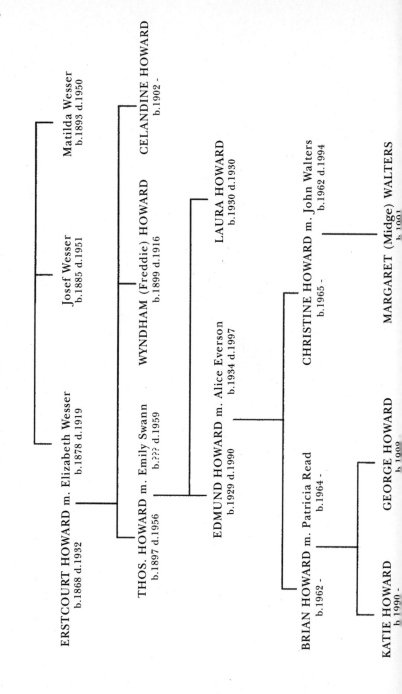

PART ONE

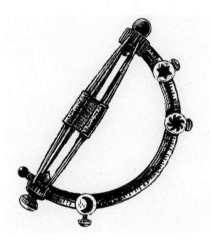

Chapter One

The tip of the bright orange float bobbed just once, no more than a twitch, a tiny bird-peck of movement, but it was enough to send a ripple circling over the water – and a jolt of excitement through George's heart. He leaned forward, gripping the butt of the rod in his left hand, willing the float to go under properly and for good. Come on . . . come *on* . . . I know you're down there, you old monster . . .

He turned the handle of the wooden reel, keeping it smooth and steady, winding in the line until most of the slack had been taken up.

Nothing more happened. The float drifted around the slowly eddying pool at the side of the weir, but remained stubbornly upon the surface.

Eventually George had to blink. He let out a little more line and allowed himself to fall back into his original dreamy trance, lost in the hypnotic roar of the weir beneath him and the strange chattering sounds that seemed hidden away in the background some-where, like faraway voices.

The constant flow of water made him want to pee

again, but he couldn't be bothered to move. He just sat on the planks, swinging his legs to and fro. Each time the float approached the main current it seemed certain to be whisked away downstream, but then it was somehow repelled, forced back towards the bank to begin its cycle once more.

George was happy to watch and wait. He resisted the temptation to interfere. This was still the best place. Down there among those tall reeds . . . that's where Old Whitey would be, if he were anywhere, silent and massive in his winter lair, biding his time. Old Whitey . . .

So old, they said, that the pigment had faded from his leathery skin and turned him into an albino. So old that he was half blind. Yes, and that could be the trouble. Pike would take just about any bait, but they had to be able to see it in the first place, surely? Maybe a bit of gristle left over from the Sunday lunch just wasn't visible enough. Maybe it was time to try the spinner after all.

George shook himself out of his reverie, and began to rummage about in the ancient canvas bag that sat next to him on the plank. The leather straps were thin and frayed, and the brass buckles were all crusty with green stuff – too far gone to be cleaned up, George thought, even if he had the inclination to try. He liked the bag, though, and he liked the rod and reel too. In the flat days that followed Christmas it had been fun to help clear out the attic and so come across all this antique fishing gear.

'It's actually a very good make,' his dad had said of

the rod. 'A split-cane Hardy. Expensive, even back in its day. Put that on eBay and you'd get a bob or two for it. And the old reel – a Shakespeare, no less. Beautiful. Worth something now.' George didn't give a hoot what they were worth; he wanted to keep them.

He found what he was looking for, the spoon-shaped spinner with its three rusty hooks, and he held it in the palm of his hand to examine it. The metal was very tarnished, black almost, with age. Maybe he ought to try and give it a polish before using it . . .

'Hiya.'

George turned round and squinted up into the wintry sunshine.

'Oh. Hi, Midge. How're you feeling?'

'OK. Bit better.'

George watched as his cousin began to make her way across the twin planks that spanned the little weir.

'Careful,' he said. 'That one wobbles.'

'Blimey. It does too.' Midge put a steadying hand on one of the big iron stanchions, part of the rusted winding gear that controlled the flow of water over the weir. 'Oh, great,' she said. 'Trust me to find the bit with grease on it.'

She sat down next to George, glanced at her blackened hand, and wiped it on the worn edge of the plank.

'Hey! I've got to sit there!'

'Sorry.' Midge rubbed her palms together, in order to spread the dirt around a little. 'Had any luck?'

'Not really,' said George. 'Just one bite. Well, I think

it was a bite. I don't mind, though. Glad to get away for an hour or two, actually.'

'Yeah, I know what you mean.'

Now that Christmas was over the builders were back at Mill Farm, and the air was once again filled with the noise of major conversion work – the clink of scaffolding, the rumble of diggers, stone cutting, wood sawing, cement lorries continuously coming and going. Midge was sure that the headache she'd had all day was from the noise of the builders.

It wasn't so bad for her cousins, George and Katie, who were only visiting their dad for a couple of days, but for Midge the constant racket had become a nightmare. 'It's driving me nuts,' she said. 'I was really excited about it to begin with, but now I just wish they could have left everything how it was. I liked it better that way, in any case.'

'Me too. But then they'd have had to sell the place, and so that'd be no good. Be worth it in the end, I s'pose. Is your room nearly done?'

'Huh. I've given up asking. They keep *saying* it is, but it didn't seem like it to me, last time I looked. And in the meantime I'm still sleeping in with Mum. You've got to be back before dark, by the way. Your dad said to tell you four o'clock at the latest.'

'Oh yeah. Sent you to keep an eye on me, more like. Make sure I hadn't drowned myself, or something.'

Midge didn't reply to that, because it was exactly what her Uncle Brian *had* said: 'Go and make sure George isn't floating face down in the weir, Midge. He's daft enough for it.'

She looked across the patchily flooded wetlands towards Howard's Hill. The shape of it was quite different from this angle, much longer than it appeared from her window back at Mill Farm. The tangled trees that crested the ridge were winter-bare, a stark dense line silhouetted against the pale blue of the January sky. The Royal Forest, she called it. An absolute stillness hung over the place, as though the hill were poised, a tufty-backed creature crouching on the landscape, waiting. No birds circled above it, no breath of air stirred those high distant branches.

Midge turned away and watched George's float for a while. She had found, lately, that she didn't want to think about Howard's Hill very much.

'So how old do you think he is?'

'Who – Old Whitey? Well, Dad says he used to come here and fish for him when he was young. Before he was married to Mum, anyway. He reckons pike can live up to twenty-five years, maybe even more. Somebody down at the pub saw him not long ago, Dad said – Old Whitey. Big as a pig, almost.'

'Hm.' Midge was unconvinced. It sounded like yet another of Uncle Brian's little stories. 'What would you do if you caught it, anyway?'

George laughed. 'Run a mile probably.'

Midge picked at a bit of moss that was growing out of a crack in the ancient planks, and flicked it into the water below. It disappeared into the tumbling foam, lost for ever.

'School next week,' she said.

'Yeah. Hey – stop throwing stuff in the water. You'll scare the fish away.'

'Sorry. Can I have a go? With the rod?'

'OK.' George sighed, but handed the rod to her. He was nice like that, always willing to share whatever he had. 'You don't have to do anything,' he said. 'Just keep an eye on the float.'

'But what if it goes under?' said Midge.

'Give me back the rod, quick. It'd be just my luck for you to catch him, after all the work I've put in.'

'Can I wind the windy thing?'

'The reel. Go on then, just a bit. No . . . the other way. That's right. Whoa . . . that's enough.'

They sat together for a while and said nothing. Midge found her attention straying from the orangey tip of the float. She glanced towards the bramble bushes that tumbled along the far bank. There was something creepy about this place, she decided. Not just the dark waters of the weir, but a feeling that everything around her was drawing a little closer, edging up on her as evening fell. Something watching, and waiting . . .

She was glad when George said, 'I'm bored now. *And* I'm getting cold. Come on, you can wind the reel in if you like, and we'll go back. Just give it a quick tug to make sure there's nothing there.'

'Like this?' Midge swished the rod up into the air, and the float leaped straight out of the water. It dangled and bounced about wildly before wrapping itself around the end of the rod a couple of times.

'Hey – look out!' George ducked away from

her. 'You've got it all tangled up now. Give it here.'

'No, I can do it.' Midge pointed the rod downwards, gave it a little shake, and the float freed itself, tumbling down into the water once more. She began to turn the handle of the reel and wound in the line until the float had almost reached the tip of the rod. Then she handed the whole lot back to George.

'Is it OK?'

'Yeah, it's fine.' George was frowning, but not in an angry way. He looked puzzled.

'Where's the thingy?' said Midge. 'The bait? Isn't there supposed to be something on there for the fish to eat?'

'Yes,' said George, 'there is.' He grabbed at the dancing piece of line and examined it. 'There's supposed to be a blimmin' hook there, as well.'

'Maybe you didn't tie it on right.'

But there were no kinks in the end of the nylon line, as might have been expected if the knot had simply come undone. It was as clean and straight as if it had been cut by a pair of scissors.

'Nothing wrong with my knots,' George said.

'So what's happened to it then?'

'Dunno.' George flicked his hair out of his eyes, and began to dismantle the rod.

It was a good twenty minutes' walk across the squelchy fields to Mill Farm, and in that time the sun had begun to sink behind the looming bulk of Howard's Hill, turning the winter skies above it to orangey pink. There was a lonely feel to the darkening landscape, a

9

sadness at the dying of the day. It had been warm for the time of year, but now Midge felt shivery, and she zipped the collar of her fleece a little closer to her chin.

'Do *you* ever think about it much?' she said.

George didn't reply for a while, but eventually he said, 'No. Not really. Try not to, anyway,' and Midge knew that he'd understood her question. The events of last summer had been so overwhelming that at first they could talk of nothing else, but after a while the memory began to fade, as though none of it had ever truly happened. It was like some weird dream, scary-weird, a dream that you didn't want to remember. And it was easy to forget, what with having so many other things to think about – the move down from London, a new school to cope with, and all the disruption of converting Mill Farm into something different. Something less wonderful than it had been, Midge felt.

She didn't like what was happening, and she wasn't as blissfully happy as she'd imagined she would be. It had seemed such a great idea at the time – moving to the dilapidated old farmhouse with her mum, dividing the property with Uncle Brian, her mum's brother, and turning it into something new and exciting. But it wasn't exciting, it was just a mess. They'd ripped the roofs off the old stables and the cider barn, knocked walls down in the house and changed the shape of the rooms, put in new staircases and smart kitchen units, tarmacked the cobbled yard. Nothing was the same any more. And her mum seemed even more distracted and stressed than when she'd been a musician. She was like a whirlwind, on the go from morning till night, haranguing the builders, nagging at Uncle Brian over this detail or that. It made Midge tired to think about it. Sometimes she wished that they'd just stayed in London.

Trudge trudge trudge. The two of them walked in single file along a rough track between a hedge and the bank of one of the open ditches – or rhynes – that criss-crossed the Somerset wetlands. The track was narrow and the hedge overgrown, so that they occasionally had to duck beneath the branches of the stunted willows that grew along the bank of the rhyne. Not so far to go now. Midge followed automatically in George's footsteps, the clump of her Wellington boots keeping in time with his. And it was no good – there was a stone in one of those boots, niggling at her. She lifted her leg and pulled off the boot, hopping about and trying not to put her foot on the muddy ground. 'Hang on, George . . .' Midge turned the boot upside down, shook it, and then stooped to pull it back on again. George had either not heard her or taken no notice. He was still walking ahead. Midge struggled with the boot, stumbling forward and almost over-balancing. As she did so, she heard a kind of whizzing sound and a *thunk* in the hedge beside her. She peered at the hedge, but could see nothing unusual – just leaves and twigs, a couple of feathers. Weird. It hadn't sounded like an animal, quite. A little surge of panic ran through her. 'George . . . wait for me!'

George turned round, and looked surprised. 'Huh?'

Midge ran to catch him up. 'It's OK,' she said. 'Stone in my boot, that's all.' But she couldn't help glancing over her shoulder.

'Oh, right. Sorry.'

They walked on in silence. Midge looked up again at the shadowy mound of Howard's Hill and at the jumbled barrier of trees and briars that kept the out-side world at bay. They guarded another world within, those thick and thorny brambles, and other existences, secrets beyond all imagining. People lived up there – tribes of little people, wild and extraordinary.

The Various.

But although Midge had met them, and knew their names and could still picture their faces, she could no longer make any of it real somehow. It was too much to carry, too much to cope with. She knew that her cousins felt the same. George had seen the little people, and Katie too – and their lives had been put in real danger – but they seldom spoke about it any more. That terrifying day when Scurl and his archers had actually mounted an attack upon Mill Farm should have been impossible to forget, and yet it was becoming more and more difficult to put the sequence of events into any order.

Why was that? thought Midge. Finding Henty and Little-Marten in the cider barn . . . burying Tojo in the lagoon . . . hiding in terror on top of the wardrobe – all of these things she remembered as though they had happened to someone else. Katie with the water cannon. Scurl's wretched crew being hauled out of the muck under Maglin's stern and unforgiving eye. And

Pegs ... the amazing and wonderful little winged horse ... whose voice spoke to her in soft bursts of colour. She could never forget him, how she had found him, and made him well again, and carried him back to the forest. But it had all become such a blur, such a confusion of vague images, like a film once watched a very long time ago.

Celandine's cup – that was definitely real, thought Midge. It stood on her bedside table. Sometimes she picked it up and looked at it, studying the figures that were engraved upon it, the little people, with Celandine herself standing tall among them, and all of them open-mouthed, singing, singing. The cup had been a gift from Henty, but it was a struggle to say when that had been exactly. Was it before or after the day of the battle? Midge couldn't remember. Perhaps she didn't want to remember. Perhaps she didn't want to remember because whenever she tried to do so another thought would take over – the thought that came to her in the darkness sometimes, and made her reach out to touch her mother's bed for reassurance. There was more to come. There was more for her to do. It wasn't over yet ...

George had stopped to open the gate to the old paddock – the Field of Thistles, as Midge liked to call it. He turned to wait for her, smiling as he pushed his fair hair out of his eyes.

'You OK?'

'Yeah.'

Together they walked down the gently sloping patch of ground towards Mill Farm. A couple of the downstairs lights had already come on, and everything was quiet and peaceful. It looked as though the builders might have knocked off early for a change.

After tea her mum said, 'Come upstairs, Midge. I've got a surprise for you.'

Midge thought that she could guess what it was. She followed Mum up to the landing, and from there towards the door of her old bedroom.

'Ta-da!' Her mum gave the freshly painted door a push, and flicked on the light switch. 'I *made* them finish it today,' she said. 'I told them – "No more excuses. Just get it done." What do you think, though? Isn't it great?'

Midge stepped into the room and looked about her. She wouldn't have recognized it. The heavy swagged curtains, the frilly lampshades and the chintzy matching valances had all gone. Now there was beechwood, and chrome, and a blue bedside lamp that shone softly against the clean white walls and made a starry pattern on the ceiling. A plain blue coverlet on her bed . . . stripped and polished floorboards . . . a creamy sheepskin rug. It was gorgeous – a picture from a catalogue. In fact it looked just like the catalogue that she and her mum had chosen all these things from. Everything new, and perfect. And different . . .

'Oh, it's lovely,' she said. 'Really lovely. Thanks, Mum.'

'Well, you deserve it.' Her mum kissed the top of her head – something Midge actually found quite annoying. 'And I'm sorry that it's taken so long. I'm afraid that everything *does* seem to be taking a bit longer than we'd hoped. Anyway, now you can move in properly. Go and get your clothes and things out of my room and start putting them away. I brought that little silver bowl of yours in and put it on the desk, next to your laptop, but I've left everything else for you to sort out. It's a very *nice* little bowl, by the way. Where did you get it?'

Midge looked across at Celandine's cup, sitting prettily on her new desk.

'Oh ... it was a present,' she said, deliberately vague. 'A friend gave it to me.'

'Really? Who was that – Azzie? It must have cost her parents a fortune. Well, they could afford it, I suppose. Um ... towels. I knew there was something else. I'd better find you some.'

Midge remained in the centre of the room for a few moments after Mum had gone, trying to take it all in. She had so loved it here when she had first come to stay – loved the silly fussiness of it, the daft curtains and the pointless frills. And now it was different and new and modern like everything else. She knew she should be grateful, and she was, but she wished that *something* could just stay the same.

The sheepskin rug didn't appear to be the kind of rug that wanted to be stepped on, at least not by some-one wearing shabby trainers. Midge walked around it and sat on her bed, jiggled up and down on it a couple of times to test the mattress. She looked at Celandine's cup, brilliant in the gentle blue light that shone onto the desk that would also serve as her bedside table. Silver, her mum had said. Silver? How could that be? Midge reached out for the cup – and immediately fumbled it, almost dropped it in fright. There! It had happened again, just like before . . . a snatch of song . . . a chorus of many voices raised in harmony. The little people singing. On and off like a radio . . . just a brief burst of sound inside her head, no time to catch any of the words.

A funny feeling spread about Midge's shoulders, and she turned round. The big old photograph was on the wall behind her. They'd put it in her room, just as she had asked them to. It was beside the new wardrobe, hidden from her view until now. The glass had been cleaned, and the lacquered frame was shiny black, polished. Celandine. That extraordinary-looking girl, gazing down upon her. The decades of kitchen grime and grease had been washed away, and now every detail of the photograph was clear and focused – the pale face, the wicker box, the sombre grandmother clock in the background. Twenty-five past ten. And the hands . . . the hands that held the little bridle. Midge could somehow feel the texture of that bridle, how the leather was smoother on one side than the other. She could hear the faint jingling sound that the three little bells made, and the deep hollow tick of the clock in the background. She knew how chilly the air had been in that little parlour, long ago, when that photograph had been taken, and how tight and uncomfortable that dress. Somehow she just knew. It was almost as though she had been there herself. Such a strange sensation, but she wasn't afraid. There was no need.

Midge waited as her racing heart began to calm itself. She took a deep breath, and let it out slowly. No, this was nothing to be afraid of. It was just a picture. A picture of a girl with wild fair hair, buttoned and booted and pinched and pinned to within an inch of her life. Celandine, her great-great-aunt. A girl who smiled with her mouth because she'd been told to, but whose eyes and thoughts were for ever elsewhere, somewhere far beyond the camera. Dark, dark eyes that looked over the shoulder of the photographer towards . . . what? Howard's Hill? This was one thing that she didn't know.

You're lovely, though, thought Midge. You're the best thing in this room, and you belong here with me. A moment of understanding came to her then – a jump of realization and certainty. This was *your* room, wasn't it? You lived here. You sat here, and slept here, and read your books here, and looked out of this window, just as I do. You lived in this room, didn't you? In this very room . . . where I was born.

The light from the blue lamp glowed softly in the picture glass, and Midge gradually saw that the hazy image of her own puzzled face was also reflected there, a shadow of her ancestor's. A big lump came to her throat, and it was hard to swallow it away. She thought, it's you and me, isn't it? Just the two of us. There's nobody else to help us in this. It's just you and me . . .

She kept staring at the photograph, lost in her own

swirling thoughts, until gradually she felt her shoulders begin to sag, a sense of comfort stealing over her. It would be all right. She shouldn't worry so much. She must just take each day as it came, and do the best she could.

Eventually she heard quick footsteps coming along the landing.

'Towels.' Her mum swept in, a brisk presence, and Midge reluctantly turned away from the photograph.

'Thanks, Mum.'

'Forgot to ask you, darling – how's that headache of yours?'

Midge considered for a moment. 'Gone,' she said.

Chapter Two

'Uncle Brian, what do you actually *know* about Great-aunt Celandine?'

Now that the photograph hung in her room, Midge's curiosity had been rekindled. And after all, there was no reason why she shouldn't ask questions. Celandine was family, wasn't she?

'What do I know about her?' Uncle Brian was making heavy work of filling the new jug kettle. He hadn't realized that there had been no need to take the lid off, and now he was searching for the plastic filter that had popped out and disappeared into the washing-up bowl.

'Um . . . well, not much really. She was my grand-father's younger sister – your great-*great*-aunt. There was always some talk . . . some suggestion . . . oh, this thing is *ridiculous*! Why don't they just keep things simple? OK, that's it – I've had enough. Hang on a minute, Midge . . .'

Midge waited as Uncle Brian put the new kettle to one side and rootled around in the cupboard beneath the sink. He found what he was looking for – the old whistling kettle – filled it at the tap, and plonked it on top of the Rayburn stove. Water glooped out of it and spat up at him from the hotplate.

'There! What could be easier than that? Stick to what you know, I say.'

Midge laughed. She liked the fact that Uncle Brian had resisted too much alteration to his part of the house. The old kitchen had been treated to some double-glazed windows and a fresh coat of paint, but by and large it was still the warm and friendly place that it had always been. The big Welsh dresser remained, and the little travel alarm clock ticked cheerfully away on the top shelf. The picture of Celandine was now in her own room, of course, and the space where it had been was taken up by a new noticeboard – already overcrowded with bills and receipts.

'So.' Uncle Brian reached up for a couple of mugs from the dresser. 'Great-aunt Celandine. Sounds like something from a play, doesn't it?' He made his voice go deep and echoey. '*Great . . . Aunt . . . Celandine.* Yes, there was always the suggestion that she was a bit . . . what's the word? . . . fey, perhaps. Believed in fairies and suchlike. Or so *my* old dad used to say. Tea? It was also said that she was run away with by the gypsies. I'd forgotten about that. Terrible really. It used to be a kind of family threat when your mum and I were kids. "If you don't do so-and-so, then the gypsies'll come for you – just like they did your Great-aunt Celandine." Total nonsense, of course.'

'But what happened to her? Is she still alive?' Midge tried to sound casual.

'Alive? No. Couldn't be. I've got no idea what happened to her. Grew up and moved away, I suppose. The farm was passed down through the sons – the way it usually was in those days. From Great-grandad to Grandad, then to my dad, then to me. Girls . . . well, girls weren't . . .'

'Important?'

Uncle Brian leaned against the sink with his arms folded, and sighed. 'It was all the farm, you see. *That* was what was important – the farm, the land. We've got a few family records in a box somewhere, but it's nearly all connected with business. So many heifers raised. So much grain bought and sold. Nothing much there to do with *people* at all. Very few photos. No letters or anything like that, not that I've ever seen. I really don't know much about those who lived here, let alone those who disappeared. One of 'em was killed in the First World War, I do know that. Some others emigrated – Grandmother's two sisters, I believe. A few of them are buried in the churchyard at Statton, including my mum and dad. Apart from that I'm pretty hazy on family history.'

'Oh.'

The kettle, which had been muttering away to itself for the last half-minute, now began to properly whistle, and Uncle Brian pushed himself away from the sink in order to tend to it.

'Why? Are you interested in that sort of thing?'

'Yeah. Sort of. I'd just like to know.'

Uncle Brian brought milk from the fridge. 'Well, I suppose there would be parish records – births, marriages, deaths, and so on. Might be worth a shot, although if Great-auntie had been buried locally then we'd probably know about it. She'd be over the same churchyard wall as the rest of 'em.'

'But if she'd moved away to London or something then there wouldn't be any records here?'

'Shouldn't think so. And you have to remember that families do lose contact with one another. More so then than now, perhaps. Just a move of twenty or thirty miles in those days might mean that you lost touch with a brother or sister altogether – and especially if you hadn't been that close in the first place. Tell you what' – Uncle Brian placed three big mugs of tea on the kitchen table – 'I could ask at the pub, if you like. There's a couple of old boys down there who know a bit about local history. Easier than going through parish records, and just as likely to turn something up. Take a mug of tea through to Katie, will you? See if you can't get her to buck up a bit. Last day of the holidays and I don't think she's spent more than an hour of it away from the sofa.'

'OK. Thanks, Uncle Brian.' Midge picked up two of the mugs, took a quick sip out of one of them, and wandered through to the sitting room.

'Hiya,' she said.

Her cousin Katie looked up from the magazine she was reading.

'Oh. Hi, Midge. Is that for me? Do you know' – Katie pushed herself into an upright position and held out her hand for the mug of tea – 'I just refuse to *believe* that it's school again tomorrow. It seems like we've only been on holiday for about ten minutes. God, I hate school, don't you? The sooner it's over and done with and I can get down to something *useful,* the better.'

Midge sat beside her cousin on the sofa, and glanced at the open magazine. '*How to tell when he's two-timing you . . .*' she read. 'What do you call useful?' she said.

'Well, something real. Something that matters a bit more than simultaneous equations and . . . and *physics.* God, I hate physics. I'm thinking of becoming a fashion editor, actually.'

'First week back shouldn't be too bad,' said Midge. Then she remembered something. 'We're supposed to be going on a trip, I think, this Friday. Some butterfly farm.'

'Oh, *that.*' Katie didn't sound too impressed. 'We went there in Year Eight. I thought I'd die of boredom.'

Midge stared out of the window of the school coach and watched the winter countryside roll by. The sun was shining, and it was dreamily pleasant to see the light dancing on the watery fields.

She had little or nothing to say to the girl who sat next to her – Kerry Hodge. What a moke. All teeth and adenoids. Kerry Hodge didn't seem to be able to breathe without making a constant gurgling sound – little bubbles of spit that popped and crackled at the corners of her perpetually open mouth.

From the rear seat of the bus came the loud chatter

of those who always occupied that privileged position: Rhona McAllister and her admirers. As a new girl, Midge had not yet achieved back-of-the-bus status. Nor front-of-the-dinner-queue status, for that matter. She was strictly in the middle for everything. It didn't bother her. There was nothing so special about Rhona's circle of buddies, male or female, that Midge felt desperate to be a part of. Most of them seemed a bit thick, really. Turnips. She missed her friend Azzie, quick-thinking, tap-dancing Azzie, who could run circles round this lot, physically and verbally, before they'd have time to blink. And she missed London, the buzz of it, far more than she'd thought she would. Everything was slower here.

There was one girl who was OK, Samantha Lewis. Sometimes she and Sam were paired off in chemistry or physics lessons, and they got on well enough. But Sam was really part of Rhona's crowd, and so that's where she was usually to be found during lunch break, or once school was over.

Break times were the hardest. Midge sometimes sought out one of her cousins, just to have someone to talk to and be with, but as Katie was in the year above and George in the year below this could be a bit awkward. And it was different at school. Katie and George each had their own friends. They weren't very often at Mill Farm during term time, and so she didn't see as much of them as she had expected.

'Shall we work on our ashignment together?'

'What?'

Kerry Hodge had turned to speak to her. Midge felt

a speckle of saliva land on the back of her wrist, and she surreptitiously drew her hand into the sleeve of her blazer in order to wipe it off.

'Er . . . maybe. I think we're supposed to try and do it by ourselves.'

'Mish Oldham saysh we can work in pairsh if we want.' The wretched girl was like a watering can.

'Does she?' Midge was non-committal. She turned back to the window and said no more, hoping that this would be enough to make Kerry take the hint. Ten minutes' conversation with that one and you'd be needing a bath towel. And in any case, she suspected that 'working together' with Kerry would simply mean that she'd end up doing her assignment for her. Plus, of course, it would be social suicide to be seen hanging around with a dreg like Kerry. It was bad enough having to sit next to her on a bus, let alone be her work partner.

But then she felt mean. It wasn't Kerry's fault that she had trouble breathing normally. Or speaking normally. Or eating, drinking, thinking . . .

'All right,' she said. 'I'll do questions one to five, you do six to ten. Then we'll meet up and swap answers.' It was a compromise, but it was as far as she was prepared to go. Also, she reasoned, if Kerry's answers turned out to be rubbish, then there'd still be time to complete the assignment by herself.

'OK.' Kerry seemed happy enough with that. 'Want some Juishy Fruit?' She offered Midge a stick of gum. 'Shtops my mouth getting dry,' she said.

Midge gave Kerry a quick glance. Was that supposed

to be a joke? But there was little to be gleaned from the expression on Kerry's goofy face, and so Midge resisted the impulse to laugh. Instead she just said, 'Er . . . no. I'm OK, thanks,' and continued to gaze out of the window. It *was* pretty funny, though, and she had to bite her lip as she imagined herself telling Azzie about it in their Friday night chatroom sessions.

The bare countryside gave way to the outer suburbs of town, and then a long straight road bordered by open parkland and a big cemetery. Eventually the coach pulled into a broad driveway, and Midge caught a glimpse of the brightly painted sign as they passed through the entrance – *Tone Vale Butterfly Farm.* The coach wound on amid high banks of rhododendron bushes and finally came to a halt in front of a large white building. There was a general bustle of movement as everyone began to collect their question sheets and lunchboxes together. Miss Oldham stood up at the front of the coach and called for quiet.

'I *hope* I don't have to remind you of the purpose of this visit – Carl, are you with us? Good. Today's exercise forms part of this term's science project . . .'

Midge had discovered that she'd trodden on a piece of gum, Kerry's probably, and was more concerned with scraping that off her shoe than listening to Miss Oldham. '. . . marked as coursework . . . sensible behaviour at all times . . . lunch in the gardens at twelve-fifteen, provided the weather stays fine . . . to either myself or Mr Edmunson . . . and leaving at two-thirty sharp . . .' The bits of teacher-speak continued to drift over thirty heedless heads, as everyone bumped and shuffled their way down the centre of the coach and out onto the sunny tarmac. '*Don't* chase the peacocks, *don't* touch the displays, *don't* all try and crowd into the shop at the same time . . .'

Midge stared up at the main building. It was big enough to be a mansion, but the white painted walls and small plain windows made it look as though it might once have been something official rather than a rich person's home. The grounds were pretty though – quite exotic – with tall yew hedges and monkey-puzzle trees and spiky shrubs. Already some of the boys were opening their lunchboxes and throwing bits of bread to the peacocks.

'Hey, Midge.' Somebody tugged at her sleeve, and Midge instinctively jerked her arm away. 'Don't worry – I'm not going to *bite* you.' It was Samantha Lewis. 'I just wondered if you'd . . . if you wanted to . . . we could go round together.'

Midge stared stupidly at Sam for a few moments. 'Oh. Yeah, sure.' She looked over Sam's shoulder and saw Rhona's crowd moving off towards the entrance to the building.

'They're all paired up,' said Sam, as though the question had been asked. 'And anyway, I get fed up with them sometimes. It's not a big deal – just that I can only talk about how gorgeous Carl Polegato is for *so* long. You don't mind, do you?'

'No, it'd be good.'

'Come on, then. We can probably get through these stupid questions by lunchtime, and then do what we like.'

Midge was struck by a sudden pang of conscience. 'I just remembered,' she said. 'I told Kerry Hodge I'd go round with her. Swap answers with her, at any rate.' She looked about her, but couldn't see Kerry anywhere.

'Kerry *Hodge*? What are you – a charity worker or something?'

'Well, you know, I felt a bit sorry for her. She can't help . . . how she is, I suppose.'

'Maybe not, but she could at least shtay out of shpitting dishtance.'

Midge couldn't help but laugh at that. And it was good to have someone to laugh with, for a change.

Sam's prediction turned out to be right. By midday the two of them had managed to complete their assignments. They'd wandered through the warm and slightly eerie rooms where the chrysalises were kept, peered in semi-darkness at the emerging gypsy moths that fluttered in vain against the netting of their cages, and answered all the questions on the life-cycle of *Ephemera*. They'd labelled their grasshopper diagrams, and identified all the European species of butterfly from the gorgeous specimens on display. Such beautiful things these were, yet sad somehow, in their neat little rows, each one daintily skewered through the thorax.

'That's it,' said Sam. 'We're done. Come on, we can bog off and have our lunch now.' They made their way back through the maze of tall display cabinets and out towards the main entrance hall once more.

Here they met the skinny figure of Miss Oldham, who looked as though she might have been on the prowl for absconders.

'Aha!' she said. 'Finished already, you two?'

'Er . . . yes, Miss,' said Midge, and then wanted to kick herself. Always a bad idea to let a teacher know you'd finished your work ahead of time – because then they simply piled more on.

And she was right, because Miss Oldham took a quick glance at their papers and said, 'Oh, you *have* worked hard. Excellent. Well, now you can do the quiz for me.'

'Quiz, Miss?'

'Yes. If you turn over the last page you'll see that I've put together a little observational quiz for you. Just things that you might see as you wander around the house and grounds.'

'Oh.'

'Don't worry.' Miss Oldham gave them the hint of a smile. 'I shan't be marking it as such. Not as course-work, anyway. But there might be a merit point for those who complete it – and you could certainly do with a few more of those, couldn't you, Sam? Yes. Run along and have your lunch, then. There's a very pretty little enclosed garden, just behind those trees. Follow that gravel pathway down, and you can't miss it.'

'Huh,' said Sam, once they were out of earshot. 'If she thinks I've been grinding away all morning just so I can spend the afternoon doing *extra* work, she can think again.'

Midge made a vague noise of agreement. She

actually quite liked quizzes, and would have been happy enough to tackle this one if it came down to it. Right now, though, she was hungry and tired of walking. 'Where *is* this blimmin' garden?' she said.

They scrunched along the path, in the chilly shade of tall yew hedges, and finally came to a little arched gateway. This opened out onto a sunny garden, circular with a white fountain in the middle. There was a winged statuette on top of the fountain, a cupid, made of bronze. Sam said, 'Look, we've got a bench. Let's go and grab it before anyone else gets here.' She hurried off, but Midge remained at the gateway for a moment, looking around her. A quick tingle of familiarity had passed through her as she entered the garden, almost as though she had known what to expect. Had she been here before? No, she didn't think so. Perhaps she had been taken somewhere like this as a baby – it wasn't such an unusual place after all. At any rate, the feeling had gone now. She followed Sam over to the bench and opened her lunchbox.

They were both starving, and nothing was said for a while as they munched through their sandwiches – a comfortable silence that made Midge think that perhaps they could be real friends.

'I can't believe this weather. It's just *freaky* for January.' Sam lay backwards with her dark head lolling against the wooden bench, eyes closed and soaking up the sunshine. She looked like a cat, thought Midge. A lazy and contented cat, happy and relaxed. Not much bothered by anything or anybody. That was a good way to be, wasn't it? Confident and cool. Clever enough to get by without having to work too hard. Friendly without being frantically demanding. Normal.

Midge half closed her own eyes and allowed her dreamy vision to rest upon the silhouetted figure on top of the fountain. Cupid, with his bow and arrow. Yes, it was good to lie back in the warmth of the sun and just think of nothing, nothing at all. To sit on a bench, with someone who you liked, and be normal. Drift away, to the sounds of the insects and the birds. Float up into the blue and forget all about . . .

. . . *the Orbis* . . .

Midge jerked upright with such a violent start that Sam jumped too.

'What is it? Wassamatter?' Sam was looking about her, wide-eyed and startled.

'Nothing. It's . . . nothing. I . . . I think I must have fallen asleep for a moment. Sorry.'

'Should think so too. Nearly gave me a heart attack.' Sam folded her arms and tilted her head back once more. 'And I was just getting comfy,' she muttered.

31

Midge stood up and looked towards the fountain. She was sure she hadn't been here before. Why did it seem so familiar to her, then? She wandered across the circular gravel path, and perched herself sideways on the edge of the fountain. Again some vague memory of this place washed over her. Sitting here, in exactly the same position. A blackbird singing, and the sun going down. And she was holding something in her hand . . .

No. It had gone again, slippery as an eel.

'Come on, Midge. Let's go and have a look at the gift shop.' Sam was on her feet and calling to her.

"K.' Midge sighed and stretched out her arms.

They met Kerry Hodge on the way back, wandering along the path towards the circular garden.

'Oh Gawd,' said Sam, beneath her breath. 'Here she comes. Get your umbrellas out, everyone.'

But Midge didn't laugh this time. She felt guilty and embarrassed.

'Hi, Kerry,' she said. 'How're you getting on?' She tried to appear cheerful, but knew what a fake she must have sounded.

'Not bad. I've done shix to ten, like we shaid. Now I'm doing the quizsh.' Kerry drew level with them and came to a halt. Sam was keeping well to one side, Midge noticed.

'Really? I haven't even started on the quiz. It's getting a bit late now. We'll, er . . . we'll go over the answers on the coach, shall we?'

'If you want.'

'Yeah. We'll sit together, like we did on the way here.'

'OK. Shee you.' Kerry started walking again.

'See you,' said Sam, and then muttered, 'Wouldn't want to *be* you . . .' once they'd moved away a few paces.

Midge groaned. 'Now I feel really mean.'

'Nah, you worry too much. And anyway, it *is* mean to pretend to like someone when you don't.'

'Think so?'

'Yeah, I do. Leading people on, it's called.'

She had it all worked out, did Sam.

The coach was quieter on the return journey. Sam had resumed her place at the back with Rhona's crowd, and Midge was stuck next to Kerry Hodge once more.

'OK,' she said. 'Let's compare papers and see what we've got.' She made an effort to sound friendly, in order to make up for the fact that she'd ignored Kerry all day.

Kerry had done a lot better than might have been expected – good enough in fact to cause Midge to make an alteration to one or two of her own answers. Maybe this hadn't been such a bad deal after all. She handed her assignment over to Kerry, and watched her copy down the answers to the first five questions, noticing how she changed the wording here and there, made little improvements to her own efforts. Kerry's hand was slow, but the finished result was clear and neat.

'You're really good,' said Midge.

'Biology'sh my favourite,' said Kerry. 'Biology and English. How did you do with the quizsh?'

'What? Oh, the quiz. We didn't . . . I didn't really get round to it. Don't suppose it'll matter much.'

'Want to copy mine?'

'Um . . . don't know. Seems a bit of a cheek. OK, let's have a quick look, then.'

Midge took Kerry's paper and glanced at the quiz page. She was surprised at the amount that Kerry had written.

'*Question One*,' she read. '*What is Cupid shooting at?*'

And beneath that was Kerry's answer: *A topiary heart.*

'What's a top . . . a top-i-ary heart?' Midge said.

'Topiary. Thatsh when they cut a bush or a hedge into a funny shape. Like an animal or a bird. There was a heart cut into the hedge of that round garden. Above the gateway.'

'Was there? I didn't notice that.'

Midge moved on to the next question.

'*Tone Vale Butterfly Farm was opened in nineteen seventy-eight. But what was the building used for before that?*'

Kerry had written, '*It was a hospital for soldiers in the First World War. Then it became a clinic, and then it was part of the local art college.*'

Midge yawned. 'Where did you *get* all this stuff?'

'In here.' Kerry pulled a folded booklet out of her pocket. Midge read the title: *Tone Vale Butterfly Farm. A Guide and History.* 'Look – Mish Oldham got all her queshtions from here. Nothing to it.' Kerry opened the booklet, and Midge saw a blurry photograph of two men and a woman – a nurse – standing in bright

34

sunshine on the front steps of the building: *Dr Sydney Lewis and Dr Josef Wesser, founders of the Tone Valley Clinic* . . . Funny name, Wesser.

But the leaflet looked boring, and so Midge just said, 'Oh, right.'

'Borrow it if you like, and do the quizsh when you get home. You could get a merit point for it.'

Midge rubbed her eyes, and leaned back in her seat. 'Nah, it's OK, thanks. I can't be bothered.'

She was tired now, and didn't want to talk any more. It had been quite a good day, though. Kerry was not as awful as she had supposed, and it had been fun to go round with Sam. But there was still something about that place that niggled at her – the Butterfly Farm. Some connection that she couldn't quite make.

Chapter Three

Ba-betts, Queen of the Ickri, was dressed in her favourite white gown, her hair neatly combed and tied back, her face powdered and painted. Very peaceful, she looked, resting in the Gondla, her wicker chair, beneath the sycamores. The little wooded glade that they'd chosen for her was silent and secluded, yet open to the skies. The birds would see her soon enough.

Aye, it was a good place, thought Maglin, nicely suited its purpose. And Doolie had done her work well. The old Queen looked better in death than she had in life. He glanced about at the quiet gathering, noting who was present and who was not. The entire Ickri tribe had turned out, as so they should, to listen in respectful silence to Crozer's speech. Just behind Crozer stood the other two Elders, Ardel of the Naiad and Damsk of the Wisp, but there were few of their tribespeople to accompany them. He noticed Maven-the-Green lurking among the bushes, and that surprised him a little, for what had Ba-betts been to the mad old hag? Of the winged horse, Pegs, there was no sign.

Crozer's voice droned away in the background, but Maglin was only half listening. His thoughts were more concerned with the immediate predicament of the tribes than with the Ickri Elder's lengthy tribute to Ba-betts. There was the future to consider, and a new responsibility to bear, the weight of which lay heavy upon his shoulders. With no heir to succeed Ba-betts, her line was over. And without a rightful King or Queen, a Steward must now govern instead. There had been but one choice. From this day on, he, Maglin, was ruler of the Ickri.

He had expected nothing less, though he knew well that the Elders would have picked another if they could. But as senior figure the Stewardship must fall to himself, and so now Steward he was, Keeper of the Stone – King in all but name, and all forest-dwellers should recognize his authority.

Aye, but who among them would? The woodlanders grew reckless in their hunger, and each now looked to his own. The Ickri hunters and Naiad farmers might listen to him for a while longer, but the fisher-folk of the Wisp lived largely by their own code and were seldom seen between dawn and dusk. There were few here today to mourn the Queen. And the cave-dwellers – the Tinklers and Troggles – they were rarely seen at all. Maglin doubted they would consider him their master, for although he was coming into power, yet that power was waning. Starvation brought rebellion, and with little to offer his people he could do little to hold them. The time had surely come for all to leave. He would talk to the heads of each tribe on the matter – beginning this very day with the one most likely to give him trouble: Tadgemole, leader of the cave-dwellers.

He must impress upon all the growing danger from the Gorji, and the urgent need of a plan. A full season and more the secret of the Various had been known to the Gorji childer. There was no reason to trust it was a secret still. And if that secret was out, then what hope was there that they could continue to live here in peace, or defend themselves from attack? How soon before full-grown giants came – and in what manner would they come? Not in friendly curiosity, that was certain. No, they would come to destroy, as was ever their way, to hunt down all that was unlike themselves. Maglin saw them in his troubled dreams, crowds of roaring men, ascending the hill with hounds and shovels, beating down the barrier of brambles that had protected the little people for so long. Aye, there was much to think on.

'From seed we come, and to seed we go' – Crozer was drawing towards the end of his speech – '. . . as we ever did, and ever shall. Let the birds now take of her, corben and magpie, as we take of them, corben and magpie. And so may she feed her people still, we who yet remain.'

'So.' The low muttered response from the crowd. A few moments more of silence, and the tribespeople began to separate and move quietly away through the trees.

Maglin walked over to where the half-dozen archers of the Guard stood, ranged in a semi-circle behind the

38

Queen's wicker chair. He spoke directly to Ictor, their captain – and sensed the animosity that lay between them. Ictor was brother to Scurl, the treacherous archer that Maglin had banished from the forest. Scurl was now presumed dead, along with his crew, and Maglin was well aware of Ictor's resentment towards him – and towards the Gorji child who had played such a part in Scurl's downfall.

'I hold 'ee under my command now,' he said. 'The Guard shall have first vigil, as is right and proper, and for as long as 'ee will. Shoot whatever might come for her, be it bird, or fitch, or rat. There be little enough in these woods that we can afford to cast aught aside. All to be shared at Basket-time, mind.'

Ictor stared him in the eye, a long and deliberate pause. Eventually he said, 'Just as 'ee command, Steward. I be in the right fettle for shooting a rat.'

The insult was plainly intended, and Maglin decided that this time he would not let it pass. Ictor had made several such remarks of late – slyly threatening, insolent, challenging. It was almost as though he sought punishment. Very well, then. Perhaps it was time to bring this captain down a rank or two. Aye, a spell as a lowly tunnel guard might help curb his tongue . . .

Royal Clearing lay silent and deserted below, as Little-Marten surveyed the scene from his high Perch in the Rowdy-Dow tree. The glade that had been chosen as the last resting place of Ba-betts was beyond his vision, hidden away in the bordering woodland, but he had caught some movement among the bare winter tree-tops and guessed that the tribute must now be over. Aye, and so it was, for there went one or two of the East Wood archers, Glim and Raim, returning to their work. Soon Maglin would come to give him orders, and then he hoped to say his piece.

Little-Marten shivered beneath his bindle-wrap, frozen hands tucked into his armpits for comfort. The day was bright, but none the warmer for that, and he was looking forward to drumming out Queen's Herald, if only to get his blood moving. The clavensticks would be cold as ice, but their sound would carry well on such a still day. Crisp and clear in the winter air, the hard rattle of the woodpecker. *Drrr-drrr . . . drrrrrr . . . drr . . .*

He closed his eyes for a moment and ran through the rhythms of Queen's Herald in his head. *Drrr . . . drr-drrr . . .*

Crack! Little-Marten sat up with a jerk as something thwhacked against the dead trunk of the Rowdy-Dow tree.

'Be you *awake*, Woodpecker?'

'Aye!' Little-Marten looked down to see Maglin there, ready to hit the tree trunk with his spear again if necessary.

'Aye, you are now,' said Maglin. 'Sound Queen's Herald, then, to mark her passing. 'Twill be the last time.' The old warrior began to walk on.

'Maglin!' Little-Marten somehow found the courage to call out. 'Have 'ee . . . have 'ee spoken yet?'

'Spoken?' Maglin turned to scowl up at him, shading his eyes against the bright light. His thinning hair looked greyer than ever in the winter sunshine, the creases on his face deeper and more numerous. 'Spoken o' what?'

'To Tadgemole. About . . . Henty.'

'Ah. The Tinkler maid. You've still a mind to wed, then? I said that I'd ask for 'ee, didn't I, come the turn of the season, and if Tadgemole were still against it. As I take it he be.'

'Aye. He'll have none o' me.'

'Hm. And what of your own father? What does Fletcher Marten say?'

'He'll not stand in our way.'

'Oh? And be those his words or your own?'

Little-Marten said nothing.

'Well, I'll tell 'ee this, Woodpecker. The day that an Ickri weds a Tinkler, then both'll be wedded to trouble, that's certain. Such a thing have never happened yet, and there's good reason for it; the two don't mix. Now there's my say. But now that I be Steward 'tis also my say to grant leave or no. And if Tadgemole will agree to it, then I shall also. Though I think 'ee a pair o' young fools, I can't see it'll bring hurt to any but yourselves. I've to speak with Tadgemole directly on other matters, and I'll put in a word for 'ee. Now that's all I can promise. To your work, then.'

'Aye. And . . . and thank 'ee, Maglin.'

'Hmf.'

Maglin left Royal Clearing and followed the narrow woodland pathway that led down towards the caves.

41

The dry rattle of the woodpecker sounded among the treetops, Little-Marten drumming out Queen's Herald for the final time. The lad was too thin, thought Maglin, his wrists no thicker than the clavensticks that he wielded. Ah, but they were all too thin nowadays, lads and maids and stewards alike.

What a cuckoo's errand this was. He was astonished at himself for agreeing to do it. Still, there it was. He had been flattered that Little-Marten and the Tinkler maid had come to him and begged him to plead their cause, and obviously thought him so powerful and wise that he could successfully do so. He found that he had a soft spot for the Woodpecker, honest little fool that he was, and the maid seemed properly respectful. But to wed! An Ickri and a Tinkler! Such a thing was unheard of, and he was not surprised that the idea had been turned down. Yet what did these things matter, when all tribes were likely to perish?

Maglin climbed awkwardly up the bank of loose shale that fronted the main cave. He waited for a moment until he had caught his breath, and then shouted, 'Ho there! Are any of 'ee about?'

He peered into the gloom. Now that he was here he felt foolish, and was in half a mind to turn on his heel without waiting for a response. The cave-dwellers were no friends of his – less so now than they had ever been – and he began to wonder what business he had being here at all. But then he saw movement at the back of the cave. A figure crept forward, some old Troggle-dame, bearing an armful of sticks by the seem of it.

'What do 'ee want?'

'I've come to talk with Tadgemole. Tell him that Maglin is here for him.'

'Maglin?' The scraggy creature shuffled a little closer, squinting into the light. 'Be you a heathen?'

'A heathen? I'll give 'ee . . . just you get back there and bring Tadgemole to me.'

'Goppo!' The old dame turned and faded back into the darkness. 'Gop! Shift thee bones, and goo and find Tadgemole. Tell 'un there be one o' they heathens at the wind-'ole. Come to see 'un.'

Maglin took a deep breath, but held his tongue. This was becoming ever more ridiculous.

Eventually, just when Maglin felt that his patience was being made mockery of, Tadgemole appeared. The leader of the cave-dwellers was dressed in grey, as always, and, again as always, he carried that air about him of one who thinks himself a little above all others.

'Maglin.' His greeting was cool, suspicious even.

'Tadgemole. I find you hale and well, then?'

'You do.'

'Only I thought perhaps to see thee abroad today. For the Queen's passing.'

'She was not my Queen, Maglin.'

''Twould have been a respect, though. Did she bring thee any harm?'

'No. Nor any good.'

It was a poor beginning. Maglin understood that he was not to be invited further into the cave, for Tadgemole took a step forward and stood at the entrance with his arms folded. It was almost as though he were barring the way. Maglin could see others of the cave-dwellers now, a little knot of them gathering in the far shadows. He thought he recognized Henty among them.

'Yet you came to the muster of the tribes, Tadgemole, this summer last when Pegs were missing. And you allowed two of your own to join in searching for him.'

'I thought that a matter of importance. A matter that might affect the safety of us all.'

Maglin let it drop. He was here to talk about the future of the tribes, not to argue. But first he would tackle that other business.

'You've a daughter,' he said, glancing over Tadgemole's shoulder. 'Henty. 'Tis her wish to be joined to Little-Marten, of the Ickri tribe. And he to her.'

'Ah. And you are here to forbid it. Now that you are King, you think to have a say in these affairs, whether they concern you or not. I wonder that you bring word in person over such a trifle, Maglin. A lowling might have served as well.'

'I am Steward, not King, and I am here to grant leave, not to forbid it.'

'Steward or King, Maglin, you seek to rule – and to be one that may grant leave or not, at your whim. Well, in this, at least, I have some say. And I do *not* grant such leave. Whilst I breathe, my daughter shall not be given to an Ickri heathen.'

'Tread warily, Tadgemole.' Maglin felt his temper rising. 'I'll not be ridden far by one of your kind.'

'One of *my* kind? You come to this dwelling with a

spear in your fist, granting *leave* that the highest of mine may be gifted to the lowest of yours – and you think it a fair match?'

'Aye – I think it a fair match!' Maglin's blood was up now. 'The Woodpecker may never make an archer, nor even a fletcher like his father, but he've a position and a skill.'

'I know full well what his position is, Maglin, and where his skill lies. His *position* was to come crawling to us upon his knees, as a seeker of refuge in our dwelling when his own were like to hunt him down. His *skill* was to entwine himself about my daughter, when my eyes were elsewhere. I was fool enough to take him in, and my daughter was fool enough to listen to his wiles. As to being an archer – he could be ruler of the Ickri, for all I'd care, and my answer would be the same. He would still be an Ickri. And I'll tell you this, *Steward*: if I see that young squab lurking about this place again, I'll not answer for his skin.'

'You think to threaten one o' mine?' Maglin shook his spear in Tadgemole's face. 'An Ickri? Then why any Ickri should want aught to do with a *Tinkler's* spalpeen is beyond my grasping. 'Tis Little-Marten that's the fool – and I a bigger one for hearing him out. And a bigger one yet to think of mixing our blood with yourn! Look out for your own, then – and to your own skins. We s'll do the same and reckon ourselves the better for it! I came here to talk o' more important things, Tadgemole, but I s'll waste no more time on 'ee. You'll not see me here again, nor the Woodpecker neither.'

Maglin turned and began to slither down the bank of shale. He very nearly lost his footing, and had to spread his wings in order to save himself. As he reached the bottom of the bank he turned again and looked upwards, thinking to hurl a last remark at Tadgemole. But the grey figure had already gone, and this incensed Maglin more than ever. Pah! He strode through the darkening woods, lashing out with his spear at any stalk or tendril that dared stray across his path. So much for his power and his wisdom. So much for his weak notions on intermingling the tribes. What had he achieved? Nothing. He hadn't even got as far as mentioning the main reason for his visit – to persuade Tadgemole that the time had come to leave. Well, let them be, then. The cave-dwellers could roast on a Gorji spit for all he cared.

A flash of white caught his eye – something lurking amid the clump of trees ahead of him. Maglin slowed his furious pace, hesitated, then deliberately changed his direction. He'd recognized the pale form of Pegs, and was in no mood for any passing conversation with that witchi creature. He'd had enough foolish talk for one day.

The following evening Maglin called a Counsel of the Elders. He had dallied for long enough. Now that the old Queen had passed to another life it was time to talk properly of the future of the Various.

Together they sat in the cramped and creaky interior of Counsel Pod – Maglin and the three Elders: Crozer of the Ickri, Ardel of the Naiad, and Damsk of

the Wisp. Their grizzled faces were lit only by the glow of the earthenware charcoal burner that hung from the wicker roof, suspended low on its long rusty chain. They each spread their palms towards its smoky warmth.

'Our time grows ever shorter,' said Maglin. 'And these woods ever more dangerous. Now that there are those who know we are here, the day must come when all will learn of it and fall upon us. We must decide: to move on whilst we can and hope to chance upon some safer refuge, or to hold until the last. Let each have his say, then. Ardel – what from you? Speak for the Naiad.'

Ardel cleared his throat. He seemed embarrassed, uncomfortable. 'The Naiad will stay,' he said. 'And the Wisp also. Damsk and I have already spoken together of this.'

'What? Spoken together?' Maglin looked from one to the other, first in surprise, then in anger. 'And you have made such a decision without me?'

'We have – and long since. There is naught to be gained in forsaking the forest, Maglin. Not for us. The Wisp already tread by night upon the heelmarks that the Gorji leave by day. They would be no safer elsewhere. And the Naiad neither hunt nor fish. We are crop-growers, travellers no more. Without our plantations we should not survive long. We shall advise our tribes to stay and meet with whatever comes.'

Maglin threw a furious glance at Crozer. Had the Ickri Elder known of this decision?

Crozer shrugged and said, 'There be other reasons to stay, Maglin. What if the Orbis should ever return? Should we not be here to take it?'

'Pah! Orbis! I've no time for such blether, and have heard too much of the like from Pegs wi' his witchi talk of Elysse and our "other lives". 'Tis this life I've to think of, and how we may act today.' Maglin leaned forward and jabbed his forefinger against Ardel's knee. 'You'd do well to keep beneath the wings of the strongest – and that's we, the Ickri. My own thinking is to quit this place whilst we may.'

'Then you think like a fool.' The reedy voice of Damsk was raised for the first time.

'What's this, you old wosbird? You name me Steward and then dare call me fool?'

'Aye. You be Steward by right, Maglin, but not by our choice. What good would it do to leave our homes? Where should we go, and how should we travel? There be those here that can scarce cross Royal Clearing, let alone cross Gorji lands to who knows where.'

'Then all should perish here for the sake of the few that be too idle to move?' cried Maglin. 'I've more skins than yours to save! What do your old bag o' bones matter when there be young 'uns that go starving? If I say the Ickri leave, then leave we shall! Aye, and along with any that will join us—'

'Maglin, Maglin . . .' Crozer intervened, raising his withered arms for peace. ''Tis no good to shout. If the tribes are to be divided in this, then so be it. But let us try to think—'

'Traitors!' Maglin was not yet calm.

'. . . to think of what may come, and act each for the best. Of what *may* come, I say – for we cannot know for sure. Do the Gorji childer keep our secret still? We have seen naught of them. Is it certain that they will bring us harm? And if the giants come, shall we not have warning? The Ickri archers are in the treetops by day, and the Wisp are abroad by night. 'Twould not be so easy to take us unawares – and the briars would keep the Gorji at bay for a half-day at the least. We might escape by whatever tunnel was furthest from 'em, if ever we truly needed to.'

'Aye, we might *escape*.' Maglin struggled to his feet, the wicker pod swaying a little as he pushed himself upright. 'But how far should we get? The giants'd be close enough on our heels to have us all skewered by first nightfall. Fools! 'Tis better we go from here *before* they come than wait till we're driven out. Now there's my say on it, and you'll either take heed or you won't. Crozer, you may stay with your fellows to argue some sense into their mazy heads if you wish, but I've had enough o' them – as they have o' me, it seems. Well, then, let them choose their own path. I'm away.'

Maglin swept aside the entrance cloth of Counsel Pod, spread his wings, and jumped down to the ground. He landed heavily, and was forced to make use of his spear for some temporary support. As he hopped and hobbled his way across Royal Clearing, Maglin spotted the humpty-backed little figure of Maven-the-Green scurrying away through the trees. She glanced over her shoulder at him, before melting into the deepening shadows. By Elysse, but that one could move quickly when she wanted to. The old hag quite put him to shame. Maglin winced as he continued with his own far slower progress home.

Ribbons of grey mist hung about the entrance of the dark cave as Massie hobbled from lamp to lamp, the lighted taper unsteady in her shivering hand. The old Troggle-dame muttered to herself as she coaxed the oily wicks, one by one, into catching the flame.

'Come on with 'ee then . . . old Massie don't have all night. Brr! I be all of a shake. Eh? What's that?' She paused, and looked about her in confusion. 'What did 'ee say? Who's there?'

Again she caught it – a soft voice that echoed in her head – yet the words came not in sound but in colours . . . bursts of blue and green and grey.

Dame, do you not hear? Bring Tadgemole to me. I must meet with him.

Massie peered fearfully into the mist that came drifting over the lip of the cave. A pale and unearthly creature was standing there, half illuminated by the flicker of the lavender lamps. It was looking at her. Some heathen thing . . . with silvery mane and tail . . . and wings. A horse!

The guttering taper dropped from Massie's hand as she backed away. She would have to give up her post as lamplighter if such outlandish beings were to keep appearing at the wind-hole.

Henty shrank back into the shadows, trying to make sure that her father didn't see her. He would be angrier than ever with her if he knew that she was spying on him, but she was curious to learn why this astonishing creature had come to the caves – the winged horse. And now that she had heard what he had to say, she could not leave.

She watched as Tadgemole drew his heavy cloak about his shoulders and spoke again to Pegs.

'How did you learn of this?' he said. 'And why should I heed the word of one such as you?'

I speak the truth, Tadgemole, and I learn as you do – from that which I see and hear. You will be deserted. All that dwell in the forest fear the coming of the Gorji, and now Maglin makes plans to leave. Not this day, perhaps, nor the morrow, but within a moon he is like to go, and all his tribe with him, to seek for safer lands. Many others of the Wisp and Naiad may follow him also in the end, I fear.

Tadgemole turned from Pegs and stared at the ground. When at last he raised his head again, his expression had changed. The deep lines around his jaw had hardened, and his voice cracked with anger.

'So. Maglin would run. We come to this then – aye, and as I always knew in my heart that we should. The heathen Ickri would desert us all to save their own skins. They were ever thus – faithless cowards, for all their braggartly talk. And Maglin has shown himself to be the worst of them. So now they plan to steal shameless into the night. Fools.' Tadgemole took a deep breath. 'Like scavenging foxes they came here, and like foxes they run. Well, away with them, then. Why should I care? I'll not be sorry to see their tails.'

You should not wish to see them go, Tadgemole. Without the Ickri archers to guard the tunnels and keep watch from the treetops this will be a more dangerous place. There will be no warning if the giants should come. And remember this: if the Ickri leave, then the Stone will leave with them also. Though Maglin has no belief in such things, yet he is Keeper of the Stone by right, and he will take it with him.

Tadgemole looked at Pegs once more. 'Ah yes. The Touchstone. And what of you, *horse*? Where is your purpose in this? I cannot recall that you have ever shown a care towards my people before. Why do you come to warn us now? What do you seek to gain?'

My purpose is common to yours, Tadgemole, and becomes ever clearer to me as the seasons pass. I seek only what you seek, and hope but to gain what you would gain – the return of the Orbis, and the pathway to Elysse.

'The Orbis? Now there is a word I rarely hear, and I wonder to hear it now from so strange a one as you. The Orbis was lost to us longseasons ago, my friend – taken from here for safekeeping when the thieving

Ickri first returned from the northlands. What would a Naiad horse know of such things?'

I am not of the Naiad – nor alike to any animal of their breeding. I know that the Orbis was carried to safety by a Gorji maid, lest Corben, false King of the Ickri, should steal it from the cave-dwellers. The maid was named Celandine, and a friend she was to your kind. You sing of her still.

'Aye, we do.' Tadgemole put his head to one side and studied the winged beast before him. 'I have given thought to you many times,' he said, 'and often wondered at your being. I know your name – Pegs – but I never saw nor heard the like of you before. Nor ever read of such a creature in our almanacs. What *are* you?'

I am a traveller. A wayfarer. I am one who began a journey long ago, yet failed to reach its end. I was upon this earth before, Tadgemole, though never in this place. We live and die and are born to live again. And across the reach of time we live still, in so many other lives that truly we are all but one. One life in many forms. I am here to finish the journey that I once began, and to that same early purpose: to bring my fellow travellers home.

'Home? To Elysse?'

Aye, to Elysse.

'Then you believe that Elysse exists.'

Look upon me, Tadgemole. Am I of this world, do you think? Are you? Or any trapped in these woods?

'No, we are none of us of this world. You are a believer, then, and so a rarer creature than even you seem. But if the Orbis were here now, we should still be as far from Elysse as ever. Perhaps you have forgotten this, or never knew it, but without the Touchstone the Orbis has no power. And now the Stone may depart these woods yet again.'

If the Orbis were found, Tadgemole, then I would bring you the Stone.

'You would bring it to me? How? Why? The Stone is in Maglin's keeping.'

Maglin has no faith in the Touchstone, nor the Orbis, nor in Elysse itself. He believes only in the strength of his own arm – and that strength is fading. So let us be joined together in this, you and I alone. Help me to find the Orbis, and I will keep my promise. I will bring the Stone to you, and it shall rest in your hand, not Maglin's.

'Ha. We may all make idle promises, Pegs. But come. Follow me into the warmth of our chambers, and you shall at least tell me what you want of me.' Tadgemole led the way across the broad expanse of the main cave, and beckoned Pegs into the side passage that would take them down to the inner chambers. The lavender lamps threw wild shadows across the roughly pitted walls of the tunnel as they entered.

Henty emerged from her hiding place to watch them go, listening as the distant *tink-tink* of hammered metal sounded an echo to the fading footsteps of the winged horse.

In a daze she wandered over to the main cave entrance, her woollen shawl wrapped tight about her shoulders as she stared out into the misty night.

The Ickri were leaving. Of all the words that Pegs

had spoken, these were the only ones that held any meaning for her. *Not this day, perhaps, nor the morrow, but within a moon . . .*

Within a moon the Ickri would be gone, and so Little-Marten would be gone with them. He would have no choice but to follow his own tribe. And now that he and she had been forbidden to meet, there might be no chance to speak before parting. Parting! She could never bear it. The thought of it choked her, plunged her into deep black waters so that she could scarcely breathe.

Why was this happening? What harm was there in her and Little-Marten being together, and by what right were they torn apart? What did it matter that they were of different tribes? When Little-Marten had first come to the caves – seeking refuge from Scurl – her father had been kind to him, and had taken him in. And when Little-Marten had brought her back safe from the lands of the Gorji, her father had been grateful. But now that the two of them wished to wed, everything had changed, and her father would have none of it. 'Twas one thing, he said, to shelter an Ickri from his own murdering kind, but no daughter of his could ever be wed to a heathen. How she hated him for that!

Perhaps she should go now, at this very moment. Perhaps she should defy her father, and run from here, and seek out Little-Marten, and . . .

'Henty? Be that you?'

Henty turned towards the dim light of the cave.

It was Pank, the young tinsy-smith, walking towards

55

her. Lately he seemed to be at her back whenever she looked round.

'I . . . I came to see if 'twas you. Is all well?'

Henty glared at him, angry that he should interrupt her thoughts.

'Are you sent to spy on me, Pank?' The words came out instinctively, with no special thought behind them, but she saw in an instant that they had hit home. Pank lowered his head and looked embarrassed. He couldn't meet her gaze.

'Your father . . . Tadgemole . . . he wondered where you might be.'

'And so you be sent to keep watch over me. To see that I don't stray too far. Be this now the way of it?'

Pank put on an air of surprise, and seemed about to deny this, but then his shoulders dropped and he gave a little sigh. He ran his fingers through his long dark hair. 'Aye,' he said. 'You'm not so far wrong. Tadgemole says that I've to see thee safe about. But 'tis no task o' my choosing, Henty, I can tell 'ee that.'

Henty put her hands on her hips and took a deep breath. Anger welled up inside her afresh, but it was not directed at Pank. This was her father's doing – and all her pain was caused by him. There was no reasoning against his stubbornness, and it was pointless to try. Let him be cursed, then, and she also if ever she spoke to him again. From now on she would make her own plans – and her own life.

'Come, then, Master *Pank*. To your duty. If you've to see me "safe about", then you may see me safe to my chamber and stand guard there the night, so that I be safe from myself. We s'll see how quick about you be on your toes – and how many nights of sleep you may do without.'

Henty swept down through the centre of the cave, her thoughts already leaping ahead of her, the stumbling footsteps of Pank already lagging behind.

Chapter Four

Midge awoke suddenly in the night. She propped herself up on one elbow, and looked around her, startled for a moment by the unfamiliarity of her surroundings. The blue lamp glowed faintly at her bedside, the dimmer switch turned down low. It was OK. She was back in her old room again, that was all. Weeks and weeks it had been since she was here, and she had grown used to sleeping in with her mum. Now it felt strange to be on her own once more. That must be why she had woken up with such a start. Wasn't it?

Midge . . .

A sunburst of pink and yellow exploded inside her head, softly spreading, like watercolour paint dropped onto wet paper. There was no sound.

Midge sat bolt upright now, perfectly still, listening hard. Nothing but the faint rhythm of her own pulse, thudding in her ears.

'Pegs?' She whispered his name, half expecting the magical animal to step out of the wardrobe, or from behind the shower door. But no. All was silent and still. With her heart in her mouth, Midge drew back the duvet and got out of bed. She padded over to the window and peeped around the curtains, but could see only the dim shadow of her hesitant self, reflected in the pane.

Midge . . .

No, she had not imagined it. Certain, now, she undid the stiff catch and pushed at the window. The cold night air made her gasp as she leaned forward to look out into the darkness. And there he was. Standing by the balustrade wall, looking up at her, his mane silvery white beneath the winter moon. Pegs.

All her memory came flooding back to her then, and all that had seemed so hazy and unreal was brought into focus. It had gone away for a while, this other world that she was somehow part of, but now it had returned to claim her and she was to be caught up in its dance yet again.

'Pegs?' She could see the whispered cloud of her own breath coming out of her. 'What's happened? What do you want?'

I must talk with you, maid.

'What, now? Do you want me to come down? But it's freezing . . .'

No. Meet with me tomorrow. Come early to the byre – alone, if you will.

'The byre? You mean the pig-barn?'

Aye. Where first you found me, look for me there again.

The pale shadow of Pegs faded back into the night and disappeared. Midge remained at the window, watching, until the pain in her frozen fingertips brought her back into the present. She closed the latch. Her whole body was shuddering quite uncontrollably now with the cold. In two seconds she was across the room and back into bed, squirming beneath her duvet, buried in its warmth. She rolled herself up into the tightest ball possible against the chilly world and her own troubled thoughts. Hibernation. What a brilliant invention that was. If only it could be for humans as well as for hamsters.

She found it easy enough to get away. Her mum was as distracted as ever with the business of Mill Farm, and Uncle Brian seemed to have made himself scarce sometime after breakfast. There was no reason for anyone to take much notice of Midge as she slipped around the corner of the old stable block and began to cross the Field of Thistles. The ground was still sodden from the winter rain, so that she had to keep one eye on where she was putting her feet, whilst keeping the other on her destination.

The Summer Palace, she had called it – that shabby little barn – when she had first spotted it from her bedroom window. Perched up there on the sunny slopes of Howard's Hill, it had seemed a good place for a picnic. Midge winced at the memory of it. Some picnic that had turned out to be. Her fear and amazement at what she had found there came flooding back to her, along with a whole gallery of images: the sliding door that wouldn't budge, the dark interior of the barn that smelled of oil and hay and animal ammonia, and the strange and awful sight of the winged horse, Pegs, trapped and bleeding beneath the spiked wheels of the hay-rake . . .

Midge reached the sheep-gate at the end of the Field of Thistles, and stopped there for a moment. It was a stiffish climb from here up to the pig-barn, but she hadn't paused just to catch her breath. The low hamstone wall that circled the base of Howard's Hill seemed like a barrier in more ways than one. It was the outer boundary to a foreign land, a line to be crossed or not. Once she stepped through this gate, she felt, there would be no turning back. Did she really want to do this? Was she really going to dive in headfirst all over again?

She might have decided against it after all, but then a brief squall of wind buffeted her neck and shoulders, so that it felt as though she were being nudged forward, encouraged to carry on. All right then, she would. The sheep-gate clanged behind her, and she began the climb that would bring her to the barn, now temporarily hidden from view behind the brow of the hill.

The little concrete building looked dismal and uninviting as Midge approached it. Part of the corrugated tin roof had come loose, a rusty sheet of metal that flapped and rattled in the early morning wind. The galvanized sliding door was still hanging at an awkward angle, just as it had been when Midge had last seen it. Not so very long ago, though it felt like years. She remembered how fearful she had been, creeping towards that door, ready to flee at any moment, yet drawn by the unearthly sounds from within. Some of that fear returned to her now, and she came to a halt.

'Pegs?' She called his name – not so much expecting a reply as warning him of her arrival. 'Are you there?' The wind had dropped momentarily, and there was silence.

Midge looked at the gap at the side of the door, hoping that Pegs would appear, but there was no sign of him. She stepped onto the concrete platform upon which the barn was built and noisily scraped some of the mud off her boots, whilst keeping a hopeful eye on the entrance. Still nothing. Oh, all right then, have it your way. A final scrape of her Wellingtons, and she clumped over to the sliding door.

'Pegs?' She cautiously put her head through the gap and peered into the gloom. The old grey tractor was still there, more cobwebby than ever, still lurching sideways onto its punctured wheel. Beyond that she couldn't see much.

'Pegs . . .' Her voice was a little shaky now. 'You're scaring me. Are you in there?' She took a step forward and waited. A renewed gust of wind battered the eaves of the barn, and then – *whoosh* – the whole interior of the building was filled with sudden daylight as one of the tin roof panels flipped upwards. The rusty corrugated sheet rose as though it were on a hinge, teetered in the wind for a moment, then came crashing down again. Midge jumped at the sound of it. The barn was plunged back into darkness – but it was as though a flashlight had been turned on and off, a bright snapshot of her surroundings. The image remained. Dust everywhere. Thick grey dust. The blue plastic sheet, still laid out on the floor, just as she had left it. The heavy hay-rake with its spidery wheels, still jacked up at a crazy angle. The bits of stone, the broom and the bucket – every reminder of that incredible summer day was still here, all as it had been.

And Pegs was here too. She had seen him – over by the far wall. He was standing next to . . . what? Something that *hadn't* been here before . . .

The effect of sudden darkness began to wear off, and Midge was able to pick out the shapes once more. She could see the hay-rake, and yes, there was Pegs, but she couldn't quite make out . . .

Do you come alone, maid?

The word-colours burst inside Midge's head and she blinked – still unable to take such a peculiar sensation for granted.

'Yes,' she said. 'I've come alone. But have you?' She felt wary, and certainly wasn't about to move any closer for the moment.

I have brought a companion. One who would speak with you. This is the maid, Tadgemole. A friend she has been to me, and is kin to the one who was friend to your kind. She is here alone, as I promised. Come, then, both. Neither need have fear of the other.

Pegs stepped forward, towards the light that fell through the doorway, and Midge was shocked to see that there was someone with him – an extraordinary little figure, dressed in grey, different somehow from the others she had seen.

But one of *them*, nevertheless. One of the Various.

Midge began to back away. She had not been pre-pared for this. Visions of similar figures flashed before her – Scurl and his crew, with their bows and arrows, and their murderous little eyes . . .

Maybe this one was different, though. He was certainly a lot older. White-haired, and gaunt about the face – and so pale, now that he stepped directly into the light. He carried no weapons that she could see.

'Wh-what is it?' she said. 'What do you want?' She was speaking to Pegs, but her eye remained on the strange little newcomer. Old he might be, but he wasn't feeble-looking. There was a toughness about him that reminded her a bit of someone else. Yes, the leader of the Ickri – Maglin – that was it. They both had that same upright stance, the same proud and fearless way of looking at you. They could almost be brothers, if it wasn't for the colour of their skin. And the fact that this one had no wings . . .

Then she remembered something.

'Tadgemole?' she said. 'Aren't you . . . I mean, are you the one who gave me . . . are you Henty's father?'

The grey eyes looked up at her – a long careful study. At last he spoke.

'I am,' he said. 'Henty is my child. To you she came, maid, when she was in trouble, and was brought safely to her home. I was grateful, and a gift I sent. Now I am here to see you for myself, and to join with Pegs in ask-ing your assistance on another matter.'

Midge was trying to take in Tadgemole's words, but at the same time she couldn't help wondering at how he spoke. Where on earth did he get that accent? He sounded so unlike any of the others she had heard. Even his own daughter didn't speak in that strange formal way. What a mixture they all were – the pompous old Queen, and the Elders, and Maglin, and Little-Marten, and now this one, Tadgemole, the leader of the cave-dwellers. All seemed to have their own peculiar ways of speaking. And as for Pegs . . . well, Pegs was from another planet, no doubt about it.

She tried to focus.

'Well . . . what is it you want?' she said.

To be gone from here, maid. We must find what we have lost, and so return to our own.

Midge turned from Tadgemole, and looked at Pegs. He seemed changed from when she had last seen him, not just older, but with an even deeper wisdom in his dark glistening eyes. And as Midge stared into those eyes she became hypnotized by the little pinpricks of light that were reflected there. Twinkling like far-off stars . . .

A strange feeling slowly came over her. It was as though she were being lifted up and carried away from this place, rising into the darkness. She was floating, tumbling end over end among the milky heavens, a windblown straw in the vastness of the universe.

'What do you mean?' she whispered, and her own voice seemed to be coming to her from a long way off. 'What is it that you've lost?'

The Orbis, child. We seek the Orbis. Our time has almost come, and we must leave this world and travel to Elysse. If we stay longer we shall perish. Help us to find the Orbis. Do you know what it is that I speak of?

'The Orbis? Yes . . . the Orbis.' And again Midge could hear her own voice, echoing through the darkness. Then came a picture, a memory. She sat by water – a pool or a fountain – and held some object in her hand, felt the cool weight of it, the smooth curve of metal against her palm. A sun, and a moon and a star. The Orbis.

'I . . . remember it.'

You remember it. And now you must find it and bring it home.

'But . . . where shall I look?'

The picture-memory began to fade, and Midge was floating back through space, returning from wherever she had been. She blinked, and became aware of the wind rattling the rusty panels of the barn roof. *Tap-tap . . . tap-tap . . .*

'Where shall I look?' She said it again, and her voice was back where it belonged. But now her head felt all spinny. 'Sorry,' she said. 'I'm going to have to . . .' She moved shakily over to the grey tractor, and perched herself against the front wheel. With a hand on each knee to steady herself, and her head lowered, she felt better. This was just too weird, though.

Tadgemole, show the child what you have brought.

Midge raised her eyes. What now? Tadgemole was reaching into his rough cloak and bringing something from it. A piece of paper – quite large. He carefully unfolded it, looked at it for a few moments, then moved towards her, offering it to her.

Midge automatically leaned forward to take the paper from Tadgemole's outstretched hand, but now she felt self-conscious at being so close to him – and so huge and awkward by comparison. His head was only a little higher than her knee. She found herself staring dizzily at the silver-grey stubble on his face. How did he keep it so short? Did he have scissors? And where did he get his clothing from? He wasn't dressed in the rag-bag of oddities that she had seen on others of the Various – the scraps of sacking and cut-down shirts and waistcoats that had so obviously started life beyond the forest. The material of Tadgemole's cloak was coarse and loosely woven, but it fitted him properly and might have been made especially for him. Did they weave their own cloth, then? How? She caught his eye and realized that she was being studied in return, a look of grave curiosity that took in her hair, and the zips on her fleece, the blue charity bracelet that she wore on her wrist. And the sheer size of her, she supposed, would make her as much an alien to him as he was to her. Another wave of dizziness passed over her, and then receded. She shook her head and took a deep breath before trying to focus on the piece of paper.

It was a double sheet, ruled – perhaps from an old exercise book. There were words on the left-hand page, very tiny, written in pencil, and a drawing on the right. The drawing was of a girl, or a woman, wearing a long dress and some sort of funny headgear. There was a big cross about her neck. A nun?

The words on the left-hand page were carefully

printed, with serifs and curly g's, as though somebody had copied the shapes of the letters from a book. 'At my going . . .' Midge began to look down the page. The words blurred, and then came back into focus. It was like a will, or a testament.

'Read it aloud to us,' said Tadgemole, 'so that Pegs may hear again what is written there.'

'All right, then,' said Midge. She went back to the beginning.

' "At my going, I, Micas, now task Loren to write my words for me, my eyes grown too weak to see. The leadership of our tribes I pass on to Bron, here present this day, and would also pass on the care of the Orbis, if it were still with me. But the Orbis has gone, longseasons since. To Celandine I gave it, when our tribes were in peril, and I have seen it no more, nor she who keeps it safe for us. Yet still I know that the Orbis will be brought to this place again, by her hand, when sun and moon and stars fall aright. The day will come. This I have been told by one who knows more, and such is now my belief. And this belief shall be passed on from leader to leader, and from heart to heart, so that all our tribe shall carry it with them. The good maid was sent to us as a sign from Elysse, to prepare us for our return. And to Elysse we shall return, when we are deemed ready. Celandine will know the day. Until then we must follow the teachings of the almanacs she gifted to us, for therein lies all the knowledge that we shall need. Come for me, when you make your journey, my friends. I shall be waiting for you along the way." '

Then there was a very scrawly signature – 'Micas' – at the bottom of the page. Midge stopped reading. What was this all about? It talked about her great-great-aunt as though she were like a saint or a prophet, or something.

'I don't understand it,' she said. 'What does it all mean?'

Tadgemole bowed his head briefly, before raising it to speak. 'These are the words of Micas, who was leader of the Tinklers and Troggles when Celandine first came among us longseasons ago. Celandine taught us our letters, and how to sing. All our knowledge she brought to us, that which sets us apart from other tribes. Then the Ickri came and would have stolen the Orbis from us, aye, and murdered us all. The Orbis was given to Celandine for safekeeping, and she fled the forest in danger of her own life. She was seen but one more time, and that from a distance, by my brother Loren. 'Twas he who wrote the words and made the drawing you see before you.' Tadgemole's voice became firmer, almost as though he were issuing an order. 'Find her, child, and bring her back. Bring her back, and the Orbis with her, so that all may be made right.'

'*Find* her? But . . . but Celandine must have died years ago. She'd have been about a hundred by now, if she was alive. Maybe more.'

'A hundred? A hundred fourseasons?' Tadgemole's heavy eyebrows rose in a look of faint surprise. 'Is that such a long life, then, for a Gorji?'

'Er . . . well, yes, actually. It is. Not many of us reach a hundred.'

Yet some do. Have faith, Midge. Celandine may be in this life still.

Pegs took a step forward, and Midge began to feel that she was being hemmed in.

'I really don't think she is. You see, I've . . . well, sometimes I think I've seen her . . . or at least felt' – she didn't like to say the word, but could think of no alternative – 'felt her ghost.'

Her ghost?

'Yes. Her . . . spirit. I can't explain it. It's like she's here sometimes. With me. Or I'm with her. Oh, I don't know. But I'm sure it means that she must be dead.'

We all of us have many lives, child. The spirit of a traveller may move from one life to another, and from one part of a life to another. Perhaps Celandine is such a one – a traveller, who comes to you from elsewhere. Find her. Speak with her when you see her, and she may answer.

Midge didn't like the thought of that at all. It was too creepy. Much too weird. And sitting here in the draughty gloom of this old barn, talking such impossible talk – this was too weird also. She wanted to escape, now, to get away.

'Well, I could try and find out what happened to her, I suppose,' she said. 'Maybe.' She could hear the lack of conviction in her words, even as she spoke, but what did they expect – that she could work miracles? She gave a shrug of her shoulders.

Nothing more was said for a few moments, and Midge was conscious of the disappointment hanging in the air. Tadgemole reached up and gently took the piece of paper from her hands. He began to fold the sheet along its original creases, handling it with such care that Midge felt her heart suddenly go out to him. His strength and pride had disappeared, and he no longer looked like the leader of a tribe. He looked like an old man, tired and worried and worn down by care, a man who had lost his way. All of them had lost their way. Midge watched the top of the aged head, bent in concentration, and knew that she could not ignore the pain that she saw there, or just walk away from it. There was no escape after all, and there never had been. She made a decision.

'All right,' she said. 'I don't understand any of this, but I'll try. Honestly I will. I'll do everything I can.'

She meant it, and she saw a new expression in Tadgemole's grey eyes as he lifted his head to look at her – a glimmer of hope, perhaps, and gratitude. And renewed curiosity.

Pegs came up to her and briefly nuzzled her hand, the warmth of his breath passing softly across her fingers. How miraculous he was. She remembered how she had cared for him, brought him back to life in this very barn when he lay crushed beneath the hay-raking machine. She shyly reached out to touch one of his wings, feeling once again the curious texture of the velvety membrane and the long quill-like bones beneath. So fine and delicate. And so beautiful that she felt suddenly awkward, as though she had no right to be so familiar with him. She withdrew her hand.

Do you see, Tadgemole, why this maid has all my faith? If not for her I would have passed from this life long ago. Midge was sent to our aid, as Celandine, her kin, was sent before

*her. We hide from the Gorji, and go in fear of them. If we
cannot escape them we know that we shall perish. And yet we
are helped on our way by their own childer.*

Tadgemole nodded. 'Aye. This is a strange world.
And a stranger day than ever I thought to see.' He
hesitated for a moment and then said, 'Take this,
then, maid – Midge. Perhaps it will help you.' He held
the folded piece of paper out towards her.

Midge briefly wiped her palms on the knees of her
jeans, and stood up – rather shakily. She had the sense
that she was being trusted with the care of something
precious, and as she gently slid the piece of paper into
the inside pocket of her fleece she said, 'Thank you.
I'll look after it, I promise.'

'Aye. It is all that our tribe have of Celandine, and
all that remains to me of my brother's hand. If it can
serve a purpose, then I am glad that you should take it
– but I should like to see it safe again.'

'Did your brother . . . I mean, is he . . . ?'

'Loren died young. The winters were ever a hard
time for us.'

It was plain that Tadgemole had no wish to say any
more. Midge pulled up the collar of her fleece and
turned hesitantly towards the doorway of the barn.

'But what shall I do,' she said to Pegs, 'if I find out
anything? About Celandine, I mean. Do you want me
to come and tell you?'

*You must keep away from the forest, Midge. Much has
changed since you were there, and little for the good. The old
Queen has gone, and now Maglin rules in her stead. All
tribes are divided, and there is much foolish talk . . .*

'Pah! Treacherous talk!' Tadgemole's pale face had begun to redden. '*Heathen* talk!'

Midge looked at Tadgemole, surprised at his sudden anger. What was all this about?

. . . which things do not concern you, maid. Do your part, if you can, and all will be made right. If you would speak with me, then come here. Come to this place, and at this light of the day if you can, and I shall do the same if I can, each day and at this light until we meet again.

Midge wanted to learn more, but decided that it might be better not to ask. And besides, she had quite enough to think about as it was. 'All right, then.' She sidled through the barn doorway, narrowing her eyes against the sudden bite of the wind. 'Brr! I'll, um . . . well, I'll see you . . .'

Briefly parted, maid. And soon united.

'Yes. At least . . . I hope so.'

But as Midge stepped away from the barn, it seemed hardly likely that this parting was to be a brief one. She thrust her hands deep into the pockets of her fleece and started to negotiate the steep descent of Howard's Hill, dodging among the coarse tufts of wet grass. How did you go about tracing long-lost ancestors? Where on earth would you even begin? No, she didn't think that she would be seeing Pegs again for a while. She looked over her shoulder for a moment or two as she clumped down the slope, in order to take one last glance at the pig-barn. The Summer Palace. There wasn't much that was summery about it today. Or palace-like. But what amazing secrets it held. Just so amazing . . .

A few paces more and the little building had bobbed out of view. *Tap-tap-tap*. Midge heard a last faint rattling of the tin roof, an eerie sound floating away on the January wind. Maybe there was something unsettling in that sound, or maybe it was just the need to get warm, but at any rate she turned and gave in to gravity, allowing her legs to be carried forward in ever larger strides, one . . . two . . . three . . . four, until finally she was running – and very quickly running out of control. Arms flailing, she leaped and bounded down the hillside, kept upright only by a series of miracles, saw the sheep-gate rushing towards her and just managed to grab at one of the rails as she crashed up against it. She hung there for a minute, horribly winded, her heart thumping painfully in her bruised ribcage.

Midge stared down at the buildings of Mill Farm until her vision stopped pulsating and she was at last able to catch her breath. Stupid. Stupid, stupid. She'd been lucky not to break her neck.

Chapter Five

Midge sat on the corner of her bed, studying the pencil drawing that Tadgemole had given her. It wasn't a very good drawing, and that was part of the trouble – the work of an eight-year-old perhaps, or maybe someone even younger. The lines were sketchy and hesitant, and if she hadn't been told that this was a picture of Celandine then she would never have guessed it. Where was the long wavy hair, for a start? Hidden under that weird piece of headgear, presumably.

The figure *did* look like a nun, though, with that big cross about her throat. And so maybe this was what had become of Celandine. She'd joined a convent.

It didn't seem much to go on. Midge had looked at the drawing many times now, and had read the words on the opposite page over and over, but she could find nothing there to help her. And yet sometimes, just *sometimes*, she felt as though that rough little sketch had . . .

Had what? Had some detail in it that she'd seen before? Or something that she was missing? The harder she looked, the more certain she felt that the image held no meaning for her. But then if she laid it aside for a while and looked at it again later, a brief flicker of recognition would sometimes flare up inside her. And instantly die away.

Midge shook her head. She got up from the bed and went and stood before the photograph of Celandine that hung upon her wall. She knew every detail of that photograph now, every shadow and highlight on that pale little face, every button that pulled and pinched, every strand of unruly hair.

'But where are you?' she whispered. 'And how shall I ever find you? Can you hear me?' Then she felt foolish, because of course there was nobody to hear her at all.

The eyes always seemed to be looking past her, concentrating on something just over her shoulder. What was it that they had seen that day, when the photo had been taken? Midge glanced behind her, as though the answer might be here in this room. Nothing but her own modern possessions: the little blue lamp at her bedside, the new office chair, the blank grey screen of her laptop. She sighed, and wandered over to plonk herself on the edge of the bed again. The bounciness of the new mattress threw her off balance, and Midge's hand jiggled the corner of the desk as she reached out to steady herself. This was enough to bring the laptop to life from stand-by, and after a few gentle whirrs and clicks, the screen brightened.

Midge looked at the wildlife scene that she had chosen for her desktop image: the magpie, perched among the winter brambles. It was such a beautiful thing. She had always thought that a magpie's plumage was plain black and white, but here were electric blues and emerald greens that were just as startling as the colours in a peacock's tail.

The picture drew her into a trance, and after a while she was gazing through it and thinking of something else entirely. How and where to begin. How and where . . .

'*Watch the birdie . . . quite, quite still . . .*'

Midge sat upright with a jolt. What was that? What had she heard? She frowned at the computer screen. Had the sound turned itself on?

No. It took her a few moments to be absolutely sure, but the words had not come from the computer. They were more like a memory, a thing triggered inside her head. *Watch the birdie.* A half-familiar phrase. Something that somebody had once said, or used to say. But where could she have heard those words? A photographer . . .

Midge dragged her attention away from the light of the screen, and turned towards the photograph of Celandine, hanging in the shadows beside the wardrobe. The eyes were looking past her, as always. She followed the direction of that distant gaze, and found herself led back to the laptop. How weird. Again she looked at Celandine, and again at the laptop. There was no doubt about it: the girl in the photograph was looking straight at the magpie onscreen. Celandine was watching the birdie.

The room seemed cold, just for a moment, and the

brightness of the computer screen reminded Midge of looking through a window – sitting in a chilly room and looking out of the window, at a bird. Was this something she had seen before?

No, it was no good. She couldn't get it, couldn't quite bring it back somehow. But at least the experience had given her an idea. Or perhaps it was Celandine who had given her the idea, a place to begin. She sat herself on the blue swivel chair and clicked onto her home page. Then she moved the cursor across to the Search box.

'Midge, are you up there?'

Her mum's footsteps on the stairs, coming halfway up and then stopping. Listening for her reply. Midge turned her head towards the door.

'Yeah. I'm in my room, Mum.'

'I'm just finishing off the ironing. Is your school uniform all ready for Monday?'

'Um . . . yeah. It's in the wardrobe.' Go away, Mum.

'Are you sure? What are you doing – homework?'

'Yeah. I'm on the computer.'

'OK, then. Katie and George have just arrived, and tea'll be ready in about ten minutes. We'll eat at Brian's tonight.' The footsteps receding.

Midge gave it another few moments more before clicking onto the Search box. She typed in 'Celandine Howard', moved the cursor over to Go, and hit the button. Then she rested her chin in her hands and waited.

Nothing. All that came up was *'no entries under this name'*.

Midge tried typing in 'C. Howard' instead. This, at least, produced a few results. A doctor in Wisconsin, a logistics company, a paper manufacturer . . . Midge worked her way through the meagre list. She could find nothing that suggested even the remotest connection to Celandine.

This was useless. Midge didn't even know what she was looking for, or hoping to find. What had she expected – a handy record of her ancestor's life, together with a current address and phone number? A website dedicated to Celandine Howard? Not very likely.

And yet she couldn't escape the nagging thought that there was an answer waiting to be found in there somewhere, hidden deep in the ether, far beyond the window of her laptop screen.

Midge rubbed her eyes and rolled back her chair. She leaned across to the bed and picked up the drawing once more. A nun. A-nun-a-nun-a-nun. Was it really worth even *thinking* about trawling the internet for convents . . . monasteries . . . ?

'Midge, come on! Tea's ready.' Her mother's voice again.

'OK, Mum. I'm coming.' Midge shut down the computer. It was a relief to be able to give up.

The five of them sat around the kitchen table: Uncle Brian, Katie, George, Midge and Midge's mum – Christine. It had become a loose arrangement, whilst all the building work was going on, to eat together in whichever room was the most habitable. Now that

both kitchens were more or less complete, the two families still occasionally shared meals – and especially if Katie and George were staying over.

Uncle Brian ladled out five plates of stew and said, 'Well, I learned something down at the Crown last night, Chris. Our family's part-German. Or it could be part-Austrian. Can you believe it?'

'What? Who told you that?'

'Albert Hughes – one of the old boys who plays crib on a Sunday. His grandad was the farm foreman here during the First World War. I already knew about that. Hadn't realized that Great-grandma was German, though. Apparently it caused some bad feeling locally. Not surprising, I suppose, considering that we were at war with Germany at the time.'

'Hm. Funny that we never heard about it before, though.' Mum seemed to be taking this news with a pinch of salt.

'Well, it's not so strange, if you think about it. We were back at war with Germany again just a few years later. You probably wouldn't go broadcasting the fact that your family was linked to the fatherland, if you had any sense.'

'Perhaps not. So what prompted this conversation then?'

'Well, it was Midge really. She was trying to find out a bit more about Great-aunt Celandine. So I asked Albert Hughes and old Wilf Tucker if they knew anything. Like walking history books, those two are. Pass the pepper, George, would you? Thanks.'

'And did they?' said Midge. 'Know anything, I mean?'

'No, not really. Nothing that we hadn't already heard, that is. "She were away wi' the fairies" and so on. No proper details. Wilf reckoned she might have ended up in an asylum, but it was only hearsay. Funnily enough, Albert Hughes thought that Great-grandma's brother *worked* in an asylum. Knew his name and everything – Wesser. Quite well known, apparently. That was what convinced me that it was probably true. But there was nothing about Celandine, I'm afraid. Sorry, Midge. Not much help.'

'It's OK. I was just curious, that's all.' Midge looked down at her plate, and tried not to let her disappointment show.

Mum said, 'Well, it probably wouldn't be too difficult to check up on. What was the name again – Vessar?'

'Wesser – with a W.'

'We ought to try and make up a family tree,' said Mum. 'Go on one of those ancestry sites on the internet.'

'Mm. Expect it'd cost money, though.' Uncle Brian no longer seemed particularly interested.

Midge pushed the remains of her food around her plate. Wesser, with a W. She was tired, and she didn't seem to be able to think straight, but that name stuck with her for some reason. It was visible. She could picture the way it would look on a page. Wesser, with a W.

Dr Wesser. Yes, that was it. Dr Josef Wesser. Standing on the front steps of a building. The Butterfly Farm . . .

Midge scraped back her chair. 'Can I get down?' she said.

Her first thought was to phone Kerry Hodge, but then she realized that she didn't have Kerry's number. There must be dozens of Hodges in the directory, and so there would be no point in trying there. She needed to have another look at that Butterfly Farm brochure now, though. Yes, but how? Maybe there was a website.

Midge ran upstairs to her room and restarted her laptop. She typed 'Tone Vale Butterfly Farm' into Search, and up it came – with a web address. Good. She clicked on the address and after a few clicks and whirrs the site logo appeared. Midge looked at the menu: *Site Map . . . North American Species . . . European Species . . . History. History* – that was what she wanted.

She scrolled quickly down the history page, speed-reading little sections as she went . . . 'built in 1858 to house a private collection . . . taken over during the

First World War and used as a recovery clinic for the military ... Lewis and Wesser later becoming well-recognized pioneers in alternative therapies ...'

And suddenly there it was – the same photograph that she'd seen on Kerry's brochure. This was much bigger and clearer, though. The two men and the nurse stood on the steps of the white building, gazing out at her. Dr Sydney Lewis and Dr Josef Wesser, founders of the Tone Valley Clinic. One of the men was quite stout, balding, with a big moustache and glasses. The other was taller and darker, bearded, with surprisingly long hair. Perhaps a bit younger. But which one was Dr Wesser? Midge peered closely at the two faces, trying to spot some sort of family likeness. Could one of these men possibly be related to her? She struggled to work out what that relationship would be. So, if one of them was her great-great ... great ... grandmother's *brother*, then that would make him ... what? Celandine's uncle? Was that right? Maybe she could figure it out on a piece of paper.

But what then? Even if this Josef Wesser did turn out to be some sort of distant relative, how would it help her? Midge glanced at the clock in the corner of the screen. She ought to be thinking about getting her school stuff organized for the morning. Perhaps this would all have to wait.

And yet there *was* something here, she knew it, something playing hide-and-seek with her memory. Something that she wasn't quick enough to catch. She had felt it as she sat in the gardens with Sam that day, and she felt it now. Maybe she was searching in the wrong place, after all. She rested her chin in her hands and let her eyes wander where they would.

How young that little nurse looked, standing there all proud and upright, arms at her side. The dark uniform was at least a couple of sizes too big for her – very nearly scraping the ground – and the white pinafore sagged slightly, so that you could only just make out the sign of the red cross on her chest. Hair tucked away under some complicated piece of head-gear. A bit like a nun. Yes, a bit like the drawing that—

Midge was jolted backwards in her chair, her whole scalp tingling with the shock of realization – and recognition. She looked across at the piece of paper that still lay upon her bed, and then back at the computer screen.

'*Oh my God . . .*' The words came out of her in a whispered gasp. 'It's *you*. I can't believe it. You're right *there . . .*'

How could she have missed it? How could she have not seen it straight away? The dark eyes gazed out at her from a face that had grown a little thinner, a little older. The extraordinary cloud of hair had disappeared altogether, either cropped short or hidden away beneath the nurse's headdress. And the smile looked different too – more relaxed maybe, not so forced. But it was still her. Absolutely and un-mistakably *her*. Celandine.

Midge gaped at the screen, her head turning somersaults, quite unable to believe her luck. If she hadn't sat next to Kerry on the coach that day, she'd *never* have discovered this. Never in a million years.

And if Tadgemole hadn't given her that funny drawing, then the similarity to the girl in the photo might never have been noticed. But there she stood, Celandine, as clear as day.

At last she had a lead, a real starting point. This one amazing photograph told her so much. Celandine had not just disappeared, or gone 'into an asylum' – not as a patient, anyway. Here she was, out in the world, with a proper job and an identity. She had become a *nurse*, not a nun, working in the same clinic as her uncle, Josef Wesser. He was quite a well-known man, it seemed, in which case there would surely be records of what had happened to his niece?

Tomorrow she would email the Butterfly Farm, and make a start. But for tonight Midge was content to just sit and gaze in wonder at the picture on her screen, amazed at how much she had discovered in such a short time. This was all meant to be, she was certain of it now. It wasn't just down to pure luck.

With that thought, Midge turned round and looked at the other picture of Celandine, the one that hung in shadows upon her wall.

'You *want* this to happen, don't you?' she whispered. 'You want me to find you, I know you do. Well, I'm trying.'

Chapter Six

Midge finished writing her email and signed it 'Margaret Walters'. It sounded more grown up than 'Midge', she thought, and so it might be taken more seriously.

Dear Sirs,

I was very interested to see in your Butterfly Farm brochure that there's a picture of Dr Wesser and also a picture of a nurse whose name is Celandine Howard. Do you have any information, especially on Miss Howard? Only she is a distant relative of mine and I'm trying to find out more about her. Do you know what happened to her when she was working at the clinic, and when she left, or anything at all? I would be very interested to know, and perhaps you would email me. Thank you for your help.

Yours faithfully,
Margaret Walters

Yes, that seemed OK. Midge went through the email for spelling mistakes, and then hit Send.

What now? There was nothing much more that she could do, other than wait for a reply. It was exciting, though. The Butterfly Farm *must* have kept records of some sort, otherwise how could they have got the information to put into the brochure? She looked again at the onscreen photograph of Celandine in her oversized nurse's uniform. How old would she have been then – fifteen? Fourteen? They surely wouldn't have let her work as a nurse if she'd been much younger than that, and yet she looked tiny next to the two men. Small for her age, probably. Midge nodded to herself. She knew what that felt like.

But she must not waste this time, whilst she was waiting for a reply. She must think. It was important to keep thinking.

Brmmmmm – blatt-blatt-blatt . . . The cement mixer had started up. That meant the builders were here. Already. Midge growled with frustration – so much for being able to think. She left her room and clumped down the uncarpeted stairs, edging past the open toolboxes and sheets of plasterboard, the tubs of emulsion, the tubes of sealant . . .

Would they *ever* be finished? It was like some kind of torture, living in this perpetual noise and mess. It seemed especially unfair to have to put up with it on Saturdays, when she was supposed to be *relaxing*, for goodness' sake.

Mum and Uncle Brian were having one of their talks in the cluttered hallway. Here was a kind of no-man's-land between the separate partitions of the house – their bit, and Uncle Brian's bit – and it was here that the two of them often stood, planning the day's operations.

'So, you can pick up the printer then?' Her mum.

'Yeah, I can do that. I'm seeing the chap about the kitchen equipment at eleven, then over to talk to Alan Lavers about wine at two-thirty. I can get the printer on the way back. What about you?' Uncle Brian was wearing his tweed jacket, and for some reason he had a pair of binoculars around his neck. He looked more like he was off to a day at the races than a series of business meetings.

'I'm on the phone for the next two hours at least, trying to get some sense into Stubbing's lot. Useless twerps. I'm tempted to ditch them altogether. Why do they make these promises if they can't keep them? It simply isn't professional. Oh, hi, Midge. What are you up to, darling?'

'Thought I might go and throw myself into the cement mixer,' said Midge. 'Or make a cup of coffee. I haven't decided which.'

Mum laughed. 'Poor baby,' she said. 'It does all get a bit fraught, doesn't it? Never mind. Just keep thinking ahead to May the first. That's when we open for business – come hell or high water. While I think of it, Brian, we need to talk about shrubs . . .'

Midge began to wander off. This was all too dull for words.

'. . . and I thought maybe we could go over to that new place at North Perrott – Almbury Mills? Barry was telling me about it. It's huge, apparently . . . garden centre, furniture, cafés, bookshops.'

Midge pricked up her ears. This wasn't the first time she'd heard that name: Barry. Yes, it had come up a couple of times lately – Barry this, and Barry that. Barry says we could have got it in Argos at half the price. Barry thinks that white's a far better choice than magnolia. Midge grabbed her jacket and paused by the front door, pretending to search her pockets – trying to appear as though she might have to go back upstairs for something she'd forgotten.

'Oh, yes,' said Uncle Brian. 'I know where Almbury Mills is. Must be about twenty miles away, though. We could make a day out of it. Maybe the kids'd like to come. What do you think, Midge?'

'Sorry? What did you say? I wasn't listening.'

'Your mum says perhaps we could . . .'

'Who's this "Barry"?' Midge said. She just blurted it out, and saw the quick look of confusion in her mum's eyes. So. It was as she'd suspected, then.

'Barry? Well, he's a friend, darling. A friend.'

'What, like a boyfriend, you mean?'

'Well, not exactly. But . . . you know. I'll tell you later, sweetheart. We'll have a proper conversation.'

'Is he going to be moving in with us, then?'

'Whaaaaat? *No*, he's not going to be moving *in* with us. Midge . . . where are you—?'

But Midge was off. She opened the front door, slid through the gap, and immediately pulled the door firmly shut behind her – not slamming it exactly, but not far short.

The cold morning air was acrid with diesel fumes from the cement mixer, and now the big digger thing had started up as well. What a racket. And honestly – *Barry*. Who in their right mind would allow themselves to be called Barry? Nobody. Didn't she have enough to worry about already, without all this?

One of the workmen gave her a cheery wave as she hurried down the front path, and Midge had to wave back at him just out of politeness.

Two days later, on the Monday evening, she had an email from the Butterfly Farm.

Dear Ms Walters,

How interesting that you should be related to Dr Wesser and Miss Howard! Unfortunately, most of the information that we have concerning the history of the Butterfly Farm is already in the brochure. However, I've attached a file with the few remaining snippets. You'll see from these that Miss Howard apparently ran her own clinic here in the main building for many years. It seems to have closed in 1976, shortly before the premises was taken over by the art college. I imagine that she would have retired then, if not before, as she must have been in her early seventies. We have no record of what happened to her beyond that point. That was almost thirty years ago, and so if Miss Howard were still alive she would be a very old lady indeed!

Have you tried the local library, or perhaps the County Gazette*? They may have more information on the history of the clinic. Do let me know how you get on.*

With best wishes,

Nigel Epps (Dir.), Tone Vale Butterfly Farm

Midge clicked on the email attachment and opened the file. There were three or four newspaper clippings about the clinic. One of them had a picture of some men – airforce pilots apparently – all sitting in wheelchairs and looking unaccountably cheerful. There was another picture of a group of art students at work, who by contrast looked rather serious. No pictures of Celandine. Midge quickly scanned the columns of text, searching for some mention of her great-great-aunt. There was only one, and they'd got her name wrong.

Clinic to Close

Tone Valley Clinic, a private hospital since the Great War, is to close its doors this autumn. Servicemen from both the First and Second World Wars were treated at Tone Valley, many for shell shock, and it was here that pioneering treatment was developed by Drs Sydney Lewis and Josef Wesser. Part of the clinic was opened as a centre for alternative medicine as early as 1936, and this was run for forty years by Wesser's niece, Miss Geraldine Howard. Former governor Tommy Palmer (79) said today, 'It's a great shame that the clinic is to close, but the development of newer facilities at the main hospital (Staplegrove) has made it redundant, and the expense of upkeep is too great. Miss Howard is a personal friend, very well respected in her field, and her work has greatly benefited the local community. I'm sure that the building and grounds will be put to good future use.'

And that was it. The other articles were about Dr Lewis and Dr Wesser, and about the art college leasing the building in 1978, but there was no other reference to Celandine.

Midge sat back in her chair and stared at the screen. She was so disappointed.

Finding this link to Celandine had seemed such a breakthrough, but now she felt as though she was just as far away as she had ever been. How could she hope to track down someone who had disappeared nearly thirty years ago, and who was an old lady even then? And how old, seriously, would Celandine have to be if she were still alive? Midge tried to do a quick bit of mental arithmetic. A hundred and two? A hundred and three? Something like that. Something ridiculous.

But she couldn't give up. Not yet. Not until she really knew that she was beaten. Maybe she'd email the local gazette and see if they had any more information, go to the library perhaps . . . or maybe she should try and persuade her mum to fork out for a search on one of those ancestry sites. Not tonight, though. There was homework to be done.

On Wednesday evening Katie came over, and the two of them had supper at Uncle Brian's. Midge felt envious of Katie, chatting away, nothing more on her mind apparently than shoes and mp3 players, and the 'amazing' exploits of some celebrity or another. Didn't she ever wake up in the night and gasp with fear and wonder at the *truly* amazing things that had happened to her? Didn't she ever think about that day when she had actually seen the little people? If she did, then she never let on.

As the supper things were being loaded into the dishwasher, the subject of Celandine came up again, in a roundabout way. Uncle Brian pulled open the drawer of the Welsh dresser and took out some sort of package – a brown envelope, folded, with an elastic band round it.

'While I remember it, Midge, here are those papers I was telling you about. You know, the old farm bills and what-have-you. I had another quick flip through them myself, and can't see that there's anything that'd be of much use to you. But you never know. Might be worth a look.'

'Oh. OK. Thanks.' Midge took the bundle and felt slightly self-conscious. Should she open it up now? 'I'll have a look later,' she said.

'Bet *that*'ll be interesting,' said Katie. 'Want some coffee? We can go and watch *EastEnders* together.'

'All right.'

They sat side by side on the living-room sofa, the TV switched on, and to Midge's surprise Katie mentioned the little people – sort of.

'I don't know why you keep picking at it,' she said. 'You know . . . what happened. You can't tell anyone, or do anything about it. Are you up to something?'

Midge took a sip of her coffee. She half wished that she could talk to Katie about what was going on – *why* she was searching for Celandine, and how she had become involved with the Various all over again. It would be good to tell someone. And yet she knew that she never could.

'No, I'm not up to anything. I'm just interested in Aunt Celandine, that's all.'

Yet now that Katie had acknowledged what lay between them, Midge couldn't resist going a step further.

'It's funny how we never talk about it,' she said.

'Not funny at all, really,' said Katie. 'We only talk about what we think about. And I never think about it. It's easy. I just make myself not think about it and then it doesn't bother me. You ought to do the same.' She sounded tetchy.

'Yeah, maybe you're right. Does George ever talk to you about it?'

Katie shook her head. 'Never mentions it. Oh! That Billy makes me so *mad*. He needs to get his act together, or they'll be splitting up again – you just wait and see.'

'What?' said Midge. But then she realized that Katie was lost in what was happening on the screen. The goings on in Albert Square were apparently far more real to her than her encounter with the Various.

Midge slipped the rubber band off her envelope and drew out the contents. There was a long slim book of some sort, with a grey marbled cover, and a few folded pieces of paper. The pieces of paper were mostly bills, by the look of them, or receipts: Lopen Feed Mills, Allen Bros., Blacksmith and Farriers . . . J. L. Bright and Partners, Solicitors . . . veterinary bills . . .

It was strange to see everything written out in such neat sloping handwriting, the sums and figures all in the old money that they'd used before decimal came in. *To treating a sick horse (Beamer) . . . £1 . . . 4s . . . 4d. To repairing an iron gate and making good . . . £0 . . . 3s . . . 9d.*

Quite interesting, but not likely to get her anywhere. Midge opened the book and saw that it was a farm ledger. More dry facts and figures: so many calves born, so many loads of hay sold. But again everything was beautifully written out in a rich black ink, some of the words painstakingly underlined in red. Copperplate handwriting – was that what they called it? . . . *Income for the month of August . . . Expenditure for the month of September . . . Mount Pleasant School for Girls . . . Fees: 2 guineas.*

What was a guinea? Midge paused, holding the corner of the page between finger and thumb. And what was this 'Mount Pleasant School for Girls'?

She sat there looking at the words for a while, then glanced up at the top of the page, to where the date was written out: September 1914.

September 1914. Would Celandine have been a schoolgirl then? It seemed about right. So maybe this could be where she went to school: Mount Pleasant School for Girls . . .

'*Do what, Peggy? You're 'avin' a larf, incha . . . ?*' The telly blared on. Katie tucked her legs up onto the sofa, and Midge shifted along a bit.

Perhaps this school still existed. And if it did, then perhaps they'd have kept a record of what had happened to their former pupils. Schools sometimes did, and particularly where pupils had gone on to do things that would make the school proud of them, as

95

Celandine surely had. Also . . . yes, *also* . . . there was the possibility of reunions, pupils keeping in touch with one another – an Old Girls Association, maybe. She could try one of those 'friends united' sites! Now that would definitely be worth a stab.

Midge closed the little ledger, feeling better now that she had a new plan to work on. There was another folded piece of paper protruding from the book, inserted between the last page and the back cover. Midge began to tuck it in, but then changed her mind and pulled it out to take a look.

It turned out to be two pieces of paper – one inside the other – both headed 'Mount Pleasant School for Girls'. But how amazing . . .

The first was a bill, addressed to Mr E. V. Howard:

To repairing wilful damage to school property, and redecorating: £14 . . . 8s . . . 0d.
To full recompense for wilful damage to pupils' property: £31 . . . 11s . . . 10d
Total: . . . . £45 . . . 19s . . . 10d

Please pay this account promptly.
R. D. Ainsworth (Bursar)

Wilful damage? This didn't look good. Midge moved on to the second sheet of paper – a hand-written letter.

Dear Mr Howard,
    Please find the enclosed bill for damage and expenses. As I

96

have said in my previous correspondence, your daughter's disgusting and abominable behaviour has been quite inexcusable. If I hadn't the school's reputation to consider, I should have certainly pressed for serious charges in this matter. Indeed I have only been able to persuade others not to insist upon my doing so by pointing out that it would not benefit their own daughters to have the school's reputation for high standards compromised. I have also asked them to take into consideration the recent loss of your son to the War, and that you should thus be spared the embarrassment of a legal suit at such a time.

Naturally there can be no question of Miss Howard returning to continue her education at Mount Pleasant.

I trust that you will settle the enclosed account immediately in order that the school can reimburse those parents affected for the considerable trouble and costs that they have incurred.

Yours sincerely,

A. Craven (Headmistress)

Wow! Midge rested the letter in her lap and gawped at the TV screen. What on earth could Celandine have done that was so terrible?

'Find anything?' Katie yawned as the programme came to an end and the credits began to roll.

Midge handed the letter over. 'Yeah. This.'

Katie yawned again and looked at the letter – then sat up straight as she began to read through it.

'Yipes! I can't believe this! Sounds like she was a right little madam. Wonder what she did, though? "Disgusting and abominable behaviour . . ." Maybe she was round the back of the gym with one of the gardeners.'

'No. Read it again. It's actual damage. There's a bill here – forty-five quid.'

'Doesn't seem *that* much.' Katie looked at the bill.

'Yeah, but that would probably have been like hundreds in today's money.'

'Suppose so. Well, well, well. Great-aunt Celandine – nothing but a hooligan! A vandal! What are you going to do now?'

'Well, I *was* going to see whether the school still existed, and whether there was like a reunion site or something for old pupils. Doesn't seem much point now, though.'

'Noooo. Sounds like she might have blotted the jolly old copybook. Eh what, me old sport, me old spiffy?'

'Ha! Just a bit.'

Yes, and that was a blow. It seemed unlikely that Celandine would ever have been a welcome member of any kind of old girls' club after what she'd done . . . whatever it was that she *had* done.

Midge picked up the ledger and the bits of paper, and put them back in the envelope. So. That was that.

Saturday rolled round again, and Midge was getting nowhere. She'd gone on a computer search, just for the lack of any better idea, typed in 'Mount Pleasant School for Girls', and found to her astonishment that there were loads of them. Or at least there were loads of schools with Mount Pleasant in the name, but they were all much too far away to have been possible candidates: Switzerland, Auckland, Delaware . . . even the one in Hampshire would surely have been a non-starter.

The local paper had responded to her email kindly, but regretfully, saying that they had nothing in their files on the Tone Valley Clinic that she hadn't already seen. It was all beginning to get her down a bit. And now she had to waste her whole Saturday afternoon doing something she did *not* want to do: meeting Barry.

They were going on a shopping trip to this Almbury Mills place, to look at shrubs, of all things. Barry knew a lot about *shrubs*, apparently, and so he would be coming along to advise her mum and Uncle Brian on what to choose. Also it would be a chance to say hallo, and get to know one another. Great.

Normally she could have just said no to such a boring excursion, and stayed at home, but of course that wasn't an option in this case. Because of *Barry*.

'Come on, Midge,' her mum said. 'It'll be an afternoon out, and Barry's really looking forward to meeting you. And Brian, of course. Play nice, eh? I think he's a bit nervous about it, actually.'

Yeah, so he should be, thought Midge. But she just sighed and said, 'OK.'

Well, he had a pretty flash car, that was something. She heard the toot of the horn and looked out of the sitting-room window to see a new silver Saab pulling up in front of the house. It looked very out of place, and vulnerable, as it nosed between the diggers and the piles of rubble that cluttered the yard. Cool, though.

Midge watched as the car door opened and a man got out. Blimey. He was *ancient*. Or maybe it was just the white hair. Not very tall, either.

She stayed where she was as Barry disappeared from view, heard the knock on the front door and her mother's voice in the hallway.

'Midge, are you ready? Come on!'

Oh well, there was nothing else for it. Midge arrived in the hallway, just as Uncle Brian came out of his kitchen door, and then there was the whole embarrassing confusion of who was to be introduced first.

'Barry, this is Brian . . .'

'Oh, hi . . .'

'And Margaret – Midge. This is Barry . . . Barry – Midge, Brian . . .'

'Hiya.' Did she shake hands? Yes, apparently she did. A quick impression of pale fingers, a very light squeeze of her hand. Then the inevitable awkwardness of everybody trying to speak at once.

'Found us OK, then?'

'Yes. No trouble, thanks, Brian. Well . . . ap-part from . . .' (Was that a stammer? How nervous could he be?)

'Don't tell me – the Ilminster roundabout . . .'

'Yes . . .'

'What, no SatNav? I should have thought you could go to sleep in that thing and still arrive safe and sound . . .' Her mum chipping in.

'Yes, there's just one exit too many, isn't there . . .' Brian again.

And then they were all out on the front path, and Barry looked at Uncle Brian and said, 'I have to say, I c-can't see much of a family resemblance.'

'Haha!' Uncle Brian laughed. 'No. I *think* you've probably made the right choice when it comes to looks.'

'Well, I sh-shan't argue with you there.'

He *did* have a bit of a stammer, then. Wonderful. What a catch. Midge trailed behind the grown-ups, and they all got into Barry's car – Midge and Uncle Brian in the back, of course, and her mum and Barry in the front. The happy couple. Still, there hadn't been any gruesome kissing, so that was a plus. And it *was* a very nice car. Like an aeroplane in there, with all its lights and dials.

She was glad that her Uncle Brian was coming along. He broke the tension somehow, talking easily to Barry about the plans for Mill Farm, how the old cider barn was to become a teashop, with a licensed bar, and how the former stables were being turned into holiday apartments for those who were interested in coming to see the wetlands. He made everybody laugh by saying, 'And of course, I shall be able to laze around swigging claret all day, and getting paid for my hobby.'

At one point Uncle Brian reached across and gave her hand an understanding little squeeze. He was a pretty cool guy, thought Midge. Barry, she wasn't so sure about. She studied the back of his head, occasionally caught his eye in the rear-view mirror and quickly looked away. She knew absolutely nothing about him. What was he – some kind of salesman? She and her mum had never had that promised conversation. There never seemed to be any time to talk.

'So how's the music business then, Barry?' Uncle Brian apparently knew more than she did.

'Not bad. Plenty of work, at any rate. Get a bit f-fed up with the touring sometimes. And the egos.'

'Yes, Chris used to be the same, I think.'

'Mm.' Her mum made a little sound of agreement but said no more. Still a touchy subject, maybe. Or maybe she regretted giving her music up to become a businesswoman.

Nobody spoke for a while, and Midge stared out of the window as the miles passed. So Barry was a musician. Another orchestral player probably – although hadn't her mum said something about all this months ago, hinted then that she was seeing someone, but *not* someone from the orchestra? Yes. She'd forgotten all about that. Maybe this was serious, then, if it had been going on since the middle of last year.

The town, when they finally got there, was packed with shoppers. It took ages to get through, and Midge felt more resentful than ever that she'd been dragged along on this trip. What a waste of a Saturday afternoon. The traffic crawled along nose to tail, and even when they'd got past the town centre and out onto the road to North Perrott, it didn't ease up. *Everybody* seemed to be on their way to Almbury Mills.

'Not far now,' said Uncle Brian. 'It's just at the top of this hill, on the left.'

They'd stopped yet again, caught in the long queue of cars that would be turning off to the garden centre. Midge leaned her elbow against the car window, her chin resting on her hand. She found herself staring up at a big old building, set back on a hill, with shrubs and spiky palm trees and neat lawns that swept down towards the road. That couldn't be anything to do with the garden centre, could it? No, far too old. The building was very imposing, with high windows, and a central clock tower. 3:20. Could that be right? By the time they arrived it would be time to go home again.

'See, *they* look nice,' said her mum, looking up at the place, 'those shrubs there. Don't they have yellow flowers later on? What are they again?'

Barry glanced across. 'Forsythia. They're OK. Bit b-boring.'

But then the traffic began to move again and Barry had to look away. They picked up speed, and as they passed the driveway to the building Midge caught a quick glimpse of a sign – 'Mount Pleasant Residential Apartments'. Large black letters on a white background, and then in smaller letters underneath: 'A *caring* home.'

Midge spun round in her seat and tried to look out of the rear window, but the sign was no longer visible. She faced front again, and now the car was pulling into the broad entranceway to Almbury Mills, following the stream of traffic heading for the car parks.

Midge blinked as she tried to remember the details of what she'd seen. Mount Pleasant Residential Apartments . . .

Could it be possible? *Might* that big old building have once been a school?

'There!' said Mum. 'Just over there, Barry – a space.'

'Yes!' Barry swung the car into the vacant space, and turned off the engine. 'Brilliant. The p-parking fairy is smiling upon us.'

As they entered the crowded and echoey complex – all glass domed roof and potted palms – Midge felt Mum's arm go round her shoulder.

'You're very quiet, love. Everything all right?'

'Yeah, I'm fine. Can I have a drink, though?'

'Um . . . well, shall we go and have a look at some plants first? It's taken a bit longer to get here than we expected, and we do need to get a few things sorted out. We can stop for tea in an hour or so.'

'Tell you what, Chris,' said Uncle Brian. 'Why don't

you and Barry go on ahead and make a start, and I'll get Midge a lemonade or something? To be honest, I'm going to be about as much use in the shrub department as a duck in a desert, and I could do with a cup of tea myself. Also, I wouldn't mind a nose around the bookshops. We can catch up with you later.'

'Well, you lazy old b . . .' Mum's voice was loudly indignant, but Midge could see that she wasn't seriously angry. 'So *we* do all the hard work, while you loll around the cafés scoffing buns!'

'Ooh – hadn't thought of that,' said Uncle Brian. 'But now that you mention it, I *could* go for a bun. What do you think, Midge?'

'Well, I might be able to force myself.' Midge looked up at Barry, and saw that he was laughing.

'Come on, Chris,' said Barry. 'It doesn't have to be a p-penance. I don't mind.'

'Sure? Oh . . . all right, then. We've all got mobiles, I suppose. Let's aim to meet up at five, then, if we don't bump into each other before then. See you later.'

'Ruddy plants,' said Uncle Brian, once Mum and Barry were out of earshot. 'Don't see why we need 'em in the first place. I'd be happy to tarmac the lot, frankly, but there you go. I suppose that's the difference between having good taste and not. Come on, let's see if we can bag one of those tables.'

They sat at one of the little café tables that spread out into the busy main concourse, and ordered up drinks and a couple of cakes.

Uncle Brian said, 'What do you make of Barry, then?'

'Um . . . don't know, really. Seems OK, I suppose. A musician, is he?'

'Yes. Quite well known in the business, I think. He puts backing bands together for when big American artists come over here to tour. It's cheaper than bringing their own musicians across if they can use local guys, so I gather they call on Barry to pull in the right people for the job. How's your cake?'

'Good.' Midge took a bite of her chocolate muffin and leaned over her plate to catch the crumbs. She looked up as she did so, and saw someone coming towards their table – a tubby man in a waxed jacket, creeping up behind Uncle Brian. The man winked at her, raised his hand and then slapped it down onto Uncle Brian's shoulder, as though he were a policeman nabbing a convict.

'*Howard*, you old layabout! What the devil are you doing here?'

Uncle Brian spluttered into his teacup, and looked round at his attacker.

'*Clifton*, you appalling specimen! Well, I was enjoying a peaceful spot of tea with my favourite niece, but I can see that it's goodbye to all that. Come and join us, why don't you.'

They spoke to each other in a jokey old-fashioned language, as though they had once been fighter pilots together, or something. Probably just schoolfriends, thought Midge.

'Excellent idea!' The man took off his jacket and draped it over the back of a chair. 'I think I might try one of those chocolate muffins, as it seems to be having such a health-giving effect on your young companion here.'

'Midge, this is Cliff Maybank,' said Uncle Brian. 'Old chum of mine. Shocking type. Well, we've come to buy plants, Cliff, believe it or not. What are *you* doing here?'

'Running a bookshop.' The man looked around for a waitress, waved a stubby finger at one of them, and then sat down. 'Though God knows why I bother. The rates in this place are criminal.'

'Imagine they would be. Given up on the antiques business then?'

'Given up the premises, at any rate. Got a shop on eBay now, selling all sorts.'

'Have you really? Hm. Well, this could be good timing, then, finding you here. We might be able to help each other out. I've got a stack of old stuff on the farm that I could do with getting shot of. Now then . . .'

And away the two of them went, chattering like a couple of schoolboys, so that within half a minute Midge had given up listening. She finished off her muffin, and the last of her lemonade, and then said, 'Uncle Brian, is it OK if I go and have a look in one of the shops? They've got an Accessorize here, and I need to think about getting Katie something for her birthday.'

'Oh Lord, is it that time of year again?' said Uncle Brian. 'I'd forgotten. Um . . . well, yes, I suppose that'd be all right, love − as far as I'm concerned, anyway. Would your mum let you go if she was here?'

'Yeah, she wouldn't mind. It's only just down there.'

'Well, all right, then. I imagine we'll be here for a while yet – I'm not desperate to go wandering through the heathers, that's for sure, or whatever it is that Chris and Barry are doing. Got your mobile?'

'Yeah. It's switched on.'

'OK. See you back here in a bit, then. Don't get lost, or I'll be lynched!'

'I won't.'

Midge made her way back towards the main entrance. She did what she'd said she was going to do, and walked into the little accessories shop that she knew Katie liked. But although she spent a few minutes looking at the bangles and the beads, she wasn't really concentrating on those things at all. She was thinking about that place she had seen just down the road – the Mount Pleasant Residential Apartments. The building *did* look as though it could have once been a school, with its high mullion windows and its parapets and its clock tower. And the distance from Mill Farm would have been reasonable, if it had been a boarding school. A far more likely bet than Hampshire, at any rate. Or the States. How could she find out more about it? Maybe there was a phone number on that signboard, or a web address.

Midge looked at her watch. Four o'clock, not even that. She could be there and back in a few minutes. And her mum wasn't expecting to see her before five, anyway. It would be awful to drive home and then find that the place wasn't in the phone book or on the web.

But if she went now, without any dithering, then nobody would even miss her. It was only just around the corner, and there wasn't even a road to cross. There couldn't be any harm in that, could there?

She went over to the shop doorway and looked back towards the café. There were so many people about that Uncle Brian and his friend were only occasionally visible, and both of them had their backs to her in any case. Come on, then, let's do it.

It felt cold out in the car park after the warmth of the shopping complex, and Midge stuffed her hands into the pockets of her fleece as she hurried along the zig-zagging pavements. She got down to the main road, turned right, and kept on going. The traffic had eased up a bit, but there were still plenty of cars and lorries about and she was glad that she didn't have to try and cross over. Only another hundred yards or so to go. She glanced at her watch again as she reached the driveway that led up to Mount Pleasant. Barely five-past. Good.

But this *wasn't* so good: the painted sign had no telephone number on it, and no web address either. 'Mount Pleasant Residential Apartments. A *caring* home,' it said. And then in quite small letters at the very bottom: 'Strictly Private. Residents access only'. That was it.

Drat. Midge stared up at the big building, and now she felt more certain than ever that she was on the right track. It looked *so* much like a school. She could just imagine Celandine cooped up in there with hundreds of other girls, toiling away. And maybe those higher windows would have been dormitories, where they all slept . . . or wept . . .

It *had* to be the right place. But what was she going to do now? Just forget it and hope that she would be able to phone or email, in order to learn more?

No. She wasn't going to risk it. She'd go in and ask – right now – whilst she was here on the spot. It wouldn't take a minute, and at least she'd know whether she was wasting her time or not. If she only came away with a phone number, that would be something.

It was daunting, though, walking up that steep curving driveway. Midge felt that the eyes of the building were looking down upon her, asking her what business she thought she had being here, accusing her of trespassing. When she got to the top, the drive flattened out, and there was a green-and-white sign that said 'Reception' pointing left towards the main entrance. She felt very small, climbing the steps up to the high arched doorway. There was an intercom system, too modern-looking in its ancient surroundings – and another test of Midge's nerve. She hesitated for a moment, but then pressed the button and waited.

'Yes?' A crackly female voice.

'Er . . . Margaret Walters.' Midge didn't know what else to say.

The buzzer went, and Midge pushed at the door. It wouldn't open.

'Pull.' Another burst of static from the intercom.

Midge pulled at the big brass handle – which, as she now realized, had a very clear sign right next to it saying 'Pull'. The door swung back, and Midge stepped inside. She saw the reception desk immediately, but it was right on the other side of a large open space, which she would have to cross. The girl behind the desk was already looking over at her in surprise. There was a big staircase, a square spiral that seemed to go right the way up through the building, and some lifts, obviously quite new. Midge wiped her feet on the mat and walked towards the desk, feeling very conscious of her grubby trainers on the thick blue carpet. She was aware too of the silence, and of a vague aroma – a mixture of air-freshener and cooking.

'Yes? Can I help you?' The girl behind the desk had lots of make-up on, but she actually looked quite young. Perhaps she'd be friendly.

'Um, yes. I was wondering – did this place used to be a school?'

'A school? This is a retirement home. Private apartments.'

'I know, but was it ever a school? I mean, years ago?' Midge's heart was already sinking. The girl didn't seem too bright.

'Oh. Years ago. I wouldn't know. Might have been, I suppose. But I wouldn't know – I haven't been here that long.'

'Would there be some way of finding out? Only I'm trying to trace someone, you see. I think she might have been at school here.'

'Oh.' The girl thought about it for a moment. Then an idea came to her. 'I could ask,' she said.

Brilliant, thought Midge. You could ask. 'Thanks,' she said. 'It'd be really helpful.'

The girl picked up her phone, very efficient, now that she knew what she was doing, and tapped in a couple of numbers. 'I'll ask the manager,' she whispered, her hand to the phone. 'She's been here for . . . Hallo? Hallo? Is that Carol? Carol, it's Helen. Carol, there's someone down here at reception who wants to know if this place was ever a school. Yes. A girl. Was it a school? she wants to know. Oh, was it? Oh, it was. Thanks.' She went to put the phone down, but Midge quickly said, 'Could you . . . thanks . . . could you just ask if they still have any school records at all? Anything to do with pupils that used to be here.'

'Carol, are you still there? Hallo? Yes. She wants to know if we still have any school records at all. Anything to do with pupils. No. All right. Thanks, then. Bye.'

The girl put the phone down, and said, 'No. Sorry. We don't have any information on that. Schools, or anything. There *are* quite a lot of schools around, though. Have you tried those?'

'It's OK.' Midge tried to bite her tongue. 'I had an aunt, that's all – a great-great-aunt. She might have been at school here, I think. But it was years and years ago.' She stepped back from the desk. 'Anyway, thanks.' She turned to go.

'What was her name?' said the girl. As though her knowing that might help.

'Celandine Howard,' Midge muttered.

'Oh. We've got a Miss Howard here. Her name doesn't begin with an S, though.' The girl laughed. 'And she's a bit too old for school.'

'Celandine begins with a C, not an S,' said Midge. She zipped up her fleece, and glanced at her watch at the same time. Nearly quarter past four.

'Does it?' said the reception girl. 'Oh, well, ours is a "D", anyway. I know that, because she hates it if you call her by her Christian name – Dinah. She hates it even worse if you call her Di. Gets *really* mad, then, the old bat. Sorry. I shouldn't say that about her.'

'Well, thanks anyway,' said Midge. 'Bye.'

'Bye. You have to push the door quite hard to close it properly.'

'OK.'

It was freezing outside, and already beginning to get dark. Midge hurried along the front driveway. She reached the corner of the building, so wrapped up in her own anger and frustration that the sudden glimpse of a big shadowy figure lurking in the bushes nearly made her jump out of her skin.

'Oh!' Her own gasp of alarm was immediately echoed.

'Oh my G—!'

It was a woman – quite a large woman – smoking a cigarette. The woman put her hand to her chest, as though she were having a heart attack.

'Lord, you gave me a fright!' she said. Her breathing was all thick and wheezy.

'Sorry,' said Midge. She stood there for a moment, trying to recover herself.

'Phew!' The woman blew out a puff of smoke. 'What are you doing here, anyway?'

Hey, I could ask you the same question, thought

Midge, but what she actually said was 'I've been looking for a relative. Trying to find someone.'

'Oh, I see. Who's that, then?' The cigarette end
glowed dimly as it was flicked into the bushes.

'Someone called Celandine Howard. Not having
much luck, though.'

'Aren't you? I'd have thought she'd be around at
this time of day.'

'What? Who do you mean?'

'Dinah Howard. Or Celandine Howard, to give her
her proper name. Though she likes us to call her *Miss*
Howard. She'd be getting ready for her tea, I'd have
thought. Isn't she there, then?'

Midge just stared at the woman. 'What – you mean
you *know* her?'

'Well, yeah, course I know her. I don't have much
to *do* with her, like, but I know her. She's our oldest
resident. Didn't you ask at reception?'

Midge felt that her head must be about to spin off
altogether. 'Well yes, but the girl there – Helen, is it? –
she said—'

'Oh, Lord, *that* one.' The woman threw up her
hands in exasperation. 'She's only been here about
ten minutes. Still learning her *own* name, that one is.
Come on, lovey, you come back inside with me. I'll
soon find Miss Howard for you – but one good turn
deserves another, all right? Nothing to anyone about
the cigarettes. It's not allowed, and quite right too –
horrible habit. But giving up's not so easy, either.'

The woman waddled along the drive and Midge
followed her, up the steps, through the arched

114

doorway and back into the building again, feeling completely out of her depth. She saw the reception girl's expression turn from vague surprise to annoyance as the big woman marched wheezily over to the desk and, with no word of acknowledgement, picked up the phone.

'Hallo? Elaine? It's Joan. Hiya, love. There's a girl here in reception come to see Miss Celandine Howard, if you please. Yep, that's right. Eh? Oh, I don't know . . . eleven maybe. Twelve. Can't tell nowadays. Yes? OK. I'll leave her here for you then.'

She put down the phone, still with no word to the girl at the desk, and turned to Midge.

'Elaine'll be down in a minute. She looks after Miss Howard, mostly.'

'Oh. Well . . . thanks. Thank you very much.'

'No trouble, love. *Just* a matter of knowing what you're doing, that's all.' The woman did throw the girl a quick glance, then, before walking over to the open lift. She pressed the button, gave Midge a wink as the door closed, and disappeared.

Midge was so stunned, she didn't know what to do. She'd been totally unprepared for the idea that Celandine might actually *be* here. The possibility hadn't even occurred to her. She stood awkwardly in the centre of the reception space, trying to imagine what might be about to happen, and how she was going to deal with it. The girl at the desk seemed very busy with her computer now, and gave her no eye contact.

There was a faint *whoosh* from the lift, a *ping*, and one of the doors opened. A woman was standing there. She paused for a second before stepping out, her movement almost hesitant. Younger and smaller than the woman in the garden had been, wearing the same sort of light-blue shift. She raised her hands to her glasses, lowered them for a second as she looked at Midge, then put them back where they were. The expression on her face, as she came closer, was more than just one of curiosity, or even surprise. She looked really quite shocked.

'Hello, love,' she said. 'So you've come to see Miss Howard, then. Is that right?'

'Um . . . well . . . I've been trying to find out more about her. I wasn't expecting to actually *see* her.' Something of the woman's apparent nervousness seemed to be catching, and Midge found that her voice was actually quite shaky.

'Weren't you? Well, she's been expecting to see *you*, I can tell you. What's your name, dear?'

'Midge. Midge Walters.'

'Midge? Right. Well then, Miss Howard's just about to—' The woman broke off for a moment, and called to someone over Midge's shoulder. 'Carol? Carol – could I trouble you for a moment?'

Midge turned round and saw another woman crossing the open space behind her. This one was dressed in a dark-grey trouser suit, very smart, and looked as though she might well be the one in charge around here.

'Yes?' The smart woman changed direction and

came over to where they were standing, bringing with her a faintly perfumed air of authority.

'Carol, this young lady is here to see Miss Howard.' The words of the first woman hung there, spoken as though they had some sort of extra meaning to them.

The smart woman stared at her colleague. Then she looked directly at Midge.

'To see Miss Howard? Well, I'm . . . er . . . I'm' – she gave a quick laugh – 'caught off-guard, as you can see. Absolutely astonished, in fact. Um . . . OK, then, Elaine. You'd better go and break this news to Miss Howard, and then bring her down for her tea as usual. In the meantime I'll take our visitor along to the day room, and we'll see you both there. What's your name, dear?'

'Midge Walters.' Midge caught a last glance of amazement from the first woman as she returned to the lift. What was going *on*? Why was everybody so surprised to see her?

'Right then, Midge,' said the smart woman. 'I'm Carol Reeve – the manager here. Are you some sort of relative of Miss Howard's?'

'She's my great-great-aunt. But . . . see . . . I really wasn't expecting her to just *be* here. I didn't even know that she was still alive. This is all such a . . . I mean, I don't know whether I actually want to—'

'You mean you didn't know that she lived here?'

'No! I just knew that she used to be at a school called Mount Pleasant, that's all. I'm supposed to be round the corner on a shopping trip, with my mum. At Almbury Mills. I only came in to see if this maybe

117

used to be Cel— my great-great-aunt's old school.' Midge was feeling overwhelmed, upset at how everything seemed to be running away with her. This was all happening much too fast.

'But she's been expecting you. You didn't know that?'

'What? How could she be *expecting* me? That's what the other woman said. I didn't even know anything about this place until today.'

'My dear, let me tell you something. Miss Howard has been expecting you for at least as long as I've been manager here. And that's . . . what . . . getting on for twelve years now. Every day she tells us that you'll probably be dropping by, around four-thirty. It's little wonder that we're surprised to see you actually turn up.'

Chapter Seven

Miss Howard opened her eyes as the last fragments of her dream floated away. Sharply focused, these dream images always were, like scraps of brightly patterned cloth. The edges of the real world that now surrounded her were blurred and fuzzy. Sometimes it was the only way of telling whether she was asleep or awake – the clarity of her vision. If everything was clean and sharp and bright, then she knew that she was dreaming.

Her dreams repeated themselves, over and over, just as the routines and conversations of her days were repeated, over and over. She was so tired of waiting.

'*Thank you for telling me, Celandine. This means very much to me . . .*' Her mother's voice, still echoing in her head. It had been *that* dream. The one where she told her mama the 'truth'. Comforting, because it had helped to put her mother's mind at rest, and disturbing because it wasn't the truth at all.

The events of that day had been real enough, she was sure of that. She was coming home to visit Mama, though she was not due any time off from the clinic until the end of the month. She saw herself walking through the front door of Mill Farm, and then through to the kitchen. Mama at the sink, throwing carrot peelings into the slop bucket, turning at the sound of her footstep on the red brick floor.

'Celandine – is you! *Look* at my girl – so grown up you are in your uniform. But you should say when you are coming. I have nothing done for you.'

'There was no time to write, Mama. And it was quiet this week, so Uncle Josef said I might come home early and see you.'

'Ach. That is a good man, to think of me.'

She saw her mother's face, so tired and frail and thin. And always so worried.

Then they were in the parlour, drinking coffee. Such a treat to drink coffee. It had made her want to cry, the thought that her mother would never spoil herself like this if she were sitting here alone. The smell of the coffee, hot and milky, was with her now – as was the overwhelming feeling of wanting to reach out and bring some comfort to that poor woman. She had lost her youngest son to the war, fighting the Germans, and yet she was still whispered about by those around her for being German herself.

'Mama, I wanted to tell you something. I wanted to tell you about what happened to me that time when I . . . when I ran away.'

And then her mother's ringless hands raised quickly to her mouth, the little gasp of apprehension. They were too thin, now, those ivory-yellow fingers, to safely

120

wear wedding and engagement rings. The risk of losing them was too great.

'I was so unhappy at school, Mama. I hated it there. And then when Freddie was killed, I just had to leave. I couldn't bear it any more – but I knew that I couldn't come home either. Papa would have only sent me back again. And so I went . . .' The words were half-rehearsed, but always they stuck in her throat at this point. 'So I went to Burnham Common. I caught a train to Withney Halt, and I walked the rest of the way from there.'

'To Burnham *Common?* Where those *gypsies* come each year?'

'They looked after me, Mama. They were kind and good to me. And they never hurt me, I promise. They gave me food, and let me stay with them.'

'Oh! But this I can't believe! Is so terrible! My own child was taken . . .'

'No, Mama, I wasn't taken. I went to them. *To* them. And they're just people, like anybody else. Just ordinary people. They mean no harm.'

'And they cared for you all those weeks? But when we found you . . .'

'I know. That was my own fault. I just fell, that's all. It was an accident. I was coming home, across the hill I think, and I just fell down it somehow. I honestly can't remember it very well. And my head hurt, and I was so upset about Freddie, and I didn't know what was happening to me . . .'

'But why have you not said this before, Liebling? Why must you have such a secret from me?'

'Because I knew what you would do – what Papa would do. He'd go marching up to the common with men and dogs and guns, and make such a fuss, and chase those poor people away. And all they ever did was look after me, as if I was one of them. *Please* don't say anything to Papa about it. Even now he might be too angry to listen properly.'

'Ah, is true. Erstcourt is a kind man, but his temper is too bad sometimes. I shall say nothing. But listen to me – are you *sure* nothing wrong has happened to you with these people? Do you promise to me?'

'Yes, I do promise. And everything's different now, Mama. I'm happy working at the clinic, and I feel so much better.'

'Then I am glad. Josef said that you would speak of this when you were ready, and now you do. Thank you for telling me, Celandine. This means very much to me. But what did you eat? And those clothes that you were wearing . . .'

The conversation had really happened, but the story wasn't true. She had not gone to stay with the travellers on Burnham Common at all. In her dream she was still a child, and as a child she knew what the truth was. In her dream she understood perfectly well why she was lying to her mother, but when she was awake the reason for it had gone – always slipping back into the shadows just as consciousness returned.

It was to do with protecting someone else. She had pretended that she had gone to stay with the travellers so that someone or something else should not be discovered. That was as far as she could ever get.

Miss Howard looked out of the high apartment window. She thought that it might be raining again, but there really wasn't much she could see – just a blurry impression of bare trees and the stone-grey afternoon sky. Soon Elaine would come to make the toast, and they would have their conversation.

'When I was young, Elaine, I once stood in the door-way of this very room, and watched the big girls making toast by the open fire. I wondered then whether I should ever be eighteen myself, and allowed such a privilege.'

'And now here you are, Miss Howard. With as much toast as you could wish for.'

'Yes. I'm still not allowed to make it for myself, though.'

'Well, it can be a bit of a dangerous thing to be doing at your age.'

'I know. But you'll let me hold the toasting fork for a while.'

'Course I will. Just wait while I cut the bread for you.'

It was a gas fire now – made to look like coal, but gas nevertheless. You could make perfectly good toast on it.

Elaine always called her 'Miss Howard', as was proper and right. The nurse who came in the middle of the week had been inclined to call her 'dear', or 'love', or even 'Di', and that she would *not* have. She was an old lady, for goodness' sake – not a little child, and certainly not prepared to be jollied along like some of those feeble folk downstairs. She was to be accorded due dignity and respect. Miss Howard, if you don't mind.

Had Elaine been and gone? Or had she just imagined it?

'I'm half expecting a visitor, Elaine. Some time this afternoon perhaps.'

'Oh, that'd be nice for you. Who's that, then, Miss Howard?'

'A girl. You might take me down to the day room at around teatime. Only I shouldn't like to miss her.'

'OK. I'll pop back up at four-thirty and help you into the lift.'

'Thank you.'

She didn't like the day room much. Too many old people there. She had tried to advise them, some of them, on how they should be treating their various ailments but they didn't listen to her. Not now.

'Oh, she's a marvel, our Miss Howard,' the care staff said – purposely loud, so that she could hear. 'And a *very* clever woman, when it comes to medicine. She used to run a clinic in Taunton. Alternative therapies, wasn't it, Miss Howard? You know, healing hands, and herbal remedies and all that. You should take her advice, Mr Lickis.'

'Alternative' therapies! An alternative to what? Pills, pills and more pills? What did they understand? Nothing. And as for herbal medicines, well! She had forgotten more than they would ever know on that subject. Let them follow their own path, then, and she would follow hers – continuing to diagnose and treat her own ills, as she was more than qualified to do.

Today she would instruct Elaine to fetch her a sprig of rosemary from the herb garden. An infusion would do her stomach good, and help calm her nerves for this afternoon. She always felt a touch of anxiety before entering the day room – in case the girl should be there. Or in case she shouldn't.

But had Elaine already been?

The girl would be standing at the window – that same window where she had so clearly seen her, all those years ago. The day room had been the Form 2 classroom then, and this building had been the Mount Pleasant School for Girls. How she had hated the place back in those days. But that hatred had long gone. She had made her peace with the old echoing corridors, so softly carpeted now. And the draughty washrooms that had been turned into such pleasant exercise suites no longer held any fear for her. She had faced the ghosts that had haunted her – Miss Craven . . . Miss Belvedere . . . Mary Swann . . . and had chased them into oblivion. They could hurt her no more.

And her life had been good. She had helped more people than she could recall, helped them to find the healing paths that existed within themselves. She had had a gift for that, and had used it as best she could.

But there was a gap. Somewhere between running away from school and beginning her working life, something had happened to her. In her dreams she knew what it was, but in her waking hours it would not come. What could it have been that was so terrible as to completely blank out her memory? Time and again she had tried to force a picture into her mind. She imagined herself spinning round, in order to catch whatever was standing behind her. And always it was the girl.

The girl was no ghost, she was convinced of that, but both a clue to the past and a glimpse of what was to come. That day when she had seen her, almost ninety years ago, standing at the window and turning towards her, a cup in her hand, had been a vision of something that would surely occur. She wished that she could make it happen, today. She wished that she had a fishing rod like Freddie's, so that she could cast her line out across the years, and reel the future towards her, or give the girl a thread to follow. She knew exactly what the girl would be wearing. Why was it taking so long for her to get here?

She must remember to tell Elaine to be sure and help her to the day room at around four-thirty. Just in case.

Had Elaine already been, though? Or was that yesterday?

Chapter Eight

'I can only stay a few minutes,' said Midge. 'I shouldn't really even be here. I've got to be back for five, at the latest, or my mum'll kill me.'

She felt nervous, walking along beside the manager lady – Carol – and not a bit sure that she wanted to be doing this. It was all too sudden.

'Yes, I understand. But now that Miss Howard knows you're here, I think that you must just say a very quick hello if you can – even if it's just for five minutes. She'd be so disappointed to have missed you. I wouldn't want you to stay for long in any case. She's rather fragile.'

They came to a set of double doors at the end of a long corridor, and Carol pushed one of these open in order to let Midge through. The door squeaked loudly as it swung back behind them.

'This is the day room,' said Carol. 'Some of the residents have their tea in here – those who prefer not to eat later on.'

It was a large open space, brightly lit, and dotted about with tables and chairs, a few of which were laid out with cloths and crockery. At these sat little groups of people – very old people – whose heads slowly turned towards the door. Perhaps twelve or fifteen in all. Carol gave a wave of acknowledgement to the room in general. 'Hallo . . . Hallo!' and led Midge over to a table set out for two by the far window.

'Have a seat,' she said. 'Can I get you a sandwich, or a drink or something? Or would you rather wait?'

'Um . . . no, I'm OK, thanks.' Midge wished that she had the courage to leave. This was just awful. But when Carol sat down, she felt obliged to do the same, and so she perched herself on the edge of the chair, her hands gripped between her knees. She noticed that the two cups and saucers on the table didn't match. One was plain, but the other had a picture on it. A fairy.

'Midge . . . I can see that this isn't a very easy thing for you to be doing. You're a bit shaken up, aren't you?' The woman was looking at her, and as Midge met her eye she saw the genuine sympathy and understanding there. Behind the smart outfit and the perfume and the neat hairdo was someone who could be trusted, she felt.

Midge bit her lip and nodded, too uncertain of her voice to try and speak.

'Well, now. Let's see if we can put your mind at rest. Where is it that you're actually supposed to be? At the Almbury centre? Is that where your mum is? Yes? And you need to be back for five?'

Again Midge nodded.

'Listen, then. I'm very happy to walk you back there

myself. It's only two minutes away – in fact you can see the car park from these windows – and you won't be late, I promise. Give your mum a quick call, if you're worried, and tell her exactly where you are. Or I could speak to her myself and explain. But now that you're actually here . . . um, how shall I put this: I don't think Miss Howard would be able to understand if you suddenly *weren't* here. Can you see that? Miss Howard's an extraordinary woman, brilliant for her age, but quite frail. And she can be difficult. And easily upset. Now, she's not a fool – very far from it – but she does get confused and I wouldn't want to—'

There was a loud bump and a squeak from the double doors, and the big woman – Joan – put her head into the room. She glanced quickly round, a worried expression on her shiny face.

'Carol!' She beckoned to the manager. 'It's Mr Lickis – he's having a bit of a do, I'm afraid. You'll need to come.'

'Oh Lord, again? OK, Joan, I'll be right with you.' Carol stood up, smoothed down her jacket, and said, 'Sorry, Midge. This won't take long – nothing serious, but I do need to be there. Now *please* don't go anywhere, OK? I'll be right back, and everything'll be fine. Don't worry!'

Carol hurried across the room to where Joan was holding the door open for her. The two of them disappeared, and the door closed again with another squeak.

Midge let out a long breath. This wasn't supposed to be happening. She had never imagined, or even tried to imagine, that she would ever actually *meet* Celandine. She had promised to try and find her, yes, but by that she had supposed that she might have been able to discover what had happened to her, perhaps piece together some details of the past – nothing more. Not once had she pictured a scene where they would truly be together, in the same room, at the same time. Talking.

And that was another thing: what on earth was she going to say? 'Hallo, Aunt Celandine. Do you know where the Orbis is by any chance?' It was ridiculous. And too weird. She felt that everyone in the room was watching her – all those watery old eyes, staring and staring at her. She risked a quick glance. Yes, most of the heads were turned in her direction, some bald, some silver-haired. All of them nodding and smiling.

Midge smiled back as best she could, and then turned away again. She picked up the cup that had the picture of the fairy on it. It looked as though it might be quite old – or perhaps it was just old-fashioned. The fairy was very pretty, all dressed in green and yellow, and holding a big yellow flower. Midge turned the cup upside down and looked at the base. 'The Celandine Fairy', she read. 'Cicely Mary Barker'. But how wonderful that there should be such a thing. A Celandine Fairy. Her great-great-aunt must have bought this for herself, as a reminder of what she had seen – although the winged Ickri looked as unlike this delicate creature as was possible. Still, it was an encouraging sign.

Midge got up from her chair, unable to just sit

there, waiting. She wandered over to the big window. Carol was right. You could see the Almbury Mills car park from here, just on the other side of that line of trees. The streetlights were all on, misty orange in the cold night air, shining down on the rows and rows of cars. She looked at her watch, and realized that she still had the fairy cup in her hand. Twenty to five. Just a couple more minutes, she'd give it, and then she really would have to . . .

The squeak of the swing door made her turn from the window. She hoped that it was the manager, Carol, returning to rescue her – but no, it was someone in a wheelchair. Another old relic, being manoeuvred through the doorway by one of the staff.

Then she recognized the woman who was pushing the wheelchair. It was the one who had come down in the lift to see her. Elaine? Yes, Elaine. *Oh my God.* And so that must be . . .

That must be . . .

Celandine.

Midge put out her free hand and groped for the window sill beside her. She needed something solid to touch, something to hold onto, just for a moment. It was too bright in here, and too hot, and everything was out of her control. The wheelchair seemed to have got stuck, half in and half out of the room. Elaine was struggling to push the thing and hold the swing door open at the same time. Midge moved away from the window sill, and guiltily replaced the china cup on its saucer. Should she go and help? No, they were safely through.

But then the figure in the wheelchair raised an arm, and there was a murmur of sound. Elaine was leaning forward, head bent low, and Midge heard her say, 'What? What is it?'

Midge allowed herself to look – to properly look – at her great-great-aunt, for the first time. Celandine.

She was tiny. As tiny as a child. She could have been a nine-year-old for all that there was of her. Except that she wasn't a child at all. She was a shrunken old woman, in a white blouse, crisply pleated at the front . . . a blue brooch . . . tartan rug over her knees . . . and shiny little black shoes that peeped out from under the rug, so that Midge was reminded of a miniature Scots doll that she'd once owned. But her hair . . . what had happened to . . . ?

The arm was moving. Beckoning to her? Midge hesitated. But no, this was apparently a signal to Elaine because the chair began to move again, rolling

across the room towards her, the wheels silent on the thick grey carpet.

Midge stood up a little straighter. The approaching face was so heavily creased about the mouth, the eyes so deeply buried in wrinkles, that it was difficult to read any expression there. Midge didn't know what to say, or how she was even going to begin.

'I'm *so* glad you could come.'

'Oh. Oh, yes . . .'

The old lady had surprised her by speaking first. Celandine. And yet not Celandine. Midge just couldn't see how this person could be the girl in the photograph, the girl on the wicker box, clutching a tiny bridle in her pale hands. It seemed impossible.

One of those hands was extended now, and Midge awkwardly reached out.

'Yes, I'm . . . I'm glad too. Glad to meet you.' How silly the words sounded. She held the thin hand for a few seconds, felt the skin, warm, but so loose and separate from the tiny bones within. It made her think of Pegs, and of Little-Marten, for some reason. Yes, that same strange touch of bone and membrane. Wings.

And something else? Some brief jolt of recognition . . . picture-memories. Midge withdrew her hand, unsure of what it was that she had felt in that moment. And uncomfortable with it.

'But I really can't stay,' she said. 'Not for very long.' She was dizzily aware that everyone in the room was looking in her direction, still curious at her presence.

'Elaine, could we have some tea now, do you think?'

said the old lady. 'And please' – she turned back to Midge – 'do take a seat, dear.'

Her voice was quiet, and the words came out slowly and carefully. Yet her speech was clear – and she was clearly used to being in command of those around her.

Elaine said, 'Right you are, Miss Howard. I'll just see to a couple of the others, then I'll be back.' She gave Midge a quick smile and moved off. Midge sat down at the little table once more, her hands in her lap. She found it hard to look directly into the wrinkled face opposite her. Such terrible old age was too scary, the shock of it too much to take in. Could that beautiful child really have turned into *this*?

But then she had to look up, because the low voice said, 'I've seen you before, haven't I? We've already met.'

'Have you? I mean, have we?' Midge was taken aback, and answered without thinking. Yet there *had* been times, hadn't there, when she had definitely sensed . . . what . . . a connection. A presence. But it had been the presence of another girl that she had been aware of, a girl of her own age, not this strange person. She could see the old lady's eyes now, gypsy-dark beneath the sunken papery eyelids. And then came the first glimpse of something that she could recognize, something that began to convince her. It was that same faraway look she knew so well, that same gaze into the distance beyond her shoulder. This *was* Celandine. It really was. The truth of it caught at her heart and her throat, so that her voice shook as she tried to answer again.

'Yes,' she said. 'I sometimes think we've sort of met before, too. I've . . . I've got a picture of you, in my room. A photo. Of when you were a girl. And sometimes it's like . . . it's like . . .'

The dark dreamy eyes shifted slightly, so that they were looking directly at her, and Midge didn't know how to finish the sentence. She took another breath and changed tack. 'You're sitting on a kind of wicker box thing. And there's a clock in the background, and you're holding a thing with bells on it. It looks like a toy bridle. And you've got really long hair.'

But then she felt embarrassed as she said the words 'really long hair', because this was perhaps the most shocking thing of all about Celandine's appearance. She was very nearly bald. Just a fuzzy sprinkling of thistledown, all wispy and thin, was the little that now remained of that amazing cloud of curls. You could see the shape of her head quite plainly, her scalp all mottled, pink and brown.

'A bridle? A toy bridle? No, I don't believe I ever— oh!' Celandine stopped mid-sentence. Her mouth remained in the shape of that little 'oh', and her eyes were again fixed somewhere beyond Midge's shoulder, scanning the distance.

'Yes, I *do* remember,' she said at last. 'Mr . . . Tilzey. The photographer. *Boof!* . . . it went. And there was a magpie . . .'

Midge felt the hairs prickle at the back of her neck.

'And then I was somewhere else. It was so very bright. And just for a moment I was . . .' The old lady's voice had become troubled, more frail and uncertain.

'Who *are* you?' she said. 'What's your name, dear?'

Midge let out her breath, and took another before answering. It was *so* hot in here, and her tongue felt dry. 'My real name's Margaret Walters,' she said. 'But everybody calls me Midge. I live at Mill Farm – over at Withney. Where you used to live.'

'Ah.' A wrinkled hand reached across and brushed Midge's arm. 'I *saw* you there, you know, when I was little. You were up at my bedroom window, looking out over the paddock. And I saw you once from a train. And I saw you here too, years and years ago, when this was my school. Yes, most definitely.'

'Here? But I've never been here before. I'd have remembered . . .'

'Well . . . I don't think you were *really* here. Not then. I think I was seeing . . . what was to be. What would happen someday. Today.'

Midge thought about that for a moment. 'You mean like seeing into the future?'

'*Yes.*' Celandine leaned back in her chair for a moment, her voice seeming to express a sense of relief – either because she had been understood or because she had finally understood something herself. 'Like seeing into the future. I knew what you would be wearing, my dear, and where you would be standing – just here by the window. Oh, I've waited so long, and wondered about it so often. Whether you'd come. And now here you are. Tell me' – she shifted sideways onto one arm, and gently pushed herself into an upright position again – 'could we be *related* in some way, do you think?'

Midge laughed, despite the tension she felt.

'Well, yes,' she said. 'Didn't you know? You're my great-great-aunt.'

'*Am* I? How funny. A great-great-aunt. No, I never knew that. So are you one of Thos's . . . no, that can't be right. Oh dear. I'm afraid I can't work this out. What's your father's name?'

'His name was Walters. No, we're related on my mum's side, I think. Her dad was a Howard. Maybe it was . . .' Midge struggled to picture what their family tree might look like. 'Did you have children?'

'No. No, I never had children. My elder brother had sons, though. Two, I believe. You must be descended from one of them.' There was silence for a while, the old lady looking down into her lap, puzzling over the past perhaps, lost in her own thoughts.

Eventually Midge said, 'What should I call you? Would "Aunt Celandine" be all right? Only, "Great-great-aunt" seems a bit . . . you know. A bit much.'

'You see, what I don't understand' – the old lady raised her head again; apparently she hadn't heard Midge's question – 'is why. Why you're here. And why I kept seeing you, when I was young. Those are dungarees you're wearing, aren't they? Green dungarees?'

'What?' Midge had lost the thread.

'Because when I first saw you, I wouldn't have known what such clothes were. Dungarees. Stripy T-shirts. There were never such things around then. I had no name for them. And yet I saw them.' Celandine's hand came up to her mouth as she talked, fingertips resting on the bottom edge of that dark empty circle, eyes searching the distance. Midge looked at the moving mouth, and then at the folds of skin across the knuckles . . . and at the wrist . . . and more folds of skin above the crisp white collar. Too big, the collar, so that the wrinkly neck looked like a tortoise's neck, coming out of its shell. How weird to be so ancient, and to have so much extra skin. Maybe people shrank when they got old, but kept the same amount of skin they'd always had, and that's why it got so creased.

'Sorry?' she said. 'What did you say?'

'I said, I don't know why this is happening, dear. I've pictured you so often, and imagined this day so many times. And talked about it too. I knew you'd come, but I still don't know why I knew, or how. I'm sure the staff here think I'm off with the fairies.'

Celandine looked straight at her, as she said the word 'fairies'. Was this a hint, Midge wondered, a cue that she should respond to? The dark-shadowed eyes were focused upon hers, waiting perhaps.

She decided to take a chance. A quick glance around the room, and then she leaned a little closer, resting her fingers on the arm of the wheelchair.

'Well . . . it's all to do with the little people, isn't it? The Various.' There. It was out.

'What? What was that you said?'

Maybe she hadn't heard properly.

'The Various. I know you've seen them too.'

'The *various*? The various what, dear?'

Midge felt her heart begin to collapse in dis-appointment, but she tried one more time.

'The tribes of little people that live in the woods . . . and the Touchstone . . . and the Orbis. You know all about it . . . all about them. I know you do. You remember, don't you?'

'Little people?'

Celandine had leaned closer still, so that Midge caught the faint scent of her – something of soap and eucalyptus. But then the dark eyes turned away from her in puzzlement, and as they caught the light Midge saw that they were covered in a bluish film – like the eyes of Phoebe, Uncle Brian's poor old spaniel. Yes, like Phoebe, who could scarcely see a yard in front of her nose nowadays. Aunt Celandine was probably almost as blind, Midge realized. She swallowed, as much shocked by this revelation as at the lack of response to her mention of the Various. The old lady could barely see, and it was plain that she had no idea what this conversation was about. Not the first clue.

Midge didn't know what else she could say.

'Tea?'

It was as though all the lights had been switched on anew. The room was hot and bright, and there stood Elaine, with a little aluminium trolley. Sandwiches on a plate, and a brown teapot, and some fairy cakes. Then Carol Reeve was crossing the room towards them, pointing to her watch as she approached.

Midge looked at the sandwiches. 'Um, no. I'd better not. I have to go. Sorry . . .'

'Sorry.' Carol's voice echoed her own. 'Got a bit caught up. We should make a move, Midge, if you want to get back to the Almbury centre before five. I'll walk you over. How've you been getting on? Everything all right?'

'Yes,' said Midge. 'Thanks.' But everything wasn't all right at all. She stood up and reached for her fleece.

'*What* little people?' Aunt Celandine was looking around her. Her voice sounded agitated now, and her hands were gripping the arms of the wheelchair.

'Sh,' said Elaine. 'Look – I've made you sandwiches. Tuna mayonnaise. You like them.'

'Where's the girl? Is she there? Has she gone already?'

'No, she's still here. But now it's time for her to go home.' Elaine bent low and put an arm around the old lady's shoulders. She looked up at Midge, over her spectacles. 'Better say cheerio now, dear.'

'Yes. All right, then.' Midge moved over to the wheelchair, and hesitantly rested one of her hands on top of Celandine's. 'Goodbye, Aunt Celandine. It's lovely to have met you.' She could feel the tremor of the thin fingers beneath her palm, and worried then that perhaps she'd said too much too soon – had succeeded only in upsetting this poor old woman. The balding head lolled backwards, rocking awkwardly, as though out of control, and the filmy eyes looked up at her, blank.

'Oh.'

Again the mouth held the circular shape of the sound it had made, a neat little 'o' of surprise and bewilderment. But then Midge felt her own hand being covered by Celandine's, a hesitant touch at first that became a great squeeze – as if of communication, recognition. The strength in that grip was really quite amazing. A curious tingly sensation ran through her, warm, and wonderfully uplifting. Her Aunt Celandine's face crinkled into a thousand criss-cross patterns, the lines as intricate as leaf-prints or bees' wings. A huge and delighted smile.

'Lovely,' she said. 'Yes, lovely indeed, and I'm sorry you have to go so soon. But we shall talk some more. And you're quite right – "Great-great-aunt" sounds perfectly ridiculous. You must simply call me Aunt Celandine from now on. You'll come again, won't you?'

'Yes,' Midge said. 'Of course. I'll ring next time, though.'

Another warm squeeze of her hand, and then Midge withdrew, backing away and turning to follow Carol across the room. She heard her Aunt Celandine say, 'That's my great-great-niece, you know,' a clear voice above the clink of teacups. Carol held the squeaky door open for her to pass through into the corridor, and then the sounds of the room faded away. It was over. As quickly and as bewilderingly as that.

They hurried across the windy car park and Carol said, 'I hope we haven't got you into trouble. It's just gone five.'

'It'll be OK.'

'Do you want me to come and explain to your mum?'

'No, it'll be OK, thanks.'

'Well, I'll stay with you till I know you're safe.'

The shopping mall was less crowded now, and it didn't take long for Midge to catch sight of her mother. Uncle Brian was still sitting at the café table with his friend, and Mum and Barry were standing next to them, chatting. Barry had his arm around her mum's shoulders. That was a bit weird.

'She's just over there.' Midge pointed towards the table, and looked up at Carol. 'I'm OK now.'

'Sure?'

'Yes. Thanks for walking me back.'

'You're very welcome. Um . . . did you mean it when you said you'd visit Miss Howard again?'

'Yes. I'd like to, anyway. Not sure when it'd be, though, or how I'd get here. I'll ring first, like I said.'

'Well, I'm sure that she'd always be delighted to see you. We'll wait till we hear from you then.'

'OK. Bye. And thanks.'

'Bye, Midge. Keep safe.'

'Yeah.'

Midge watched Carol walk away, her dark two-piece suit looking out-of-place smart somehow, amongst all the winter shoppers in their jackets and jeans. She turned to see that Mum had spotted her, and that there was already a questioning little frown on her face.

Better be prepared, then. Midge put her hands in the pockets of her dungarees and walked towards the café. What was she going to say? Tell the truth, as far as she could. Usually the simplest thing. But everything had happened so quickly in the last hour that it was hard to accept that it *was* the truth. She had found Celandine. Could that really be right? It made her head spin.

'Hallo – where have *you* been? I was just about to give you a call, missy. Brian says you've been gone almost an hour. Who was that woman you were talking to?' Mum had disentangled herself from Barry's arm, the better to get serious with her.

Midge smiled. They were never going to believe this.

'You're never going to believe this,' she said. 'I've been having tea with Aunt Celandine. Not that I actually *got* any tea, though. There wasn't enough time. Can I have another cake or something? I'm starving.'

It was great to see their faces. She wished she had a camera.

Her mum said, '*Whaaat?*'

Chapter Nine

Maglin had made his decision. He would gather together the Ickri tribe, along with any of the Wisp and Naiad who were willing to follow him, and quit the forest as soon as was possible. All others would be left to their fate.

The Far Woods might provide a temporary haven. He would take his people and sit out the rest of the winter there. Then, when better weather came, he would move north, sending out scouts to search for lands that were less overrun with giants. There was no knowing whether such lands existed, but any chance was worth taking when the alternative was simply to sit here starving and waiting to be discovered.

With his shoulders hunched against the cold, Maglin entered Royal Clearing and walked towards the Rowdy-Dow tree. How miserable the Woodpecker looked, crouching up there on the Perch, all huddled beneath his bindle-wrap. Little wonder that he seemed so wretched. With no permission to wed, the lad hadn't even the comfort of his thoughts to keep him warm.

Maglin tapped the shaft of his spear against the tree trunk.

'Come, Woodpecker – rouse up. I've work for 'ee.'

Little-Marten hastily pulled his bindle-wrap aside, looked down at Maglin, and fumbled for the clavensticks.

'Aye, Maglin. I be ready.'

'Then muster the tribes.'

'All tribes?'

'All tribes. 'Tis time we were gone from here. You'll have heard the talk, I don't doubt. Well now you hear it from me. The Ickri be leaving – along with any others that will. Sound the Muster, then.'

'Don't 'ee do it, Maglin!'

Maglin stared up at Little-Marten in astonishment – then realized that it was not the Woodpecker who had spoken. He swung round, spear at the ready. From the back of the shattered beech tree stepped the fantastic figure of Maven-the-Green. By Elysse! Maglin jabbed his spear at the hag, quite prepared to run her through there and then for giving him such a shock.

'You old *witch*! Do 'ee ever stop creeping about? Get back from me, if thee've a mind to live this day through!'

Maven slowly raised her arms as a sign of peace, but Maglin just growled at her and thrust his spear further towards her skinny throat. The crone looked more outrageous than ever – the sight of her was enough to make a rock jump. Her face and arms were daubed in what looked to be rough green clay, so thick that it had cracked and split upon her skin like willow-bark.

Her hair too was caked in clay, matted into great twisted hanks that snaked down over her forehead so that the peering red-rimmed eyes were hardly visible. A terrible creature she was, hump-backed and wreathed in winter ivy – ancient as the very woods she haunted. And mad as a nest of adders.

Maglin cautiously withdrew his spear.

'This be a dangerous amusement, hag, to creep up on one such as I. Eh? Now I warn 'ee: keep such japes for those with softer tempers and thee might breathe a while yet, but try 'em with me and I'll have 'ee wriggling on the end of this spear like an eel. Too often I find 'ee lurking where thee've no business.'

''Tain't such an easy thing, though, maister.'

'Eh?'

'To spear an eel.' Maven's voice was a creaky whisper. She lowered one of her arms, but kept the other one half raised and began moving it gently to and fro, in a lazy snaking motion. There was something graceful in her actions – the hypnotic movement of her arm so clearly imitating an eel, moving back and forth in a slow current. ''Tis plain enough to *see* 'un' – Maven moved a little closer towards Maglin – 'and so thee reckons thee shall *have* 'un.' Her voice was lowered to a softly rhythmic croak. 'Thee bides . . . and thee bides . . . and then – when 'ee has 'un just right – thee *throws* the spear . . .'

In one startling movement Maven's arm shot forward, grasped Maglin's spear, and flung it to the heavens. The weapon flew straight up towards Little-Marten's high Perch, hit the underside of the broken

146

limb with a solid *thunk*, and hung there, quivering. Little-Marten's squawk of fright drifted down from above.

'And then what 'ee be left wi', maister? No eel. And no spear, neither.' Maven shrugged her skinny shoulders. Her mouth cracked open into a horrible grin – a flash of pink against the green of her encrusted face.

She stood her ground, waiting almost, as Maglin recovered himself from his shock to come roaring down upon her.

'Dost think to make a mock o' *me*, you old drab?' Maglin lunged forward, grabbed Maven by the arm, and shook her from side to side. '*Here's* what I be left with – a bundle o' dry twigs as I might snap into kindles! A handful o' last season's nettle-stalks as I might trample down just to hear 'em crackle! By Elysse, I'll have 'ee tied to the Whipping Stone for this!'

But Maven, instead of struggling to escape, yanked herself closer to Maglin – clung to him so that her face was thrust up against his cheek, her breath hissing into his ear.

'Dost think I be mad, maister? Dost reckon me witless? That I be mazy in the head? No! 'Tis thee, Maglin, that be too crack-nogged to reason aright. 'Tis *thee* that've lost all sense. Do 'ee not see where the true path lies? Then let me show 'ee . . . let me aid thee . . .'

'Get . . . get *away* from me!' Maglin managed to wrench himself free of the bony green fingers that clutched at his tunic. He sent Maven staggering back against the trunk of the beech, and raised his head to shout up at Little-Marten.

'Woodpecker! Do 'ee just bide there gawking? Get me my spear!'

Little-Marten, sitting astride the Perch, began shuffling further along it in order to try and get at the weapon. He hooked one of his legs beneath the broken tree limb, and gave an awkward push at the spear with the ball of his foot – very nearly unseating himself in the process. The spear swung sideways, dislodged itself and tumbled downwards . . . end over end . . . to drop straight into the waiting grasp of Maven-the-Green.

With astonishing agility the old hag snatched the spear from mid-air, and had it pointed at Maglin before he'd even begun to move. Little-Marten gawped down at the scene, barely able to see how such a thing could have come about.

'Maven – none o' your games! You give me that!' Maglin advanced towards the crone, arms outstretched, snarling with fury.

'Don't 'ee wish thee may get it, then?' Maven retreated, but kept the spear pointed at Maglin, feinting, thrusting, holding him at bay. From left to right Maglin dodged, always advancing, but never able to move quickly enough to get around that vicious jabbing blade.

Away from the Rowdy-Dow tree and back across the frosty clearing the two of them moved, locked together in their circling dance, the still air alive with the threats and roars of the one, and the mad cackling

148

of the other. Always Maven was too quick to be caught – yet Maglin could hardly give up and allow himself beaten. He was Steward of the Ickri!

Little-Marten watched dumbfounded as Maven-the-Green finally backed into the dead undergrowth that surrounded the clearing, and Maglin continued to pursue her. Occasional bellows of outrage were audible for some time after the two of them had disappeared into the trees.

Was there no one else to hear all the clamour? Little-Marten turned wide-eyed towards the plantations of Great Clearing, and yes, here were a few of the Naiad farmers peering through the gap that separated the two clearings, come to see what the matter was. But now the noise had ceased and all was silent again. The Naiad looked about them for a few moments longer, glanced in Little-Marten's direction, and then withdrew. If the Woodpecker was on his Perch and had sounded no alarm, then all must be well.

Should he be sounding an alarm? Little-Marten was at a loss. There was still no sign of Maglin – but surely such a great warrior as he would be able to retrieve his spear from a feeble old crone without the need for drumming up companies of archers? Maglin might not thank him for sending aid, at that. He would not want to be seen as a laughing stock.

Aye, Maglin would soon be back, Little-Marten felt sure, and then he could get on with sounding the Muster . . .

The Muster! In all the mayhem he had forgotten

the nature of Maglin's order and what it meant. The Ickri were leaving. He had heard the talk and had refused to believe it – hadn't wanted to believe it. But now that Maglin himself had said that it would be so, then so it would be. The Ickri were leaving, and he would be forced to leave with them. And without Henty.

Little-Marten dropped his head. He tapped one of the clavensticks lightly against the barkless stump of the Perch as he tried to think. Could he refuse to go – or beg to stay behind? But even if that were allowed, what then? There would be no home for him here. Tadgemole would never let him near Henty, and he would be all alone. Could he take Henty with him, then? No, for his own were as against the cave-dwellers as the cave-dwellers were against his kind. Henty would have no life among the Ickri.

What could he do, then? What *could* he do?

Tap-tap . . . tap-tap. So often he had sat here, and for so long, that the sticks had beaten a smooth hollow in the weather-bleached limb before him. The Woodpecker. How proud he had been of his post and his work. Here he had dreamed his dreams, high above the world, scorched by summer sun and drenched by autumn rain. Dreams of all that might be. And were they now over? What did he have to offer Henty? If not a future together, then perhaps she would give him up. She might already have done so. He'd not seen her for days. If only he could truly fly, like his namesake the woodpecker, then he would carry her far away . . .

Some skirmishing movement in the bushes on the far side of the clearing caught his eye; a figure, pushing aside the low branches. Maglin, returning? No, it was . . . Henty! *Henty?* What was she up to?

Across the clearing the Tinkler maid came running, skirts hitched up, long dark hair streaming in the wind – but then another figure appeared behind her, stumbling through the rough tangle of undergrowth. It was that little tinsy-smith, Pank! What was *he* doing so far from the caves, and in broad daylight?

Little-Marten sat open-mouthed as Henty made straight for the Rowdy-Dow tree. She passed directly beneath the Perch, but didn't stop or even look up at him. She muttered a few breathless words, and kept right on going.

'Come to the caves at moon-wane – and be ready to journey. Whistle me down. I'll be waiting.'

'Eh?'

But Henty was away, with never a pause and no other acknowledgement. Little-Marten turned in wonder to watch his old friend Pank come bringing up the rear, pink in the face from his exertions.

'See what I be brought to, Woodpecker? This be all your doing, you great zawney! I hopes you can keep up wi' her, for I be troggled if I can.'

Pank passed beneath the Rowdy-Dow tree also, and made off across the clearing without stopping.

Little-Marten blinked. Some wondrous sights he had seen from this position, but never anything as likely to tumble him from his Perch as all this. First Maven-the-Green and Maglin, then Henty and Pank . . .

A cold gust of wind sprang up, billowing around his oilskin wrap and lifting its corners up like broad wings. Little-Marten leaned back against the trunk of the Rowdy-Dow tree and smiled to himself. Let the wind blow, then. Let icy rain and hail fall from the skies and soak him to the bone. His heart was warm again. Henty had not given him up, and he was sure now that she never would. She had risked the wrath of her father to come and find him, and to let him know that their future was to be together come what may. He was to meet her at moon-wane, ready to journey, perhaps to fly away after all. Whatever plan she had in mind, he would gladly follow.

Little-Marten looked out over the clearing, watching the low strip of cloud that rose over the bare treetops. Soon it would be dark, and his duty would be over. He would sit here till then, waiting for Maglin. And for moon-wane . . .

*   *   *

'There. Thee may take it, then. I've done playing wi' it.'

Maglin saw the spear being tossed towards him, but he missed his catch, and the weapon landed in the dead leaves a little behind him. He turned and pounced on it, furious that he should have to retrieve it in such a shameful manner.

It was in his hand at last, though – and now that old witch would pay for her insults!

He whirled round to face her, spear drawn back in readiness to strike . . . but Maven was not there. Or not where he had expected her to be. She had moved around to his right. Maglin was forced to step sideways in order to shift his balance, and in that moment he saw that Maven was holding a weapon of her own. It was pointing straight at him.

He had never actually seen the thing before, but he knew instantly what it was – and what it could do. One dart from that witchi little blowpipe could drop a grown archer straight into the dust. Both Tulgi and Benzo had fallen to its effect, and neither of them had ever got up again.

Maglin remained motionless, spear poised high, for just a little longer. Then he slowly brought his arm down, letting the spear-shaft slip through his fingers until the blade rested upon the earth.

'Be this your purpose then, Maven? To see me dead?'

Maven took the slim blowpipe away from her mouth, but kept it upright, holding it in both hands, still pointed directly at him. She could fell him in an instant if that was her whim. Maglin looked along the deadly pipe and into the black eyes of Maven, trying to fathom her tangled mind, seeking for some way out of this. *Why* had he not properly dealt with this creature before?

'I've watched 'ee since 'ee were a wean, Maglin. From a wean to what thee be today – Steward of the Ickri. Thee've a brave heart, and a true 'un. No, I've no wish to sithee dead.'

'Then I be glad to hear it.' Maglin was puzzled. A subtle change had come over Maven. She seemed calm, normal almost, in her speaking. *Was* she as mad as she appeared? 'What do 'ee want of me then?'

'To show 'ee something. And to tell 'ee a tale. To help 'ee.'

'To *help* me? Is this a help, then, to rob me of my spear, and dance me into the trees where thee may put a dart in my neck?'

'Would 'ee have listened to me, without you were made to?'

'No.'

'But you listen to me now.'

'Aye.'

'Then listen, while there be no other ears to hear. Thee've a greater power than 'ee do reckon, maister. Now that 'ee be Steward, the Stone be thine to hold. And yet thee pays it no mind. Dost think to take it from here when thee goes a-journeying?'

'The Touchstone? What's that to you, crone? Aye, I shall take it, as'd only be my right and duty.'

'You'm wrong, then, for 'tis your duty to bide here.

154

And the Stone belongs here also. Turn theeself around, Maglin, and walk to the pods. I shall tell 'ee a tale upon the way.'

'What's this? You think to tell *me* of what my duty might be – and to give *me* orders?' Maglin's voice rose in anger, and he took a step closer to Maven.

'Turn theeself around, Steward. I told 'ee that I'd no *wish* to see thee dead, but it may happen so yet.'

The rawness had returned to Maven's voice, and once again she seemed capable of any deed. Maglin growled in frustration, but did as he was told. He turned round and began to walk down through the silent woods, with Maven following at his back.

''Twere before your time, Maglin, when the Stone were first brought back to these lands, but I were there, on all that long journey . . .'

Maglin could hear Maven's low voice as he picked his way among the dark trees, but her footsteps were as light as a renard's. No crackle of twigs or rustle of grasses echoed his own clumsy progress. Had she really been there, all those seasons ago? How had she survived for so long?

'. . . aye, and for many a moon we travelled, four-season upon fourseason, down from the northlands. Avlon were King then, and 'twere he who vowed to join the Touchstone with the Orbis, as 'twere split from, when Ickri and Naiad first quarrelled. Avlon carried the Stone part way of the journey. But though the Stone were his to hold, there were one who under-stood it better – his daughter, Una. She were a wise chi', witchi, and she had the true Touch. I were a friend to she, and she to me. Aye, she learned much from old Maven. In Una's hand the Stone showed its power, and so guided her to where it would be. The Stone led the Ickri to these woods – back to the Orbis, that waited here so long to be joined with its brother. Do 'ee see?'

Maglin grunted, still raging at the ignominy of being herded along in this fashion.

'No,' he said. 'I see naught but the mazy tale that were told us as childer.'

'Ah, but 'tis a true tale, Steward, for I were there at the start and at the finish.'

'How did it end then?' Maglin couldn't help but ask the question.

'Avlon had a brother – Corben – who wished to take all for himself. Aye, and so he did. Corben poisoned his own brother, the King, and told all that 'twas Una who had done this thing, that she might gain the queenship. They believed him and sent archers to slay the child in the night. I saw she who were my friend die at their hands. Then Corben took the Stone. 'Twas he who first entered these woods, and brought the Touchstone home – Corben, *King* of the Ickri. Pah!'

'And so he joined these things together – Stone and Orbis?'

'No. The Orbis were wi' the cave-dwellers. Corben would've robbed 'em of it, but they were too slippy for he. They sent the Orbis out into the Gorji lands wi' a maid, and 'tis long gone. With the Gorji still, perhaps. We shall see. Bide there, Maglin.'

They had reached the grove of oak trees where the

pods of the Ickri archers hung. Maglin came to a halt and looked about him, half hoping that there would be some of his company here to aid him, half hoping that there would not. He hardly liked the idea of being seen in such a position as this. All was silent and deserted, however, the blackened willow pods hanging motionless from the spreading branches of the oaks. The light was already fading, but the archers would be at their work until true darkness fell, patrolling the woods for whatever game they could find.

'The Stone, Maglin. Bring it to me.'

Maglin turned to find that Maven still held the blowpipe pointed directly at him. By Elysse, but if he ever lived this day through, he would strangle the old crone in her sleep.

'The Touchstone?' He had to think for a moment. Was it still in the Royal Pod – Ba-betts' old home? No, the Elders had brought it across, along with the mapskins, all bundled together in a pecking bag. The bag lay where it had been left, just inside the entrance to his own pod. He had barely glanced at the contents, such things being of little interest to him. Nevertheless it was his duty to protect the relics of Ickri power, and he would refuse to now hand them over to Maven, though it cost him his life.

'The Stone ain't for thee, Maven. Nor shall you touch it – blowpipe or no.'

'Ah, there speaks the true Steward. And you be right, Maglin. The Touchstone were never for old Maven. I'll make 'ee a vow, then. Only bring out the Stone, and I'll not lay finger on it, nor try to take it from thee. But I would show 'ee what it can do.'

Her voice had grown softer. Maglin tried to look past the twisted hanks of hair that covered Maven's eyes, but could divine nothing of what might be going on in that wild head. Sometimes she seemed deadly dangerous, and sometimes the madness seemed temporarily to slip away from her. He would play her game a little longer, and perhaps in doing so the opportunity would arise to snatch that blowpipe from her. Then she would see what 'twas like to be on the other end of such a thing.

''Tis in my pod,' he said. 'But I warn 'ee, Maven, I'll not let go of it. Not while I be Steward and 'tis trusted to my keeping.'

'Lay the spear aside, then, and fetch out the Stone. I s'll not take it from 'ee, though I could have had 'un for myself long ago, if so I wished.'

Aye, that was true enough, thought Maglin. The Stone could have been taken a hundred times over for all the attention he had paid it. Ba-betts had always kept the Queen's Guard close to her pod, but he had not thought such protection necessary. In future he must post a couple of archers also, if this was to be the way of things, rather than send them all to hunt.

Maglin moved across to his pod, aware that Maven was still close behind him and that the blowpipe was pointing at his back. He rested his spear against the wickerwork, drew aside the stiff oilcloth and reached his arm over the curved lip of the entrance. The pecking bag was still there, just to one side. It was heavy. Maglin looked at Maven as he gripped the leather straps of the bag. He was tempted for a moment to swing the thing out of the pod and hurl it straight at her. The heavy stone would crush her skull if he caught it aright. But no. He would never be fast enough to beat one of those deadly little darts of hers. One quick puff from those stained green lips and he would be joining Benzo and Tulgi, wherever they might be.

He slowly brought the pecking bag out into the evening light.

'Here 'tis, then,' he said. 'What would 'ee have o' me now?'

'Fetch out the Stone.'

Maglin reached into the bag, fumbled around for a moment among the sheaf of mapskins, until his fingers closed upon the Touchstone. He had never handled the thing before, and was surprised at its weight as he drew it forth.

'What do 'ee think to it then, Steward, now that 'tis yourn to hold?'

Maglin looked at the Stone, hefted it in his rough palm, still inclined to view it as a possible weapon. The surface was highly polished, a deep orangey red, with flecks and veins of darker colour here and there. Two small indentations had been cut into the globe, at opposite poles, so that he could just grip the whole between thumb and middle fingertip. He turned it on this makeshift pivot a couple of times, saw how it might fit within some other device and thus rotate.

'A bauble,' he said. 'And a pretty thing, no doubt. For a chi'.'

'Aye, a pretty thing.' Maven's voice had dropped to a low murmur. 'And a pretty weight for a chi' to carry – as a chi' once did. For many and many a season.'

'As you've said. The one that was slain. Little good it brought her then, and little good may it bring me also. Tell me why we stand here, Maven, and what your purpose is with me.'

'My purpose? To make 'ee see, maister. To make 'ee see.'

'I see well enough, hag.'

'Do 'ee? The Stone sees more. The Stone sees what lives and what does not, what yet exists and what does not, and it'll tell 'ee true. It can answer many questions for thee.'

'What questions?'

'Do 'ee mind the time, Maglin, when that winged horse were gone – lost among the Gorji? None knew whether he were dead or no. I told all of 'ee that the horse were still alive, and so he was. Do 'ee remember what happened that day?'

Maglin thought back. Aye. Pegs had flown to the Far Woods, on some foolish errand, and had failed to return. There was a Counsel held. The old Queen dropped her bauble – the Stone – and Maven picked it up . . .

'I remember,' he said. Maven had performed some piece of witchery, noted by him at the time, but then forgotten. 'You asked the Stone a question, and made a mark upon it.'

'No. I asked the Stone whether the horse did live, Maglin, and the Stone answered me. I made no mark.'

'Then I saw wrong. What's this to me?'

'Wet your finger, maister. Like this.' Maven stuck out her pink tongue, a livid sight against the coarse green of her face, and licked her skinny middle finger. Then she raised the blowpipe to her lips once more.

Maglin hesitated for a moment, but the end of the blowpipe jabbed threateningly towards him and he had no choice but to do as he was bidden. He licked the tip of his finger.

'Now ask a question, maister. Take a name, from any that 'ee knows or did ever know, dead or alive, and ask "Do this one live?" Then lay thee finger upon the Stone.'

Maglin sighed. Without enthusiasm he said, 'Ba-betts. Does she live?' – and drew his wet finger across the surface of the Touchstone.

'Do 'ee see anything?'

'No.' Maglin saw nothing but his own fingermark, a damp streak upon the red of the stone.

'Ha! All to the good, then. For we shouldn't want *she* back again.' Maven gave a horrible cackle, and lowered the blowpipe a little. Maglin kept his eye on the thing, inwardly measuring its distance from him, judging the extent of his own reach.

'Now wipe 'un clean and ask this time of one that *lives*, "Do this one yet exist?"'

'Maven, this be naught but foolishness . . .'

'Ask!' Again that threatening little jab with the pipe – closer now . . .

Maglin wiped the Touchstone upon the front of his jerkin, and licked his finger for a second time.

161

'Fletcher Marten. Does he live?' He drew his finger across the Stone and watched. Almost immediately a bluish streak appeared, a mottled imprint of where his touch had been. Maglin started backwards in surprise, glanced up at Maven, and then back at the Stone. The blue mark slowly faded, evaporating to nothing, so that the fiery jasper was once more unblemished.

'How did 'ee . . .' Maglin couldn't see how Maven had managed this piece of witchi-pocus. She stood there grinning at him, her blackened teeth making her look more outlandish than ever.

''Tis naught to do wi' I, maister. 'Twere all thee – for the Stone'll only talk to they with eyes to see. And a heart to believe.'

'Believe? I believe in no such tricksy. This be your doing, Maven.'

'I tell 'ee it ain't, then. Try 'un again. Ask again – and whichever might please thee – one that exists, or one that exists no more.'

Maglin growled in disbelief that he was tied up in such nonsense.

'What a fool's game this be.' Nevertheless, he licked his finger, and touched it upon the Stone. 'Maglin,' he said. 'Does Maglin exist? For I begin to wonder . . .'

Again the mottled blue streak was plain to see, and Maglin, for all his suspicion, was shaken. *Could* there be some strange power at work here? Then how did it happen? He watched as the misted blue mark faded away to nothingness.

'Another,' said Maven. 'Dead or alive.'

'Very well,' Maglin growled. 'Benzo. Does he live?'

He half hoped that the dark shadow might appear again, and show the Stone to be wrong – for Benzo had died at Maven's own hand – but this time there was nothing. Just a faint damp mark where his finger had touched the jasper.

Maglin shook his head, still unconvinced.

''Tis a pretty trick,' he said, 'but 'twould be more a help to me to learn something I don't already know. Aye, let it tell me what may come – now *that* would be a wond'rous thing.'

'The Stone can only tell us what is, and what is not. It casn't say what will be.'

'Hmf. More's the pity, then.'

'Do 'ee reckon so? If we sees clear what is today, then we may better guess at what shall come to-morrow. And is all that exists alive? Thee've to find the right questions.'

'Tell me then what I should ask.'

'No. Maglin. You be Steward, not I. 'Tain't for I to tell 'ee what thee should know, nor ask it for 'ee. But I'll tell 'ee this: thee've seen naught yet of what the Stone can do. If the *Orbis* were joined wi' the Stone again, then the hand as held both'd need fear no enemy, such a power it would have. And the Orbis will come to thee, Maglin, I vows it, if 'ee would but bide a little. To your hand it shall come, I can promise 'ee. Think on that. Be it your proper duty to leave such a thing behind, when it may not be so far off? Talk to the Stone, maister. 'Twill always answer thee true. Turn away from me, so that I casn't see, and ask some question that I casn't hear. Goo on.'

Maglin looked down at the Touchstone, and wondered at it. Perhaps he'd been wrong, after all – too quick to dismiss the old tales of the past, too stubborn to question how the tribes had ever come to be in this place. And perhaps others had been right . . . Pegs . . . and Maven. They surely knew more than he of the history of these things. But could there really be truth in the notion that their future was somehow tied to a bit of rock? Should he risk staying a while longer in the forest, to see if this Orbis did indeed come to him?

Ach! He scowled up at Maven-the-Green, and was irritated all over again at the way she kept the blow-pipe pointed at him. Little enough chance he ever had of snatching the object away from her.

'Very well.' He turned away, so that Maven was unable to see the Touchstone, and stood in thought for a moment. This time he would find a question that neither he nor Maven could know the answer to. But what might that be? All who lived or died in the forest were known to him, and he could think of none in the world beyond . . .

. . . save Scurl. Aye, *there* was a name he had wondered about. Scurl and his archers, Flitch and Snerk and Dregg – they that had been banished for their treachery, doomed to wander the wetlands until they froze or starved. What of them now? Dead? Half choked and drowned they had already been when he had sent them away, and unlikely to last more than a night or two. Dregg! What a slack-jawed zawney that one had been. Maglin licked his finger, and drew it

over the Stone. 'Dregg,' he whispered, 'does he live?'
The Touchstone showed no mark. Dregg was dead,
then, as he might have supposed.

But as Maglin wet the tip of his finger a second time,
a shivery feeling stole about his neck and shoulders, a
creeping sense that the mad hag at his back was up to
something.

Perhaps she meant him harm in the end, and this
had been all her purpose from the start. Perhaps even
now she was about to bring him down, and take the
Stone for herself.

Maglin spun round . . . and found that he was alone.

Maven had gone, disappeared into the falling night.
But just in front of him, lightly resting on the coarse
winter grass, was the blowpipe. Maglin turned this way
and that, peering into the black shadows of the woods
behind him, and then again across the deserted
expanse of Royal Clearing. There was nothing to see,
no sign of any movement. Maglin stooped to pick up
the blowpipe – just a simple hollowed-out reed, by the
look of it. He raised it towards the darkening skies and
looked along its tunnelled length. The pipe was
empty.

At moon-wane, Little-Marten arose and crept towards
the entranceway of the pod. He held his breath as he
drew aside the heavy oilcloth – the thing was so stiff
with frost that he was frightened that it might crackle
and thus wake his father. The cold night air rushed in
and Little-Marten made haste, lowering his bundle of
belongings to the ground as quickly and gently as he

could. Then he followed, hopping lightly over the lip of the entranceway and down onto the frozen patch of earth below. He remained crouching in the darkness for a few moments, his head turned up towards the looming bulk of the pod, listening for sounds from within. Nothing but the distant rhythm of his father's snores, muffled through wicker-and-daub and thick winter coverlets. Good. He hoisted his bundle across his shoulder and hurried across Royal Clearing, wincing at the crunch of his footsteps on the frosty grass.

The clearing had been dark enough, but once Little-Marten entered the woodland he could see nothing. In total blackness he edged forward, relying more on memory than on sight, one arm cautiously extended in front of him. The pathways that led down to the caves, so simple and familiar by day, seemed to have twisted themselves into another arrangement altogether come nightfall, full of unexpected humps and hollows and protruding roots, all slippery with the frost. Little-Marten began to wonder whether he had lost his way entirely, and had perhaps strayed into a part of the forest completely unknown to him. More than once he stopped in fright, convinced that some great pit or ravine lay before him and that one more step would send him spinning to his doom. Almost worse were the sudden rustles from the undergrowth that surrounded him, the startled squeaks and low grunts of such dread creatures as would only be abroad at moon-wane. Brocks, perhaps . . . renards . . .

Little-Marten gulped and pressed on.

166

By the time he found himself to be close to the caves, his forehead was damp with perspiration despite the freezing night air. He peered upwards into the darkness, knowing by the shale beneath his feet that the entrance to the main cave was just above him. Was she there? Little-Marten cupped his hands together and gave a low owl-hoot, a breathy *twoo-twoo* that sounded far too loud in the frozen stillness. He waited, heart pounding, head cocked to one side as he strove to listen. Was that something? Yes! A tiny sound . . . that of a stone rolling down the bank of shale. And another, and another. Her footfall was light, but it was impossible to descend that slippery pile in total silence, and Little-Marten was in agonies lest someone else should hear. A final slither of shale and Henty was with him, grasping for his arm in the darkness, the smell of lavender in her hair.

There was no time to delay, and none for talk, but as Henty took his hand and began to hurry him away, Little-Marten had to pull back and whisper, 'Henty, wait! I can't see a hemmed thing . . .'

'No? I can, though. I be used to the dark. Come.'

She led him away into the night, so sure-footed and confident that Little-Marten was happy to put all his trust in her, to give himself up to fate and blindly follow.

They didn't speak until they were clear of the forest, standing beyond its bounds, high upon the cold hillside that looked down over the lands of the Gorji. A hint of light had crept into the sky. If they were to find a place of safety, then it would have to be soon.

'Where shall us go?' said Little-Marten. The vastness of what lay out there was overwhelming, and he hadn't given the first thought to what they might do beyond the act of escaping.

'Down to the Gorji settlement – where we were before. 'Tis dangerous, but 'tis the only place we know. We can sleep in one of the byres till night comes again. Then we can plan to find somewhere safer. And if the Gorji childer do find us, then I don't reckon they'd bring us harm.'

Henty obviously had given the matter some thought, and Little-Marten nodded as he considered the idea. It *was* dangerous, but it couldn't be any worse than the last time they'd been on Gorji territory together. At least they wouldn't have Scurl to contend with – or that great felix. Little-Marten shuddered at the memory of the beast, and of how he and Henty had stood side by side in order to fend it off.

The Gorji byres . . . aye, perhaps they could stay there safe for a night or two. He put his arm about Henty's shoulder, happy as long as she was happy, ready to face anything that might come if they could only face it as one. They were well used to danger – had lived each day of their lives in the shadow of it, and likely always would. And if they were now putting themselves in even greater danger, it seemed worth the risk. A single season together, if they could survive so long, would surely be better than a lifetime apart.

He could just see her face now, and so realized that dawn was beginning to break.

'We'd best go down, then,' he said.

'Aye.' Henty shivered and put her arm around his waist, tucking it beneath the bindle-wrap that he carried. 'What did you bring? Anything to eat?'

'Load o' cobnuts,' said Little-Marten. 'Some flatbread. Bit o' baked meat – squirrel . . .' They began to make their way down the hillside. 'Couple o' tiddies I got from the Naiad – cooked. A smoked eel . . . dried crab-apple . . . some honey-root . . .'

Henty laughed. 'We shan't starve, then.'

'No,' said Little-Marten. 'We shan't starve. Not this day.'

Chapter Ten

'We must make the effort, though,' said Mum, 'now that Midge has actually managed to find her. It's only right that we go over and say hello. Oldest living relative and all that.'

But Katie didn't want to go, and George couldn't – he was off on a weekend school trip – so the planned family visit to meet Aunt Celandine was a bit depleted: just Uncle Brian, Midge and Mum.

Perhaps it was just as well. Carol Reeve, the manager at Mount Pleasant, had been enthusiastic about a get-together, but had warned that Miss Howard was uncomfortable amongst crowds of people – disliked the fuss of birthdays and social gatherings, or any situation where she was the centre of attention.

And so it turned out to be. Friday afternoon tea at the retirement home was a brief and awkward affair, Aunt Celandine so vague and distant that she seemed hardly to be there at all. She obviously remembered Midge, and was glad to see her again, but showed no more than polite interest in Uncle Brian and Christine, or in their inevitable talk of family history.

She became a bit more engaged when questioned on her work at the Tone Valley Clinic, but even so her replies were short. Dismissive almost. It was a relief when Elaine came to clear the teacups away and it was time to leave.

Midge had felt embarrassed throughout this non-event, and yet, just as they were saying goodbye, there was again that fierce squeeze of the hand, and the sense of something being communicated. She thought she understood, and when Aunt Celandine said, 'You'll come again?' she said yes, she would try.

'Amazing woman,' said Uncle Brian, on the car journey home.

'Wouldn't want the job of looking after her, though,' said Mum. 'Did you see how she gave that Elaine the runaround? Still, she seems well cared for, and that's a blessing. Must have money, I suppose. Places like that don't come cheap. Anyway, at least we don't have to worry about her. Not sure I'd bother going again.'

'I wouldn't mind going again.' Midge spoke up from the back seat. 'I think she's really interesting. I like her.'

'Do you? I thought she was a bit . . .' Mum's voice trailed off. 'Well, we'll see. I don't know how you'd get over here, though. It's a bit of a trek.'

There was a pause. Then Uncle Brian cleared his throat and said, 'Er . . . I might be able to bring you across, if you like, Midge. I'm coming back over this way again on Sunday, and probably a couple more times during the next few weeks.'

It seemed like a loaded remark, and Mum said, 'Oh? Why's that then?'

'Cliff Maybank,' said Uncle Brian. 'I'm doing a spot of business with him. He's got this shop on eBay and he's going to help me shift all the farm gear out of the Stick House. Should make something on it.'

'What? Haven't we got enough to do without messing around with auctions? And is this guy really a businessman, or just some old school chum?' Mum wasn't ready to let go of this yet.

'No. He's a friend of Pat's – well, a former employer, really. She still does a bit of work for him here and there. Accounts and whatnot. In fact she sometimes pops across to the bookshop herself on a Sunday, so I gather. Just to keep the paperwork up to date. I shouldn't be surprised if we bump into one another.'

'Really? Pat knows him? Oh. Oh well. I suppose we *do* have to get rid of all that junk somehow . . .'

Midge heard the instant change of tone in her mum's voice at the mention of Auntie Pat. If there was the slightest chance of Uncle Brian getting back together with sensible Auntie Pat, then Mum would be all for it. Most definitely. And so that meant that Uncle Brian would get his way. He'd be driving over to Almbury Mills on Sunday afternoons – he could drop her off and pick her up again. Good.

Midge tried to deflect any possible argument about this by going off on another tack.

'Why do we call it the Stick House?'

The ramshackle lean-to that was tacked onto the back of the cider barn was hardly a 'house'. Nor was it made of sticks.

Uncle Brian laughed. 'It was where we used to store the winter kindling for the old stove. We kept sticks in it. So we called it the Stick House.'

'Oh.'

'This used to be the sixth-form study when I was a girl. They were allowed to make their own toast, on this very fire. It was a *proper* fire then, of course. I was very envious.'

Aunt Celandine seemed more relaxed this time, happy to chat as Midge wandered about the neat little apartment, looking at all her odds and ends. And it was nicer here than down in the day room. She liked the ticking clock on the mantelpiece, and the bamboo plant that stood in the corner. That was pretty.

'Who's this?' she said. 'Your husband?' There was a photograph on top of the television, of a soldier, very smart and proud in his uniform. A bit young, though, surely. Perhaps he was only a cadet.

'No, I never married. That's my brother Freddie. Just sixteen when that was taken. He died in the Great War.'

'Oh. Sorry . . .'

'Stupid . . . *stupid* business.' Aunt Celandine was looking down into her lap and shaking her head. 'All those poor boys . . .' She stopped talking and stared into the fire.

'Sorry,' said Midge. Again.

She continued her tour of the room. There were a couple of other photographs – one of a middle-aged Aunt Celandine sitting at a huge wooden desk, with lots of medicine bottles arranged on shelves behind her. Presumably this was taken at the clinic. And there was another of two young women on a beach, arm in arm, each holding on to their hats and laughing. There were donkeys in the background, and a pier. Weston-super-Mare?

Some of the objects in the room seemed slightly out of place: a glass case containing a dusty and faded collection of birds' eggs; a very old-looking cricket ball perched on the end of a shelf; a rusty penknife . . .

It was interesting, but Midge reminded herself that she wasn't here just to look at birds' eggs. She needed somehow to re-introduce the subject of the Various.

Aunt Celandine was still staring into the fire, her mouth moving as though she were chewing on something, or talking to herself. Midge sat down opposite, in the wing-backed chair, and looked at the plate of toast that lay on the little table between them. She hadn't yet been offered anything to eat, but she really wasn't hungry. Elaine had been present to oversee the making of the toast, and Midge had got the impression that this was some sort of daily ritual. Perhaps the new jar of jam had been brought out in her honour – or perhaps it was placed there every day, the paper seal remaining unbroken.

'Aunt Celandine – how old were you when you were at school here?'

'Hm? Oh . . . thirteen, I would think. Twelve or

thirteen. It was a *horrible* place. I ran away, you know.'

'No! Did you? What, properly ran away?'

'Oh yes. Ran away and never came back. There was a lot of trouble.'

Midge remembered the letters she had seen, detailing the damage to school property, and the bills for expenses. Had that been connected to this running away episode?

'Did you do something wrong?' she said. 'I mean, were you caught . . . I don't know . . . caught smoking or something?'

'Smoking? No, I've never smoked. I did light a cigarette once, but only once. Dreadful. It was for someone else.'

'So why *did* you run away?'

'I poured paint everywhere, you see. I was so upset. All around the dormitory, over people's clothes and into their shoes. On the bed linen . . . oh, it was a mess. Two bucketfuls that the decorators had left behind.'

'What? You poured paint . . . ?' Midge was struggling to grasp this picture.

'Round and round. *All* up the walls . . . *all* over the floor' – Aunt Celandine was rocking from side to side, her voice a little sing-song of remembrance – '*in* the laundry bag, *in* the locker drawers. Ooh no. I haven't forgotten that, dear. Do you know – I never got a splash on me.'

'Blimey. So . . . then you ran away?' Midge felt a little surge of glee, envy almost, at the thought of performing such an act of outrage.

'Oh yes. Never came back. Well, I did come back years later. To live here. Isn't that funny?'

'So when you ran away, where did you go?' Midge tried to keep her voice calm. She was beginning to think that perhaps she could guess the answer to this.

But Aunt Celandine was silent then. She turned back towards the fire, and shook her head. After a while she said, 'I told Mama about how I'd gone to Burnham Common, to stay with the gypsies, and how they'd looked after me. Kind people, who never did me any harm. They come there every year, for the fruit picking. They used to.'

'Oh.' Midge was disappointed that she'd apparently guessed wrong, but she continued to be intrigued – it was such an amazing story. She backtracked a little, and said, 'What were you so upset about that made you do all that damage?'

'I had a letter from my father. It was about my brother, Freddie. How he'd been killed in France. I don't think I *knew* what I was doing – but I knew I couldn't go home. They'd have just sent me back again. And I hated it here.'

'Oh. And so' – Midge could see it then, could almost feel what that lonely schoolgirl might have felt, all those years ago – 'so you ran away, and stayed with some gypsies. Were they friends of yours? Did you already know them?'

'Eh? Know who, dear?'

'The gypsies.'

'Gypsies? There were never any gypsies. That was

just a story I told my mother. She was so worried about what had happened to me. Didn't know *where* I was, poor woman.'

Midge's head was going round and round. 'But you said . . .' She tried again. 'Then where did you go?'

'I don't *know*.' The words were out almost before Midge had asked the question, and there was exasperation in Aunt Celandine's voice. Anger even. 'I don't know.' She said it again, a little more softly. 'And that's the trouble. I've tried to remember, but it's all gone now. Disappeared years ago. The silly thing is, I *used* to know. That's what makes me so cross. I remember that it was all a secret, something that I wasn't supposed to tell, and so I never did. I never even told my dearest friend. But I think I must have kept it a secret for so long that in the end it became a secret from me too.' Aunt Celandine gazed over Midge's shoulder, the light from the window reflected in her watery eyes. 'I had my work, I suppose, and a new life once I'd left home. I tried to forget about the war, and school, and Freddie and, oh . . . all the unhappy things. I *had* to put everything behind me, and I did just that. But now there are bits that won't come back, even though I want them to.'

'Is that why you came to live here?' said Midge. 'To see if it might . . . remind you?'

Aunt Celandine blinked at this, and her head jerked back, a little spasm of movement.

She turned to stare at Midge, and after a while she said, 'You're a very perceptive child, my dear. Midge. How old are you?'

'Twelve.'

'Twelve. Yes, I always thought you'd be about twelve.' Aunt Celandine leaned forward, reaching out across the little coffee table. 'Let me hold your hand for a moment. Don't worry, it's nothing to be frightened of.'

Midge shuffled to the edge of her seat, and stretched out her arm. She swallowed, nervous all of a sudden, but allowed her fingers to be found and enfolded by Aunt Celandine's own searching hand. Warm and dry, the skin felt, against her own. The pressure of the thumb firm and steady on her palm.

'I really can't see you very well at all, you know,' Aunt Celandine said. 'My eyesight's so poor nowadays that I'm more or less blind. And yet I know what you look like, because I remember you so well. I know that you have blue eyes, and a few freckles, and fair hair – quite long, but with a spiky fringe. Now then: why do I remember a girl I could never have really seen, and still can't see properly, and yet not remember things that I truly did see? Why can I recall things that never happened, and not recall those that did?'

Aunt Celandine closed her eyes. Midge sat in silence, staring at her great-great-aunt, wondering how she ever came to be in such a strange situation as this. She became aware that her hand was starting to feel curiously warm – not on the surface, but somehow from within.

'I spent hours of my life like this.' Aunt Celandine's voice was no more than a murmur. 'So many hands

I've held . . . dozens and dozens, over the years. And all of them with stories to tell.'

Silence again.

Midge said, 'Is that what you're doing now? Reading my hand?'

'No. I'm hoping you might be able to read mine.'

'What? But I can't do that.'

'I think perhaps you can. I think perhaps that's why you've been sent to me.' Aunt Celandine half opened her eyes, just fleetingly, then allowed them to close once more. 'Let me tell you what I remember, and then we'll see if you can see more. So. I ran away from school, as I told you – this school, yes? – and I went to the railway station at Little Cricket. See if you can picture me there, on the platform. I caught the train home, and got off at Withney Halt. Then I walked across the fields to Mill Farm. Close your eyes, dear, and watch me walking across the fields. I know that I was carrying a heavy bag, and it was getting dark. I stopped when I reached Mill Farm and looked at the lights, but I didn't go in. I was sure that there would be no welcome for me there. Instead, I put a letter on the gatepost and I weighed it down with a stone. It was a letter to my mother, telling her that I would be staying with friends and not to worry about me. I started to climb Howard's Hill. Do you know it – the big hill? Well that's where my memory disappears. All of it just fades away. I don't remember ever getting to the top. Later they told me I'd fallen *down* the hill, and hurt my head. I think I must have broken my ankle as well. I do recall being on sticks, and that it took me a long time to get well again. There were bad dreams too, although I can't remember what they were about. And I wouldn't speak for days and days after they found me. So they said. But I don't know why that was.'

Midge didn't close her eyes. She didn't need to. She thought she could already see where that runaway schoolgirl had gone on that dark night so long ago.

'I did get better, in the end,' Aunt Celandine said. 'Yes, in the end. I remember sitting by a fountain. I think it must have been the one in the gardens of Hart House – the clinic where my uncle worked as a doctor. It was so long ago, now, but I can see myself there, throwing things into the water. Pennies for luck, perhaps. And then I *was* lucky. My uncle brought me to work at the clinic, just as an assistant at first. But he encouraged me. He said I had a gift. A touch, he said. They called me Witch, you know, when I was at school.'

Aunt Celandine's eyes opened again, and Midge wanted to take her hand away. The bones of her fingers felt as though they were being heated up from the inside. It didn't hurt, but it was just so strange – and she didn't like this talk of witches. Weirder still was the sudden image that came to her, of Aunt Celandine as a girl. She saw it, like a video clip, a real picture, flashed in front of her eyes and then whisked away. A girl, sitting by a fountain, holding something. Dropping something into the water . . .

Orbis. That word again. It floated into her head, and remained there, teasing her. The fountain at the Butterfly Farm. Could this thing be hidden there, buried deep in the mud?

180

Perhaps she was looking too far ahead.

'So when you fell down the hill,' she said, 'and they found you . . . how long had you been gone for? That wasn't the same night?'

'No. I'd been missing for ages. Weeks, I think. The thing is, I believe I knew at the time what had happened, but I had to keep it a secret for some reason. It was only later that it all started to fade, like somebody rubbing out a pencil drawing, until there was nothing left to see any more. It's been ninety years, now. All that time . . . wondering . . .'

Midge could feel her hand being squeezed tighter.

'Where *did* I go? What happened to me?' Aunt Celandine's voice had become louder and more agitated, almost panicky.

Midge didn't know how to begin. This poor old woman might have a heart attack or something if she said the wrong thing. The responsibility was frightening. But the truth would have to come out somehow, and who else was there but her to tell it?

She withdrew her hand, as gently as she could, and said, 'I think I know where you might have gone, Aunt Celandine. But it's scary to talk about. I was scared when I . . . when I first saw what I saw. You know the woods on top of Howard's Hill? I think you went there.'

'What? That tangled-up old place? No. No, I don't think so . . .'

'You did. I know you did. The people who live there can still remember you. They talk about you.'

'People who *live* there? What people?' Aunt

181

Celandine was staring at her, obviously still at a loss.

'I'm not the only one who's seen them,' said Midge. 'My cousins have too – George and Katie. They're real. Honestly they are. And if I brought George and Katie here, they'd tell you so too.'

'But who on earth are you talking about, dear? What people?'

Here it was again, then. Well, there was no other way of saying it.

'Little people, Aunt Celandine. *The* little people. There are tribes of them, living up there in the woods.'

'Oh, what nonsense! Little people? Do you mean fairies? No, no. You surely don't believe in that kind of thing at your age?'

Well, at least the news hadn't brought on a heart attack. Aunt Celandine seemed likely to survive a little longer. But of course that was because she didn't yet understand, or believe, or remember. Midge persevered.

'No, they're not fairies,' she said. 'Although some of them have . . . well, they have wings. But no, they're just little people. About this big.' She held her hand a couple of feet above the carpeted floor. 'There's two tribes that live in caves, and another lot that live in the trees – the Ickri – and some of them fish. And they grow beans and things. Potatoes . . .' She stopped talking, aware of how ridiculous the words sounded. But how *could* she make it believable?

Aunt Celandine put her head back and gazed at the ceiling. Something had apparently occurred to her.

'You know, I *do* remember going up there' – Midge's heart gave a little lift – 'but that was another time. With my brother Freddie. Yes. I could only have been about seven or eight. I was following Freddie, and we were walking and walking – right the way round the wood, I think – all through the long grass and the nettles and dock leaves. It was hot, and I was very tired and thirsty. We couldn't get in there. That's right! Freddie was trying to find a way in. But there were so many brambles and briars that there just *wasn't* a way in. I'd forgotten all about that.' Aunt Celandine nodded to herself. Then the concentration faded from her expression for a few moments, as though she'd lost the thread of what she'd been saying. She squeezed her eyes shut, and pinched the bridge of her nose, obviously tired now. 'So you see, I really don't think I would have gone to those old woods when I ran away. Not if I already knew that there was no way in.'

There's a tunnel. The words hung there, in Midge's head, but she didn't say them. There's a tunnel, and I bet that's how you got in. Same as me. But you just don't remember, do you? And there's no point trying to force it. She looked at her watch.

'I'd better go,' she said. 'I'm supposed to be meeting my uncle at five.'

She was disappointed – not just because she was getting nowhere in her search for the Orbis, but also because she had so hoped to be able to talk to someone who had shared her own experience.

'I'm sorry.' Her Aunt Celandine was reaching out

for her hand again. 'I simply can't . . . simply can't . . . get it back.'

'I wasn't making it up, Aunt Celandine.' Midge felt that she had to get that clear. 'I know it seems impossible, but it's the truth. There *are* people living there, on Howard's Hill. I'll try and come over again next Sunday, and then maybe I could tell you more about it.'

'Yes. Do come and see me again. It's lovely to talk to you, even if . . .' Aunt Celandine didn't grasp her hand in parting this time. Instead she just patted it, and said, 'Well, even if I can't make any sense of it. But I'll try. Yes. I know that I have to try to remember more. Would you do me a favour before you go, and tilt my chair back? I'm suddenly feeling rather tired. There's a lever . . .'

'What, this chrome one? How does it work – like this? Is that far enough back?'

'Yes, that's lovely. Thank you, dear.'

* * *

'You're very quiet, Midge,' said Uncle Brian, as they drove back home in his rattly old estate car. 'Everything OK? How was Aunt Celandine?'

'Oh, she was fine. Quite chatty this time.' Midge made an effort to perk up, although all she really wanted to do was think. 'How about you?' she said. 'Successful day on the auction site?'

'Yes, not bad at all. It's taken a while to get things organized, but we seem to be more or less up and running. I think I may have already sold the Fergie.'

'What, your old tractor? That's good, isn't it?'

'Well, yes it is. Funny thing, though – I sort of miss the old gal already.'

Yeah, thought Midge. I know what you mean. Already she was thinking ahead to next weekend, trying to come up with some way of jogging Celandine's memory. Today had been a setback, but she was *not* going to give up. Not when she'd come this far.

'Miss Howard?'

Her name. But she ignored it. Not now. Not now, not now . . .

'Miss Howard, are you OK? Having a little nap, dear? That's right. I'm just going through to rinse the tea things, and then I'll run your bath. Won't be long.'

Elaine. Fussing around as usual.

Celandine kept her eyes tight shut, and tried to hang onto the memory of whatever it was that she had seen . . . or dreamed. Freddie. They were walking around the woods on Howard's Hill. And they were shouting, calling out. *Halloooo! Are you there? We've brought you some food.* But she didn't want to be doing this. There was nobody to hear them, and she was tired of walking, and her head still hurt from falling down the hill. Her temples throbbed and she wished she was lying in the baby carriage, the bassinet . . .

The bassinet! She remembered it! Oh, what bliss that had been, to lie beneath the shady trees, her head on a pillow, and to gaze up at the pretty green patterns of the leaves. All the birds singing, and the cheerful sounds of voices drifting towards her from below. The Coronation party. And cake! Yes, she could see a piece of cherry cake, floating through the air, as she held it aloft. Dark red cherries against the fluttering green of the foliage. And the skinny arm that came to take it from her . . . tiny brown fingers, desperately reaching down towards her own pale hand . . .

Cake-cake-cake . . .

'Righty-ho, then. I think we're all ready now. Miss Howard? Are you awake? We'd best get a wriggle on, or it'll be bedtime before we know it.'

Celandine opened her eyes to see the blurred and bespectacled face of Elaine before her. A different face entirely from the one she'd just pictured so clearly, staring down at her from the trees . . .

Chapter Eleven

By the time they reached the Gorji settlement, Henty and Little-Marten were able to see more clearly than felt good for their safety. The sky had turned from black to grey, and the shapes of the dwellings loomed before them. They crept among the thistles and peered through the bars of the metal gate that led into the giants' enclosure. Something had changed. The very atmosphere was different. A smell of raw timber hung about the place . . . and fresh stone dust . . . and other less recognizable scents, sharp and oily.

Little-Marten whispered, 'Bide here, whilst I take a glim.' But Henty shook her head. They were in this together. She made the first move, slipping easily beneath the lower bars of the gate and looking about her as she waited for Little-Marten.

The mossy stones that had once paved the enclosure were gone, and the whole area was now covered with a smooth black substance, strange to feel beneath the rabbit-skin soles of their boots. Piles of stone blocks were stacked here and there, and between these they dodged, making their way along the line of byres. But the byres, where they had hoped to find some rest, now turned out to be roofless and open to the elements – as was the building where they had encountered the terrible felix. They stood in the doorway of the old cider barn, and looked up in wonder at the dark patterns of wooden beams silhouetted against the breaking skies. There would be no shelter for them here.

''Tis no good,' Henty whispered. 'We shouldn't have come.' She was shivering, perhaps from the cold, or perhaps from the memory of what they had witnessed on this spot. Little-Marten put his arm about her shoulders, and together they turned to look back along the way they had come, each at a loss as to what they should try next. These byres were no longer the neglected places that they remembered, thick with grime and season upon season of undisturbed cobwebs. The Gorji were busy making changes, and the scent of them was everywhere.

Little-Marten felt Henty's shoulders flinch. A light! From high up on the largest building, a brilliant square of yellow cut through the dawn. A fuzzy shadow, huge and ominous, moved back and forth across the light, then disappeared. The giants were awake.

Without a word Little-Marten grabbed Henty's upper arm and together they hurried back towards the metal gate. *BrrrrrrmmmMMMM!* Too late! A terrible rumbling sound erupted at the far end of the enclosure, and they were caught in the glare of some monstrous lit-up contraption that came swinging in through the main entrance, filling the world with its roar and stench.

To the left they dodged – their instincts identical – and into the shadow of the pillars that fronted the main building. Panic drove them onward . . . up the steps . . . across frosty stones that crunched and skittered beneath their feet . . . through clumps of shrubs and bushes . . . anywhere to escape that blazing clanking terror.

They reached the corner of the dwelling, scuttled across an open area of grass, and headed for the welcoming shadows of nearby trees. A copse. At last it was possible to take a breath. The monster could still be heard, bellowing its way around the enclosure, but they were no longer in its sight.

What now, though? They backed further into the trees, still shaken by what they had seen. Little-Marten felt something brush at his shoulder and let out a squawk of fear. Argh! He automatically ducked and lashed out with his hand. But as the thing danced off into the shadows, and then swung back towards him, he realized what it was. Rope.

Rope and bits of wood – a ladder – dangling from the branches above.

Little-Marten had seen this object before. He remembered it. 'Henty!' he whispered.

'What is it?'

Little-Marten grabbed at the rope ladder, put a foot on the lowest rung to steady it, and then looked over his shoulder at Henty. 'I were here afore,' he said. 'Just bide still, while I make sure 'tis safe.'

'Eh?'

Hand over hand Little-Marten climbed, whilst Henty stood at the bottom, peering up into the trees. She could see a construction of some sort – a platform? – among the branches. The noise of the Gorji machine grew momentarily louder, and Henty glanced nervously towards the direction of the sound. When she looked back, Little-Marten had disappeared into the foliage.

''Tis all right.' She heard his whisper from above. 'Come on up.'

Henty swung her bindle-wrap a little further around her back, grasped the wooden rungs, and began to climb. It wasn't easy. The ladder swayed and twisted, and her fingers were too frozen to grip properly, but she managed to get safely to the top, hooked her arm over a branch and hung there for a moment in order to get her breath back.

Little-Marten was edging towards her, holding out his hand. 'Grab hold o' me,' he said. 'Don't be feared.'

Henty grasped his wrist, hauled herself up among the branches, and followed his lead. A short hop, a pause for balance, another little jump, and they had gained the platform.

It wasn't just a platform, though. Here was a dwelling – of sorts – made of wood. And though it had but three sides it did at least have a roof.

'We s'll be safe here,' said Little-Marten. 'For this night, anyways.'

'This *day*,' said Henty, for now the true light of

morning was filtering down through the trees, and the copse was alive with birdsong. A little longer out in the open and they would have been exposed to any with eyes to see. All the more fortunate, then, to have found this shelter – if it was indeed safe.

'Do the Gorji not dwell here, then?' Henty sounded doubtful.

'Don't reckon so,' said Little-Marten. ''Tis empty, and I can't smell 'em. I seen 'em here last summer, but there's naught of 'em now winter've come.'

There had been more to this place, he remembered, on his previous visit: sleeping arrangements, and bits of clothing and the signs of cooking. Strange objects. Things that made frightening noises when you touched them . . .

Now there was just a single box, a big wooden crate, pushed deep into one corner. Little-Marten sighed. A warm byre, with some hay perhaps to sleep on, would have been better. They might stay dry beneath this roof, if they were lucky, but there would be no escape from the freezing winter air. 'Twould have to do, though.

Henty was wandering about inside the hut, touching the walls, looking up at the roof, but Little-Marten stepped to the edge of the platform to see what he could see. Not much, and that was all to the good. The tree was a blue cedar, its winter foliage as thick and concealing as it would be in the summer. And although part of the main dwelling was visible, and some of the byres, and stretches of the landscape beyond, Little-Marten felt that this was as safe a place as they were likely to find – unless the Gorji returned by chance. A thought occurred to him. He could pull the ladder up into the tree. Aye, that would give hindrance to any that might come, and 'twould allow some warning . . .

'What's this?'

Little-Marten turned to see that Henty was kneeling by the big wooden box. She had the lid open.

'What've 'ee found?' Little-Marten stepped over to take a look, blowing on his fingers to try and get them warm.

The box contained a solitary object: a big black bag, curiously shiny, and so tightly stuffed that it looked as though it was about to burst. Henty prodded it with her finger.

'Hsst! Don't 'ee fool wi' it!' Little-Marten's previous experience of Gorji possessions had made him wary, but Henty could see no danger. She tugged at the bag, and found that it was light for its size – light enough to be lifted from the box and placed on the wooden planking. As the bag rolled over to one side a small hole was exposed, and from this bulged a scrap of some softer material, bright red. This too Henty prodded, and found that the little hole could easily be made bigger. And bigger still . . .

It was as though whatever was in that bag *wanted* to come out. Little-Marten looked on, still agitated, as Henty used both hands to pull the stretchy black substance apart. Like a burgeoning flower the contents emerged – a great roll of padded material, thick and soft, and warm to the touch.

Confident now that there were no nasty surprises to come, Little-Marten ceased his fretting and helped Henty to unravel the object. They laid it out flat, then stood back to take a proper look. Henty was the first to recognize how valuable this thing might be to them.

'Better'n a bindle-wrap,' she said.

'Aye! You're right – 'twould be.' Little-Marten knelt down again. 'And look. 'Tis like a gurt sack. See?' He lifted a flap. 'We could get *inside* 'un, and be snug as a nest o' throstles.'

'The box,' said Henty. 'We'll put it in there – 'twould be warmer yet.'

A good idea. They folded the padded sack in two and stuffed it into the big wooden box. With a bindle-wrap placed at one end for a bolster it was perfect – such luxury for themselves as they could never have imagined or hoped for on this icy morning.

'Jump in and get theeself warm,' said Little-Marten. 'And find us a bit o' food. I be going to pull up that ladder.'

Was there ever shelter as welcome as this? Little-Marten and Henty lay wrapped up in their box, and thought they had never been as warm and comfortable in their lives. Those giants surely knew how to winter, if this was the way they did it.

Little-Marten hung one of his rabbit-skin boots over the edge of the box, and then gently lowered the lid onto it. Now there would be some air, and enough light to let them know when evening had come again. Then perhaps they would have to make some other plan – or perhaps they wouldn't. There was no hurry. As long as they were safe and warm, and together, nothing else mattered.

'How long can we stay here, dost reckon?' Henty voiced the thought.

'Dunno. I should be happy to wake up when 'tis spring.'

'Yes. Like the hotchi-witchi.'

'Heh. You ain't so prickly as one o' they.'

It could rain or sleet or do what it liked now, they felt. Better if it did, for then the Gorji were less likely to be abroad. Let the winter storms come, then, and howl across the landscape, so that even giants must give it best and stay a-bed till the season turned. A peaceful vision, but an unlikely one, and as Little-Marten and Henty fell asleep it was to the dull growl of the Gorji machine, still patrolling the distant enclosure.

Chapter Twelve

Maglin woke in confusion, hauled from his slumbers by the sounds of angry voices outside the pod.

'You'll let me pass, or I'll crack both your heads open!'

'Will 'ee? Step back, old 'un, and hold thee peace. Bist deaf? Step *back* or 'twill be the wuss for 'ee! Maglin!'

What was happening? Maglin grabbed for his spear in the darkness and lurched towards the entrance of the pod. His fumbling hands made heavy work of the oilcloth, and as he finally managed to yank it aside the winter sunshine streamed into his eyes so that he was near blinded by it.

'So. At last we behold the great Maglin – mighty Steward of the Ickri.'

It was Tadgemole.

Maglin shielded his eyes against the dancing sunlight and saw that the leader of the cave-dwellers was being held at bay by the guards – Glim and Raim – their spears thrust towards him in defiance.

'What's this, *Tinkler*?' Maglin was aware of how

ridiculous he must look, half naked and shivering –
and caught so late a-bed – but this only made his anger
the more bitter. 'Do 'ee come seeking a crust? Tain't
yet Basket-time, I think.'

'A crust? When have I taken aught from you?'
Tadgemole raised his staff in a threatening gesture
and the guards prodded their spears at him anew. 'I
don't come here seeking crusts, heathen. I come here
seeking my daughter, Henty! Tell me what you know
of the matter.'

'What matter?' Maglin was thrown. Had something
happened that he hadn't been told about?

'She's gone!' roared Tadgemole. 'That's the matter!
Gone in the night – aye, and I can guess in whose
company, *and* with whose blessing! Is this your doing?'

Maglin looked towards the Rowdy-Dow tree. The
Perch was unoccupied. Small wonder he'd slept so
late, then, with no Woodpecker to herald the dawn.

'Glim,' he said. 'What of this?'

Glim glanced quickly over his shoulder, then turned
back towards Tadgemole.

''Tis true,' he growled. 'We've seen naught of
Woodpecker. And we took over watch at moon-wane.'

'And neither one of 'ee thought to wake me?'

Glim shrugged. 'This be a new game for we, Maglin.
We be archers, leastways by our reckoning. Now we're
to play at lookout, it seems. Must we look out for
Woodpecker too?'

'Ha!' Tadgemole snorted in disbelief, and thumped
the butt of his staff upon the hard earth. 'A fine set of
fools you are! Is this the tribe that call themselves

guardians of the forest? And do you, Steward, reckon to be the one that should lead us all? Go back to your bed, and sleep the day away. 'Tis plain you know nothing. Yet you shall know this much: my daughter has gone, stolen from me by a heathen, and I hold you to blame for it. A true leader would be able to keep his own raggle-tags in check. A true leader would know the true path for all, and hold all to it. Well, mark me – such a one may come yet. But for now I must seek my child.'

'You'll not leave the forest!' shouted Maglin. 'Do 'ee hear me? Go back to your hole and stay there, till I've thought on this!'

But Tadgemole had already turned to walk away. He lashed out with his staff as he did so, cracking it against the spears of Glim and Raim.

'I'll do as I please.' Tadgemole threw the remark over his grey-cloaked shoulder. 'Without let from you.'

Maglin was speechless. He watched the cave-dweller stride across the clearing, moving like one half his age, his staff more weapon than support. Tadgemole disappeared into the far trees, and Maglin then caught sight of something else lurking there – a flash of white among the dark winter brambles. Pegs?

The freezing air reminded him once again of his undressed state, and Maglin shook himself free of his thoughts. He turned his attention to the guards.

'Bide there, till I'm mantled,' he said. 'I've not finished with 'ee yet.'

The Touchstone lay heavy in his hands, the weight of

it a solid comfort somehow, when all else seemed blown to the winds. Maglin sat cross-legged at the entrance to his pod, rolling the polished orb from palm to palm as he considered his problems.

Little-Marten and Henty had gone, quit the forest, evidently, in order to be together. Should he risk chasing after them – sending others into danger that the young fools might be dragged back to safety? No. Not this time. But what if they were discovered by the Gorji, and so brought disaster down upon them all? Maglin didn't see what he could do to prevent this. Could the Stone help him? Perhaps. But Little-Marten and Henty were not his only concern. There were others.

Tadgemole, for instance. Something in that cave-dweller's manner had changed. A season ago he would never have spoken as he did now. '*A true leader would know the true path for all, and hold all to it. Well, such a one may come yet . . .*' What threat was hidden in those words? Did Tadgemole imagine that some new power, or leadership, was about to come his way?

And then there was the Orbis to think about, that missing piece of the Touchstone's history, ignored by him until now. Did it truly exist? Many times Pegs had tried to persuade him that the Orbis would free the Various from the lands of the Gorji, and return them safe to Elysse. But where and what was Elysse? Aye, and who or what was Pegs?

Maglin shook his head, as far away from any answer as ever. But of one thing he felt a new and growing certainty: Tadgemole and Pegs had joined together, fallen into some alliance with one another. He saw again Tadgemole's purposeful stride, heading for the trees on the far side of the clearing, and the pale shadow of the one who waited for him there . . .

'. . . *a true leader may come yet . . .*'

What did those words mean? Were Tadgemole and Pegs plotting some treachery against him – hoping to see him overthrown? It was possible, for Tadgemole would surely see him dead and think it no pity. And as for Pegs, who knew?

But by what power could the likes of Tadgemole ever hope to lead the Various? What could even begin to put him in such a position?

Possession of the Orbis . . .

Maglin ceased rolling the Stone from hand to hand, and looked out across the clearing. Now he saw it. Aye, now he understood. His tracker's instinct had not yet deserted him. Longseasons it had been since he had hunted these woods, a young archer in those days, but his eye was still sharp – still capable of seeing the unseen. The twitch of a leaf, the brief rustle in the undergrowth . . . such things always gave away the game that was hidden there.

And now he could sense the game that was hidden here. If Tadgemole and Pegs had indeed thrown in their lot with one another, it could likely be for but one reason: to find the Orbis. And if they should succeed in finding it, Tadgemole would certainly never hand it over to the Ickri. Yet the Orbis would be of no use to him without the Stone. So was Tadgemole planning to get his hands on the Touchstone also?

Aye, there it was – the hidden game – given away by that brief flash of white amongst the brambles.

Maglin breathed deeply through his nostrils to quell the outrage that rose within him. His first thought was to gather his company and descend upon the traitors before the day was out! But no. He would beat down his anger and say nothing – at least until he was sure of his suspicions. He would watch that pair . . . see what he could see . . . learn what he could learn. And if he should once catch them skulking together, plotting against him, then look out both.

In the meantime there was yet another matter to consider: the Stone itself.

What should he make of this thing? Here was magic, seemingly, his to hold and his to make use of. Yet he was still mistrustful of such witchi-pocus, still inclined to believe that it was all that mad hag's trickery.

Let it be put properly to the test, then, whilst my lady crone was elsewhere.

According to Maven, the Stone could tell neither the future nor the past, only what lived or existed today.

Very well. He would ask questions that only he could know the answer to. Maglin licked his finger and drew it across the Stone. 'My father, Zorn – does he live?'

Nothing but a damp smear on the jasper globe. Maglin wiped it clean and tried again. 'And my younger brother, Hazlin, does he live?'

Again there was naught there to see. Maglin tried a third question.

'Hazlin's daughter, Zelma. Does she live?'

The fingermark on the surface of the Stone turned a deep blue, darkened further, then became mottled and faded away to nothing. Maglin shook his head. The Stone had answered aright, but *how* did this happen? Again he tried, and again, working his way through those that he knew and those that he had known, the living and the dead. The Stone answered and was never wrong. For those that lived a blue mark appeared, and for those that were no more – nothing.

Perhaps, then, he must trust the Stone with questions he himself did not know the answer to. Maglin thought about this for a few moments, then wet his finger.

'Little-Marten. Does he live?'

Aye, according to the Stone, the Woodpecker had met no ill fate as yet. Henty too was still apparently alive, and this was good to learn. But what else should he ask?

Maglin knew the question he would most like to learn the answer to: shall the Various survive? But in this the Stone could not help him. Nor could it tell him whether there were those who plotted against him, nor whether the Orbis would come to his hand, nor even whether he would live this day through. Such things were for the future.

What exists and what does not . . . what exists and what does not . . .

Maven's words returned to him: '. . . is all that exists alive?' So could the Stone tell him about the existence of things that did not live and breathe? He would test the idea. Maglin glanced about him, and his eye fell upon the old pecking bag wherein the mapskins were kept. He knew they were there. Could the Stone divine it also?

'The mapskins,' he said, 'they that guided the Ickri from the northlands – do they exist?'

And there was the mark upon the Touchstone, darkening and fading as before. So.

Maglin wiped the surface clean, and prepared to ask a far more important question.

'The Orbis . . .' He drew his finger across the Stone. 'Does it exist?'

Strong and clear, the blue fingermark appeared.

Maglin felt then that the world about him had changed, and he with it. He had thought himself a hunter, one with an eye to see beyond what was visible. And yet how much he had missed. How much was hidden from him still, for lack of faith.

But the Orbis was real, and if it was real then it must be joined once again with the Touchstone. It must come to him, and to no other.

Maglin's hand shook as he raised a finger to his mouth for the final time, the hardened skin rough against the tip of his tongue.

'Elysse . . .' He paused for a moment, trying to prepare himself for what might come. 'Does it truly exist?'

Dark as night the fingermark bloomed upon the deep-red surface of the Touchstone, and to Maglin's wondering eyes it seemed to remain there longer than before, a misted cloud that hung among the heavens of some great planet, before slowly melting away.

Maglin let out a deep breath. It was true, then. All

of it true. The power of the Stone was real, the Orbis existed, and Elysse was waiting – waiting for him to bring his people home. The task was his, and although he didn't yet see how it was to be accomplished he knew that he must make it so.

Maglin lowered his head and closed his eyes – a believer at last.

Chapter Thirteen

'Pegs? Are you there?' Midge put her head around the door of the pig-barn and peered into the darkness. The outside world was crisply cold and bright, and this made the barn interior seem doubly gloomy.

She heard a brief scrabble of movement from somewhere beyond the hay-rake, and then the voice of Pegs blossomed inside her head.

Midge?

He sounded as though she'd startled him.

'Yes, it's me. Are you alone?' Midge sidled through the doorway. The place had the faint smell of livestock about it, and she realized that Pegs might have been in here for some time. He appeared from the far shadows, shaking out his mane. And walking very stiffly, Midge thought.

'Were you asleep?' she said. 'You were, weren't you? Pegs, that's really dangerous! Anything could wander in here – dogs . . . or anybody. You need to be more careful.'

Aye, 'tis true. But the nights are cold in the woods, and I sleep ill. I find more warmth here, and have been glad of it – and glad to have reason to come each day. What have you learned, though, maid? Have you news?

He looked different today, thought Midge. The brilliant sheen of him had dulled. His coat was scruffier – grey with dust from the barn. There were blackened hayseeds and bits of straw in his mane. But she liked him this way. It made him seem less other-worldly somehow, and it made this situation seem more . . . normal.

But then when he moved again she saw that his limbs were not just stiff from sleep. He was limping – quite badly – one of his forelegs barely touching the ground. His normal grace had gone, and he was obviously in pain.

'What's the matter?' she said. 'What's happened to you?'

When I flew down here in the morning darkness I lost my footing on the grey stone that surrounds this byre. It was icy, and I fell. I am unused to landing on such stuff.

'Oh no! Again? Do you want me to have a look at it? Can I help?' Midge was worried now.

No. This time I will mend – and there will be aid for me when I return to the forest. I have broken nothing and can walk a little. But I durst not fly, for fear that I should make matters worse when I come to earth. I may not be able to meet with you here for a while. But you said there was news?

Midge wasn't at all happy at seeing Pegs so disabled, even if it was only temporary. But she perched herself on the front wheel of the tractor, and said, 'Yes, I do have news. Amazing news – though it's good and bad. Celandine is alive, Pegs. Can you believe it? I found

205

her! Almost by accident really, although I'd been trying really hard.'

She lives? Truly lives?

'Yes! I've seen her three times now. I haven't had a chance to come and tell you before today, what with school and everything. I can only get up here at weekends, at least in the daytime. It's half-term next week, so that might be a bit easier. And anyway, I wanted to be able to talk to her properly first.' She was gabbling, and she could see that words like 'school' and 'weekends' and 'half-term' would make little sense to Pegs.

But she lives. Nothing could matter more, my friend. Nothing.

'I know. I still can't believe it's happened. The trouble is, though – and this is the bad news – she's *ancient*. Really really old. And she can't remember anything. I've tried telling her about the Various, and everything, but it's hopeless. She doesn't even remember going to the forest – in fact she's sure that she's never been in there in her life. It's like she's just blanked it all out. And so now I don't know what to do.'

Ah. She has forgotten us then. I have heard it said before – that those who see us do not believe what they see, and so forget. Perhaps this is to our good.

Pegs hobbled a little closer to the light of the doorway, and stood for a while looking out on the world.

The writings that Tadgemole gave you – have you showed these to Celandine?

'Um . . . no. No, I never thought of that. I don't

know whether it would do any good, though. She's almost blind, so she wouldn't make much sense of it. I could read it to her, I suppose, and see if she recognizes any of the names. I'm going to visit her again tomorrow – as far as I know.'

She is without sight? Then we must seek for some other way to stir her memory. Let me think on this and talk . . . with others. For now it is enough that Celandine is found. I may not be here for a while, Midge, and I cannot fly to you. It would be better you do not come to the forest. Wait, then, till I improve, or if there be aught that needs be more quickly said or done, then I shall try and send word. But now I have other news.

Pegs turned from the doorway and limped over to where Midge sat. Her heart sank to see him in such discomfort, but if he didn't want her help she didn't see what she could do.

Aye, and a poor tiding it is: Little-Marten and Henty have left the forest. None can tell where they have gone. Not to thee, I trust?

'What? No, I haven't seen them. They've run away? Why?'

They sought leave to wed, but Tadgemole would have none of it. Now he is in yet more of a fury, so that he talks of searching the Gorji lands himself. I have persuaded him to remain in the forest, until I have spoken to you at the least.

'Well, I haven't seen anything. I'll have a look around the barns, if you like, but there's so much going on and so many people about that I don't think there'd be anywhere for them to hide.'

Ach. Do we not have troubles enough, without this foolish

pair adding to their number? Look for them if you will, then, maid. And I shall try and keep Tadgemole from bringing harm to himself.

'All right.' There didn't seem to be anything left for her to say or do. 'Shall I go then?'

Aye. Go now, child, and let me rest a little. I shall wait for darkness to come, then return to the forest.

Midge didn't like to leave him this way. He was so delicate and fragile, so ill equipped to exist in this hard-edged world. And it wasn't just this new injury that worried her – Pegs was thinner, she realized, beneath that coarse winter coat. What did he do for food at this time of year? Maybe she could bring something to the barn for him, next time she came, just to make his life a little easier. Was there even anything for him to drink in here? Her eye fell on the old bucket that she had once used to bathe his wounds.

'Can I get you some water?' she said. 'Are you thirsty?'

Aye, some water before you go. That would be a kindness.

Chapter Fourteen

Carol Reeve wanted a quick word. In her office.

'I've noticed a change in your aunt this week,' she said to Midge. 'And I'm just a little bit concerned about her. She's not eating as she should, and that's never a good sign. But she also seems to be . . . I don't know. I shouldn't use the word "dippy", I suppose. Excitable, perhaps. Doesn't seem to know what day it is, quite. She keeps asking for you, and we keep explaining that you can only come on a Sunday, but . . . well . . .'

The office intercom buzzed, just once. There was a red light that continued to flash. Midge looked at it, and said, 'It's still all right for me to see her, though?'

'Yes, of course. She loves to see you, and the last thing I'd want to do is frighten you off. Sorry, Midge, I'd better just take this.' Carol picked up the phone, and said, 'Carol. Oh, hallo, Elaine. Yes, she's here now, actually. Yes, with me . . .'

Midge looked around the neat office. It was an odd mixture of old and new. The shelves and cabinets were all very modern, stacked with box files and hard-looking reference books. But Carol's desk was a big old antique thing, dark wood, with a green leather top. There was a photograph of two young boys – twins, by the look of them – and a little cut-glass vase with a sprig of pussy willow in it. Midge put out her hand and touched the polished wood of the desk.

'It was here when I arrived,' said Carol. She put down the phone. 'The desk, I mean. This used to be the headmistress's study, when the building was a school, and I couldn't resist the idea of having a real headmistress's desk. I imagine there would have been a few poor girls quaking in their boots on the other side of this old thing – your aunt being one of them, possibly. Right. Elaine's just on her way down, and Miss Howard's all ready for you. Now I don't want you to worry, but just keep bearing in mind that she is *very* old, and that sometimes old people . . . well, they can be off in a world of their own. OK? Go and say hello, then. I'm sure she'll be delighted to see you.'

Midge felt apprehensive, despite Carol's friendly manner, and Elaine didn't help matters much. In the lift, she said, 'Well, I've heard Miss Howard come out with some funny old stuff, but nothing like this week. Weird things. And do you know what she's just said to me? "Don't want any toast. What do I want with toast?" Well! We *always* make toast.'

Elaine left Midge at Celandine's apartment door,

and said, 'You go on in, dear. I've got to pop along and see Mrs Doble. I'll come by in a bit, and just make sure you're all right.'

By now Midge was imagining that her aunt had turned into a mad woman, and was likely to be standing behind the door with a poker. She hesitated, but then reasoned that it might be best to enter whilst Elaine was still within earshot. She turned the door handle.

There had been no need to worry. Aunt Celandine was sitting by the fire as usual, the top of her fuzzy head just visible over the back of her wheelchair.

'Aunt Celandine?'

'Ooh! Is that you, Midge?' The head turned slightly. 'Come and sit down, dear.'

'How are you?' Midge walked across the room, and sat in the wing-backed chair opposite her great-great-aunt. The little round table that stood between them was empty, she noticed. No tea, and no toast.

Aunt Celandine was already leaning forward, her hand reaching out and vaguely flapping in Midge's direction, searching for her. Midge perched herself on the edge of her chair and took her aunt's hand, surprised as always by the strength of grip in those frail-looking fingers.

'I've *seen* one! I've remembered. Yes! Yes!' Aunt Celandine squeezed Midge's fingers again and again as she spoke, each squeeze an emphasis of her words. Then she let go, and sat back in her chair.

'I've thought of his name too. Fin! You were quite right, my dear. Yes. Quite right.'

'What?' Midge was struggling to catch up. 'You mean, you remember going into the forest and everything?'

'No. I don't. I don't remember going in there at all, but I do remember seeing one of them. I was lying in a pram beneath the trees, and I saw a little boy looking down at me, hiding amongst the leaves. He was *very* little. I gave him some cake. Then his father came shouting for him . . . *Fin* . . . *Fin*. His father had a beard.'

'Really?' said Midge. 'And you don't mean that you just saw an ordinary little boy? He was . . . they were . . . you know, *little* people?'

'Oh, they were tiny. I think I said to someone afterwards – "Who are those little people living in our woods?" '

'What – you *told* about them?'

'I think I did. I don't remember that anyone believed me, but I do remember walking around the outside of the woods with Freddie, and shouting up at the trees. We didn't find anything.'

'Well . . . it's a start,' said Midge. And it was too – a very good start. 'Anything else?'

'No, nothing else. But you see, it's *there*, isn't it? It's in there somewhere – and it means that you were right. Oh, if I could just find more . . . remember more . . .'

Aunt Celandine looked smaller, Midge thought. More shrunken into her chair somehow. And yet there was a new restlessness about her, a continual movement. Her fingers tapped the arms of the wheelchair,

212

and her eyes seemed bigger and brighter than before as they travelled the room.

'One funny thing that happened . . . yes, that was funny . . . I woke up in my bed the other night and looked at the ceiling and there were all these *things* up there. Like barnacles. I thought I was in a cave. And somebody shouted, "Blinder!"'

'*Blind* her?' Midge didn't like the sound of that.

'Yes, "Blinder!" It was a child's voice – as though there were children playing outside in the corridor. And I suppose there *might* have been children playing in that corridor once, when this was a school.' Aunt Celandine gave a little chuckle. 'The ghosts of 2B.'

Midge didn't like the sound of that either.

'Oh, and I thought I heard hoofbeats as well, but that was out in the garden. They like to sit us on the patio for an hour if the weather's fine. Yes, I had my eyes closed, and I heard all these little hoofbeats trotting by. Tum-tum-tum-tum-tum. Quite close. Oh, that'll be the horses, I thought. Going off to be milked. Now why would I have thought that?'

Er . . . right. Midge didn't know whether to laugh or be alarmed. She had Tadgemole's letter in her pocket, and had intended to try and use it to jog the old lady's memory. Perhaps now wasn't a good time. Carol was right: Aunt Celandine had changed. Her thoughts seemed to be flitting about all over the place.

'It's always somewhere between sleeping and waking,' said Aunt Celandine. 'I can't remember my dreams any more, but just as I'm waking up there's sometimes a chance . . . a chance . . .' She closed her eyes. 'I had a little horse once. He was called Tobyjug. But then he died. That was before I cut off all my hair . . .'

It was as though she were talking to herself, off in a world of her own like Carol had said. Maybe that wasn't a bad thing, thought Midge. Maybe something would come through, if she just left her to it. She was getting a numb bum from sitting on the hard edge of this chair.

'Big scissors they were . . . and bushes. Oh! A picture in the bushes . . .' Aunt Celandine's head rocked from side to side. Midge watched her, and felt a sudden wave of affection for her. And sadness. She was such a nice old thing, really – always glad to see her, always sorry to see her go. And she was bright and clever, obviously a person who had been respected for the work that she'd done. It was a shame to be treated differently just for growing old and being a bit . . . dippy. And it was a shame to keep pushing her to remember stuff. Maybe it was time to give it a break, thought Midge. She stood up.

'Don't worry about it, Aunt Celandine. It'll be OK. Do you mind if I wander about a bit? I've got pins and needles.'

'Mm? Oh yes. Yes . . . like a picture puzzle . . .'

There was a stick propped against the side of the fireplace, a walking stick, painted white. Midge had never noticed it before. Was it Aunt Celandine's, and did she still use it? No, it didn't seem very likely. That must have been from before she was in a wheelchair. Midge picked up the stick, and held it out in front of her, trying to imagine what it must be like to be blind.

'*Schnnnick!* I can remember the sound, but I don't know where I was . . .' Aunt Celandine was still talking, eyes closed. Midge wondered whether she could get from the door to the far window, with her own eyes closed, just by using the white stick, and without tripping over or banging into anything. She'd give it a go.

It was almost impossible not to cheat, that was the trouble. She couldn't help but open her eyes just a tiny bit, and that rather defeated the point of having a stick.

'Oh, but it did feel wonderful. Thos said I looked like a boot brush . . .'

'Did he?' said Midge, just to be polite. She went back to the door in order to start her journey again. This time she was determined not to peep until she reached the opposite window.

Amazing how unsteady and insecure walking with your eyes closed made you feel – like you were about to tumble into a pit . . . or an open fireplace. Midge hesitated at this thought. But no, she couldn't have changed direction so very drastically, and anyway, that was what the stick was for, to warn of any such hazard. She inched forward.

'. . . like a green jigsaw. Where could I have been, though, when all this happened?' Aunt Celandine's murmuring voice gave Midge a bit of help as to direction.

But the stick wasn't making contact with anything, and that *didn't* help. It just waved about in thin air. Aha! Here . . . yes, here, she'd found something. Midge kept her eyes tight shut and made exploratory movements with the stick.

Tap-tap . . . tap-tap-tap . . .

What on earth was it? A rustling, swishing sound accompanied the tapping of her stick. Midge became aware that the room behind her had frozen into silence. She reached out again.

Tap-tap-tap-tap . . .

'*No . . . don't!* Please no! Don't . . . don't . . . don't . . . *don't* . . .'

Midge jumped in alarm at the sound of Celandine's terrified voice. She spun round.

'What? What is it?'

Aunt Celandine was crouching forward in her chair, her hands over her face, wailing and wailing.

'No! Don't let them . . . don't let them!'

Midge couldn't even move. What had she *done*? What was happening?

'Oh! They'll get me . . . no . . . don't let them . . .'

Midge remained motionless, locked solid, absolutely at a loss as to what was wrong or what she should do. And then the door opened, swinging back against the bookshelves, bump, and Elaine was there, hurrying across to the wheelchair, already bending over to put an arm around Aunt Celandine's tiny shoulders.

'Miss Howard? Miss Howard! What's the matter?'

Midge managed to take a couple of steps forward, still reeling with confusion. But she stopped as Elaine's spectacles flashed up at her.

'And what are you doing with that stick?'

'Nothing! I don't know what's . . . I haven't *done* anything!' What was she being accused of?

'No . . . no, course not. Sorry, love. It just looked . . . Miss Howard? Yes, that's right, it's only me. Now calm down, dear. It's all right. Everything's all right.'

'They'll get me . . . they'll get me . . .' Aunt Celandine had taken her hands away from her face, but she was still distraught.

'Oh no they won't. There's nobody here *to* get you – only me and Midge. And we'd never hurt you, now would we?'

'No . . .'

'No.' Elaine gave Midge a little nod of reassurance. Don't worry, don't worry. She kept a shielding arm about Aunt Celandine's shoulders, and continued to murmur words of comfort, as one might to a small child. 'Sh . . . it's all right now . . . everything's all right.' Gradually Aunt Celandine became calmer, and the worst appeared to be over. Elaine looked up at Midge again. 'Better tell me what's been going on, then. What happened exactly?'

'Well, I was just . . . walking about.' Midge hardly liked to say that she had been pretending to be blind. 'Wandering around . . . not doing any harm. I was over by the window. Over by . . .' She turned round. What *was* it that she had tapped with the stick?

217

She still didn't know. 'Over by that . . . that big plant. The bamboo plant. Then suddenly Aunt Celandine started . . . you know. She got upset. And I'm so sorry if it was me, Aunt Celandine. Was it me? Did I do something?'

Midge went across to the wheelchair and crouched down beside it. She put her hand on top of her great-great-aunt's and squeezed it tight. 'If I did anything to frighten you, I'm really sorry. Are you OK now?'

'I don't suppose it *was* anything to do with you,' said Elaine. 'She's been sort of funny all week – going on about prams and little boys in trees, and I don't know what. Poor old duck. I've had a feeling she was building up to something. Well, they can all get a bit confused, like, and it's hardly surprising at her age. She'll be OK.'

Even Elaine did it sometimes, Midge realized – talked about Aunt Celandine as if she weren't there or couldn't hear. And Elaine was really fond of her, you could tell.

'Can you remember what it was?' said Midge. 'That scared you so much?'

She looked up into Aunt Celandine's face and saw that the watery eyes were still troubled, still staring at something in the distance, beyond her shoulder. Her mouth was moving, but Midge couldn't hear anything.

'Sorry – what did you say?'

Aunt Celandine leaned a little closer.

'Is . . . *get* you . . .' she whispered.

'What?'

Elaine straightened up, and smoothed her hands across the front of her blue tunic. 'I think it'd be best if you went home now, love. She's probably had enough for today. But listen – try not to worry. She'll be fine now. I'll look after her.'

'Yes. Yes, all right.'

Midge stood up, and realized that she was still holding the white stick. She gently put it back where she had found it, resting it against the corner of the fireplace. Before she left she took a last glance at the bamboo plant. It was just a normal-looking plant, and the stick was just a normal stick, but she was convinced that these things had triggered some dreadful memory for poor Aunt Celandine. She wondered what could possibly have been so terrifying about that sound – the tap-tap-tapping of the stick, and the rustling of the leaves . . .

She had to say something to her mum about it, once she was home. There was no point in pretending that everything was fine when it wasn't. But at the same time she was careful to filter the information, to bend the facts a little.

'Yes, she got really upset. I still don't know why, because I wasn't *doing* anything much – just sort of wandering about. You know, looking around. I had pins and needles.'

'Hm. Well, listen.' Mum closed the door of the dishwasher, and leaned against it, arms folded. 'I think perhaps you should keep away for a bit. I've never been all that comfortable about you going over there, and if you're the cause of any kind of upset – even when it's not your fault – then you're doing more harm than good. And besides, you shouldn't have to be coping with geriatric problems at your age. Psychiatric . . . whatever.'

'She's not just some old *nutter*, Mum. I *like* her. I *like* going to see her.'

'Well, I'm still not sure that you should. But I think that what I might do is have a talk to that manager woman about it – Carol Reeve. Yes? Let's get a proper professional opinion on this, and take it from there. Happy with that?'

'No, not really. Wish I hadn't said anything now.'

Midge sat up in bed, her arms about her knees, and scowled at the photograph of Aunt Celandine. Why didn't things just go right for once? It wasn't *her* fault that Aunt Celandine had been so scared. She'd only been mucking about with a stick, for goodness' sake. And now her mum was threatening to keep her away. Well she wasn't going to keep away, and there was an end to it. She sighed, as she stared at the picture, try-ing to let the anger drain out of her.

It was possible now to spot the likeness between the child that she'd never met, and the old lady that she had come to know. The eyes and the mouth, even the hands, were somehow recognizable. How strange it must be to grow so old, and to have seen so many changes. No mobile phones back then, on the day that photograph was taken. No televisions or computers. The girl sitting on that wicker box would never have seen such things. Maybe she'd never even been in a car. Horses and carts – that was how they got about in those days, wasn't it?

Horses being milked . . . where could such a funny idea have come from? And barnacles in a cave. Midge thought about the caves that she'd seen in the Royal Forest, and a flash of intuition came to her. Yes, she'd bet anything that was where the runaway Celandine had stayed – among the Tinklers and the Troggles.

Aunt Celandine's memory *would* return, she was sure of it. But would she be strong enough to bear it? Something horribly frightening had obviously happened to that girl in the photograph. Was it just cruel to be trying to bring it all back again? It was too late to stop now, that was the trouble.

Yes, and it was too late at night to be sitting up worrying about it. Midge turned the dimmer light down, so that there was just a faint blue glow. She snuggled beneath the warm duvet and closed her eyes.

3:20. It was the first thing she saw – the illuminated face of her clock radio. Why was she even looking at it? Why was she awake? Midge pulled back the duvet a little and listened. There! A rustling sound. And again. Here in the room? Midge sat upright, nervous now.

Tap-tap . . . tap-tap-tap . . .

No, not in the room. Outside! Oh my *God*, there was something out there . . . something perched on the broad stone window ledge . . . rustling . . . tapping against the window pane!

Tap-tap-tap . . . tap-tap . . .

Aunt Celandine's urgent whisper came rushing into her head, the strange words echoing above the roaring pulse in her ears.

'Is . . . *get* you . . .'

Chapter Fifteen

'Is . . . get you . . .'

Celandine chased the words round and round in her head, trying to imagine where they might have come from. But it was like chasing tadpoles in a tin bath, the things wriggling through her fingers just as she thought she had them, disappearing into the murky swirl once more.

And the harder she tried, the murkier those waters became. She should stop and think of something else – let things settle for a bit.

Celandine gazed at the soothing patterns in the fake coal fire. They were very blurry patterns, her eyesight being what it was, but patterns nevertheless – shapes and sequences that repeated themselves. The flames danced their same little dance over and over. There . . . and gone . . . and back again. There and gone . . . back again. Just like her own thoughts: too fleeting to catch for more than an instant, but always returning to tease her.

She started once more: the tiny boy in the trees, staring down at her. The piece of cake, snatched from her fingers. The voice of the older one . . . '*Fin!* . . . *Fin!*'

'Is . . . *get* you . . .'

Celandine blinked and turned away from the fire. Was it one of *them* who had spoken those words? A picture came to her of that little brown face, the eyes so wide and fearful – but not in the trees this time. No, he was on the ground, head barely rising above the tall grass. Then grabbing at her sleeve . . .

'*Gorji* is get you!'

Gorji? Who or what was Gorji? Celandine pinched the sleeve of her cardigan between finger and thumb and tugged at it, closed her eyes and felt again the sensation of being pulled forward, scrambling to her feet and following . . . following . . .

. . . through the dock leaves and the nettles and the long summer grass, stumbling around the crest of Howard's Hill, the tiny figure always ahead of her, and then . . . he just disappeared.

He was gone, and her memory gone with him. She could recall nothing beyond that point.

Oh, but this was progress! At least she had something more to work with – another few steps to add to her dance. She would whirl through those steps again and again, and perhaps her feet would remember more and carry her forward of their own accord.

Back to the beginning of the sequence, then: Fin, standing in the tall grass, reaching forward to grab at her sleeve . . .

She saw him in more detail this time, and some of her original emotion swept through her. The realization that such a being had truly existed, and that this had truly happened to her was overwhelming. This was no longer just a picture-memory, or some half-forgotten dream. This was real. The little bead of blood on his shoulder . . . the long black hair all dusty with summer pollen . . . the ragged waistcoat . . . she was not imagining these things. This was recollection, as real as her memory of Freddie, clumping down the wooden stairs in his new army uniform.

'Is *Gorji* come! Is *get* you!'

She caught something of his voice – a throaty little whisper – and it was both exhilarating and frightening to hear. She was getting somewhere, she really was, but who knew what terrors might be lurking along this dark pathway? Is . . . *get* you . . .

Tap-tap. It was only a brief knock at her door, but the sound made her jump.

Carol Reeve put her head into the room.

'Miss Howard? Are you awake?'

Celandine wished that she could pretend that she wasn't. She liked the woman well enough, but she didn't want company. Not right now.

'Yes. Come in, Mrs Reeve.'

Carol crossed the room and sat on the arm of the wing-backed chair, her hands in her lap. She had brought a waft of floral scent into the room. Something new . . . different to the perfume she normally wore. Freesias? No . . .

'I've just been talking to Elaine, and she was telling me about your upset. How are you feeling now?'

'Oh. Much better, thank you. It was just . . . oh,

some silly thing. I think I must have been half asleep and having a bit of a bad dream. I wouldn't want to be the cause of any worry.'

'Hm. Well . . . it's our job to worry – or rather to care. What was the dream about? Can you remember?'

'No, not really.' She wished that Carol would go away, and let her *think*.

'Elaine wondered if it had anything to do with Midge. She thought that perhaps the girl had . . . frightened you in some way.'

Yes, she had. Something that Midge had done had frightened her very much. That tapping sound had terrified the life out of her, and yet she couldn't say why. Even now her heart was beating a little faster at the memory of it.

She realized that she'd paused for too long.

'No! Nothing to do with Midge at all. It was just a dream.'

'Would you rather she didn't come here for a while? Midge, I mean. You see, I'm beginning to think—'

'No! Of course she must come! I *must* see her!'

Carol stood up. 'Well, if you're absolutely sure, then of course I wouldn't want to upset you by keeping her away. All right, then. I'd better carry on and do the rounds. I'll tell Elaine that I've had a chat with you, and that as far as I'm concerned it's business as usual. Anyway, I'm glad you're feeling better. So. I'll say goodnight, then, and see you in the morning? Elaine will be along in half an hour or so, to help you to bed.'

'Yes. Thank you, Mrs Reeve. See you in the morning.'

'Night, then, Miss Howard.'

'Goodnight.'

As Carol closed the door behind her, another faint trace of perfume was wafted on the air. It reminded Celandine of something so strongly: someone that she had once known, perhaps, or some place that she had once been . . .

'Blinder . . .'

Where *had* she heard that word before? Celandine sighed. It was no good trying to force anything to come through. She could only sit here with her eyes closed and wait. Sit here . . . and be calm . . . breathe in the sweet scent of lavender . . .

Lavender. Of course – how silly of her not to have recognized it straight away. Carol Reeve's perfume was lavender.

But the smell of lavender didn't make her think of Carol Reeve. It made her think of . . . darkness. Yes, of darkness, and the muffled sound of children's voices, playing quietly somewhere. But that could be anywhere. Celandine breathed slowly in and out. The scent of lavender was fading now, and the half-memory that it had triggered was fading too. She couldn't catch it, couldn't put herself in that place where she had once been. Perhaps it was unimportant, and unconnected to her search. But if anyone had asked her what the smell of lavender reminded her of, she might have said, 'Underground.'

Chapter Sixteen

Little-Marten and Henty had never been as warm and comfortable in their lives. The box-crib that they had made for themselves was well sheltered from wind and rain, and the open-sided wooden tree-dwelling was as safe as any place they could hope to find on Gorji territory. From this high viewpoint they could watch the comings and goings of the giants, and if sudden danger should arrive they were prepared for it. They had planned an escape route along one of the low-spreading branches of the cedar tree. Their combined weight at the end of this branch caused it to dip close enough to the ground for Henty to be able to jump without hurting herself. With a little practice of this manoeuvre they were certain that they could be out of the tree and away into the thickets soon enough, should it become necessary. Little-Marten could of course have floated straight down from the platform itself, but that would have meant leaving Henty to fend for herself and he would never do that.

The soft Gorji bindle-wrap would go with them, they had decided, when the time came. It was too precious a find not to keep, although too bulky to carry easily. They solved this problem by cutting off the end of the sack, so that it was of a length more suited to their size. Little-Marten spent some time hacking the thing apart with a tinsy knife, and Henty then folded the rough edge and stitched it with fishing thread. It was good – not rainproof, but wonderfully warm. And they could always cover it with one of their own oilskin bindle-wraps to keep out the wet.

The birds in the trees about them, they noticed, were far tamer than the few that now remained in the Royal Forest. It was plain that the ruddocks and throstles that dwelt here had less to fear from the Gorji than their forest cousins did from the Ickri. No archers prowled this peaceful copse, ready to shoot down anything that moved, no snares were set for the coneys that fed unconcerned at the very borders of the settlement.

And so it was with them. Henty and Little-Marten had been among the Gorji before, and had suffered no hurt at their hands. Consequently they were wary, but unafraid. Even the great roaring machines that came and went, so alarming at first sight, seemed to pose no real danger. Such things were apparently con-fined to the enclosure, and never ventured beyond those bounds.

The distant voices of the Gorji became familiar to them, after a day or two. Midge they immediately recognized – the maid who had come to the woods – and the other maid and youth who had been there on the terrible day of the felix. But this was the first time they had been able to observe full-grown giants going about their business – those who commanded the machine monsters, and the man and woman who gave them their orders. Were they such a fearful race? They carried no recognizable weapons, built no fires upon which to roast their victims, dealt none of the death and destruction that all childer of the little people were told was the Gorji way. The Wisp, who nightly fished the Gorji wetlands, returned with tales of such deadly encounters and hair's-breadth escapes as would freeze the blood of the listener. So brave those fishers were, to dodge the giants' flashing blades and skip beneath the bellies of their ferocious hounds for the sake of a string of eels. But the one old hound that Henty and Little-Marten saw looked scarce able to walk. Perhaps the fishers' tales were exaggerated after all.

A string of eels, though. What wouldn't they give for a nice piece of baked eel now? Warm and dry they might be, but they were becoming desperately hungry. Their store of food had long gone, and there was very little in the trees and bushes about them that they could eat. Little-Marten was no hunter – had never used a bow and arrow or killed in his life. His position as Woodpecker had excused him from such tasks. Neither was Henty any expert forager. She had picked mushrooms and blackberries, but the daughter of Tadgemole had not been expected to seriously grub for survival. Both had relied on others to provide for them. Come the spring and summer there would be roots and nuts and fruit for the taking, but how should they live until then? To escape, and to be together – this had been their only thought. Beyond that there was no plan. Now they were going to have to learn how to winter off the land.

'What do the Gorji eat?' Little-Marten wondered. 'Do 'em grow tiddies like the Naiad?'

It was worth finding out – though how they would cook a potato should they find one was an unanswered question. They could hardly be lighting fires so close to the Gorji settlement.

'We'll go and see,' said Henty, 'come moon-wax.'

It was late into the night before the last of the bright lights of the settlement was extinguished, and even then there remained a faint blue glow from one of the high windows. But now was the time, if they were to risk it at all.

Little-Marten and Henty descended the rope ladder, and silently made their way through the copse. The air was cold and still – dangerous, for any little sound they made would carry clearly on such a night. High up on their platform perch with a view of the world about them they felt safe enough, but down here on the ground and in darkness was a different matter. They would not want to meet the Gorji hound at this level, old and feeble though it might be.

As they stepped from the copse onto an open stretch of short-cropped grass, a pale moon appeared, slyly showing its face from behind the clouds. More danger – for now they could be seen as well as heard. The pair quickly crossed the grass and moved around towards the back of the dwelling, where the shadows were deeper.

Henty grabbed Little-Marten's arm. 'Hst! What's this?'

Little-Marten looked down at the ground. A cabbage. And another . . . and another. They had stumbled upon a vegetable patch, and so quickly that they could hardly believe it. Their instinct had been proved right: the Gorji lived as the Naiad did, cropping the land for their food.

But when they crouched down to examine this treasure, they were disappointed. The cabbage plants were ancient, with leaves as tough as snake's hide and already reduced to tatters by slugs and winter frost. Little-Marten and Henty moved around the frozen plot, the soil solid and lumpy beneath their feet. They found other plants – tough stalks and half-exposed roots that they didn't recognize – but all of them the neglected remains of a season long gone. There was no food for them here.

Move on, then. They tiptoed along the pathway that surrounded the massive building, and came to a stone construction that jutted out, like a smaller dwelling added to the first. Here there was an open entrance-way. Little-Marten and Henty peered inside as they moved past, hanging back, ready to run if necessary. The enclosed space was dimly illuminated by some circular object fixed to the far wall. They saw that there was another door, this one shut, a wooden bench . . . some long garments hanging above it . . . and a row of giants' boots, arranged into pairs, the biggest of which were almost as tall as themselves. Henty and Little-Marten lingered for a few moments, fascinated by this glimpse into the Gorji world. But they could see nothing here that was of any practical use to them, and so they pressed on, retreating from the light and silently rounding the darkened corner of the building . . .

Hssssssschhhhhttt! A ferocious explosion of hissing and snarling burst upon them from the shadows, so sudden that they fell against one another in terror. Fiery yellow eyes glaring down at them from above . . . fangs drawn back, spitting hatred . . . their enemy, their nightmare, here to haunt them again. The eyes widened, fixed them to the spot in their chilling gaze, then seemed to shoot straight out into space. Henty and Little-Marten instinctively ducked, but the beast had already launched itself. To their amazement it flew straight over their heads. They saw it land in the light of the open doorway behind them, a shock of black-and-white fur, frantic claws scrabbling for purchase on the frosty stone. In an instant the thing had gone, a final yowl of outrage trailing its disappearance into the night.

Henty and Little-Marten rose unsteadily from their crouching position, still stunned and weak-kneed with fright. A felix! Memories of the savage barn animal that they had encountered the previous summer should have made them more wary of venturing abroad at night – and yet this creature had plainly been terrified of *them*. It had been much younger and smaller, they realized now, than that other monster.

Had its yowling roused the giants? They stared up at

the dwelling, ready to flee if any light should appear. Nothing. All remained quiet and still.

Little-Marten let out a deep breath, and ran his fingers through his hair. 'Ffffffff . . .' He drew Henty towards him and they stood for a while in the cold moonlight, waiting for their beating hearts to subside. When they finally moved apart, Little-Marten saw the puzzled expression in Henty's eyes. She tilted her head back a little, as if to focus, then put her hand up towards his shoulder.

'Bide still,' she whispered.

Little-Marten craned his neck sideways, trying to see what she was doing. 'Eh? What is it?'

Henty had a fragment of some pale substance between her finger and thumb. She sniffed at it, held it away from her, sniffed at it again. Then she cautiously put it to her mouth and tasted it.

'What've 'ee got there?'

'Try it and see.'

Henty raised her fingers to Little-Marten's lips, and put a scrap of something into his mouth. Little-Marten chewed at the morsel between his front teeth, explored the texture of it with the tip of his tongue. It was . . . fish? Aye, fish! But like no fish that he had ever eaten before . . . a delicious salty flavour, with none of the earthiness of the eels and gudgies that the Wisp provided.

How could a piece of fish have found its way onto Little-Marten's shoulder? It must have been dropped there by something. The felix . . .

Simultaneously the pair of them turned towards the

place that the felix had sprung from. They saw a large black container, square edged and taller than them, with a lid that had been thrown open. From the top of the container protruded torn scraps of a shiny material that they recognized – the same type of black sack that had held the Gorji bindle-wrap. They sniffed at the air, and looked at each other, as if to confirm what they were both thinking. There was food in that thing. They could smell it, for certain, and they were beginning to guess at what it was that they had discovered – a food store. This must be what the giants used for their Basket-time.

The container had handles – very useful – and Little-Marten found that by standing on tiptoe he could just reach one of these. He tested the weight of the thing, rocking it to and fro on its base.

'I reckon I can tip 'un up,' he whispered to Henty. He put one foot against the base and leaned back, pulling the handles towards him. Henty stood beside him, ready to help take the weight. Between the two of them they managed to lower the object onto its side, more or less in silence. They hauled the black sack from the open mouth of the container, and began their exploration.

What they found was scarcely believable: pieces of fruit, vegetables, meat – more food than all the Various tribes had seen brought to their own Basket-time in a moon. Crusts of toasted bread, some already spread with honey . . . half-full metal containers, one of which held the delicious fish . . . some strange curving yellow fruit that had been peeled back, bitten into, and then put aside for later . . . and all of it jumbled together in a glorious heap. They feasted as they foraged, gulping down mouthfuls of cooked potatoes, greenstuff and those things that they recognized, poking experimentally at those they did not, sniffing, tasting, offering, sharing. Did the Gorji truly live thus, with so much food to spare that they could leave such a basket out for a single felix? No, there must surely be others who would come to take of this.

In the meantime how much could they take for themselves, without it being missed? They had a whispered discussion.

'Enough for the morrow,' said Henty. 'No more, or they might come a-hunting for it.'

'Aye, agreed,' said Little-Marten. 'We'd likely end up as meat ourselves if they catched a hold of us.'

They sorted out a few crusts, some small round pieces of dark fruit – of which there seemed to be plenty – and part of a bird carcass. The rest of the food they carefully put back into the black sack, trying to arrange things as they had been before. Then they grabbed hold of the handles of the big container and tilted it upright once more.

'Should we close the top?' Henty wondered.

'No. Best leave it as 'twas.'

Back to the tree-dwelling they hurried, carrying enough spoils to see them through the following day, delighted at their success. Provided that the giants raised no alarm on discovering their loss, there seemed no reason why this shouldn't become a nightly expedition.

'We s'll see the winter through yet,' said Little-Marten, as they reached the foot of the rope ladder. 'And never need turn a hand. Go on up with 'ee, then.'

'Oh no, Master Woodpecker. It's those idle hands that I don't trust. You first.'

Chapter Seventeen

Midge was sitting bolt upright in bed, her pulse banging in her ears.

Tap-tap-tap . . .

Again that terrifying sound from beyond the drawn curtains, louder now, more insistent. Midge wanted to run – to leap out of bed and dash to her mother's room – but she dared not move. One twitch from her, and whatever monster was out there would surely come bursting through the window . . . roaring through the shattered glass . . .

Tap-tap-tap-tap-tap-tap . . .

Although if there *was* a monster, then it might not be quite so polite as to knock for permission to come in. Midge felt the use of her muscles returning to her, along with her reasoning. It would take no more than a moment for her to be through that door and out of here, if she wanted. She turned her bedside lamp up a little higher, then edged over to the far side of the bed, swinging her legs out in readiness.

Tap-tap . . . *tap-tap* . . .

Could it be Pegs? The thought occurred to her.

Maybe he'd flown up to the window ledge and was perched there, trying to get her attention. Maybe it was him. No. Pegs would speak, as he had done before, whisper to her in those strange colour-words. But then something that Pegs had already said came back to her, about Little-Marten and Henty. How they'd run away . . .

Maybe it was Little-Marten, then.

That seemed more possible. Midge stood up, still undecided as to whether she should run to get her mum or go over to the window and see for herself. It couldn't be anything that dangerous out there, could it?

Tap-tap-tap . . .

Well it wasn't going away, whatever it was. Midge crept silently over to the window. She hesitated a few moments longer, before gingerly twitching the edge of the curtain, keeping it at arm's length, ready to jump back. She couldn't see a thing.

Closer, then. She leaned forward and pulled the material aside a little more, to make a bigger gap.

'Oh . . . !' Midge gasped and instantly let go of the curtain.

A hand! She had glimpsed a pale hand, flat against the glass, a waving movement. The hand was quite small, though, and its gesture unthreatening. Perhaps it was Little-Marten after all. Midge forced herself into decisive action. She drew the curtain aside properly, grasped the catch and pushed the window open.

'Agh!' Midge heard a grunt of alarm from outside, felt the resistance of the window as it bumped against some living thing, and realized to her horror that she'd shoved whatever it was off the window ledge.

'Oh no!' She peered out into the darkness below, and saw something scuffling about among the shrubs near the balustrade wall. 'Spick it! Spick . . . spick . . .' Low muffled curses drifted up from the shrubbery. It didn't *sound* like Little-Marten.

The figure straightened and turned to look up at her. Midge could see a face now, furious eyes that glinted white in the moonlight. It took her a moment or two to realize who it was – and even then she could scarcely believe it.

'*Maglin?*'

'Aye, Maglin.' The hoarse whisper came back to her. 'Or what be left of him. Do 'ee mean to see me dead, maid? Well, no matter. I be down here as'd have to come down anywise.'

'Yes . . . um, sorry. I didn't mean to push you like that. But what do you want?'

'Look on the ledge, maid, beside 'ee. There be a pecking bag – see it?'

'A what? Oh. Oh, yes. I've found it.' Midge looked along the window ledge and saw a rough bundle of material. 'Do you want me to throw it down?' She still didn't understand what this could be all about.

'No, maid. 'Tis for Celandine. Thee must take the bag to her and tell her that 'tis a gift from Maven-the-Green. Can 'ee remember that?'

The freezing night air was making Midge shiver so much that her whispers came out in shaky gasps.

'Wh-what?' She couldn't believe she was having this

conversation. 'This is f-for Celandine?' She dragged the bag towards her.

'Aye. And only for she. From Maven.'

'But what is it?'

Maglin didn't reply. He'd turned away from her and was looking intently towards the far end of the building. Midge heard a muffled yowl from the other side of the house. Probably one of the cats messing around in the bins again.

'I be gone,' Maglin hissed up to her. He began to back away towards the shrubbery. 'Mind what I tell 'ee, now. The bag be for Celandine – from Maven. To help her remember. And when 'ee've learned whatever there is to learn then bring word to me. To me. Come to the tunnel and ask for Maglin – no other.'

'No . . . wait. What about Pegs? Have you seen him? Is he all right?'

But Maglin was already clambering over the balustrade wall. He disappeared into the darkness with no other word. Gone.

Midge picked up the bag and put it under her arm for a moment as she closed the window. A quick tug at the curtains and back to her bed she scuttled, shaking with the cold. She threw the bag on the bed, and sat with her knees up and her duvet pulled around her shoulders, as she studied it. The material seemed to be of soft animal skin, a bit like roughened chamois leather, but darker in colour. It had a single carrying strap, again made of leather, and a flap that had been tightly fastened with waxy twine so that the contents were hidden. Midge reached forward and prodded its

241

lumpy shape. There was a round object in there of some kind . . . a couple of other indeterminate shapes . . .

Midge was becoming aware of a pervasive smell beginning to fill the warm room. She lifted the bag and brought it cautiously towards her. Yipes, the thing *stank*. A deep earthy smell, overlaid with a sweeter perfume . . . sort of musky. Lavender?

She was going to have to do something about this, and quick. Her mum was sure to notice the smell when she brought in her morning mug of tea. And then there would be awkward questions. Midge hopped out of bed and went across to her wardrobe. She rummaged about and found two or three scrunched-up plastic carrier bags, remnants of past shopping trips. They might help contain the strange odour. She put the leather bag inside one of the carriers, tied it up as tightly as she could, then put that bundle inside a second bag and did the same. Get out of that, she thought, and stuffed the whole lot back into her wardrobe.

What could be *in* there, though, and why had it been Maglin who had delivered this strange package? He was the last one she would have expected to see. 'To help her remember,' Maglin had said. They knew, then, that Celandine's memory had gone – probably from Pegs. But how had Maglin known whereabouts in the house to find her? And what on earth did that weird old Maven-the-Green have to do with all this?

Too many questions, as always. But tomorrow was Sunday, and so perhaps she would soon learn some answers. Uncle Brian was going over to Almbury Mills again, and she'd be able to visit Aunt Celandine. The bag would go with her.

Midge turned her lamp down low, and lay back down on her pillow. She closed her eyes. You just couldn't think too much about all this stuff, otherwise you'd go nuts. That was one thing she'd learned already.

Maglin paused at the gates to the Gorji settlement, listening for any further sounds of danger. Nothing. If there were a felix about, it was nowhere to be seen.

He glanced back up towards the blue light in the Gorji child's window, marvelling at what he'd just achieved. It had been no easy matter to land on that narrow ledge . . . fly-hopping from the swaying branches of the nearby fir tree. And no easy matter to balance there once landed. Drat the girl for then shoving him from his perch . . .

But he'd done it – flown down from the woods, soaring through the black night, to deliver the pecking bag at Maven's behest. He shook his head, still unable to see how the hag had known exactly where the child would be. And still wondering how she'd managed to persuade him to take on such a task.

'If thee would hold the Orbis, maister, then thee has it to do.' Maven's words came back to him. And her meaning had been plain: he could not simply wait and hope for the Orbis to come to him. He must act to help bring it about.

'And you think it *my* task to run this errand?'

'Name another that should do it for 'ee – or could. Celandine lives, Maglin, but she ails. She be old and near-blind, and have no remembrance of her time amongst the Various. She've long forgotten the night she left the forest, and what she carried with her. Unless she be given some reminder, the Orbis s'll not be found. I've gifts for her that may aid her memory. Bring them to her, maister. Put them in the hands of the Gorji child, and tell her they be for Celandine – for Celandine alone, mark 'ee – and for none but she to open. From Maven-the-Green.'

'What? Shall Celandine know your name, then?'

'Aye, she'll know my name. I told her long ago as this day would come.'

'You *spoke* with her?'

'Once. She were but a maid then. 'Twere I who helped her flee the forest, carrying the Orbis with her, when Corben and the Ickri would hunt her down . . .'

Such revelations. Maglin was lost in the wonder of it. How little he had understood of his own tribe and all their history. How little he had seen and heard of what was in the very air around him, and how little he had cared. Only a short while ago he would have given Maven the rough side of his tongue for even daring to step close to him. Now he did her bidding, it seemed. He was to fly to the Gorji settlement bearing gifts for Celandine, from Maven-the-Green.

And still he had hesitated. 'Maister', she called him. Yet who was maister here, when Maven seemed to know so much, and he so little?

'How shall I find the child?' he had said.

'Look for a blue lamplight. Beyond that lies her chamber.'

'A blue light? How do 'ee *know* all this?'

'I knows what I knows, maister.'

And there it was. He had put his trust in Maven and in his own powers, and that trust had been proved well founded. Faith and belief. This must be his way forward.

Maglin took one last look around the settlement, then climbed through the bars of the gate to begin the long journey home.

Chapter Eighteen

A new sharpness in the morning air told Little-Marten that something had changed. He put his hand against the lid of the box-crib, raised it a little, and listened. The birds sang as usual – the throstle in the nearby rowan tree, the wood pigeons further away at the edge of the copse. But their sound was different, flat and muted, the air itself unnaturally still. Little-Marten raised the box lid completely, sat up, and looked towards the open side of the tree-dwelling. Now he understood. The branches of the cedar were heavy with snow.

He clambered out of the crib, pulled on his chilly jerkin, and wandered over to the edge of the platform to take a look at the world.

'What is it?' Henty's voice, sleepy and muffled from within the box.

'Come and have a glim,' said Little-Marten.

They couldn't remember when they had last seen a fall as heavy as this. The trees and bushes were thickly laced, bowed down by the weight of snow, and on the ground below there was barely a blade of grass showing. Beyond the copse they could see the smothered rooftops of the Gorji settlement, and beyond that the silent stretches of wetland, flat and uniform beneath a coverlet of white, dark rows of willows protruding here and there.

In the old forest such a snowfall would be viewed with dismay. Hunting and trapping, fishing and foraging, all would be made the more difficult. There would be no time or inclination to stand and admire the wonder of it, only grumbles at the hardship it brought. But for Henty and Little-Marten, this was not so. They had fallen on easier times. Warm and dry and well-fed, they could afford to gaze out in delight at the transformation.

Little-Marten kicked at the ridge of snow that lined the edge of the platform, so that a small avalanche of it fell to the ground below with a satisfying *flump*.

'Hst!' said Henty. 'Don't!'

'Why not?'

'The Gorji might see it.'

Little-Marten was about to say that this wasn't very likely, when something far more important occurred to him. He peered down at the smooth and unbroken surface of the snow that surrounded their tree – a surface that would be similarly unbroken all the way to the Gorji dwelling. If he and Henty were to go on living here in secret, then that covering of snow would have to remain as it was: undisturbed.

'This don't look so well,' he said.

'What do you mean?'

'Well don't 'ee see? We can't get to the Gorji basket

for food without we leave tracks all the way there. Aye, and all the way back.' He scanned the surrounding copse, trying to see if there was some route by which he could hop and glide from tree to tree, and so keep off the ground. He wasn't hopeful. The cedar where they now dwelt was by far the biggest tree between here and the dwelling; those nearby were mostly hollies and rowans – too spindly and bushy to be able to land upon, not enough height to be able to stay aloft. And the slippery snow-covered branches would make it harder still. He'd likely end up on his back at the first attempt.

Henty could see what he was thinking. 'No good?'

Little-Marten looked up into the high branches of the cedar. 'That'd be the only way,' he said. 'Climb up to the top of 'un and do it in one. 'Twould only be a crack-nog as'd try it in the dark, though. And if I got there I should still leave tracks all around that gurt basket – and have to get back, somewise. No. I reckon we'm stuck here for a bit.'

They clambered back into the box-crib and sat huddled together, watching the skies. For the time being they were trapped, but perhaps the snow would melt before too long. They weren't so badly off.

But by mid-afternoon the weather looked as though it might worsen if anything. The sky was a flat grey colour, with a band of darker cloud on the horizon – no hint of sunshine to melt the snow – and it was plain that they would have to go this night at least without taking food from the Gorji basket.

'Wish we'd not been so careful, though,' Little-Marten grumbled. 'I could go a couple o' tiddies, now.'

But Henty put her head to one side, and raised a finger to her lips. Little-Marten looked at her. What had she heard?

Voices. Coming down through the copse.

'Yes, if it's still like this tomorrow we'll get the old toboggan out for you, eh? Where is it – in the Stick House?'

'Think so. Haven't used it for about three years.'

A man and a youth by the sound of it.

Then another voice: 'I've never even been on a toboggan. There weren't really any hills around where we lived, in London, and we never got much snow. Nothing like this, anyway.'

It was the Gorji maid, Midge. So there were three of them altogether – a man and two childer.

Little-Marten and Henty got out of the box-crib as silently as they could, and quickly began to gather their belongings: pecking bags, clothing, the Gorji bindle-wrap . . . hurry . . . hurry . . .

'Yeah, we could build a snowman. Or an igloo! That'd be better still. I've always wanted to . . . hey! That's funny. Where's my rope ladder?'

'What?'

'The rope ladder – it's gone!'

'What do you mean, gone?'

Crunching footsteps coming closer to the tree.

'No, it's still up there, George. Look, see that bit of blue rope?' The man's voice.

'But I didn't leave it like that! How could I have got up there again?'

'Well you must have done.'

'But I didn't!'

The voices were directly beneath the tree now. Little-Marten and Henty were ready to go, but dared not move for fear of being seen.

'Well it doesn't matter right now, does it?'

'Course it matters right now! I'm going to find a branch or something. See if I can get it down again, and find out what's going on.' More crunching of footsteps.

'Well, hang on a minute, George. Listen. Go to the shed and find a rake, or a hoe – it'd probably be quicker in the long run. And some gardening string. Get some string, and Midge and I can try and find a stick in the meantime. We'll tie the rake to the stick, and I'll probably be able to reach it, then.'

'OK. Back in a tick.'

Little-Marten moved silently towards the edge of the platform, risked a quick glance, and then drew back again. He saw the boy, George, beginning to run towards the dwelling.

'Come on, Midge.' The man spoke again. 'We're going to have to humour him, the nutter. Help me hunt around for a stick, and then we can think about going over to Almbury Mills. That's if you still want to.'

'Yeah, course I do. George is right, though, Uncle Brian. He *couldn't* have left the rope ladder up there like that.' The girl sounded puzzled, and it was a moment or two before the crunching footsteps moved away from the tree.

'Brr! Bit of a wind blowing up.' The man's voice had become more distant. 'Shouldn't be surprised if we get another dose of this before long.'

Henty and Little-Marten waited, peeping down from the platform, dodging back out of sight again, trying to keep track of the whereabouts of the Gorji. Finally, Little-Marten whispered, 'Now!' and the two of them began to make their way down through the branches. They took the route that they had planned, continually looking over their shoulders in order to keep an eye on the giants. Along the lowest branch they shuffled, horribly aware of the lumps of snow that kept falling to the ground. But the giants were further down the copse, and still they had managed to avoid being seen. They took the final jump, landed on the soft snow, and hurried away towards the thicket that bordered the copse. Little-Marten fairly pushed Henty into the undergrowth and took a last look behind him as he followed her. He glanced through the trees and saw that the girl Midge was turning in his direction. Had she seen him? It was hard to tell, and too late to do anything about it. He scuffled beneath the hedge, and crouched next to Henty.

'Got one!'

The boy was back, waving some long implement.

Little-Marten and Henty stayed where they were. Perhaps the giants would fail to get up into the cedar, and just go away again.

'OK, well I've found a stick. Let's give it a whirl.'

It didn't take them long. The man simply tied the stick to the long pole thing, reached up towards the platform, and after a couple of attempts the ladder came tumbling down.

'There you go.'

'Thanks, Dad.' The boy climbed up the swinging ladder and scrambled over to the platform.

'Hey – all my stuff! It's all messed up! Come and have a look, Midge. I can't *believe* this!'

The boy disappeared from view, as the girl began climbing the ladder.

'Look at this!' The boy was back, standing at the edge of the platform and holding up the remains of the soft red bindle-wrap. 'Somebody's hacked my sleeping bag in half! And there's old tin cans up here . . . bits of cabbage stalk . . . chicken bones . . . *hell* of a mess . . .'

The girl paused at the top of the rope ladder, to look at the bindle-wrap. Then, as the boy disappeared once more, she turned and stared at the exact spot where Little-Marten and Henty were hiding.

'We'd best be gone,' Little-Marten whispered to Henty, and she nodded. The two of them pushed their way through the hedge and began to struggle along the snow-filled ditch on the other side. The easy times were over.

They had barely got away from the settlement before the weather turned. Perhaps the whirling clouds of sleet that now came sweeping across the wet-lands would help keep them hidden, but it made the going that much harder. Little-Marten and Henty stayed close to the hedges and ditches, ducking low, their eyes narrowed against the icy sting. No word was spoken, but both knew that there was only one direction left open to them: the Far Woods.

They dared not set out across the open fields, although there was little chance of their being seen in this weather. Instead they kept to the borders and the banks of the rhynes, dodged along the lines of willows, finding what cover they could. Their zig-zagging progress was slow and dispiriting – made worse whenever they were forced to backtrack because of some hedge too thick to penetrate or some rhyne too wide for Henty to jump. Exhaustion finally brought them to a standstill. Henty sank into a crouching position at the base of a willow, her back to the wind.

'Just let me rest a little,' she said. 'Then we'll go on.'

But Little-Marten knew that neither of them were able to go much further. They would have to find shelter, and soon, if they were to survive the coming night. He turned and looked beyond the narrow rhyne from where the willow stood, searching what little he could see of the swirling landscape. There were dark shadowy shapes out towards the middle of the next field. Little-Marten couldn't tell from here whether these were bushes or pieces of Gorji machinery, but he would go and investigate.

'Bide here,' he said.

The wind threw him off balance as he spread his wings in order to jump the rhyne. Little-Marten teetered on the edge for a moment, but then launched himself and managed to land safely on the opposite side. He scrambled up the snowy bank and leaned into the wind, battling across the field towards the objects that lay there.

It was a tree – or the remains of one – an old oak that had been cut down. The rotten stump remained in the ground, whilst all around lay stacks of logs and branches. It looked as though the Gorji were in the process of sawing and sorting the wood, ready for some future use. Little-Marten moved among the piles of snow-covered tree limbs, looking for a likely place to shelter. As he circled the area, eyes screwed up against the biting sleet, he saw that there was a great split in the main stump of the tree – a deep hollow. He pushed his way towards it, and crouched down to take a closer look. Immediately his heart lifted. The hollow was big enough for both him and Henty to crawl into. It looked fairly dry in there, and better still it was to the leeward side of the wind. That was enough. He would go straight back and get Henty.

She made a better job of crossing the rhyne than he had, jumping lightly from bank to bank as he stood with his hands outstretched ready to catch hers. Her face was desperately white, though, and the touch of her fingers was like ice.

'I've found somewhere,' he said. 'And 'tis just a step.'

Little-Marten was already unpacking the bindle-wraps as they approached the tree stump. He ducked into the hollow, quickly spread an oilskin on the ground, and laid the soft Gorji sack on top of that.

'Get theeself in there,' he said.

They buried themselves deep inside the red bindle-wrap, their limbs aching and shaking beyond control, their faces so numb that they could barely speak. The very air inside them was frozen. It seemed impossible that they could ever be warm again.

But eventually their teeth stopped chattering, and a little feeling returned to their fingers and toes. The amazing Gorji wrap had begun to work its magic. Little-Marten was the first to surface, lifting his head from beneath the soft material and squinting out at the wild landscape. They were protected in here from the worst of the weather, and though the wind growled around the entrance to their makeshift cave it could no longer gnaw at their bones. He shivered at the thought of what would have become of them if they had not found this shelter.

The inside of the tree smelled musty, and was so rotten that the slightest movement caused crumbling lumps of wood to fall upon them, lumps that could be pinched to dust between their fingers. Little-Marten and Henty lifted the corners of the oilskin wrap beneath them and grubbed around to see if there might be a few acorns that they could eat. Nothing. Not even a beetle.

They were warm now, and relatively dry, but darkness was falling on a day that had been without food, and it was plain that they could not live for long like this.

'We could go back to the forest.' Little-Marten voiced the thought that he knew to be in both their heads.

'No,' said Henty. 'I'd rather be frozen here with you than alone there and warm. I shan't go back – not unless my father should change his stubborn thinking. And I never knew that to happen yet.'

'Heh. You be his daughter then, right enough.'

Little-Marten caught a dig in the ribs for this remark, but he'd already braced himself for something of the sort, and at least it showed that Henty's spirit was far from broken. They would see what tomorrow would bring. In the meantime it had stopped sleeting outside, and the wind was dying down. It looked as though the worst of the storm had passed.

Chapter Nineteen

'Yes, it's a bit disturbing,' said Uncle Brian. 'All that business with the tree house and George's rope ladder.'

'Mm.' Midge rubbed her elbow against the misted car window, and looked out at the sleet that came billowing across the moors. 'He often does pull the ladder up, though. Maybe he climbed down the tree, last time he was up there, or jumped or something instead of using the rope ladder. And then just forgot.'

'Well, yes. But that doesn't explain all the mess, or the ruined sleeping bag. I'm a bit concerned, frankly. It looks to me as though we've had intruders.' Uncle Brian glanced across at her. 'Not that I'd want you lying awake worrying about that, mind. It'll be just lads, probably. Half-term . . . kids with too much time on their hands . . .'

Lads. Midge smiled to herself. She knew better. Yes, it was pretty clear to her who'd been camping out in the tree house. She was sure she'd caught a glimpse of the culprits, scurrying away into the hedge. But where would they go now? she wondered. The passing countryside looked desperately bleak, a miserable prospect for anyone caught out in this weather. She hoped they'd managed to find somewhere – or better still come to their senses and gone back to the forest.

'Can you smell something sort of . . . pongy?' Uncle Brian was making a face and sniffing.

'I think it might be me.' Midge had her reply ready. 'Sorry. I stepped in some compost. I needed it for a school project thingy.'

'Ah. That's OK, then. Thought something had crawled into the heater and died.'

Midge pushed her carrier bag a little further into the footwell.

It had only been a few days since she'd last seen Aunt Celandine, but her appearance had definitely worsened, Midge thought. She looked thinner and more frail than ever. And sadder too, somehow. Usually there was a big smile for her whenever she turned up, but today Aunt Celandine just seemed exhausted.

'I haven't been sleeping very well,' she said. 'And the truth is I don't want to be sleeping all the time. The doctor comes round and tries to give me pills, but I don't want them. I want to think, I tell him, not sleep.'

Midge took up her usual perch on the wing-backed chair opposite her great-great-aunt. 'But you need to rest,' she said.

'No.' Aunt Celandine's voice was tetchy. 'There'll be time enough for that. I can't be . . . peaceful . . . not in my mind, until I've untangled everything. I keep getting close, you know. I remember little bits and pieces of things that happened to me . . . faces and voices . . . sounds. But then they fade away again. Do you know what I wish now? I wish I'd spoken at the time. I wish I'd told people, whilst I still remembered, where I'd been and what I'd done. But I didn't. I never even told Nina. And now it's too late. I don't think it'll ever come back.'

'Who's Nina?' Midge had never heard this name mentioned before.

'Nina?' Aunt Celandine looked at her for a few moments. 'Nina was my . . . well, she was my friend. My very dear friend.'

Midge blinked, and in the silence that followed she thought that she understood something about her aunt that she had not understood before. Oh.

'Oh,' she said. 'And, er . . . and . . .' But she could find nothing else to say about this, and so she picked up the carrier-bag bundle that she had laid beside the chair.

'Aunt Celandine, I've got something here for you. It's a present. Well, I think it's a present. It's not from me, it's from someone else. I'll, um, I'll just see if I can get it out of these bags.'

Midge tore apart the knotted plastic bags, glad to be able to occupy her hands. She would look again, she thought, at that photograph. The one with the two young women on the beach, laughing and holding onto their hats . . .

'A present?' Aunt Celandine leaned forward in her

chair, trying to see. 'But what on earth is it? And who's sent it?'

'Here you are.' Midge lifted the leather pouch and placed it in Aunt Celandine's outstretched hands. 'It's from Maven-the-Green.' Midge came right out and said it. She watched her great-great-aunt's face – to see if there was any reaction.

'Maven the . . . *what* did you say . . . Green? Maven-the-Green?' Aunt Celandine rested the bag in her lap, and sat staring down at it. 'Maven-the-Green . . . Maven. Maven . . .'

Midge said nothing, but she could feel her heart beating faster. Was there a glimmer of recognition there?

Aunt Celandine lifted the bag a little higher towards her, and sniffed at it. She closed her eyes, and remained like this for a while, slowly breathing in and out. 'Caves . . .' she said at last. Midge noticed the tremor in the pale mottled hands. 'Yes – I can smell the caves! And horses. The little horses. Lavender . . . and camomile . . . wild garlic . . .' Aunt Celandine raised her head, but still kept her eyes closed. 'And mushrooms . . . nettles . . . wet leaves . . . oh, and all the forest. It's all here in my hands. So clear, now. *So clear . . .*'

The old lady sat as though transported to another time and place, her eyes closed, a smile of pleasure on her wrinkled face.

Midge was amazed at this sudden breakthrough. She waited for a while, then said softly, 'There are things in the bag for you, Aunt Celandine. Gifts.'

260

'Gifts . . .' Aunt Celandine murmured. '*Thee'm one wi' a gift . . . a gift to be given.* Who said that? Maven-the-Green. Yes, Maven. I was so frightened. But she was there to help me. I had a gift, she said. A gift to be given . . .' A slight frown crossed Aunt Celandine's face. 'But there was another gift. *A gift to be hid, till better times than these,* she said. *Thee shall know the day.* And I can't . . . I can't remember what that was, or what it meant.'

'Shall we look inside?' Midge was really excited now. She should have brought some scissors, though, to cut the twine that had been used to fasten the bag shut. Stupid. Aunt Celandine was beginning to look agitated. Her eyes had opened, and the spell was in danger of being broken.

Midge didn't want to disturb the moment by asking where a pair of scissors might be found. She stood up and quickly scanned the room. There had been a penknife somewhere – she remembered it. Yes, over there, on the shelf next to the cricket ball.

'I'll use this,' she said, not waiting to ask for permission, and grabbed the little knife. The thing was ancient and it was a struggle to get the blade open, but she managed it.

'Shall I, er . . . ?' Midge stooped to gently take the bag from her aunt's hands, and began to hack through the bits of string. Her fingers were impatient, and she was lucky not to stab them with the rusty blade. Finally she got the bag open, and placed it back on the old lady's lap.

But Aunt Celandine was staring off into space now,

her mouth silently moving, and Midge had to prompt her.

'The bag, Aunt Celandine. Don't you want to see what's inside?'

'I was running away, and they were after me. All of the . . . all of *them*. Chasing me through the darkness. Through the vegetables . . . like an allotment. And tapping with sticks, the way that beaters do to drive the pheasants.' Aunt Celandine was still somewhere else, still remembering. Midge was desperate to find out what was inside the bag, but she had to be patient. And this was good, wasn't it? She could see that Aunt Celandine was actually back in the forest, talking about what had happened to her.

'And they were so close, so close . . . and then this wonderful little person . . . Maven-the-Green. She helped me. I climbed a big tree. It had been struck by lightning.' Aunt Celandine lifted the bag and breathed in its odour once more, as though this was the fuel for her memory. 'I thought they were all coming up the tree after me . . . the little people. Yes, the little people. *Tap-tap-tap*. And I jumped down from the tree, and escaped. And then it was hailing. I ran *down* the hill. Hailing like bullets, it was, as though I was going over the top, like all those poor boys.' Aunt Celandine put the bag back in her lap and sat there nodding. 'Poor boys. That's all they were. Just boys. Ours and theirs.' She looked down at the leather pouch. 'And I was carrying a bag. Just like this one.'

Aunt Celandine put her hand inside the bag. Her

movements were slow, and shaky. Midge struggled to contain her impatience.

'Oh . . .' Aunt Celandine drew out what looked like a handful of old leaves. She lifted them to her face and sniffed at them. 'Oh yes,' she said. 'Feverfew. I used to use this a *lot*. And lavender, of course . . . groundsel . . . and here's a bit of silverweed. Very good for the kidneys, is silverweed, and also, well . . . ladies' problems.'

Midge wriggled in frustration. Was that it? Just a bunch of smelly old plants? No, Aunt Celandine's hand was in the bag again, and this time she seemed to have got hold of something more interesting.

'Ooh. What's this?'

She held up a round object, about the size of a small coconut. At first glance it looked like a scrunched-up bundle of oily canvas. But there was apparently something wrapped in this material – the thin strips of it, wound round and round.

'Oilskin,' said Aunt Celandine. 'Yes, I remember they had a kind of oilskin. It does go a bit rancid after a while, though.' She picked at the end of one of the strips and began to pull it away, unwinding it, slowly and carefully.

There seemed to be an awful lot of it. Midge was agog, wondering what could possibly lie at the centre of all this stuff. But then Aunt Celandine stopped pulling at the material. Her face looked puzzled. 'I've seen this happen before,' she said. 'I *know* I have. It's . . . oh, it's . . .' She resumed her work, untwisting the lengths of oilskin. It reminded Midge of a black-and-white film she'd once watched, where somebody was unwrapping the bandages from somebody else's head, and then in the middle there was nothing at all. Something about an invisible man.

But this wasn't invisible. Aunt Celandine pulled the last bit of oilskin away, and held up a . . . pine-cone.

Midge couldn't have been more surprised. Or disappointed. A *pine*-cone? She stared in disbelief at the thing, and was then startled as Aunt Celandine let out a hoot of laughter.

'A *piney*-cone!' she squealed, and for a moment she sounded just like a little girl. '*I* remember now! They all thought it was going to be the Orbis, and it turned out to just be an old pine-cone! Oh, you should have *seen* Corben's face. Ha! He was *furious*. And that's when I fell out of the tree, and had to start running. And of course, it was me that had the Orbis all along, though I never knew it till later. Yes, a pine-cone, just like this one.' Aunt Celandine rocked back and forth in her chair, gurgling away, and fumbling in the sleeve of her cardigan until she found a hanky. She wiped her eyes, and tucked the hanky away again.

Midge just gawped at her. 'You remember that?' she said. 'About having the Orbis and everything? It's really true?'

Aunt Celandine had calmed down a bit. 'Yes,' she said, and now there was surprise in her voice, as though she'd only just realized what this meant. 'Yes, I *do* remember. Isn't that funny? The Orbis was in my bag – a bag just like this one. They'd put it there without my knowing. It was the cave-dwellers who did that.

They wanted me to carry it away and keep it safe for them.'

'You took it away with you? Well, then . . .' Midge asked the big question. 'What did you do with it?'

'What did I do with it?' Aunt Celandine was looking horribly blank again. Her dark filmy eyes moved around the room, as though searching for clues. 'I . . . don't know. It's gone.'

Midge had suffered so many setbacks in this quest that she had almost grown used to it. And she had learned that there was no point in getting upset, or in trying to push Aunt Celandine along any quicker than she was able. Nevertheless it was very hard to have come so far only to fail. She desperately wanted to move forward, but for the moment there was no alternative but to take a step back.

'Oh well. Perhaps it'll come eventually,' she said. 'Is there anything else in the bag?'

Aunt Celandine sighed and shook her head, obviously confused and disappointed with herself. She rummaged around in the leather bag, pulled out a few

more leaves, or herbs, or whatever they were, put them back and rummaged some more. Midge watched her and thought how tired she looked. Perhaps it was time to give up and call it a day. They really had made some progress, and so this visit could hardly be written off as a failure.

Something else had appeared from the bag. Midge couldn't quite see what it was . . . feathers?

'Oh . . . oh my word . . . I *never* imagined I'd see this again! Oh but this is wonderful. Just wonderful! Look, Midge.' Aunt Celandine held out her cupped hands. Midge peered at the object in front of her. It was a little homemade toy, a walnut-shell boat with a tiny figure sitting in it. The figure looked as though it might be made of wax. It had wings – two feathers sticking out of it – although perhaps these were supposed to be oars. The figure might be flying or it might be rowing. Either way it was beautiful.

'Oh, that's so *sweet*,' said Midge. 'It's lovely.'

Aunt Celandine pressed the object to her chest for a few moments, but then she had to search for her hanky again. 'This means so much to me,' she said, and this time she was really crying. 'So much. I just can't tell you.' She dabbed at her tears, and cradled the strange little toy to her.

Midge sat and looked at her, dumbfounded. What should she do?

'I lost it years ago, you see, just after I'd left home. They made it for me as a leaving present – the cave-dwellers. It meant so much to realize that they cared about me, when I thought that they didn't care at all.

And then I lost it. All the other things I just put in my jewellery box and forgot about, and I'd meant to put this in there too, but I didn't. I kept it with me, just for a little while. And then it simply disappeared, some-how, as things do. And I suppose I must have missed it at first, of course.' Aunt Celandine wiped her nose on the hanky. 'But since then I've forgotten all about it, the way I forgot about everything else, and haven't given it a thought. But I remember now that this was one thing that really mattered to me at the time, and I can't tell you how happy it makes me to see it again. Oh dear.'

Midge felt her own eyes prickle with tears, and she wished that she had a hanky too. But she quickly drew her sleeve across her face, and then said, 'I'm really glad, then, that it's come back to you. And it *is* lovely.' At the same time she couldn't help wondering how this could possibly be the same little toy. Perhaps it was better not to point this out, or question it.

'Tell me about the cave-dwellers,' she said. 'Is that where you stayed, in the caves?'

'I read stories to them . . .' Aunt Celandine was staring into the distance again. 'And we had singing. I wrote letters on the walls, with chalk. The alphabet. And songs. I showed them how to make words from the letters . . .'

Midge remembered something. 'Was there one called Lor . . . Lorril . . . Loren?'

'Oh . . . *yes*! Loren. Of course . . . Loren! He was so clever. But how did you know about him?'

'I've got something he wrote,' said Midge. 'And a

drawing he did – of you. But it's in my other jacket. Next time I'll bring it, though.'

'Little Loren. Oh, he was a marvel. I wonder what happened to him.'

Midge thought of Tadgemole, and the sad expression on his face. Loren had died young, so Tadgemole had said. But again it might be better not to mention this. Instead she said, 'I've met his brother – Tadgemole. Did you know him?'

'Tadgemole . . . Tadgemole. Yes! He was the baby! A *tiny* little scrap. Is he really still there?'

'He's the leader of the cave-dwellers now. He looks pretty old.' Midge was thinking of something else as she spoke. She wanted to ask so many questions about Celandine's life among the Various, but there was something more important niggling at her . . . yes, she'd got it.

'Aunt Celandine, you said that you'd kept the little toy boat, but that you'd put everything else that they'd given you into a box . . . a jewellery box?'

'Yes, I did. I *called* it my jewellery box, although I can't remember that there was much jewellery in it. It was mostly ribbons and hairgrips . . . one or two little bracelets, perhaps . . .'

'But' – Midge tried to stay on track – 'the Orbis. Did you put *that* in there too?'

'Um . . . yes, that's right. I did. Yes, the Orbis . . . and a letter. A little wooden comb, I think. But I kept the boat with me, for a while.'

Midge took a breath, and tried to keep her voice steady. 'And what happened to the jewellery box? What did you do with it?'

'Oh, that's easy enough.' Aunt Celandine's voice was confident. 'It stayed on my mantelpiece. I'd always kept it there, because there was a mirror above it. I never opened it again, though, not after what happened.'

'Oh.' Midge's heart was beginning to sink again. 'So you didn't take it with you when you left home?'

'No. I liked to know that it would always be safe, you see, in my old room. No, the jewellery box never left Mill Farm.' Aunt Celandine smiled. Her eyes had come alive and she no longer looked so tired. 'Do you know, Midge, so much of it is coming back to me now. Those little horses that they used to milk . . . I knew I was right about that . . . and how I cut all their hair . . . and the time I helped Micas put the pine-cone into the hollow tree . . . I haven't got it all in order quite, but it's there now. At least it's there.' Aunt Celandine was obviously far less interested in the fate of the Orbis than in her own returning memories. 'And after a while it seemed almost *normal*. They *were* normal, really. Just people. It was only when those others came . . . the ones that had . . . wings . . .'

Midge listened, but she was trying to think at the same time. 'What did it look like, the jewellery box?' she said.

'Oh, it was nothing very special, that I can remember. Dark wood. Yes, about the size of a shoe box . . . and the sides sloped inwards. A casket. It had a key. Oh . . . I've remembered about that game, now, that the children used to play . . . Blinder . . . yes, they flicked these little stones . . .' Aunt Celandine was off again.

Midge was mentally running around the rooms of Mill Farm. Had she ever seen a dark wooden casket that could once have been a jewellery box? She didn't think so. And what were the chances, really, that it would still be around after all these years – and especially since the recent upheaval? It just wasn't possible. So what was she going to *do*?

'You had to try and get the stones to land inside the sheep's skull. Ugly-looking thing, it was . . .'

There was a soft knock at the door, and Elaine put her head into the room. 'Mr Howard's here,' she said, and there was Uncle Brian, standing out in the corridor, all muffled up in his thick winter jacket. He looked a bit embarrassed.

'Sorry, Midge,' said Uncle Brian, over Elaine's shoulder. 'I need to get back a bit earlier today. I made sure that you had your mobile, then realized I'd forgotten mine, so I couldn't ring you. Hallo, Aunt Celandine. How are you?'

'Oh. Who's this?' Aunt Celandine was trying to turn round in her chair. 'Is it the doctor?'

'No, it's me, Aunt Celandine. Brian Howard. I'm your, er . . . I'm Midge's uncle. We've met before.' Uncle Brian came a little further into the room.

'*Have* we?' Aunt Celandine didn't seem entirely convinced.

Midge exchanged glances with Uncle Brian and shook her head. She stood up. Far easier to be on her way than get into lengthy explanations as to who was related to whom.

'I'd better go, Aunt Celandine,' she said. 'I hadn't

realized how late it was. But listen . . . it's been a lovely afternoon, and I'll, um . . . see you soon, yes?'

'Oh . . . must you go?' Aunt Celandine held out her hands. 'Midge, come here. Come here a moment, dear. There's something I want to say to you.' She grasped Midge's fingers, and then glanced across at Elaine and Uncle Brian. It was plain that she wanted to speak privately, and Midge bent closer. 'I'm so grateful . . . for what you've done.' Aunt Celandine's voice was a low whisper. Midge was aware that Uncle Brian and Elaine had discreetly moved away. She was aware also of a deep warmth beginning to spread through her fingertips, a strange sensation. As though something was being passed from her great-great-aunt to her.

'Yes, *thank* you.' Aunt Celandine was focused now, squeezing her hand tight, seeking her full attention. 'Thank you for coming to see me, and for putting my mind at rest. Today has been a *wonderful* day. You've helped me to find so much of what's been missing, and I don't think I could have even begun without you. You're a very special girl, and you've made me very happy. I was told when I was young, Midge, that I had a gift. A gift to be given. And perhaps it was true. I held many hands, just like this, and I did what I could.' Aunt Celandine's eyes closed. 'And whatever this gift was, I would sometimes recognize it there in others – in their hands too. Just occasionally. And I've recognized it in yours. Yes, right from the very first time. I know that it's there. No . . . no . . . don't be frightened . . .' Aunt Celandine opened her eyes, as Midge instinctively drew away. 'It's nothing to be frightened of. Just do what you can, dear. It's all we can ever do. There now. That's all I have to say.'

This sounded alarmingly like a goodbye, and Midge was completely taken aback.

'But we'll be seeing each other again, won't we? In a few days?'

'Yes, of course, dear. Certainly. Now don't you worry. We'll see each other again, I promise.'

A last big squeeze of her hand, and Aunt Celandine sat back in her chair. She raised her voice again. 'And when you find that old jewellery casket, you let me know.'

'Yes. I will. Bye then, Aunt Celandine.'

'Bye-bye, Midge.'

'Ready, then?' Uncle Brian was zipping up his jacket.

'Yeah.'

'Cheerio then, Aunt Celandine. Take care of your-self.' Uncle Brian gave Aunt Celandine a smile and a wave.

'Oh. Yes. Goodbye . . . er . . . Brian.'

As they stepped out into the hallway, Midge heard Elaine say, 'Poo! What's all this stuff then, Miss Howard?' She meant the bag and its smelly contents.

'Oh, it's just some herbs and things that I asked Midge to collect for me. I've been telling her all about plant remedies . . .'

Aunt Celandine's voice faded away as the door closed. She was a pretty good liar, thought Midge. For her age.

* * *

'She doesn't look at all well to me,' said Uncle Brian as he turned the car ignition key. '*Much* thinner than she was last time. There's nothing of her.'

But Midge didn't want to hear that. 'No, she's all right, I think. Just tired. She hasn't been sleeping very well.'

Well, perhaps Aunt Celandine would sleep better tonight, now that her mind was more at ease. And it *had* been a good day, Midge thought. A wonderful day in many ways, although the Orbis was still as elusive as ever. She realized with a jolt that there was one question that she hadn't even thought to ask: what did the Orbis look like? She still had no idea what it was that she was searching for! How stupid could you get? It could be sitting in the kitchen cupboard with all the food processor bits for all she'd know. And as for ever finding this jewellery casket . . .

'What was all that about a jewellery casket?' Uncle Brian's question made her jump.

'Oh! Well . . .' Midge couldn't see that there was any harm in telling him. 'Aunt Celandine used to have this wooden box, when she was a girl. She left it at the farm, years ago. It was dark wood, she said, like a casket, about as big as a shoe box. And it had a key. It would be really nice if we could find it again, that's all. I don't suppose you've noticed anything like that, have you?'

'Ha! No, love. And I think that a spare nineteen-twenties jewellery box is something that I *might* notice, if it happened to be kicking around. So what was in it?'

273

'Oh, just bits of ribbon and hairgrips and stuff. No jewellery. Nothing valuable at all.'

'Ah.' Uncle Brian had obviously lost interest. He reached over to turn on the radio. 'By the way,' he said, 'that's probably my last trip to Almbury Mills for a while. Cliff and I have got everything listed now, and he's shown me how to do the online auction thing. I can sort the rest out on my home computer.'

'Oh. Oh . . . right.'

Mum wasn't in a great mood when they got back. She was sitting at the bottom of the stairs, surrounded by piles of paperwork, some of it stacked beside her, some of it spread out on the floor around her feet.

'Brian, I'm simply not coping with all this,' she said. 'And we can't afford for you to be playing around on the internet every Sunday. It's just not fair. You need to be here – and as for *you*, miss' – Midge had tried to edge past her mum in order to get upstairs – 'you need to be doing your homework for tomorrow.'

'Already done it,' said Midge. 'And anyway we don't go back to school till Wednesday. There's two extra "inset days", or whatever they're called, in case you'd forgotten. And Wednesday's only some rubbish school trip – that steam engine thing. So there's no need to take it out on me. *I'm* coping, even if you're not.'

'Hoy! Don't you talk to me like that! If you had any *idea* of what I have to deal with . . .'

But Midge had managed to get past her mum, and was already stomping up the stairs. Yeah, she thought. And if *you* had any idea of what *I* have to deal with . . .

'Listen, Chris, it's OK. It's OK.' Uncle Brian had put on his calm-and-soothing voice. It was actually very irritating. Midge could imagine him using this technique on some angry customer and getting a bop on the nose for his pains. 'Listen. For starters, I don't need to go to Almbury Mills again. I've got all the stuff listed now. And as for the paperwork, well . . . I saw Pat again today. She said she's willing to give us a hand with it . . .'

Midge stormed along the landing and into her room, cutting off the voices below as she slammed the door behind her.

Drat the lot of 'em, with their stupid planning permissions and builders and . . . shrubs and wine merchants and . . . *paperwork*. She had more important things to worry about. What was she going to do about the Orbis? What . . . what . . . what . . . ?

She sat on the end of her bed and tried to calm down, tried to think. Not rage, but think. The Orbis had been left here, in this very room, on that very mantelpiece. It was unbelievable. And yet Aunt Celandine had been quite clear: she had put the Orbis in her jewellery box, and as far as she was concerned it had never left Mill Farm.

Except that it must have done, because it certainly wasn't here now. An awful empty feeling began to fill Midge's heart. Her sole plan all along, she realized, had been to try and find the Orbis through Aunt Celandine. What other plan could there have been? And she had succeeded, that was the terrible thing. She'd done so well. She'd found her great-great-aunt, against ridiculous odds, and had helped her as best she could to remember her past. And Aunt Celandine *had* remembered, at last. She'd left the Orbis here, in a casket, on the mantelpiece. Brilliant.

But eighty or ninety years had passed since then, and the Orbis certainly wasn't here now. So it could be anywhere. Anywhere in the world . . . buried deep under acres of landfill . . . lying at the bottom of an ocean . . . or just simply rotted away to dust.

That was it, then. This day had gone so well in so many ways, but now there was nothing else that Midge could think of doing that made any sense. She'd reached the end of the line.

Celandine's face glowed softly down at her, a pale shape, suspended among the shadows of the corner alcove. Midge leaned sideways onto one elbow, and in that shifting movement it seemed that Celandine's eyes briefly met hers. It was just a change of the light, a twinkling reflection upon the glass, but Midge felt that she had caught a glimpse of the real person behind the photograph, a flash of understanding from one who knew her well. Sympathy from a friend.

Silly. The faraway gaze was over her shoulder now, as always. But at least she knew now what that child was looking at, and something of what those eyes had already seen. There was some mutual understanding there, and they were friends, in a way.

'And we did try,' Midge whispered to the empty room. 'We did what we could.'

PART TWO

Chapter Twenty

'Brother . . .'

Ictor spun round at the sound – a familiar voice at his shoulder, low and rasping.

'Sh!' he whispered. 'Bist here again? And in day-light? I've told 'ee, 'tis too dangerous! Get back in there where none can sithee!'

The shadowy figure retreated a little into the dark mouth of the tunnel. Ictor looked quickly from right to left, making sure that there was nobody else nearby, then stepped onto a rock amid the trickling waters of the stream so that he was positioned directly in front of the wicker entrance.

''Tain't safe to keep coming here,' he muttered, still facing forward. 'All do reckon 'ee dead, brother, and 'twould be best kept so. Thee must wait till I can find a way of getting 'ee back in.'

'Aye – and so starve.' The low voice behind him sounded wild, desperate. 'Have 'ee got any food? For I be shrammed.'

'Here.' Ictor pulled a crust of flatbread from his tunic and held his hand behind his back. He felt the snatching fingers of Scurl, long nails that scraped against his palm as the bread was torn from his grasp.

'What's the matter with 'ee?' Ictor grimaced at the animal sounds of Scurl attacking the chunk of bread. 'Have 'ee forgotten how to hunt?'

'Got no flint . . .' The words were broken by savage gulps and swallows. 'Lost it and casn't find another. I can hunt . . . but I've no fire. I'd scarce dare light one anywise, wi' the Gorji all around me. Whatever I kill I've to eat raw . . . and it gives I the collies.'

'Take mine, then.' Ictor took out his flint and passed it back. 'And risk a fire. Better that than die.'

More sounds of chewing and gulping. Then Scurl said, 'What news? When does Maglin go?'

'He've changed his thinking,' Ictor replied. 'He stays. And so all will now stay. 'Tain't no good, Scurl – thee casn't come back in. None of 'em are like to be going anywhere, as I can see.'

'Then I be good as dead,' Scurl growled. 'For I'll not last another moon out here. All my company be gone . . . Dregg and Snerk and Fitch . . . all starved . . . and I be next. I'll tell 'ee this, though – I s'll take that Gorji brat with me. Put an arrow through her, soon as I gets close enough.'

'Aye, do that,' Ictor sneered. 'And bring the giants down upon us all.'

'Pah! What do I care? Let 'em come . . .' Scurl took another savage bite of food, grunting and snuffling like a furze-pig. Ictor turned away in disgust, his brother's last words still echoing in his ear . . . Let 'em come . . . Let 'em come . . .

Scurl was mazy in the head, that was plain enough. His scavenging life had turned him into something unrecognizable, a beast: slobbering, filthy, stinking of the very ditches he dwelt in. Ictor stared at the black waters of the stream at his feet. Poor Scurl. Driven half mad. And yet . . .

Had what he had said made some sense? Let 'em come . . .

Was there an answer to be found here after all? Ictor raised his head towards the grey skies. He had a vision, then, of yelling giants, swarming up the hillside, bursting into the forest and slaying all before them. Raging unstoppable monsters that tossed Elders and Stewards alike onto the bonfires of their vengeance. Aye, vengeance . . . outrage at the loss of something they held dear . . . such a fury against the Various as would drive them to kill every last one they found . . .

Ictor let the evening sounds of the forest settle around him as he pictured the scene, thought it through.

'That maid,' he said, turning to glance into the shadows behind him. 'The Gorji child that were the cause of all your trouble. Dost reckon 'ee could find her, then?'

'Ptuh!' Scurl's voice spat at him from the darkness. 'Find her? I knows where she be, and I'm hemmed if I don't put an arrow through her first chance I get. I've come close to it already – but not close enough. I bides my time, though. I s'll have 'er in the end.'

Ictor nodded. 'Or I shall.'

'Eh?'

'I've heard rumour she may come here again, to the forest. Some blether o' the Orbis – this witchi thing they all be after. What'd happen, would 'ee say, if that maid were to enter these woods and never return to her own? Dost think the giants'd come looking for her? Would they come here?'

'Aye. They'd come here. There's the other Gorji brats as know of this place. Why they ain't told of it already I casn't say. But if one o' their own were missing, they'd chelp up soon enough, I knows.'

Ictor took a few more moments to think about this. 'And if she were found dead, wi' an arrow through her, what do 'ee reckon those giants'd do to all that were here?'

There was silence.

'Do 'ee see what I be getting at, Scurl? If that meddlesome child were to die, and the Gorji were led to those they reckoned brought her down . . . well, then. There'd be none left alive by the time they'd finished wi' 'em. None left save you and I, for we should have already hidden ourselves far away. And then if we should return to the forest, when the giants were gone and all were quiet once more, what lives we should lead, eh? These woods to ourselves, all the game to we two alone, and none other to plague us. Brothers, as when we were childer, afore our troubles came . . .'

'She's *mine*.' Scurl's hiss of anger brought Ictor back to the present. 'I've sworn to kill that young snip for what she've brought me and my company to, and kill her I shall.'

'Then do it.' Ictor could see clearly now how between the two of them they would achieve the same end. It mattered not who first got to the child. Either way it would be the Various who would be blamed. Their secret would come out, the tribes would surely be discovered, and all would suffer the same end at the hands of the giants.

Let Scurl seek his revenge then, and have his day, should that day dawn. And if instead the child should come to the forest, then she would find himself here waiting for her . . . standing tunnel guard . . . ready with an arrow. Ah, if only he could then stay to watch the slaughter that would follow. But there. Perhaps there would be a chance to bring down Maglin himself, just for the pleasure of watching him die, before going into hiding . . .

'Do it.' Ictor repeated his words. 'Do as 'ee've planned all along, Scurl, and kill that maid. Don't matter how or where. Drop a rock on her head if there be no other way. But hear me, brother: make sure 'ee leave an arrow in her, or with her, so that the giants'll learn from their brats who've done this. Aye, and shall then know where to seek their vengeance. An arrow, mind. So that she carry our mark.'

Ictor gazed up at the dark woodland with new eyes. All this would be his to rule. His and Scurl's. And what a bloody revenge they would have on all who had served them so ill: Maglin, the Gorji child, the very giants themselves . . . all would pay . . . all would pay . . .

'Do 'ee understand me, Scurl? Be your head clear?'

'Eh? My head be clear as day, Ictor, don't 'ee fret. I understand 'ee well enough. And 'tis good . . . 'tis good . . .'

'Then we've a brothers' pact on it. But when this be done, I s'll needs be gone from these woods afore the giants come. Do 'ee have a place for us to hide?'

'Aye. I've a place to hide . . .'

Chapter Twenty-one

Henty and Little-Marten slept deep into the following day, and when they finally awoke the world had changed yet again. Bright beams of sunshine came slanting in through the entrance to the hollow tree, and the glare of reflected light on the snow outside made them squint and shield their eyes. They could hear the drip-drip of water amongst the surrounding stacks of logs and branches, and knew that the thaw had already begun. The snow would disappear almost as quickly as it had arrived.

Little-Marten wriggled forward until his head was outside the tree-hollow. The air was clear and still, and the sky above as blue as a ruddock's egg. A perfect winter's day for those with full bellies and the ease to enjoy it, but for him and Henty there was no such luxury. They needed to find food and proper shelter. He looked across the white landscape towards the distant treeline of the Far Woods, a dark shape, threatening and unknown. Come nightfall they must make their way there. Little-Marten shook his head at the thought of it. What comfort was there likely to be in such a place, and who could say what terrible creatures might dwell there? Brocks ... renards ... and worse, for all he knew. Aye, and he and Henty must arrive under cover of nightfall, when all such monsters were up and waking ...

The deep thrumming sound of a Gorji contraption caught his ear, like that of the mighty machines that roamed the giants' settlement. But closer.

Little-Marten crept further forward and peeped around the side of the tree stump. A field away, beyond the dividing hedge, he could see the bouncing heads of men as they rode upon some moving platform. The platform was hauled by one of their machines, a great red thing that belched smoke into the clear air. The machine drew up to a gateway and stopped, its clatter slowing to a steady growl. A man jumped down and walked towards the gate. Little-Marten waited to see no more.

'Henty! Rouse up – there's giants a-coming! Quick with 'ee!'

But Henty had already sensed the danger. She was gathering up their belongings, hurriedly stuffing everything away as best she could and with no thought as to order.

'Ready?'

'Aye. Away, then.'

A final glance about them and they left the shelter of the tree stump, dodging among the stacks of logs and heavy branches until they came to the last pile. Here they turned and looked back across the field. The Gorji machine was through the gap, and had again come to a halt, waiting for the man at the gate to close it. And now they saw something that made their hearts beat faster still: the gate-man had a black-and-white hound at his side. Horribly lively the creature looked, dancing around, full of excitement . . .

'I reckon they've come for the wood,' Henty whispered, and Little-Marten nodded. It would be easy enough to hide amongst these loosely stacked piles of timber, but if that was what the men were here for then they'd soon be discovered. He looked behind him, towards the rhyne that they had crossed the previous afternoon. That was their best hope, although there was a stretch of open land to be covered between here and there.

Henty made the decision. 'Back to the ditch,' she said. 'We can't bide here.'

'Quick as 'ee can, then.'

Away they went again, stumbling through the snow-covered tufts of grass. The uneven ground made their progress seem horribly slow, and the distance far greater than it had at first looked. With each gasping step they expected to hear a cry go up from one of the men or the sudden baying of the hound . . .

But no, they were over the lip of the rhyne and scrabbling down the bank with no alarm yet raised. They kept moving, pushing their way along at the water's edge, trying to get as much distance as they could between themselves and the giants in the field above. But the waist-high grass and reeds that grew on the steep banks of the rhyne made the going almost impossible, and they were forced into climbing a little higher, and then higher still. Eventually they risked peering out over the top of the bank. The field with the men in it was behind them now. They could see the entire group, sorting through the piles of wood, lifting the rough logs onto the wheeled platform. And they could hear the voices of the giants on the still air. Loud, in a way that the forest-dwellers could never dare to be. Careless and cheerful, fearful of nothing. What must that be like?

Little-Marten and Henty turned away and surveyed the bright landscape, trying to plot a pathway towards the Far Woods. Already they could see how they had overestimated the speed of their progress, and how hard-pressed they would be to gain those woods in what remained of this day. It was too dangerous to cross the open fields and so travel in a straight line. Instead they would have to check back and forth amongst the hedges and ditches in order to keep as close to cover as they could. The journey was likely to take a lot longer than it needed to.

Henty led the way for a while, walking as close as she dared to the top of the rhyne bank, keeping to where the grass was a little thinner and the snow less deep. She seemed calm and steady. Little-Marten was apprehensive, and grew more so as the day wore on. He followed behind, continually looking to left and right for signs of danger as the true nature of their situation began to sink in. They were hungry and homeless, and deeper into Gorji territory than even the Wisp would dare venture. And in broad daylight against such a snowy background they were horribly exposed, easy prey to whatever should happen to glance their way, be it man or beast. At any moment giants might step out from behind this hedge or that tree, men with clubs and shovels and slavering hounds . . .

Little-Marten glanced behind him, fearful that some great grasping hand might be about to fall upon his shoulder. Nothing there. Nothing but the trailing wake of their own footprints in the snow. Aye, footprints that might betray them yet. And even if they should safely reach their destination, what then? What kind of life awaited them in those black woods, where there was neither Ickri archer nor bramble thicket to keep the creatures of the night at bay? A monstrous sense of dread began to descend upon Little-Marten, a feeling beyond the natural nervousness of being caught upon Gorji territory. The sunny countryside, as cheerful as it might have been under other circum-stances, now seemed to be hiding something evil behind its smile, a thing of utter darkness beneath its pretty winter mantle. Little-Marten became certain that every step they took drew them closer to a terrible and inevitable end. His instinct was so strong that he was ready to give up now, and turn back, but he knew that Henty would have none of it. Her very stride told him of her will and determination. She was unlikely to change her mind and go home just because he had a jittery feeling in his bones. Very well. They would find shelter for this night perhaps, but then he must talk to Henty properly, persuade her of his fears, make her return to the forest, even though it meant their separation. For himself he would risk all danger, but he would not see Henty walk to her death on his account – and death, he was now convinced, was where this journey was leading them. It was out there, waiting . . .

They could try again when the weather was warmer and there were easier pickings to be had. That's what he would tell her. Or he would tell her that he was simply too scared to carry on, or even that he no longer loved her. He would say anything, do anything, to turn her from whatever lurked on that darkening pathway.

'What is it?'

They could hear the roar of water up ahead. A steep bank confronted them, above which rose the top of some piece of machinery, russet-coloured against the blue sky. They scrambled up the bank and found themselves at the edge of a waterfall, a dizzying rush of noise and tumbling movement.

Two snow-covered planks spanned the broad stream before them, and out in the centre was the big metal thing that they had first seen, tall columns with toothed wheels, and what might be a handle on the top. Beneath this the swollen torrent flowed, brown and sinuous, rushing forth in a great arc before pounding itself to foam in the pool below. Here great bubbles and flecks of mushroom-coloured froth circled one another, round and round in a hypnotic dance, eventually to be whirled away downstream.

The weir-pool looked dark and deep, a fearful place. The low rays of winter sunlight could not reach it and so it seemed more gloomy than ever. The horror of falling in made Little-Marten and Henty hang back from its edge, and yet there was a pull to that swirling current that invited them to come closer . . . just a little closer . . .

'Ugh! Don't like it.' Henty stepped away, grabbing at Little-Marten's arm as she did so. 'Can we get across?'

They looked towards the treeline of the Far Woods, and saw that crossing the water would be their quickest way. Their only way, perhaps.

Little-Marten wondered whether this would be the time to tell Henty of his deep fear of going on at all. But no. She would only think he was frightened of the water. He put his foot on the end of one of the planks.

'We s'll try. I'll go first.' His voice was almost lost in the roar of the waterfall.

But Henty had heard him, and she still had hold of his arm.

'No, we go together.'

Hand in hand they began to edge their way across. No one had walked this way since the snow had fallen, and so the crunch of the unbroken surface beneath their boots was reassuringly firm. Nevertheless they took it one step at a time, both of them careful to keep their eyes on the opposite bank, rather than looking down into that crashing foam. They were approaching the metal construction at the centre of the crossing. Little-Marten stretched out his free hand to gain some support . . . and then felt the plank beneath him tip sickeningly to one side. His stomach lurched in terror as he staggered forward, thrown completely off balance. He heard Henty's squeal of panic, grasped her hand tighter than ever in response and was dragged to his knees by the sudden swinging weight of her. She was over the edge – he knew it – but still he hung on, falling flat on his belly now, all tangled up in his bindle-wrap and hopelessly clutching at handfuls of snow as he felt himself being pulled after her. His desperate scrabbling fingertips found a gap between the two planks and instantly locked into it, gripping as though they would never let go. It was enough, just, to keep Little-Marten from sliding any further. He craned his head around, whimpering in fright, and saw that Henty still had one leg crooked over the edge of the boards. Her head and body were dangling above the torrent, but she was not lost to him yet. The realization gave him new strength, and with a roar of defiance against the triumphant clamour of the waters below, Little-Marten hauled himself sideways, rolling over onto his back so that Henty was dragged bodily towards him. She was safe.

'Ah . . . ah . . .' Henty lay on the slippery boards gasping for breath, but Little-Marten would give her no pause.

'Crawl!' he shouted, and began to do so himself, moving towards the far bank on his hands and knees. He was raging at the Gorji for building so treacherous a bridge, and at himself for putting faith in any of their works. What a fool he was to take such risks, and to allow Henty to do the same. He had nearly lost her. Well then, enough. He hawked and spat far out into the roiling froth. Aye, enough.

There were tangled clumps of blackberry bushes growing on the far bank, spilling across the end of the plank bridge itself, and these had to be gingerly pushed aside before Little-Marten and Henty could feel themselves safely back onto firm ground.

'Henty, this ain't any good.' Little-Marten's words came tumbling out. 'I be taking you home. No . . . *no* . . .' He held up a hand as Henty opened her mouth to speak. 'I be done with it, I tell 'ee. There's nothing for us out here but trouble . . . and . . . and . . . danger. We've no food and nowhere to stay and there's worse to come, I knows it. Far worse to come if we carry on like this.'

Henty said nothing, but moved in close and put her arms about his neck. She was shaking. Little-Marten drew her to him, but still he stumbled on, determined to say his piece. 'I can't bear it, Henty – can't bear to sithee live so. Cold and hungry, and every step in fear o' what the next might bring. We'm like mice in a hawk's nest out here, and'll come to proper grief afore another day's out, 'tis certain. I just can't watch 'ee do it. Not any more. So I'll tell 'ee now – we're going back.'

He waited for her response, looking over the top of her head at the pale countryside. Already the sun was past its strength.

'But I'm with you,' she said at last. 'Don't you know that's all I care about?'

'Henty, I thought I'd lost 'ee. I did true. Chance were with us this time, but what o' next time and the time after that? I could be standing here alone now – or you could. What then? We must go back.'

293

She said, 'But we've come such a way that we can't turn round now. Why don't we just get to the Far Woods and see how 'tis? All we need might be waiting for us there.'

'Ha. I don't know as I want to see what waits for us there. This don't feel right, not any of it.'

'Well I'm not going back tonight.' Henty had stopped shaking and some of her spirit had returned. 'Nor crossing that water again. And if you were so for giving up, then why come over to this side?'

'Henty, I wasn't going to start some argle-bargle with 'ee out in the middle o' that lot! Listen . . .' Little-Marten sighed and looked about him. 'We ain't going to reach the Far Woods this day, even if we did carry on. We'll look for shelter now, before 'tis too late, and then talk on it.'

Henty nodded. 'All right.'

It was a compromise that each was happy to agree to – each believing that a little rest might help the other see sense.

There was a byre, a huge red building, two or three fields away. It was partially hidden by trees, but Little-Marten and Henty could see that the object appeared to have no sides – just a massive curved roof raised high from the ground on tall metal stanchions. A roof was better shelter than nothing, though, and nothing was their only other choice. They began to make their way around the edges of the fields, doubly cautious now that they were approaching a building where giants might be present.

An air of disuse hung about the place. From

beneath the cover of the last belt of trees Little-Marten and Henty peered forth in silence at the great open-sided byre, just a short distance away now, and a taller building than they had ever seen in their lives. It occupied the high end of a sloping field, and from here a rough snow-filled track ran down towards a distant gate. There were no other dwellings nearby, and no sign of movement.

The purpose of the byre had apparently been for storing hay. An uneven stack of bales still filled one corner, bales that had been long forgotten if their blackened appearance and sprouting tufts of grass were anything to go by. Low patches of brambles had spread from the surrounding field, and entwined themselves about the rusting stanchions. They had even begun to embrace a piece of machinery that stood half in and half out of the byre – some ladder-like object on wheels. It was plain to Little-Marten and Henty that the Gorji were not often in this place. They crept from beneath the trees and scuttled over to the building.

It was a better find than they could have hoped for. The floor was just bare earth, but quite dry – dusty even – towards the middle where snow and rain could not reach. And the hay bales that were beneath the shelter of the roof were also dry, though grey with age. Bits of Gorji rubbish lay scattered about here and there, things fashioned of wood and rot-metal and other less recognizable materials. Orange-coloured twine – there seemed to be a lot of that around. Little-Marten thought that he might remind himself to take a few lengths with him when they left.

They found evidence of Gorji butchery, or so they assumed it to be – a rabbit skin stretched out upon a wooden pallet. The square pallet was propped against one of the metal columns that supported the barn, and the rabbit skin was pinned to the centre of it, hooked over splinters that had been cut into the edges of the wooden slats. The pelt was uselessly ruined, slashed about as though with a blade. Why?

The two of them wandered away in different directions. Little-Marten noticed a few pale scraps of something lying on the earth floor near the ladder-machine and went over to take a look. Bits of . . . apple? No, it was the remains of a winter root, gnawed by some animal perhaps and then discarded in the dirt. It could be a wurzel, or a turnip.

'Henty – look at this.' Little-Marten stooped and picked up a piece of the grubby root, dusted the cleanest part of it on the front of his jerkin and took a bite. Wurzel! Hardly a luxury, but after two days without food it was welcome enough.

'What is it?' Henty was struggling to move one of the hay bales.

Little-Marten didn't answer. He chewed thoughtfully on the scrap of wurzel root. It was half raw, but that was what puzzled him. He looked at the bit that remained in his hand, the bit that was blackened on the outside. Not grubby after all, but . . . charred . . . cooked . . .

Henty called across to him. 'Marten, look – I've broke one of these bales open, and 'tis all good and dry. We can sleep on this.'

'Aye, build theeselves a nest, my pretty birds. And I shall see as thee sleep sound enough.'

The harsh rasping voice froze Little-Marten's scalp. He swung round, horrified, the piece of root falling from his hand.

A wild and ragged figure stood at the open side of the byre, a bow in his fist, arrow ready notched. The remnants of his tunic and breeches hung about him in tatters, and round his shoulders was draped a filthy piece of Gorji sacking, tied at the throat with orange twine. His hair had grown longer and greyer, and the once-stubbled chin was now full-bearded, but Little-Marten recognized his old enemy in an instant. Here were the eyes that could stop his heart from beating, and here was a name at last to the fears that had dogged him all throughout this day: Scurl.

Scurl, once captain of the West Wood archers, now banished from the forest by Maglin for his treachery. Scurl, who with his cronies had been cast out upon the lands of the Gorji, where it was assumed they would perish. Two seasons and more it had been since Scurl's departure and all had forgotten him. Yet here he was, still in the area, still alive, and as terrifying as ever.

Little-Marten felt his whole being go weak as Scurl raised the bow towards him, and drew back the arrow.

'Now then, Woodpecker. I don't know what good fortune brings 'ee here to me, but I'll tell 'ee this – I ain't likely to waste it. Not this time.'

Chapter Twenty-two

The prospect of an extra couple of days off school was always a good one, and Midge had intended to have a long and peaceful lie-in, with time to give some serious thought to the Orbis, and what she could possibly do next. But of course it was Monday morning – she'd forgotten that – and by eight-thirty the builders had well and truly arrived. The dumper truck was already roaring around the yard outside her window, and now it sounded as though somebody was trying to hammer his way up through the floorboards directly beneath her bed.

With a strangled squeal of fury Midge threw back the duvet. Was there never to be any *peace* around here? She stomped over to the shower cubicle as loudly as she could, her bare feet banging in time to the hammering below.

George was downstairs, she was quite pleased to discover, apparently having driven over with his mum.

'We're just here until lunchtime,' he said, through a mouthful of toast and marmalade. 'Thought we might go tobogganing. What do you reckon?'

The kitchen felt quite crowded. Midge's mum and Auntie Pat were sitting at the end of the breakfast table, drinking tea and surrounded by the inevitable piles of paperwork, and Uncle Brian was on the phone, staring out of the window and saying, 'Yes. Yes . . . will do . . . right-ho, Cliff . . . see you sometime this afternoon then . . .'

'Tobogganing?' said Midge. 'Yeah, OK, then. I don't mind.' Anything to escape this mayhem, she thought.

'Hiya, Midge. All right, lovey?'

'Hi, Auntie Pat. Yeah, I'm fine.'

Her aunt smiled up at her, patting at the neat little lacquered hairdo that always looked to Midge as though it could withstand a tsunami. Midge smiled back and Auntie Pat returned her attention to the list of figures that lay before her. 'So what's this then, Chris? Oh, I see . . . you've done it that way. Right . . .'

'I had a bit of a go yesterday,' said George, 'while you were out.'

'What? Oh, the tobogganing . . .'

The room was too busy, and Midge just wanted to get away. 'Come on,' she said to George. 'I'll go and find my wellies.'

The snow didn't look as though it was going to be around for long. Already the whitened slopes of Howard's Hill looked a bit patchy, and the bright sunshine – such a contrast to yesterday's weather – felt warm enough to begin melting what was left. But you could see where George had been playing the previous afternoon, a long flattened track that ran from the sheep-gate down towards the Field of Thistles, and perhaps this icy strip would resist the effects of the sun for a while yet.

'But the weather was *horrible* yesterday afternoon,' said Midge, as she and George trudged up the hillside. 'It must have been freezing out here.'

'Yeah, it was a bit.' George had both hands behind his back, pulling the red plastic toboggan along by its length of thin rope. 'Seemed a shame to waste it, though. I didn't go out until it was nearly dark, and I could only stand it for about an hour. But it had stopped snowing by then. Pretty much.'

They reached the top of the slope, close to the wall where the sheep-gate was, and George said, 'I'll go first. Just to make sure it's safe. It looks a bit more slippery than it did before.' He manoeuvred the plastic toboggan out into the centre of the flattened track, straddled it and then plonked himself down on the moulded seat bit. 'Give us a bit of a push, then, when I say "go".' He grabbed the rope, and put his feet up. 'OK – go.'

Midge stood at the back of him, put her hands on the shoulders of his padded jacket and gave him a good shove. 'Agh!' She nearly overbalanced, and slithered a little way down the track before she could right herself. She looked sideways to see George bouncing down the hillside at quite an impressive speed. Blimey. Quite a scary speed . . .

'Who-oh-oh-oh-oh . . .' George's fading yell was like that of someone riding a roller coaster, half terror and half excitement, but the sound was broken by every bump that he hit, and there were a lot of them. His head was jiggling about as though it was being used as a cocktail shaker. The toboggan shot way past the point where the icy track petered out, and ploughed on almost to the hedge that bordered the Field of Thistles before hitting a final big hummock and stopping dead. George tipped neatly forward and fell face down in the snow.

Midge could hear him cursing from where she stood. He picked himself up and stomped about rubbing his backside. 'What're you laughing at?' he shouted back up the hill – and it was true that now Midge had started she could hardly stop. She clutched at her stomach and bent over double, seriously worried that she was going to wet herself.

'Sorry . . . sorry . . . ahhhha! You just looked so . . . *funny*! Ohhhh . . .' Midge straightened up and tried to regain some control, but then the sight of George's angry red face started her shrieking again. 'It was your . . . your . . . head! It looked like it was going to fall off!'

'Oh, hilarious . . .' George's voice drifted towards her as he began hauling the toboggan back up the hill. 'Yeah that would've been *really* funny if my brains were all splattered about in the snow . . . what a laugh . . . teeth and eyeballs everywhere . . .'

But by the time he'd climbed to where Midge stood his temper had improved a bit. Now he was grinning again, and there was a glint in his eye . . .

'Right then,' he said. 'Your turn.'

'Ah, but George, no pushing, OK? Let me do it by myself.'

'Oh, but you'll need a *little* push, just to get you going.'

'No, I mean it. You let me do it by myself or I'm not doing it at all.'

'Go on then.'

'Well, you just keep away from me.'

'OK.'

Midge pulled the toboggan over to the ice slide, and gingerly lowered herself onto it.

'Hey, how do you steer this thing anyway?'

'Use the rope – look.' George came across and leaned over her shoulder. 'Hold it with your hands a little way apart. Bit more – that's right. Then you sort of pull the corner up . . . left or right.'

'Like this?'

'That's right,' said George, 'like *this*!' and Midge felt hands on her shoulder blades, shoving her forward.

'No, George! No-oh-oh-oh . . .'

In an instant she was flying down the hard icy slope, and as helplessly out of control as if she were riding a runaway horse, unable to do anything but cling onto the rope. Her feet were too far forward, so that every jarring bump of the toboggan shot straight up her spine and made her teeth rattle. *Bump* . . . *b-bump-bump* . . . *bump* . . . Midge hauled on the rope, more with the desperate idea of somehow making the thing stop than in any attempt to steer it, but then with a sideways judder the toboggan veered from the track and went bounding into fresh snow. There was a final thump as the toboggan disappeared from beneath her, the world did a quick flip, and Midge found herself staring dazedly up into an unbroken expanse of blue sky. She remained spreadeagled on her back for a few moments, catching her breath. Nothing above her but pure clear blue . . . no edges, no boundaries. Like an endless computer screen . . .

George was laughing. She could hear him in the distance, but the sound was funny somehow. Midge sat up and realized she had an earful of snow.

They experimented and found that by starting from about three-quarters of the way up the slope, there was a reasonable chance of staying on the toboggan. The compacted snow track had obviously frozen overnight, so that now it was far more slippery than it had been the day before. Again and again they took it in turns to make the exhilarating run, until they were finally exhausted and could climb the hill no more.

'*Kills* your bum, though,' said George as they headed, limping, for home. 'We should have brought a cushion or something.'

'Yeah, I can just see Mum letting me use one of the sitting-room cushions. But it was great.'

Three hours they had been out there, Midge realized, and in all that time she hadn't given a single thought to anything but the toboggan and the next ride. All her troubles and her worries had disappeared. This was how things should be, wasn't it?

When they got back to the farm they saw a big flat-bed truck standing in the yard. It looked very flashy.

'Chevrolet,' said George. 'Left-hand drive too. Whose is that?'

'I think it must be that friend of your dad's,' said

Midge. 'Cliff Maybank? Come to pick up all the junk from the Stick House.'

'Oh right. Well that's where I keep the toboggan. Better make sure they don't take it by mistake.'

They found Uncle Brian and Cliff Maybank struggling to manoeuvre a huge piece of furniture through the rickety doorway of the Stick House. Midge was startled to recognize it as being the old wardrobe that had once stood in her bedroom. The wardrobe was tilted towards her, so that she could see the top of it, and her heart jumped at the memory it brought back. That was where she had hidden, crouched in terror high up on that dusty bit of plank-ing, hoping and praying that she would not be discovered . . . Scurl and his ugly crew searching the empty room below . . .

Ugh! She blinked and shook the memory from her.

'To me . . . to me . . . OK, now your way a bit.' Uncle Brian was sweating with the strain, and from inside the Stick House there came a muffled reply. Not so muffled that it couldn't be heard for what it was, though, and Uncle Brian said, 'Kids out here, Cliff. Watch your language.'

'Oh. Sorry.'

Bit by bit the wardrobe was jiggled and coaxed through the doorway, until finally it stood in the sunlight, a shabby old monstrosity.

'Good-oh.' Uncle Brian dusted off his hands, and Cliff Maybank emerged blinking from the dark interior of the Stick House. 'I'll back the truck up then.'

'I'm just going to put my toboggan away, Dad,' said George. 'Didn't want it disappearing along with everything else, that's all.'

'No, no, that's fine, son. Make an empty corner somewhere. It'll be OK.'

Midge felt something brush against her leg and looked down.

'Hallo, darling! I haven't seen you for ages.'

It was the Favoured One.

The kitten of last summer had grown into a young cat now. Sleek and smooth her baby fur had become, and there was a wildness about her that reminded Midge more and more of her father, Tojo. Cats were not allowed in the house, and so the Favoured One lived out in the barns along with her sisters. Sometimes she was happy to be picked up and cuddled, sometimes not. Midge crouched down and stroked the pretty head, watching the eyes squeeze shut in brief appreciation. The moment didn't last, though, and as soon as Midge tried to get her hand beneath the cat's body, she skipped deftly away, trotting into the Stick House, tail up in the air.

I bet that's where you live now, Midge thought. It would make sense, what with all the work that was going on elsewhere. She stood up and followed the cat into the darkness. George was already in there, clearing a corner of some curtain poles in order to make room for his toboggan.

'Baby-baby-baby . . . where are you?' Midge peered around the cluttered gloom of the little outhouse. 'Aha!' She caught a glimpse of white fur, the Favoured One's tell-tale bib, and then the shape of the cat grew around that. She was sitting on a tall box, tucked away between an old laundry mangle and a milk churn.

'Poor baby. Is this your home now, darling? And are we messing it all up for you?'

The Favoured One seemed less jittery in the safety of semi-darkness. She allowed herself to be stroked and petted – she even purred a little.

'You're lovely. Yes you are. Lovely-lovely-lovely. Yes.' Midge picked the cat up and cradled her, tickling her under the chin, feeling the soft fur against the backs of her fingertips. But this time she would put her down on the box again, before she grew restless or tried to escape. Maybe that was the trick of it: not to try and force anything.

She saw that the top of the box was covered in soft material, a shiny swirl of raised patterns. And it was padded. A nice warm place, then, for the Favoured One to rest her head.

But what was it exactly? Midge stepped back, still cradling the cat, and considered the box. It was made out of wicker – thin woven cane – and it had obviously seen better days. Some of the cane had become unravelled, and the whole thing looked slightly lopsided, as though somebody far too heavy had tried to sit upon it.

It was the image of somebody sitting upon it that made Midge gasp out loud. The Favoured One wriggled out of her arms and slid to the ground, but Midge was barely aware of it. She just stood there, staring at the wicker box . . .

'OK. All done.' George's voice made her jump, but Midge still couldn't look away.

'What's the matter? You all right?'

'George – look!'

'What?'

'It's the *box*. The box from the photograph. You know the one . . . with Aunt Celandine sitting on it. When she was a girl.'

'What photograph? You mean that one that used to be in the kitchen? Nah . . . it can't be.'

'It *is*. I've looked at it a million times. It's hanging in my bedroom now, and I see it every day. It's the same box. *This* one.'

'Coo. Wonder if there's anything in it.' George tried to see if the top would lift up, but although it shifted slightly there was something stopping it.

'Oh, I get it. There's a sort of loop . . .' George fiddled around for a moment, then raised the lid of the box and looked inside. 'Pillow,' he said, and

307

hauled out a sorry-looking object. It was black-and-white striped, quite badly stained, and the downy feathers that now twirled in the light of the doorway told of its contents. George delved into the box and had a quick rummage. 'Yeah, just a couple more pillows. It's like a laundry basket, I suppose. Phew! Pretty mouldy down in there, though.' He took his hand out and wiped it on his jeans.

'I can't *believe* this!' said Midge. 'It's just amazing.'

'Yeah? Well I suppose it is.' George didn't seem particularly impressed. He put the pillow back in the box and shut the lid. 'Amazing that nobody's slung it out before, anyway.'

'I've got to have it,' said Midge. 'I mean, I've just got to. Do you reckon your dad'd let me keep it?'

George shrugged. 'Dunno. Don't see why not. Well, not unless it's worth something. Ask him.'

Uncle Brian was watching the truck as it reversed towards the Stick House.

'Come on, Cliff . . . bit more . . . bit more . . . OK.' He banged his hand against the side panel and the truck came to a halt, engine dying abruptly away.

'Uncle Brian, can I ask you a *huge* favour?' Midge ran across and grabbed at her uncle's arm. 'I mean a really *massive* favour. I'll . . . I'll pay for it if it's worth anything. Save up . . .'

'Eh? What is it, love?'

'There's an old wicker box in the shed. It's the box in the photograph, Uncle Brian, you know – the one with Aunt Celandine sitting on it . . .'

'What?'

'Come and see.'

Uncle Brian followed Midge and George into the outhouse.

'This one.' Midge kept her hand on top of the box, willing it to be hers. She could already see where it would stand in her room, directly beneath the picture of Aunt Celandine sitting on this very same wicker box. It would be so perfect.

'Oh *please*,' she said. 'I just love it.'

'Hey – I think you're right, you know,' said Uncle Brian. 'It must have been kicking around the place for donkey's years, but there's so much junk about that you just don't notice any of it in the end. I suppose it's been up in the attic and then brought down again at some point. It does look like the one in that old photo, though, I'll admit. Anything in it?'

'Nah. Couple of mouldy pillows,' said George.

'OK,' said Uncle Brian. 'Keep it then, Midge, if you like it so much. Bit of an heirloom, I suppose. Sling the pillows, though. Take them across to the house and put 'em in a black sack or something – saves me having to sort it.'

'Yes! Ooh – thanks, Uncle Brian! Thank you. I'm going to put it under the photo. It'll be great. Help me carry it across, George, will you?'

'OK.'

'Better get a move on, then, George. I think your mum's about ready to go,' said Uncle Brian.

''K.'

The thing was heavier and more awkward than it

looked, and Midge and George had to pause for breath halfway up the stairs.

'Blimey. What did they used to put in those old pillows,' said George, 'whole chickens? Hey – I've had an idea, though. We could use the pillows as cushions for the toboggan! One of 'em, anyway . . .'

They dragged the box up the remaining stairs, *bump-bump*, one at a time, and then carried it into Midge's bedroom.

'See?' she said. 'It'll go in this corner, right under the photograph.'

'Yeah.' George sounded a bit doubtful. 'Maybe you could paint it or something.'

The old object did look scruffy, it was true, in contrast to all that was new and modern in the room. Midge didn't care. It was the very same box as the one in the picture above it, and that was what counted. Magical.

'George – are you up there?' Auntie Pat was shouting up the stairs.

'Yeah. Coming,' George shouted back. Then he said to Midge, 'Give me one of those pillows, and I'll sling it in the Stick House on the way out. For the toboggan.'

'OK.' Midge unhooked the wicker loop that fastened the box lid down, and hauled out a pillow. 'Here.' She handed it to George. As an afterthought she reached down into the box for a second time. 'Do you want this other one as well?'

'Nah. Sling it. This one'll do.'

'Are you coming over again tomorrow?'

'Shouldn't think so. Mum's working, as far as I know, and Dad's off somewhere so there's no one to give me a lift. And then it's school again on Wednesday, so it'll probably be the weekend before there's another chance. Snow'll be gone by then, I expect.'

'Oh well. See you whenever.'

'Yeah.'

George left the room, one or two feathers floating in the air behind him. Midge scrunched up the pillow she was holding, and began to push it back into the wicker box. Then she stopped. What was that?

She pulled the pillow out again, and peered into the shadowy interior. There was something else down there. Midge moved to one side, kept hold of the basket-lid, and tilted the whole thing towards the light. She could see pale-coloured material . . . a bundled-up garment of some sort . . . but wood also . . . the edge of a wooden box. A lock. With a key in it . . .

Midge's arm jerked backwards. She let go of the padded lid and it banged shut, the wicker basket rocking backwards and forwards a couple of times before settling creakily on its base. Oh my God . . .

Oh my *God*! It was in there!

Midge put her hands up to her mouth and tried to swallow. Aunt Celandine's jewellery casket. She was sure that was what it was, certain that it could have been nothing else. It was here, in this very room. But no, that would be just too incredible. Wouldn't it? Midge had to take a few deep breaths before she felt able to lift the lid again. She was shaking now, as nervous as if this basket held a cobra. Again she

311

peered down into the musty interior. And there it was. A wooden box, turned on its side, the lock and key facing upwards towards her. The pale garment that had been rolled up and bundled against the casket might once have been a pair of cricket flannels. Midge slowly allowed the lid to fold all the way back on its hinges, and then just stood there staring. It was a long while before it even occurred to her to do anything else.

She could just about reach. Bending down into the dark mouth of the basket, her arms extended in front of her, Midge was reminded of the wicker tunnel that led into the forest. She was groping forward into the shadows, feeling for the unknown. It was smelly in here, and claustrophobic. Then her hands gripped the edges of the wooden casket, and she wriggled backwards, surfacing to the here-and-now of her warm bedroom, bringing with her treasures from another world.

Midge carried the casket over to the corner of her bed and sat there with it on her lap. It was as her Aunt Celandine had described it: dark wood, quite heavy, with sides that sloped inwards. Four round feet . . . no, three. One missing. An inlaid diamond pattern on the lid, in paler coloured wood. Midge lifted the casket and shook it very gently, bringing her head closer to listen. There was movement in there, as of something shifting slightly, but no real sound.

She put her fingertip on the little metal key, stroking the smooth rounded surface for a few moments before gripping it between finger and thumb . . . ready to turn it . . .

No. This was a moment that needed preparing for. It was lunchtime, and her mum might call up to her at any second, or even come in to see her. Which could be disastrous. She had to know that she would be alone for this moment. Be patient, then.

Midge gently lowered the casket back into the wicker box, stuffed the pillow down on top of it and closed the lid. Then she went downstairs.

'Are those things wet? The bottoms of your jeans look soaked.' Mum was in the kitchen, working as usual, papers and books spread out across the table.

'Yeah, they are a bit,' said Midge. 'I was tobogganing with George. I'm going to get changed in a minute. In fact I think I might get straight into my pyjamas. Mum, I'm really tired. Could I have a drink and a sandwich and take it back upstairs with me? I just feel like slobbing around – and I've got a bit of reading to do before Wednesday. I might have a rest first, though, while the builders are quiet.'

'A rest? Must be nice to have the time. Get yourself a sandwich or something, then. There's cheese in the fridge. Might be some egg mayo, I think . . .'

'OK.' Midge had thought that Mum might stop what she was doing and make a sandwich for her, but she was obviously too busy. She walked over to the fridge.

'How's it all going?' she said, trying to at least pretend interest.

'Oh, we'll get there,' Mum muttered. 'We have to. What about you? Everything all right?'

'Yeah, I'm fine.' Midge found herself fighting back sudden tears, and this took her completely by surprise. She pulled open the fridge door, and kept her head turned away so Mum couldn't see.

'Only, I look at you sometimes, and I do wonder. You seem . . . so far away. I never know what you're thinking about . . .' The scrape of the kitchen chair told Midge that her mum was getting up and crossing the room.

Midge kept staring into the fridge. 'I'm OK. Really. Don't worry.' She tried to pull herself together. This was no time to be weakening. Not today.

'Well, as long as you know that I care.' Mum kissed the top of her head in passing. 'But now I feel a bit guilty, because I'm going to have to leave you on your own for most of tomorrow – and it's your last day before school starts again. Brian's not around either. I'm going over to a trade show with Barry, to look at alternative sorts of heating for the holiday apartments, and Brian's seeing this wine guy, Alan Lavers. Which if I know Brian could take all week. Will you be all right? Although you *could* come with me and Barry, if you really wanted to . . .'

'Er, no, Mum. Don't think so.'

Her mum laughed as she paused in the doorway. 'Well, maybe not. But listen, the builders'll be around and about. And you know Dave, the really tall one. The foreman. He's a nice man – got kids of his own, here at the primary school. If there was ever any trouble . . .'

'I'll be fine. Can I take a yogurt up with my sandwich?'

'Go on, then. But mind the bedclothes please, miss. Get yourself a spoon, and a tray.'

'All right. I'm going to eat this and then have a rest. My legs are all achey.'

'That'll be the tobogganing. See you later, then. I'll give you a shout at teatime if you're not down before.'

'Yeah. Thanks.'

'But get yourself out of those damp clothes before you do anything else.'

'OK.'

So that had been worth doing. Now she was as unlikely to be disturbed as could be hoped for.

Midge sat on the bottom edge of her bed and took a bite of her sandwich. She stared at the wicker box as she chewed, and tried to prepare herself. But for what? She hadn't the faintest idea what it might look like, this thing she was hoping to find in the casket.

It might be something really dangerous. That thought hadn't occurred to her before. Maybe it would explode . . . or cut her . . . or be poisonous. No, that wasn't very likely. Aunt Celandine had seen it, and she'd survived the experience.

But perhaps there would be nothing in there whatsoever. Nothing but ribbons and hairgrips and empty disappointment. And that thought was unbearable. It was the reason why she was putting off the moment, Midge realized. Not knowing meant that there was hope. Once she'd opened the casket, all hope might disappear.

Midge took another bite of her sandwich and put the rest of it back on the plate. Come on. It has to be done. She stood up, dusted the crumbs from her fingers, then retrieved the casket from the wicker box.

The key didn't want to turn. It was loose enough in its keyhole, but she couldn't make it work the lock. For a good five minutes Midge struggled with the casket, holding it firmly on her lap as she tried turning the key this way and that. But it was no use. Her fingers had become sweaty and sore from the effort, and now she couldn't even get a decent grip on the thing. Maybe she should go and find a screwdriver or something. She looked round the room.

The teaspoon for her yogurt. That might do it. She pushed the end of the spoon through the hole in the key. Which way *should* it turn? To the left seemed the most logical, and she applied a bit of pressure in that direction, using the spoon as a lever. Still nothing, and now she was frightened of breaking the key. Just a tiny bit more, then. Gently . . . gently . . .

It moved. The key had definitely creaked to the left. Something was beginning to give. Midge kept up a slow steady leverage, and then suddenly the mechanism broke free. The key twisted round all the way with a jerk and the lid simply fell open. Midge tried to right the casket in order to keep the contents from spilling out, but it was too late, and the first thing her scrabbling fingers caught hold of was the Orbis.

Or at least it was the brown bundle of oilcloth in which the Orbis was presumably wrapped. Midge snatched at it as it rolled down into her lap, and there it was. In her hand at last.

Oh, but she needed a moment to recover before going any further. Her eyesight had gone all blurry, and she was shaking and sweating like anything. Midge rubbed her forearm across her brow, and then used the same free hand to jiggle the casket off her lap and onto the bed beside her. OK. Deep breath, then. Now she was ready.

The oilcloth was stiff with age, dry and crumbly. As Midge tried to peel it away, bits kept breaking off. It was mummified. The thin strips couldn't be unwound in the same way as the one that she had delivered to Aunt Celandine. But she persevered, picking gently at the loose ends, layer after layer, and putting all the bits on the tea tray beside her.

Very gradually the contents began to appear – a first glimpse of metal . . . a knurled knob . . . a curving section . . . a sliding piece with what might have been an engraving of the moon . . .

She had never been able to picture what the Orbis might look like, and so had not imagined what her reaction to it might be. But as the last few scraps of oilcloth fell away, Midge felt absolute delight. It was a gorgeous thing. Just beautiful – like something that might be found on an old sailing ship, or in a museum of astronomy. There were bits to twiddle, little screws and knobs and slidey pieces. Beautiful.

But how did it work? What did it do exactly? Midge could see that the main curve of the frame, shaped like a letter C, would be able to hold something between the two knurled knobs at either end. A globe perhaps. Yes, there was a further circular frame built at right angles to the C, and so a ball shape would fit into the whole cage construction very nicely, and spin round on the pivots, like a classroom globe. But then there were three sliding pieces on the main frame – one with a sun emblem engraved into it, the other two with a moon and a star. And a little rod that popped out on a spring. What did all these things do?

Midge found that the sliders were each held in place by a small screw. By loosening the screws, the pieces could be repositioned on the curve of the frame. Except that there was magnetic resistance to this. The sliders moved in and out of several fields of magnetism around the frame, as though the frame itself were made up of a series of magnets invisibly welded together into one curving strip. And the central slider, the one with the sun on it, repelled the moon and star sliders when you moved them close together. It was wonderful.

Midge sat on her bed for ages, playing with the Orbis, taking bits off and putting them back on again, trying different combinations . . .

George would love this, she thought. But then she had another thought, and a more disturbing one:

she might have messed this thing up completely in her enthusiasm to explore its workings. It might have been as finely set as a chronometer, for all she knew, tuned in to some magnetic astral force that she knew nothing about. And now she'd changed it all around. How had it been when she'd first started fiddling with it? Oh Lord . . .

There was no chance of getting it back to exactly how it was. But at least she'd found it, and surely that was the main thing? Surely they'd be grateful for that?

Midge decided that she'd better not make matters any worse. She reluctantly put the Orbis to one side and looked in the casket to see what else was there. A folded piece of paper . . . a few glass beads and some ribbon . . . a flowery enamelled brooch . . . a couple of wooden combs. Nothing else that was anything like as interesting as the Orbis. Midge picked up the piece of paper and unfolded it. Lined notepaper, it was, brown and mottled with age. She saw tiny words, written in pencil. No capitals and all unpunctuated – a bit like text messaging at first glance.

'*thee orbis be not saf and so it must leev this plas with thee this da I sl tel . . .*'

What?

Midge puzzled for a while over the strange formations of letters. It was English, of a sort, she realized, and bits of it made sense, but she couldn't get the entire gist of it. And who had written this?

They had. Of course. The tiny writing, the lined exercise paper . . . it was the same as the paper that

Tadgemole had given her. It was a letter, to Celandine, from the Various. But how amazing!

Midge took the paper across to her laptop, and spent the next quarter of an hour copying the whole lot out as a word processor document. She experimented with punctuation and spelling, bit by bit, until finally she thought she had made a reasonable translation.

The Orbis be not safe, and so it must leave this place with thee this day. I shall tell the Ickri that it were stolen and cannot be found, for they would take it from us if it were kept here.

There be one who knows more, and I do this with the aid of she. None other knows of this. Keep the Orbis safe for we, till better times be come and we may meet with thee again. Thee shall know the day. Thee be our true friend, as we be yours, and we shall not forget.

From Micas.

Midge rested her chin on her hands and read the piece again and again, utterly overwhelmed by her discovery. Here was Celandine's history. She had been a friend, a true friend, to the cave-dwellers. And she had fled the forest at the coming of the warlike Ickri, carrying the Orbis to safety with her. *How* could anyone have ever forgotten such a thing?

And now the Orbis was here, rediscovered at last, after all those long years. Celandine needed to know about this – and immediately. It might be ages, though, before another visit could be planned. Midge looked around for her mobile, spotted it lying on the window sill, and then hunted in her bedside drawer for Carol Reeve's card. She would phone Mount Pleasant straight away.

The number was a direct line to the manager's office. Good, thought Midge. That meant not having to talk to half-witted Helen, the girl at reception.

'Carol Reeve.' The calm voice at the other end of the line. Midge pictured her, sitting at that big old headmistress's desk in her smart suit.

'Oh hi, Mrs Reeve, it's Midge Walters – you know Aunt Celandine's . . . I mean Miss Howard's . . .'

'Midge! How are you? Everything OK?'

'Yes, I'm fine. But I might not be able to get over to visit for a while. Is my Aunt Celandine there? I wondered if I could speak to her?'

'Oh. Well, we could try, I suppose. I'm not sure how she'd cope with the phone . . . hang on, Midge. Let me just put you on hold a moment . . .' The line went quiet for a while. Midge thought about what she would say to her aunt. I've found the Orbis . . . found the Orbis . . . and everything's going to be all right now.

'Midge, are you still there? Listen, Miss Howard's asleep, I'm afraid. I've just rung down to Elaine. She has been sleeping a lot lately – Miss Howard, that is, not Elaine. And I do think it's good for her. She's been far more peaceful since your last visit, but very tired, and still not eating much. I really don't want to wake her. Can I give her a message, to say you rang?'

'Oh. Yes. Um . . . could you tell her something from me? It's quite important. Could you tell her that I've found . . . I've found her old jewellery box. She'll know what I mean. She lost it years and years ago. Her *jewellery* box, tell her. It's all safe, and . . . er . . . everything's still in it. That's the really important thing to say to her – that everything's still in it.'

'Ooh. That sounds like good news. I'm sure she'll be very pleased to hear it. And so . . . will you be bringing this box across some time?'

'Well, I'll try. But she'll just want to know that it's OK. And everything's going to be fine now. Tell her that. And tell her that I'll see her soon.'

'I certainly will. And I've got your phone number in case there's any message in return. All right? Good. Thanks for calling then, Midge. Bye.'

'Bye.'

Midge put her phone down on the bed beside her, and picked up the Orbis again. She must think about a temporary hiding place for it, and the letter also, perhaps. The presence of the wicker box and the jewellery casket could be explained to her mum easily enough, but the Orbis must remain a secret. Where could she put it? In her wardrobe? That would probably be the best place. Tuck it away in a carrier bag behind the unused rolls of Christmas wrapping paper. It would be safe there, overnight at least. Soon she would do that. And then she would have to think about getting it back to the forest.

And what an amazing moment that would be – to be able to hand this strange and magical object over, to have done with it, to walk away knowing that she had succeeded.

Yes, soon she would be able to think about all of

that. But for the moment another thought was beginning to dawn upon her . . .

Nothing that she had done over the past few weeks had actually made the slightest difference. Her meeting with Pegs and Tadgemole . . . her astonishing discovery of Aunt Celandine . . . the arrival of Maglin with his mysterious bundle of gifts . . . all of her planning . . . all of her efforts . . . none of it had had any real effect on the outcome. What had happened today might easily have happened anyway. The Orbis had been here all along, at Mill Farm, and she had stumbled upon it simply because she had gone tobogganing with George. If it hadn't snowed, she would never have found it.

And so if you looked at it like that, she hadn't really found the Orbis at all. It had simply turned up of its own accord.

This should have been such a wonderful moment, but instead Midge felt quite low and useless. It was almost as though she had been tricked.

Chapter Twenty-three

Little-Marten could feel his insides quaking. He was as terrified for Henty's sake as for his own. A dozen wild notions ran around his head, but though he might beg, or reason, flatter, or even attack, he knew that none of it would do any good. Scurl was mad. Easier to argle-bargle with an adder than deal with this one.

'Have 'ee no word for an old friend then?' Scurl's bow and arrow casually swept from one of them to the other. Little-Marten glanced across the open byre towards Henty. She was backed up against a stack of hay bales, poised as though to run, her face pale in the gathering dusk. Little-Marten caught her eye and willed her not to do anything foolish. Now was not the time for any show of spirit on her part. He knew Scurl better than she, how murderous his actions were like to be if he were ever challenged.

Scurl looked Henty up and down and shrugged. 'No? A pity. 'Tain't so often I hears any voice but my own.'

'We've quit the forest.' Little-Marten spoke up – more intent upon distracting Scurl's leery eye from Henty than with any real thought as to what he might say. 'Driven out, as thee were once driven out.'

Scurl turned towards him, thick eyebrows twitching upwards in momentary surprise. 'So? Did 'ee fall wrongsides o' that old wosbird Maglin then? 'Tis easy done, as well I knows. Ah . . .' Scurl nodded as if he began to understand the situation. 'I see how 'tis. Thee'd be together, but there be those that'd not let 'ee. All the worse then, to have run into I so soon – for 'ee've not been out here long, by the look of 'ee.'

'No, not so long,' Little-Marten blundered on. 'We were hiding at the Gorji settlement, but then—'

He was cut short as Scurl spat on the ground in front of him. 'Gorji! Do 'ee dare speak that word to me? Have 'ee forgotten what brought me to this? 'Twere that Gorji snip, and her like! 'Twere because of she that I were sent out here to die, and my company with me. Aye, and dead they now be – Dregg . . . and Snerk and Flitch. 'Tis she that I blame for that! And *thee*, Woodpecker – and *thee*, Tinkler!' Scurl swung round and trained his bow upon Henty once again.

'Well now I've the pair of 'ee, and I shall have t'other soon enough. That ogre maid'll come straying away from the settlement one time too many, and then she'll find me waiting for her. I've near put an arrow through her more'n once already.'

'Could 'ee not shoot straight then?'

Little-Marten's words tumbled out in desperation. His head was whirling, and his only conscious thought had been to say anything – *anything* – to deflect Scurl's attention from Henty. And he had succeeded, if only momentarily, for Scurl's ugly face turned slowly back

325

towards him. But now its colour had deepened in fury and the sharp yellow teeth were bared in a snarl beneath the straggled beard.

'Not *shoot* straight? Ha! I s'll let thee be the judge o' that, Woodpecker!' Scurl flicked his head in Henty's direction, and his voice lowered to a growl. 'Choose theeself one o' they pretty eyes then – whichever thee fancy – and then we shall see whether I shoot straight or no. Choose! Or I shall choose for 'ee . . .'

'There's another choice you could make.' Henty spoke for the first time. 'Which would you rather – that 'twas we who stood before you, or the Gorji maid here in our stead?'

'What?' Scurl lowered his bow a little, and some of the tension went out of the drawstring. He stared at Henty. 'How could the Gorji brat be here in your stead?'

'We might lead her here. Bring her to you. And then you might . . . let us go.' Henty's voice was quiet, calm.

Little-Marten shook his head at her. What did she think she was doing?

But Henty had Scurl's attention now, and Little-Marten could only look on. He held his breath, waiting to see how this would play out.

'Let 'ee go? I've birds in hand, maidy. I ain't likely to let the two that I hold go a-chasing after one that I don't. For how many dost reckon I'd end up wi'?' Scurl's voice was sneering, but the bow dropped a little lower still. He seemed interested, perhaps willing to listen for a few moments longer.

'What if only one of us were to go,' said Henty, 'and

that one to come back with the Gorji maid? Would you let us free then?'

Scurl took his hand from the bowstring, keeping the arrow loosely notched. He scratched at the underside of his filthy beard.

'Well here be a sharp 'un,' he said, 'for a Tinkler. Is that what they learn 'ee, down in they caves – how to horse-trade? I thought 'twere only the Naiad as were up to such tricks. Now how could either of 'ee hope to snare that ogre?'

'I reckon she'd come,' said Henty, 'if I told her . . . if I told her that Little-Marten was hurt. Trapped . . .'

'Trapped? By me? Aye, I don't doubt she *would* come. And bring men and hounds with her – I don't doubt that, neither.'

'No.' Henty looked around the byre. 'That Gorji machine . . . if I said Little-Marten was stuck under that thing, she'd come to help. She did the same for the Naiad horse, Pegs. And she've brought none of her own kind to the forest yet, nor told our secret that we know. She've been a friend to us.'

Scurl looked across at the heavy ladder-machine, considered it for a moment, then turned back to Henty.

'And thee'd stand here and watch her die, would 'ee? This *friend* o' yourn?'

'I'd watch her die – if only we might live. She've brought us no harm, but she's still Gorji.'

'*Henty* . . .' Little-Marten could hold his tongue no longer.

Scurl spun round and pointed a shaking finger at him. 'Stay out o' it, Woodpecker! This 'un might keep 'ee breathing a while yet! She've a sight more to her than thee!' Scurl held Little-Marten in his wild gaze for a few moments longer, before turning away.

'Now then. If 'ee were to bring the ogre to me, what makes 'ee think I s'd keep to my part?'

'Your word on it.' Henty looked at Scurl, a steady gaze that showed neither fear nor hatred. Little-Marten marvelled that she could remain so calm. Scurl's back was to him, thinner and bonier than it had been, but still confident in its swagger – a back that shrugged off the possibility of attack, and Little-Marten felt weak and useless. This was between Scurl and Henty. It was as though he didn't exist.

The tiny sounds of dimpsy-dusk came creeping into the darkening byre, faint rustles in the hay bales, the call of a heron from somewhere far out in the wetlands, the creak of the metal roof high overhead.

Finally Scurl sucked at his teeth, and said, 'Well, thee've a head on they skinny shoulders o' yourn, maid, I'll give 'ee that, and wits about thee. Too many wits, I'm thinking . . .' Then, in a flash of movement, Scurl drew back his bow and shot.

There had been no hint of warning. Henty squealed with pain and Little-Marten felt his heart explode at the sound. His knees sagged beneath him and he struggled to keep his vision in focus. He saw the black-and-white feathers of the arrow . . . their barred pattern mingling with the pale blur of Henty's face . . . and realized that she was pinned to the bale behind her. By her hair.

'What do 'ee say, *Woodpecker*?' Scurl's roar echoed

around the byre. 'Do I shoot *straight* enough for 'ee?' Already Scurl had another arrow at the ready, and as he drew back the bow Little-Marten could only half raise his hands in a helpless plea. He had no voice to answer the snarling monster that stood before him, nor even wits to flinch from the arrow-point that met his eye. Deep into his brain that arrow would drive, a flash of magpie feathers the last thing he would ever see . . .

'Pick me up some o' that twine!'

What?

Scurl kicked at something with his ragged foot, and Little-Marten tried to drag himself out of his shocked state. What? He turned his head towards Henty. She was struggling to untangle her hair from the arrow that was embedded deep in the hay bale beside her.

'Twine, thee crack-nogged little zawney!' yelled Scurl. 'There . . . and there! Pick it up!'

Little-Marten looked around him. Lengths of orange twine lay scattered about the earth floor of the byre – long knotted loops that had been used to tie the hay bales. Yes, he'd noticed them before. He stooped to pick one up, and tumbled sideways as Scurl's foot shoved him in the ribs.

'Pick 'em up, dammee! More!' Little-Marten scrambled away, and hastily began to gather up what he could find. From the corner of his eye he saw Scurl march over to where Henty stood, and heard her cry out again as Scurl yanked the arrow from the hay bale.

'Get over there, and kneel down. There – kneel! Woodpecker, bring me that twine . . . give it to me. Now get down on your knees. No – away from she. Over there.'

The two of them were made to kneel on the earth floor, facing each other but some distance apart, at the foot of the tumbledown pile of hay bales. Scurl pulled a knife from his belt, long-bladed and heavy, some Gorji object. He wordlessly held it before them, raised it to his own hairy throat and drew it sideways in a quick slicing movement. His meaning was plain enough. They were to understand what this thing was likely to be used for, if they gave him any trouble.

Little-Marten watched as Scurl crouched down behind Henty, the knife blade clamped between his teeth. He took a length of the orange twine, looped it about her neck in a snare noose, then brought it down her back, keeping it taut as he wound it round and round her ankles. If Henty tried to straighten her legs out she would strangle herself.

'Hands.' Scurl made Henty hold her hands out in front of her whilst he tied her wrists.

Then it was Little-Marten's turn.

'Get back'ards.' Little-Marten had been kneeling upright, but Scurl forced him down so that he was sitting on his heels. The reason for this became plain as the twine was looped around his neck, yanked tightly backwards, and attached to his ankles. There was to be as little play as possible. Little-Marten instinctively brought his fingers to his throat and tried to ease the pressure, but Scurl roughly pulled his hands away.

'Hold 'em out – wrists together!'

Little-Marten did as he was told, and in a few

moments was bound and helpless. He could still raise his hands to his neck, and by slumping his shoulders could loosen the snare noose just a little, but it was still a horribly uncomfortable and frightening position to be in. Scurl had been careful to tie his wrists so that the final knot was on the underside. Little-Marten knew that he would not be able to get his teeth anywhere near it, and that escape would be impossible.

Scurl picked up Henty's bindle-wrap, untied it so that her few clothes and possessions fell onto the floor, and then tossed the oilskin towards her. 'Cover theeself up,' he said, and wandered across the byre to where Little-Marten's bundle lay. He stood for a moment looking up at the hazy moon that now appeared among the bare branches of the trees outside. They could hear him muttering to himself.

'I shall have 'ee . . . hmf . . . what do 'ee say, Ictor? Aye. Thee'm right . . . thee'm right . . . let 'em all come . . .'

Little-Marten looked at Henty, and puffed out his cheeks. With her bound wrists, she was struggling to get the oilskin about her shoulders, but she gave him a faint smile and a nod of encouragement. They were still alive, somehow, and for that at least they were grateful.

Scurl had picked up Little-Marten's bindle-wrap, untied it, and discovered the soft Gorji material within.

'What be this, then?' He re-crossed the byre and dropped the oilskin in front of Little-Marten. Then he sat on a bale between the two of them in order to examine the red Gorji sack. It didn't take him long to realize its purpose. He put his feet into it, and drew it up over his knees.

'Stinks o' the Gorji,' said Scurl, but kept it where it was. 'Now then . . .' He looked at Henty. 'Thee reckons the ogre maid'd come here to help Woodpecker, if thee were to ask her. But what of t'other way round? What if I sent Woodpecker to go and find her? If he said that 'twere *thee* as needed aid – would she come then?'

'No.' Little-Marten spoke up immediately. He could see where this was leading, and was horrified at the thought of leaving Henty alone at the mercy of Scurl.

Scurl swung round and raised the knife high, as if to hurl it at Little-Marten.

'Aye!' said Henty. 'She would! I know she would . . .'

Scurl remained poised for a moment longer, then lowered the knife. 'Hmf . . .' He sat tapping the blade against the palm of his hand, scowling at it. 'Hmf. Then 'tis which of 'ee to choose. Or neither. Which . . . or neither . . .'

Little-Marten reached out towards the crumpled oil-cloth that lay before him. He was nervous of making any movement, but he was also freezing. The noose tightened at his neck as he leaned forward. He gasped and looked up at Scurl to see whether his effort to reach the bindle-wrap would meet with any threat of punishment. But Scurl still seemed to be lost in thought, and Little-Marten was able to drag the oilcloth towards him and flick it back over his head. He drew the cold stiff material about his shoulders, and tried to huddle himself beneath it as Henty had done.

Scurl was still tapping the knife blade against his palm, head lowered, muttering to himself. Finally he nodded. 'Aye, so be it, then.'

A moment's pause, and then Scurl raised the knife, holding it by the blade. In a smooth and practised movement he drew his arm back and hurled the object across the barn. Little-Marten's flinch of terror came as a delayed reaction. The weapon had already flashed past him and struck its target. A deep *thunk* – the sound of metal biting into wood – and the knife was now protruding from the centre of the rabbit skin that they had noticed earlier. The tattered pelt, stretched across the wooden pallet on the far side of the barn, was obviously something that Scurl used for knife-throwing practice, a way of passing the cold and solitary evenings . . .

Little-Marten tried to swallow, but the tightness of the twine about his neck made it almost impossible to do so. He turned away from the knife to realize that Scurl was staring at him – at him and through him – wild red-rimmed eyes unblinking in the faint light. Scurl's great bony forehead glistened, waxy, as though with a fever, and his unkempt hair and beard only made his appearance the more awful. He was as terrifying as that huge Gorji felix had been . . . more unpredictable, at any rate. And perhaps even madder than Maven . . .

Little-Marten shrank backwards as the eyes shifted slightly and focused properly upon him. Scurl's brow furrowed into a scowl. 'Bist hungry?' he said.

Chapter Twenty-four

Midge woke up to find George sitting on the edge of her bed.

'Change of plan,' he said.

'Eh? What are you doing here? I thought you weren't . . .' Midge pushed herself upright and put her fist to her mouth as she yawned.

George flicked his fringe back. 'My mum's come across for a couple of hours after all, same as she did yesterday. Doing a bit more paperwork or something. Anyway, it meant that I could come too. Fancy another go on the toboggan? The snow's mostly gone, but the slide's still there . . .'

'Uuuuggh.' Midge yawned again, and tried to get her brain working. This wasn't what was supposed to be happening at all. Today was going to be the day when she would hand over the Orbis. She was going to climb Howard's Hill, find Pegs or Maglin or whoever she could, and just get rid of the thing. Today was going to be the day when it all finally came to an end, this whole ridiculous, amazing, impossible business. And now George was here.

Well, maybe it'd have to wait until later, then.

'What's the time?' she said.

'Dunno. About eight, I think.'

'*Eight o'clock?* Ugh. Way too early . . .' Midge flopped back down on the bed. 'Go and get us a cup of tea or something, George, will you?'

'OK. Are you going to get dressed then?'

'In a bit.'

Midge stared at the ceiling, and listened to George's footsteps clumping down the stairs. At least his absence gave her a moment or two to think. The sense of anticlimax that she had felt the night before was still with her. After all the *trouble* that she had been to . . . the secrecy, and the worry . . . it just seemed so much pointless effort now that the Orbis had literally tumbled into her lap. And even though it was such a beautiful object, the magic of it had vanished. Now that she had seen it and held it, the Orbis was like a Christmas present unwrapped: no matter how wonderful, or how longed for that present might be, it could never quite live up to the mysterious promise of its packaging.

She felt unreasonably angry, and when George came back into the room with a mug of tea in each hand she came to a decision. Well, why not? What difference would it make?

'Can you go and get something out of the wardrobe for me?' she said.

'Huh? What am I – your blimmin' servant?' George carefully put the mugs of tea on the bedside cabinet.

'You'll like it. Go on. There's a carrier bag at the back . . . a red one . . .'

Midge took a sip of her tea, and watched George as he walked across to the wardrobe and pulled the door open. Her anger was turning to excitement now, with that thrill of anticipation that only comes from giving away a deeply sworn secret. But there was also a spark of revenge within her. Somehow, somewhere along the line, she had been made a fool of. There had been no need for all the care she had taken, no need to have suffered alone. She could have told George everything right from the start, and brought no harm to anyone. And so now she *would* tell. Maybe he could even come with her when she delivered the Orbis . . .

'Is this the one?' George had found the red bag.

'Yeah. Bring it over here. I want to show you something.'

Telling about it was almost more gratifying than the actual finding of it had been. George sat on the bed, twiddling with the Orbis, his eyes and mouth wide open in fascination. He must have said 'Wow!' about twenty million times.

It was funny, though. Midge told about Tadgemole, and their meeting in the pig-barn, and the letter with the drawing on it. She told about her search for Aunt Celandine, and how amazing it had been to find her, then how difficult it had been to get her to remember anything. She even told about Maglin coming to her window at night and delivering the leather bag –

which definitely got the biggest reaction of all from George. But she couldn't tell about Pegs. There was just no way of making that talking-in-colours thing believable. And Pegs was such a special secret, far more special to her than the object that George now held in his hands. She couldn't begin to explain, even if she'd wanted to. And anyway, George had more than enough information to be going on with. She wondered how Pegs was now . . . whether his injured leg had healed . . .

'But what does it *do*?' said George. 'What's it for? And who *are* they, anyway? Why are they still here?'

'Well, I suppose they're—' Midge started to say something vague, but then she stopped. She stared in silence at the Orbis, as the answer – or some kind of an answer – came to her at last. She hadn't been thinking especially hard about it. But now something had occurred to her for the first time, and her scalp tingled as she tried the idea on George.

'I think maybe they're aliens,' she said.

'*What?* Don't be daft. Aliens don't look like that!'

But Midge saw the puzzled expression that crossed George's face even as he spoke, and she knew what was going through his mind.

'Yeah, exactly,' she said. 'What *do* aliens look like?'

'I know. But . . .' George shook his head, not convinced.

Midge wasn't sure that she was properly convinced either. The Various were so ordinary, in some ways. So simple, and ancient and old-fashioned. And it was plain that they'd been here for decades, centuries maybe. But they didn't *want* to be here. They didn't belong. And when she thought of the Ickri . . . with those wings . . . and of Pegs . . . well, what other explanation made any sense? Pegs was surely from another world. He must be.

'I think there's a kind of round stone,' said Midge. She pointed to the Orbis. 'That fits in there, between those two screw things at the ends. And once they can put it all back together again . . . well, I don't know what happens then. But this is the bit they've been looking for. The Orbis. It's been lost for years and years, and that's why they've been stuck here.'

'Yeah, but what does it *do*?' said George. 'They can't all jump aboard and then shoot off into space on it. They're not *that* blimmin' small.'

'Well I don't *know*!' said Midge. She was getting cross again. 'And to be honest I don't really care any more. All I know is they wanted me to help them find it, and now I have. I'm just going to carry it up to the woods and give it back to them. Then that's it – I'm done. After that it's up to them.'

'When are you going to give it back?' said George. 'This morning? Can I go with you?'

Midge laughed. George looked so keen, and the whole thing was just so ridiculous that she couldn't stay mad.

'Yeah,' she said. 'I was going to ask you.'

'We could take the toboggan. Come back down on the slide. Hey – how are you going to get into those woods anyway?'

Midge laughed again. George was great – you could

tell him anything. And she wished now that she'd told him about all of this a long time ago. He'd never have let on.

'There's a tunnel,' she said.

'Wow! Really?'

'Yeah, really. Now buzz off. I'm going to have a shower. Hey – don't forget your tea.'

'We should be back about five, then,' said Midge's mum. 'Auntie Pat's here till lunchtime, and the builders'll be around all day. You OK?'

'Yeah, I'm fine,' said Midge. 'George and I are going tobogganing again.'

'Are you? Well, just be careful.'

'OK. See you later. See you later, Pat.'

Midge and George hung around the kitchen until most of the grown-ups had gone – Uncle Brian, Midge's mum and Barry all trooping out together. Only Auntie Pat remained.

'We'll see you later then, Mum,' said George.

'Yes. Mind what you're doing – and remember we have to leave at midday. Twelve-thirty at the latest. Hey, have you got a watch on?' Auntie Pat looked up from her sheets of figures.

'Um, no. Didn't bother.'

'But how will you know what time it is? What about you, Midge?'

'No . . . 'fraid not. I've *got* a watch, upstairs, but it needs a new battery.'

'Oh. Well that's not much help, is it? Come on – I need to be away on time. I can't have you just rolling

up when you feel like it . . .' Auntie Pat looked doubtfully at her own neat little wristwatch. 'Um . . . maybe
I could lend you . . .'

'I could take that old travel alarm of Dad's,' said
George. He reached up to the high shelf of the Welsh
dresser. 'That'd be OK, wouldn't it?'

'Um . . . yes. I suppose so. Better than nothing, anyway. But don't just put it in your pocket and forget
about it, all right? Maybe you should take it, Midge.
You've more sense than this one.'

'OK,' said Midge. 'Look – you could even set the alarm
for us. Make it for eleven-thirty. Then we can't forget.'

The cars were pulling out of the driveway as Midge
and George walked down the front path – Uncle
Brian's old banger, followed by Barry's smart new
Saab.

'Come on,' said George. 'We'll just go and pick up
the toboggan. Got the bag?'

'Yeah.' Midge clutched the carrier bag that held the
Orbis. How weird it was to be finally doing this. The
two of them crossed the yard, and made their way
towards the cider barn. They had to wait for a moment
as a dumper truck reversed in front of them, carting a
load of rubble away. The driver gave them a wave of
thanks for not making him stop on their account.

George pulled open the rickety door of the Stick
House and they stepped into the gloomy little building. It was almost empty now, just a few bits of rubbish
remaining. Midge looked around to see if the
Favoured One was here, but she could see no sign.

'I'll just get the— Hey . . . where's the pillow gone?' said George. The red toboggan was propped up in the corner and George walked over to it. 'I left the pillow hanging over it, to keep it off the floor.' He grabbed hold of the top edge of the toboggan and lifted it away from the wall.

Midge took another glance around the Stick House, half wondering where the pillow might be, but also thinking about the kitten . . .

'*Sheesh* . . .' Midge heard the sudden gasp of fright from George, and then the amazement in his voice. 'What are *you* doing here?'

Midge turned round. George was holding the toboggan upright, at an angle from the wall, as though it were a door. And standing behind it, very upright, like a sentry in a sentry box, was Little-Marten.

The shock of finding him there at all was made worse by seeing the state he was in. He looked dreadful. His clothing was torn and filthy, and his big frightened eyes peered out from a face that was streaked with dirt. But he was also alarmingly thin, his cheekbones sharp beneath the taut skin, his head seemingly too big for such a scrawny body. The jaunty little being of last summer had changed beyond belief.

'My God . . . what's happened to you . . .' Midge couldn't help the words from coming out.

George's reaction was rather different. 'You're standing on my pillow,' he said. Little-Marten looked up at him and flinched, but remained where he was.

'Shush, George,' said Midge. 'Can't you see he's . . .' She walked across to Little-Marten and crouched down in front of him. 'It's all right,' she said. 'We won't hurt you. Just tell us what's happened. Why are you here?'

Little-Marten's eyes were so full of confusion that Midge wanted to reach out and hug him to her. 'Come on,' she said. 'You know that we don't mean you any harm.'

''Tis Henty.' Little-Marten's voice was so quiet, barely audible, even in the stillness of the outhouse. Midge had forgotten how softly spoken the little people were, and how loud human voices were by comparison. 'She'm in trouble . . . trapped . . .'

'Trapped? How do you mean? Like . . . caught in something?' Midge was picturing snares . . . cages . . .

'Aye, caught.' Little-Marten looked nervously up at George. 'Tangled up in summat. She casn't get free.'

'Tangled up in what?' Midge tried to keep the volume of her voice down. 'Brambles? Rope?'

Little-Marten's eyes flashed back at her as she said the word 'rope'. Almost guiltily, Midge thought. But he said, 'No. She'm in a gurt byre.'

'A byre? You mean a barn? Here, in one of these buildings?' Midge half turned and circled her arm, vaguely indicating their surroundings.

'No. Away. Across the fields.'

'So she's trapped in a barn, somewhere away from here.' There was a jolt of familiarity about this scenario, and Midge immediately thought of the pig-barn on Howard's Hill, where she had first encountered Pegs. It would be very odd if the same thing was happening all over again . . .

342

'Is it the barn up on the hill?' she said. 'The one near the forest?'

'Not that 'un.' Little-Marten seemed to have been ready for this question. ''Tis a big 'un, wi' a red roof.'

Midge looked up at George. 'A red roof? I don't know any barn with a red roof,' she said. George was staring at Little-Marten's wings, obviously so astonished by what he was seeing that he was not really concentrating on what was being said.

'What? Sorry – what?'

'A barn with a red roof,' said Midge. 'Any ideas?'

'I can take 'ee there,' said Little-Marten. 'I knows where 'tis.'

George seemed to pull himself together, and said, 'Um . . . I think maybe he means Dutch Barn. That's got a red roof – sort of. Belongs to Tom Hayne's dad. He's a kid in my year. Tom Hayne, that is, not his dad.'

Midge shook her head. 'I've never seen it,' she said. 'Is it far?'

'I can take 'ee there,' said Little-Marten, again. He stepped from the pillow – which had apparently been used as a makeshift bed – and onto the earth floor. His grubby hand reached tentatively for Midge's sleeve. 'I can take 'ee there now.'

'Well, but what's happened to her exactly – Henty, I mean? Is she stuck in something, or under something?' Midge was torn between the need to do something immediately if Henty was in real pain or danger, and the uneasy sense that this all seemed a bit suspicious. But now that Little-Marten was standing in better light, she could see how red his eyes were, and

343

how drawn and pale his face. He looked as though he had spent the whole night crying.

'She'm . . . she'm . . .' Little-Marten's voice broke, and that was enough for Midge to make up her mind. It was obvious that he was genuinely distraught.

'OK. Come on, George. I don't know what's going on, but we've got to try and help if we can.'

'Uh? Oh yeah. Yeah . . . sure.' George was still looking completely stunned, and Midge judged that he wasn't capable of much in the way of thinking. She went over to the doorway of the Stick House and looked out. The dumper truck was at the nearby end of the old stable block, stationary, but with its engine running. A man was standing with his hand on the tipper bit, and talking with the driver. Neither of them appeared to be in any hurry to go anywhere. They probably wouldn't notice if she and George were to walk past leading an elephant between them, yet she couldn't take the risk of trying to smuggle Little-Marten out beneath their noses.

George appeared at her shoulder, and looked towards the builders. A third man had joined the party now. Didn't they have any work to be getting on with?

'I don't see how we can do this,' said Midge. 'It'd be better if it was raining – at least they'd be working indoors then. They'll be outside all day in this sunshine, and bound to spot us. How can we get him out of here with that lot hanging around?'

'Toboggan,' said George.

'What?'

'Put him on the toboggan. Cover him up with the pillow.'

'Who – Little-Marten?'

'Is that his name? Yeah. Lie him down flat and cover him up. We'll just make out that we're going tobogganing, like we did yesterday. Who's going to care? And in any case, we don't even have to go past the builders. Dutch Barn's over that way.' George pointed towards the distant treeline of Burnham Woods. 'Can't see it from here, but it's on the other side of the weir.'

Midge was amazed. George had gone from being an open-mouthed zombie to a man with a plan in about half a minute. And it wasn't a bad plan, at that.

'How long would it take us to get to it,' she said, 'this barn?'

George shrugged. 'Twenty minutes. What's the time now?'

Midge pulled the travel alarm out of her pocket and flipped open the circular metal case. 'Quarter to ten.'

'OK,' said George. 'Even if it took us half an hour to get there and half an hour to get back, that'd still give us . . . um . . . over an hour at the barn. Can't be *that* serious, can it?'

'Well if it was, then we'd have to get proper help, I s'pose.' Midge blinked at the thought: the very idea of actually trying to explain this to anyone . . . calling her mum on her mobile . . .

'Come on. Let's do it.' George was excited now. He walked back into the gloom, grabbed hold of the toboggan and laid it down on the floor. 'Oi,' he said, 'Little-Marten . . . lie down on that.'

'Eh?'

George put out a guiding arm, but then his finger-tips brushed against Little-Marten's wings. Midge saw George's hand recoil in hesitation and she knew exactly how that felt – the strange texture of the velvety skin, the fragile bones beneath.

'Eh?' Little-Marten looked down at the toboggan, then at Midge.

'It's all right,' said Midge. 'We're going to hide you on this so that nobody can see, and then we can pull you along. George knows where the barn is. You don't have to show us the way.'

''Twould only take one of 'ee, though, to help Henty. No need for t'other to go. No need for he.' Little-Marten looked doubtfully at George, and again Midge sensed that there was something not quite right about all this.

'What? But we need George to show us how to get there. Then you can stay hidden. Just lie down on this. Come on – that's it. No, the other way round. On your tummy.'

Little-Marten looked very unhappy and confused, but they managed to get him lying face down on the toboggan, hands outstretched and gripping the front edge. George picked up the pillow and placed it on top of the prostrate little figure. It was immediately clear that this wasn't going to work. Little-Marten's wings stuck out too much, and his hands and feet were still exposed. The pillow wasn't big enough to cover him.

Try again, then. Kneeling either side of the tobog-gan, Midge and George experimented. In the end they found it best to get Little-Marten to lie on his side, with his knees tucked up and wings folded in. With one hand gripping the front edge of the toboggan and the other hanging onto the underside of the pillow, there was a chance that he might remain hidden.

It took a while, and a lot of manipulation, to get it right, and Midge guessed that George must be feeling as overwhelmed as she was. To be viewing this extra-ordinary little being at such close quarters, manhandling the tiny limbs, tucking those amazing wings out of sight, it was just so unearthly. So . . . alien. And yet most of Little-Marten's clothing might have come from the village jumble sale. The tattered sweat-shirt, cut down to fit and tied at the waist with a plastic belt, the brown woollen leggings that looked as though they had been made from a child's jumper, worn upside down – these things were so homely and recognizable, so plainly of this world. And so ordinary. Only the fur-lined boots, stitched with the seams on the outside, like moccasins, looked as though they had been made from scratch.

'That'll have to do,' said George. He stood up and walked over to the doorway, stuck his head out and quickly pulled it back in again. 'The builders are still there,' he said, 'but they'll be too busy yakking to take any notice of us.'

The toboggan looked a bit odd. Small he might be, but Little-Marten still made a sizeable lump with the pillow on top of him. He couldn't actually be seen, though, and that was the main thing.

'Come on, then,' said Midge. 'In for a penny. You pull the sledge, George, and I'll walk behind just to keep it a bit more hidden.' She crouched down again and patted the pillow. 'Can you hear me? Hang on tight, then. Just keep as still as you can, and don't you make a sound what*ever* happens. All right? We're off.'

They left the Stick House and turned right, moving diagonally away from the builders. The toboggan made a horrible grinding noise as George dragged it across the tarmac, and from the corner of her eye Midge saw that the men were idly grinning at them. There was so little snow around, that was the trouble. If the toboggan had been a canoe it could hardly have appeared a more optimistic enterprise. But there. What business was it of anybody else's?

Once they were through the back gate and heading across the fields, Midge felt able to breathe again – although now there was a new problem. The toboggan was bouncing around so much on the rough grass that Little-Marten must be struggling to stay aboard. Midge

hurried forward a few steps, so that she was walking beside George.

'Better slow down a bit,' she said.

George looked behind him. 'Huh? Oh, right. OK. I felt like a right idiot, with those three blokes watching us. Think they suspected anything?'

'What are they going to suspect – that we're smuggling little people around?'

'Ha. No, s'pose not. God, this feels weird though.'

They managed to cross the first couple of fields without mishap, but at the gateway to the third field it was clear that they would have to stop and think. The ground was all churned-up and muddy – great furrows across it where tractors had been in and out – so that there was no chance of dragging the toboggan through without it overturning.

'We'd better get him off,' said George, 'and risk him walking this bit.' He glanced around him. 'Can't see anyone about.'

'No, let's just pick the whole thing up and carry it.'

'Do you reckon? All right, then. We can give it a go, anyway.'

The toboggan was easy enough to lift, but not so easy to keep level. With George at one end and Midge at the other, they staggered and stumbled their way across the deep muddy channels, and more than once there was a nasty lurch that threatened to tip Little-Marten into the mire. But they got through in the end, carried the toboggan onto firmer ground and laid it down.

Midge crouched beside the toboggan and lifted a corner of the pillow.

'Are you all right under there?' she whispered.

'Aye.' A muffled little sound.

'We need to go that way.' George pointed towards a line of willows. 'Then follow that rhyne along till we get to the weir . . . oh—'

He stopped talking, and Midge straightened up to see what was the matter. At the far end of the field a group of men were working. It looked as though they were stacking wood onto a tractor and trailer. One man was standing on the trailer itself, and the others were heaving logs and branches up to him.

Midge and George watched for a few moments.

'It's OK,' said George. 'We'll just keep going. They won't bother us.'

'Do you want me to pull the toboggan for a bit?' said Midge. She stood up.

'Yeah, if you like.'

George put his hands in his pockets, and the two of them walked side by side. Midge tried to keep to the smoothest ground she could find, continually looking over her shoulder to check that Little-Marten was still with them.

'Tell you what, though,' said George. 'I wish I'd brought a knife or a hatchet or something. How stupid is that? We haven't got a clue what we're going to find, or what we might need—'

'Oh no!' Midge stopped pulling the toboggan. 'I've just realized – the Orbis! I've left it behind!'

'What?'

350

'I must have put it down for a moment . . . in the Stick House . . . ohhhh . . .' Midge groaned and looked back the way they had come. 'I can't believe it! We're going to have to turn round.'

'Well, hang on a minute.' George was staring over her shoulder, giving this some thought. 'It's not as though we're going to *need* it for the moment, and anyway it'll be safe enough for an hour or—' George paused, and Midge saw his eyes widen. 'Oh hell,' he muttered. 'Here's something we *don't* need.'

Midge spun round. There was a dog – a big black-and-white thing – bounding up the field towards them. A man's voice cut sharply through the still air. 'Ginny! Gin! Come 'ere!'

One of the workers down by the trailer had separated from the group, and was hurrying after the dog.

'Ginny!' The man shouted again, but it was clear that the dog wasn't going to stop. Midge took a couple of steps sideways, so that she was in front of the toboggan and bracing herself for trouble. In another few moments the dog was upon them, a flurry of black and white, barking and scampering wildly about, mad with excitement.

'Get away!' George shouted and waved his arms around, trying to head the dog off in another direction, but already the creature was snuffling at the toboggan. There was a squawk of alarm from beneath the pillow, a wriggle of movement, and this set the dog off into an absolute frenzy of barking. Midge was terrified that Little-Marten would simply jump up and make a run for it. She screamed at the dog and tried to grab its collar – a stupid thing to do with a strange animal, but she didn't care. The dog danced away from her, still barking, then rushed in again, desperate to get at whatever was beneath the pillow.

'It's all right! It's all right – she won't hurt you!' The man came running up, red-faced and pouring sweat. 'Ginny! *Ginny!* Come *here!*' He chased after the dog and managed to get hold of its collar. 'Phew! Sorry about that. Blimey . . .' The man was young, but quite overweight, and he had to pause for breath, running the sleeve of his thick checked shirt across his brow.

'Now just calm down, whoa-whoa-whoa. Shush!' The idiot dog was still barking and trying to get at the toboggan. It was clear that the man had very little control over it and Midge was furious.

'What's the *matter* with the stupid thing?' she shouted. 'Get him away from us!'

'Hey-hey-hey! She's only playing. Just curious, that's all.' The man was looking at the toboggan, very obviously curious himself.

'I don't care!' Midge yelled. 'You should keep it on a lead if you can't . . . if you can't . . .' She felt like giving the dog a good kick; the man too.

'It's OK, Midge.' George stepped in, and put a hand on her arm. 'It's all right. There's no harm done.'

'That's right,' said the man, and he was beginning to look angry himself now. 'No harm done. But what are you kids hanging round here for anyway – looking for free firewood? This is private property. And what have you got under there, eh?' He nodded at the toboggan. 'Not an axe is it, by any chance? Or a saw?'

'What? No, we're just . . . we're just going on a picnic, that's all,' said George. 'We've got some sandwiches. Chicken,' he added. 'She probably smelled it.'

It sounded very lame, and the man said, 'A *picnic*? In February?' But the dog was wriggling around and whining, still trying to get free, and the effort of holding her back must have been tiring on the arm. At any rate the man said, 'Well rather you than me – and you don't exactly look like log rustlers, I must say. But go and do whatever you're doing somewhere else, OK? We're trying to work here. Come on then, Ginny. Back to it, eh? Come on, gal.' He dragged the dog away and started to walk her down the field. After a few yards he stooped and picked up a stick, let the dog sniff it, and then hurled it in the direction of the tractor and trailer. The dog went careering after the stick, overshot by a mile, and had to double back in order to retrieve it.

'Ruddy thing,' George muttered. 'I thought we'd had it then.'

Midge watched as the dog brought the stick back to the man in the checked shirt. Her heart was banging in her chest and she couldn't say anything for the moment. The man threw the stick for a second time, and away went the dog. Once she felt sure that the wretched beast had forgotten them, Midge sank down onto her heels and rested her hand on the toboggan. Another glance down the field and she risked a quick peek beneath the pillow.

She could actually feel the material quivering.

Little-Marten squinted up at her, plainly scared out of his wits. He was shaking, huddled into a ball, his hands clasped together. His face looked very white beneath the streaks of dirt.

'I casn't . . . I casn't . . .' he mumbled, his voice tiny and breathless.

'It's all right,' Midge whispered. 'They've gone. We'll be OK now – promise. Just hold on a bit longer, and we'll soon be there.'

How soon, though? Midge stood up and looked back the way they had come. Should they turn round?

George said, as though he'd been reading her thoughts, 'We're about halfway. We might as well keep going.'

Midge shook her head and sighed. 'OK.' She stooped and grabbed hold of the toboggan rope. 'You were great, though. Brilliant, actually. I'd never have thought of saying that about a picnic.'

'Don't think he believed me. Come on, then. Over there, by those willows.'

They reached the bank of the rhyne at last, hauled the toboggan up it, and walked parallel to the broadening stream. The grass on top of the bank had been trodden down by the feet of fishermen, so that there was a fairly smooth pathway leading towards the weir.

Long before they got there, they could hear the roar of water, and George said, 'It's up pretty high, I reckon.'

And so it turned out to be. Midge and George stood on the banks of the weir for a while, gazing at the pounding arc of water, hypnotized by the gouts of froth that endlessly circled the dark pool below.

'Too risky to drag the toboggan across the planks,' said George. 'Or carry it. He's going to *have* to walk this bit.'

'Yes. How far's the barn, then?' said Midge.

'It's just over there.' George pointed to a belt of trees beyond the weir, and Midge followed the direction of his hand.

'Oh, yeah.' She could see a reddish-coloured roof, curving above the treetops. Not far.

They took a good look about them, made sure that there was nobody in sight, and then Midge knelt down to gently lift the pillow from Little-Marten. He was still huddled in a ball, and looking more vulnerable than ever.

Midge reached out and touched the small hands, gently enfolding them in her own. 'Don't worry,' she said. 'We're at the weir. It's really not far to go now, but you're going to have to walk across the planks, Little-Marten. Can you do that?'

As Midge brought Little-Marten's hands away from his face, she was horrified to see that there was a great red welt around his throat. The skin was raw and bruised, little pinpricks of blood showing beneath the exposed flesh. In the darkness of the Stick House she hadn't noticed it, but out here in open sunlight it was unmissable. Something, or somebody, had very nearly strangled him. Was this how Henty was caught? Snared?

'What . . . what's happened to your neck?' Midge sat

355

back on her heels as Little-Marten hauled himself upright. He got painfully to his feet and stumbled from the toboggan, looking wildly about him, pushing back his long brown hair with trembling fingers. His breathing was fast, and his dark eyes looked distracted.

'No. No. I casn't do this . . . casn't do it. 'Tain't right.'

'What? You mean the water? No . . . don't worry. We'll make sure you're safe.' Midge was aware of George standing beside her. 'Tell him, George. We'll look after him, won't we?'

But George said, 'What're all those marks on his neck? What's happened to him? Did the dog get him?'

The dog? That hadn't occurred to Midge. It didn't look much like a dog bite, though.

'Little-Marten . . . Little-Marten . . . listen.' Midge reached out and caught hold of Little-Marten's wrist. 'You have to tell us what's going on. What happened to your neck? Is that . . . is that what's happened to Henty too?'

Little-Marten's eyes met hers. He stared at her for a moment, and nodded. 'Aye . . . aye . . . to Henty. She'm tied . . .' But then he was pulling away, struggling to escape her grasp.

'Tied? You mean tied up? But how?' Midge hung on as one more question occurred to her. 'Who? Little-Marten – tell me who's done this.'

Little-Marten yanked his arm free. 'Scurl! 'Tis *Scurl*! He've got her . . . over in that gurt byre . . . and I be supposed to take 'ee to 'un . . . but I casn't. I casn't do it! Don't 'ee see?'

'*Whaaat?* Scurl's not . . . he can't still be . . . Wait! Just wait a moment!'

But Little-Marten was backing away. He dodged past George, turned, and scuttled towards the planks that spanned the weir. Midge jumped up and ran after him, still clutching the pillow, with absolutely no thought as to what she was doing.

'Hang on a minute, Midge!' George's startled voice called out to her, but Midge took no notice. By the time she set foot on the weir bridge, Little-Marten was already halfway across, arms and wings outstretched for balance. Midge took a couple of hurried steps forward, then saw that there were still some patches of ice on the wooden boards ahead of her, the last remnants of the snowfall. Sense prevailed and she slowed her pace, taking each step carefully and trying to ignore the pull of the rushing water beneath her.

She looked up as she reached the metal stanchions, and saw Little-Marten weaving his way into the bramble bushes that spilled across the other end of the plank bridge. Then she stopped. What was that? George was yelling at her – 'Get down, Midge! Get down!' – and there was some sort of scuffle going on in the brambles up ahead. She couldn't see properly – the heavy locking gear was in the way. What? More voices . . . shouts and curses . . .

Midge hesitantly reached out for the nearest of the stanchions and drew herself closer to it, peering through the angled gap between the twin uprights, trying to watch the movement in the bushes that spread along the far bank. 'Agh!' Little-Marten reappeared away to the left, stumbling forward onto his knees, as though he'd been pushed. Midge ducked behind the machinery, then peeked out again.

And then, as she moved sideways in order to get a better view, she saw Scurl.

He emerged from the bushes and began picking his way along the opposite bank. He had a bow and arrow in his fist, and he was looking straight at her.

Midge clung to the cold metal for support. Her legs felt too weak to hold her up. Scurl! It couldn't be . . . it just couldn't . . .

Chapter Twenty-five

Panic jolted through her, and her muscles came back to life. For a moment she was tensed and ready to run – but then the heart went out of her and she was helpless once more. Running would do no good. The locking gear was her only protection, and if she moved away from it she would be more exposed than ever. Yet if she simply stayed where she was, Scurl would eventually reach the end of the plank bridge and so have a clear view of her.

He was getting closer. The brambles snagged at his tattered clothing, caught at his legs and ankles as he edged along the weir-side bank, but he kept his eye fixed on hers and his bow and arrow drawn. Midge clutched her pillow to her and shrank behind the rusting stanchions, waiting for the inevitable.

No. She must think. *Think.* Maybe she could reason with him. But one look at Scurl's wild appearance told her that this creature was beyond all reasoning. His hair was long now, pushed back from his bony forehead in great straggly hanks, and his grey beard looked matted with filth. Not once did he blink or allow his gaze to falter, but held her in his eye like a bird of prey . . . a snake . . . a look that was as hypnotic as the swirling waters of the weir-pool below . . .

Midge tore herself away and glanced behind her, searching for George. He was lying on his stomach, flat out in the rough wet grass near the end of the plank bridge.

'Get down!' He signalled to her with his arm. 'Down!'

But Midge was still frantically casting around for ideas, some way out of this. She looked down at the weir-pool. What if she jumped? No, that was stupid. Maybe she should just turn and run after all . . . risk the arrow that would come flying after her . . . hope that it might miss. She looked back at Scurl and knew that he knew what she was thinking. He was standing still now, arrow full drawn, just waiting for her to break cover.

And what other choice was there? Midge put her hand flat against the metal upright, ready to turn and push herself off to a running start . . . if only she dared do it. But then some slight movement off to the right caught her attention – a small figure, standing among the low briars, leaning forward to see what was happening. It was Henty.

The Tinkler girl looked towards her, pale face solemn and anxious. There was something odd about the way she stood, awkward and unnatural, her hands clasped together in front of her. She hopped sideways, a clumsy movement, and her face twisted with pain as she did so. Then Midge saw, and realized, what the matter was. Henty was tied up – her wrists and ankles bound in orange twine.

Scurl's work, obviously. What did he *want*? Midge's fear began to turn to anger. Any thought she had of running away had gone. She *couldn't* leave now. Both Henty and Little-Marten were at the mercy of this mad creature, and if she were to somehow escape he would surely take his vengeance upon them.

So this had been a trap all along. Scurl had used Henty as bait, and had sent Little-Marten to lure her away from the farm . . . to find her, and bring her to this. If she had reached the end of the bridge without any warning, it would all have been over.

Now she understood. But she still didn't have a clue what she was going to do – and Scurl was on the move again.

Midge peered around the stanchions, watching as Scurl continued to thread his way through the low tangle of briars at his feet. There would come a point, just before he reached the plank bridge, where the locking gear would block his view almost entirely. That would be the moment to run, thought Midge. Except that now she couldn't run. Did Scurl know that? Was he guessing that she wouldn't leave Little-Marten and Henty to their fate? And where *was* Little-Marten anyway? Midge looked around until she spotted him, just visible behind one of the bramble bushes. Still on his knees, clearly too terrified to move.

Scurl was almost at the bridge. His eye was upon her, as it had been all along, but just for a second his glance flickered to one side. He was judging the distance that he would have to cross with her out of his sight. For the first time, Midge felt that she had some slight advantage over him – not because she intended to run, but because she had seen his moment of uncertainty.

'It's all right,' she shouted. 'I'm not going anywhere, you little creep!' Her voice rang out above the roar of the waterfall, and she saw Scurl's brief reaction – a twitch of surprise on his ugly face.

Again he glanced sideways at the bridge, then back at her. And again. Then he jumped. In a flash he had leaped the couple of paces from the weir-bank and clambered up onto the bridge. He was to the right of the locking gear now, standing on the corner of one of the wooden planks. That was it. He had her in his sights.

Midge pushed herself as tightly as she could against the metal stanchions, seeking whatever protection she could find. She realized that Scurl was still hampered by the briars that tumbled across the planks. They were all around his feet and legs, and banked up high on his right. He couldn't move any further sideways, and so his line of vision was not yet perfect. But with just a few steps forward he would be onto the bare planking. And from then on he could shoot her at will.

She saw him glance at the pillow. The pillow . . .

Midge hadn't given it any thought. Could she use the pillow for protection? Would it stop an arrow?

'Get back, dammee!' Scurl's sudden yell made her jump. He swung the bow sideways, no longer pointing it at her but at something beyond her shoulder. Midge looked quickly behind her and then back at Scurl. In that instant she'd seen George drop to the ground. *Shot?* No . . . the arrow was still in the bow – and trained on her again. Midge raised the pillow in front of her, desperately trying to cover the half of her body that wasn't hidden behind the stanchion.

Her wrists and arms kept making little jerking movements. She fought to keep the tip of the arrow in focus . . . weaving her head from side to side . . . ready to duck . . . waiting for the moment . . .

But the moment didn't come. Why? Why didn't he just go ahead and do it? Even in her terror, Midge began to realize something: Scurl had only got one chance at this. If he were to shoot and miss, then he would have lost his control over her. She could rush forward . . . try and grab the bow before he could use it again. In fact she and George together could very probably overpower him. Scurl was all alone – no gang around him now – no other archers to back him up. All he had was that bow and arrow, and perhaps one shot at her. He had to be certain . . .

Brrrrrrrrr . . . rrr . . . rrrrrr . . .

The sound was so startling, so unfamiliar, that for a moment Midge thought it was something to do with her attacker. She stared at Scurl in bewilderment, saw him crouch a little lower, teeth bared. Then she realized what was happening and delved frantically into the pocket of her fleece. *Brrrrrr!* The sound grew even louder as Midge drew out the travel alarm. On and on it went, the high-pitched ringing sharp and insistent above the dull roar of the weir. Midge fumbled with the brass winding keys. How did you turn the wretched thing off? *Brrrrrrrrr* . . .

She found the button at last, and the noise stopped dead. Midge didn't know what else to do, so she just held out the clock in her right hand for Scurl to see. She didn't want him to think that it was a weapon. The old-fashioned object dangled from her fingers, brass case hanging open so that the winding keys were exposed, sunlight glinting on the curve of the glass. Twenty-five past ten, the hands said. Hadn't it been set for half-eleven?

Scurl kept the bow trained upon her, but his eyes strayed to the metal clock. Midge was already trying to think of some way of explaining, searching for words that would assure Scurl that there was no threat here.

'What be that thing?' Scurl's angry voice rose above the crash of the weir. 'Some Gorji trickery?'

'No, it's . . .' Midge was still hoping to show Scurl that the clock was not harmful in any way. But at the same time she could see that he was curious. His attention had been deflected, if only for a moment. Perhaps she could somehow extend that moment . . .

And then a flash of true inspiration shot through her. She grabbed at the idea, spoke without even thinking.

'Don't you know what it is?' she shouted. 'You've been searching for it long enough. It's the Orbis.'

'What did 'ee say?'

'I said this is the Orbis. I've found it.'

She waited . . . waited for his sneer of disdain, waited for him to tell her that he knew full well what the Orbis looked like and that it bore no resemblance to this piece of Gorji rubbish.

But Scurl didn't speak. He looked at the clock again. Then he lifted one of his feet, shook it clear of the brambles and took a deliberate step forward.

'And if you come any closer,' said Midge, 'I'm going to drop it in the water.' She extended her right arm so that the travel alarm was dangling beyond the edge of the plank.

Did Scurl believe any of this, or care? She couldn't tell. But he remained where he was at any rate. Midge half turned her body, shifted her stance so that she was ready to run either forwards or backwards depending on what happened next. Scurl regarded her, his eyes taking in the pillow, the position of her feet, the alarm clock dangling above the water. He was a hunter, and like a hunter he was prepared to wait for his best opportunity.

But then his thinking seemed to change. He nodded, and lowered the bow a little.

'Well, if that be the Orbis, maid, we'd best parley. Why did 'ee bring it here – to give to I?'

'Yes,' Midge improvised as best she could. 'To give to you . . . if you want it.' She brought her arm back towards her.

'Then give it,' said Scurl. 'Or do I come and take it?' He lifted his foot as if to step further forward, and Midge immediately hung the travel alarm over the torrent once more.

'No!' she shouted. 'You've got to give me something in exchange.'

'Ah.' Scurl moved back. 'I didn't think as 'twould come for naught. What would 'ee trade for such a bauble then?'

'You know what I want. You have to let us go free – all of us.'

'Agreed, then.' Scurl didn't even hesitate. 'Give me the Orbis and I'll not touch 'ee. Any of 'ee.'

Was he mocking her?

'You mean . . . you'll just let us go?'

'Aye. Now give me the Orbis.'

Their voices rang back and forth above the tumble of the water.

'But how do I know you won't shoot me if I do?'

'Well, thass just it, maid. Thee ain't likely to trust old Scurl, I reckon, so we don't get very far, do us?' He was playing with her, Midge was sure of it. Just playing for time. But then so was she.

'All right. Let Little-Marten untie Henty. Give your bow and arrow to him, and then I'll give you the Orbis.'

Scurl laughed outright at this. Midge could see his sharp yellow teeth beneath the greasy beard. 'Now that be going just a little too far down t'other path, maidy. Give my bow to the Woodpecker? And what do 'ee think he might do wi' it? No. But don't let I stop 'ee talking. I be enjoying myself – and still willing to hear 'ee out.'

Midge tried to think. There must be some way of doing this, some suggestion she could make that

366

would test whether Scurl was serious or not. He wasn't going to just give up the bow and arrow. It would leave him with no hold over her, and in too much danger. How badly did he want the 'Orbis'? He didn't seem very bothered about it, but then maybe that was the whole idea.

'Look,' she said, 'the Various have been trying to find this thing for years and years. You know how important it's supposed to be. If this was yours then you could take it to the forest, and . . . and everyone would be very proud of you for finding it. They'd forget what you did, and forgive you and everything. They might even make you King or something, for all I know. It has to be worth letting us go in exchange.'

Scurl had stopped laughing now. ''Tis thee that put me out here, maidy, to rot and to starve – as all my company did rot and starve – and I s'd be glad to put an end to thee in return. Aye, and I've tried to do it more 'n once. I casn't stand to look at 'ee, nor these rag-tags that hang by thee, nor any such traitors. But I'll tell 'ee this true. If I was to hold the Orbis then I'd give up my hold on thee, and never think on 'ee again. Now there's my word on it. Find the way, and I'll make the bargain.'

Midge had seen enough of Scurl to know that his word was hardly to be trusted, but she wanted to believe him nevertheless. He made no attempt to hide his hatred of her, yet he would put that hatred aside for the sake of something that meant more. She had to make this work. It was their only chance.

'What about this then,' she said. 'Let Little-Marten

untie Henty, and let them come over to this side of the weir. Then put down your bow and arrow, on the bridge, where you're standing now. And then come and meet me here in the middle and I'll give you this.'

'No,' said Scurl. 'For as soon as I got to the middle, thee'd all turn tail and run – and take the Orbis with 'ee. My bow'd be back here, and I'd lose the lot of 'ee.'

'Well, you think of a better way, then.'

'Woodpecker and the Tinkler stay this side,' shouted Scurl, 'I ain't letting go of 'em. Not till I gets what I want.'

Midge tried to think this through. How could she keep Little-Marten and Henty safe? Maybe if Scurl were to put down the arrow . . . or give it to Little-Marten . . . keep the bow . . .

No, she just couldn't seem to find any way of . . .

'Tell 'ee what I'll do,' Scurl's harsh voice called out again. He took the arrow from the bow, and held both of them up for Midge to see. Then, with a sudden swing of his arm, he flung the bow far out into the weir. Midge watched in astonishment as the bow twirled out across the water, a bright spinning arc, to be swallowed up into the tumbling foam. She couldn't believe it.

'There. What do 'ee think to that?' Scurl was grinning at her. 'Now thee've naught to fear. But hark 'ee – I've still got this 'un.' He held up the arrow in his fist. 'Aye, and more like it. So if either of 'ee try to come at I – thee or that other Gorji snip – then thee s'll find I've a sting yet. And if 'ee were to run, or keep the Orbis from me, then I've still got the Tinkler maid.

She ain't going anywhere, nor Woodpecker neither, not whilst she'm snared. And I s'll stab this arrow through her eye, or worse, I can promise 'ee, if there be any Gorji tricks. Woodpecker!' Scurl turned round and shouted for Little-Marten. 'Come up here – away from that maid! Get theeself up here, where I can sithee!'

Little-Marten was still on his hands and knees beside one of the bramble bushes. He rose hesitantly to his feet, but remained where he was, looking completely dazed.

'Up here, dammee!' Scurl watched for a moment as Little-Marten began to stumble forward, then he turned back to Midge.

'Now then, maidy. Here be the way of it. I s'll come to thee – and I warn 'ee, thee'd best not run. Then we shall make our trade – the arrow for the Orbis. Agreed?'

Midge couldn't get her thoughts straight. This was all moving too quickly. She needed to work this out, but she was being given no time. Already Scurl was beginning to step forward.

'Don't trust him, Midge!' George's voice called out from behind her.

'Stay out o' this!' Scurl roared back. 'And stay down! I ain't coming across with two of 'ee on the bridge!'

'It's all right, George, he can't hurt me,' said Midge. But her words sounded more confident than she felt. *Could* he stab at her with that arrow?

'Hold the arrow the other way round,' she shouted to Scurl. 'With the feathers pointing towards me.'

369

Scurl nodded. 'Agreed, then.' He held the arrow by the tip, loosely pinching it between finger and thumb so that it dangled harmlessly downwards, the feathers tilted in Midge's direction.

Midge was still nervous, still trying to see how Scurl might use the arrow to harm her. He couldn't shoot her with it, and she didn't think he would be able to throw it hard enough to do much damage. She still had the pillow clasped to her body if he should suddenly try to stab at her. Would he really risk losing what he was after just for the chance of wounding her? Would he have thrown the bow away like that, if he wasn't serious about trying to do a deal? No, he had kept the arrow for his own defence, not to attack her. Once he had what he wanted he'd go away, surely? And as long as she and George stayed here, Henty would be safe enough.

'Come on, then,' she called to him. 'But keep the arrow like that.'

He looked so awful, that was the trouble. As Scurl stepped out above the pounding waters and drew closer to her, she saw how disgusting he really was. His hair and beard were matted into great clumps, solid with grease, and there were fingermarks smeared all down the front of his leather jerkin. Around his feet and legs were wrapped bits of old sacking, cross-tied with orange binder-twine. As he spread his tattooed wings and edged along the planks towards her, Midge caught the animal scent of him – strong as a monkey house. It turned her stomach over, filled her with fear and revulsion just to be anywhere near him, but at the same time she couldn't help feeling a stab of pity for this terrible creature. He looked so completely derelict.

Then she caught sight of the oilskin quiver, slung around his back. She'd forgotten about that.

'Those other arrows,' she said, pointing. 'I don't want them near me. Put them down.'

Scurl said nothing, but once again he did as he was asked. With his free hand he unslung the quiver, bringing the leather strap over his head and lowering the bundle onto the planks at his feet. Then he stepped over the object.

'Bist ready?'

'Yes.'

Scurl was almost within reaching distance now. Every sense in Midge's body was alive, straining to stay sharp. She was aware of the crash and rumble of the weir beneath her . . . the anxious figure of Little-Marten hovering near the other end of the bridge . . . Henty, white-faced and helpless among the briars . . .

She knew that George would be tensed and alert on the bank behind her, waiting, trying to be ready for whatever might come. There was nothing more she could do but get it over with.

Midge gripped the pillow closer to her body and leaned forward, holding the clock out towards Scurl. Her hand shook with nervousness, and the scuffed and battered little object looked pitifully unconvincing in the bright sunlight.

But Scurl didn't even glance at it. His eyes were on her, and they were still the eyes of a predator, unblinking, fierce in their concentration.

'Take it,' he said, and held the arrow out, raising it so that the feathered flights were pointing towards her. Midge hesitated. Unless she let go of the pillow she would have to take the arrow in the same hand that the clock was in. She didn't want to do that in case he grabbed her, but nor did she have any intention of dropping the pillow.

She shook her head. 'No. I'm going to have to put the cl— the Orbis down.'

It was a gamble. Midge lowered herself into a half-crouching position, feeling horribly vulnerable. Her eyes were almost at Scurl's level as she let the alarm slip through her fingers. It tumbled forward onto the boards with a soft clunk. Midge quickly stood up again.

'*Take* it.' Scurl thrust the arrow towards her. He still showed no interest in the clock. Midge didn't want the arrow – didn't want even that minimal contact with this awful being – but this was the deal that they had struck, and the look in Scurl's eye told her that she had no choice. She reached out and grasped the arrow, feeling the bristly texture of the trimmed feathers sharp against the palm of her hand.

Scurl didn't immediately let go of his end. He resisted her pull just for a moment – enough for Midge to know that it was deliberate, and enough for her to know that she'd made a mistake. As Scurl released his hold on the arrow, he took a step forward, placed his foot next to the travel alarm – and kicked it into the weir.

The clock skittered across the boards and was

immediately gone, lost in the broil of froth and spray.

Midge was still frozen in position, holding the arrow out in front of her like a fencer. She looked down in horror at the water, then back at Scurl. What was he—?

'Dost think me a *fool*?' Scurl roared. His red face danced just beyond the sharpened point of the arrow. 'Dost think I don't know yellow-metal when I sees it? And glass? These be *Gorji* things! Gorji work!'

He'd known all the while, then. Right from the very start he'd known, and had played her along in order to get as close to her as he could.

Midge felt her legs going. She tried desperately to keep the arrow upright, pointed at Scurl's face. It was her only chance. Just keep jabbing . . . and jabbing . . .

Scurl retreated, but remained calmly beyond her reach. He let her take a couple more feeble little stabs at the air, then he hitched aside his leather jerkin, crooked an arm behind his back – and drew out a knife.

In his hands it looked like a sword . . . some great military thing . . . curved and horrible. Scurl grinned at her.

'Now we be matched,' he said.

Midge thought that she would faint. The dizzying roar of the water was all around her, and the sunlight seemed blazingly bright. She saw the arrow drop from her helpless fingers and bounce towards the edge of the planking.

'Thee'd best run, maidy.' Scurl's voice was like a whisper in her ear.

'No!' Another voice, shouting, from far away. Henty. 'Don't run! Don't show your back to him!'

Don't run? Midge looked at the knife. Scurl was changing it from one hand to the other, holding it by the blade now, raising it high as if to throw it. She turned from him and felt the pillow slide from her grasp. Don't run? But she must. She must run and run . . . faster than a knife could fly . . . faster than it could cut through the air . . . blade spinning end over end . . .

She must run. And yet she couldn't move.

Little-Marten *was* moving, though . . . dashing along the planks . . . and then flying . . . soaring upwards to land on Scurl's shoulders, grabbing the arm that held the knife. '*Nooooo!*' Midge heard his furious yell – and felt the boards tilt beneath her. She saw Scurl and Little-Marten tumbling sideways, locked together in a dark tangle as they fell from the bridge, and knew that she was falling too, helplessly off balance on the rocking planks. Midge flung out her arms as the water rose to meet her, but was then swinging back round and crashing against the boards. She landed on her knees with her arm twisted up behind her. George was there, gripping her wrist, hauling her back to safety.

'Agh . . . agh . . . let go. Little-Marten . . .' Midge gasped, and staggered to her feet, frantically scanning the weir. She heard Henty's screams from the other bank, but couldn't take her eyes from the seething waters.

'There!' shouted George. 'Over there!'

A head had bobbed up, midstream. It disappeared

for a moment, then came up again, sweeping away from the main current and into the slow circling eddy at the far side of the weir-pool. A clumsy splash of arms and wings and the head turned round. Scurl. He cursed and spat, thrashing at the water, his attempts to stay afloat hampered by the fact that he still held the knife in his hand.

'He's gone! Little-Marten's gone!' Midge was beside herself with anguish. She tried to push past George, but George shouted, 'No! Look!'

And there he was – Little-Marten – miraculously coming to the surface in a flurry of movement, coughing and spewing water, not two feet from Scurl. He was facing the opposite bank, and immediately began trying to paddle towards the heavy clumps of reeds that grew there, grabbing at the water in panicky little strokes.

Little-Marten was obviously unaware of the danger that was right behind him. But Midge saw it, and grabbed George's arm in horror as she realized what was about to happen. Scurl gave a great surge forward, lunging out with his free hand and grasping at Little-Marten's ankle. The two of them disappeared for a moment, and when they rose again Scurl was roaring with fury. He lifted the knife high into the air, plunged it into the foam, lifted it a second time . . . and then his whole body seemed to scoot sideways, propelled across the weir-pool by a hidden force.

The waters heaved and the long pale flank of some great creature broke the surface, a glistening torpedo of solid muscle, delicately mottled in green and white.

Up it rose, wheeling majestically through the sunlight, diamond droplets scattering heavenwards from the lazy flick of its broad tail. Its motion was smooth and unhurried and unstoppable, the gleaming arc of its body as bright as metal, machine-perfect in its power.

Midge and George were locked in the moment, open-mouthed. The huge pike seemed to hang in mid-air, pausing at the top of its flight, before descending into the boil of the weir-pool.

The monster had shown itself at last. It had arisen from the gloom of its underwater lair to burst upon the brightness of the upper world in a breathtaking display of savage grace. Then with a heavy swirl of its tail it was gone, returned once more to the dark mysteries of reed and river-bed.

And Scurl was gone with it. A single gurgling scream, and Scurl was pulled beneath the waters, his white face fading into darkness like a moon behind the clouds. Nothing remained but a rising string of bubbles, and a final ripple broadening across the pool.

Into the blank vacuum that followed came the rush of the weir, and the sound of Little-Marten. He was still there, still trying frantically to stay afloat, and it was his loud kicking and splashing – together with Henty's screaming – that dragged Midge and George from their shocked state.

They ran across the bridge and scrambled through the bramble bushes in order to get down to the water's edge.

'He's all right!' Midge shouted in Henty's direction

– although she could no longer see her. 'Don't worry. We'll get him!'

'You go and help her,' said George. 'It's OK. I can pull Little-Marten out.'

'Shall I?' Midge was reeling, helpless and uncertain, as she looked across at the weir-pool. Little-Marten was among the rushes now, and already more or less safe. 'All right, then.'

Midge threaded her way through the bushes as quickly as she could, though all her movements were clumsy and disconnected. She was surprised by Henty coming the other way. The Tinkler girl had apparently managed to break free, and was still untangling her-self from trailing lengths of orange binder-twine as she went. Midge could see what the effort had cost, though. Henty's wrists and neck were red raw where the twine had cut into her, and there were a couple of nasty bramble scratches down the side of her face, beaded with blood.

'Henty – are you all right?'

'Aye . . .' Henty fought to catch her breath. 'But Marten . . . Marten . . .'

'He'll be fine. Come on. Can you walk – do you want me to carry you?'

'No. I can walk.'

They stumbled down to the weir-bank to find George leaning out over the reeds, reaching towards Little-Marten with a long willow branch. 'Just hang on to this,' he was saying. 'I'll do the rest.'

Little-Marten grabbed the far end of the branch, clung on tight, and in a few moments George had hauled him staggering and splashing through the reeds and back onto firm ground. Henty ran straight to him and took him in her arms, soaked through though he was and plastered in river mud. The two of them clung together for so long that George started to get fidgety.

'Come on,' he said to Midge. 'Let's go and find that pillow. We can rub him down a bit with that.'

'What? OK.'

They walked back up to the bridge and stood there for a while, looking down into the endlessly foaming water. Midge had to lean against the locking gear as reaction to all that had happened began to set in. She felt horribly sick and shaky. Her mouth filled with water and she had to keep swallowing.

'That was awful,' she said. 'Just . . . awful . . .'

'I know.' George's voice sounded normal, but his face was very pale. He shook his head and let out a deep breath. 'Old Whitey,' he said. 'I just can't believe that he's really . . . real. Really down there. And he's huge. Big as a pig, just like Dad said. *God*, that was horrible, though. When he—' George stopped for a moment, gazing out across the weir, remembering. 'And when you were up here with Scurl, that was horrible too. I couldn't believe what Little-Marten did. He was amazing. I thought you were going in with them, though.'

'Yeah . . . so did I.' Midge let out a long breath. She couldn't seem to get her lungs or her heart back into rhythm. 'I would have done too, if you hadn't grabbed me.'

'Huh. I should've been thinking quicker in the first place. But it was like I just *couldn't* think. I didn't know what to do.'

'Nor me. I was too scared to run even. Anyway . . .' Midge let out another juddering breath, and pushed herself away from the stanchion. She had to occupy herself with something in order to keep this whirling dizziness at bay. 'We'd better see if we can get Little-Marten cleaned up a bit. I still don't understand what's been going on.'

'No. I thought Scurl was supposed to have been waiting in the barn.'

'Maybe that's what he wanted us – me – to think. He knew that I wouldn't have been expecting anything to happen here.'

George picked up the pillow, and they walked back across the bridge. Midge stopped and looked down at the quiver of arrows that Scurl had dropped. She put one foot forward, kicked sideways and swept the whole lot into the weir. Her balance was so unsteady that for moment she thought she was going to go with it.

The pillow didn't help much. They rubbed Little-Marten down with it as best they could, but he still looked as bedraggled and mud-smeared as ever. His saturated woollen leggings sagged at the knees and his hair stood on end like a chimney-brush.

'What shall we do with him?' said Midge to George. 'He's going to catch his death out here if we don't get him dried off properly. We can't take both of them back

to the farm, though. Not on the toboggan at any
rate . . .'

'We'm going *home*,' said Little-Marten. He was
shuddering with cold, but his voice was firm – as
though putting an end to any argument in the matter.
'Agreed?' He looked at Henty.

'Yes,' she said. 'But 'tis you that must talk to my
father, for I shan't.'

Midge looked at them. 'Well . . .' she said. 'I think
it'd be best if you did go back. And if you *are* going,
then you can take a message from me. It's very
important. Tell Tadgemole – or Maglin – that I've got
the Orbis. I found it. Tell them that I'm going to bring
it to them later on. Today.'

'The Orbis?' Little-Marten stopped wringing out his
sleeves. 'Thee've *truly* found it, then?'

'Yes. Truly. And I'm going to bring it to the forest.
You can go and give them the news.'

Little-Marten blew out his cheeks. 'Well if that don't

make old Tadgemole smile on us then I dunno what would. Eh, Henty? What do 'ee reckon to that?'

Henty took Little-Marten's arm and looked up at Midge. 'You've been a friend to us,' she said. 'And we shan't forget. If you hadn't a-come . . . then I don't know what would . . . what Scurl would have—'

'Well he's gone now,' Midge cut in. Her mind shied away from Scurl and from the terrible things that had happened. She didn't want to think about it, or talk about it.

'We thought you were supposed to be in the barn,' said George to Henty.

Henty nodded. 'Scurl reckoned Little-Marten might give warning, so he brought me to hide here, where you'd not think him to be. He had the bow – and the knife. I couldn't say aught, nor shout out.'

'I saw 'un, though,' said Little-Marten. 'And tried to call to 'ee. But he got a hold on me . . .'

'Well, it was enough to give me some warning,' said Midge. 'And then George saw him and shouted too. So I knew that *something* was going on over on this side of the bridge. I wasn't that surprised to see him here.'

Little-Marten hung his head. 'I shouldn't ha' done it, though. Shouldn't have brought 'ee. I could've gotten 'ee killed . . .'

'But he'd have got me anyway, in the end.' Midge tried to make him feel better – yet at the same time the thought of Scurl made her stomach tighten again. 'I think he's tried once or twice already. If you and Henty hadn't been around, and none of this had happened, then he . . . he would have just waited until

381

I was on my own some day . . . walking in the fields or something. I wouldn't have known he was still alive until it was too late. So really you've saved me from him.' She took a shaky breath. 'But what are you doing out here in any case? Have you run away?'

Little-Marten looked at Henty. 'Aye. We'd be together, but Tadgemole'll have none of me.'

'What? Why not?'

'I be Ickri and she be Tinkler.' Little-Marten shrugged as if it was obvious.

'Well . . . what difference does that make?'

''Tis like raven and magpie. We ain't o' the same feather.' Little-Marten's teeth were chattering, and Midge thought it better to stop asking questions.

'Listen, then,' she said. 'Go back to the forest and tell them that I'm bringing the Orbis—'

'Tell them *we're* bringing it,' George interrupted. 'I'm coming too.'

'OK, then. *We're* bringing it,' said Midge. 'And then I'll talk to Tadgemole, if you like. He owes me a favour or two, I reckon.'

Henty and Little-Marten looked around the land-scape, uncertain of their bearings. George said, 'The quickest way is just to follow this rhyne. It's a straight line nearly all the way there – see? Stay close to the water and you should be safe.'

Little-Marten took Henty's hand. 'Come, then. We'm away. And I s'll be glad to be out o' this, I can tell 'ee.'

'Don't forget,' Midge called after them. 'We'll come to the tunnel as soon as we can. Make sure there's somebody there to meet us – Maglin or Tadgemole. Doesn't matter which.'

'Aye.' Little-Marten's voice drifted over his shoulder as he and Henty disappeared among the brambles. 'One or t'other shall be waiting for 'ee.'

'Think they'll be OK?' said George, once the pair had gone.

'Yeah. Hope so. And I hope the Orbis is still safe, now that I've promised to bring it to them. Come on. We'd better get back.'

'Do you really want to do this today, though?' said George. He was walking ahead of her as they began to cross the weir. 'I mean, haven't you had enough?'

'Yeah – I *have* had enough. That's exactly it. I've had more than enough, and that's why I want to get it done. It's school again tomorrow, and so there won't be another chance until the weekend. I just don't want to have to be thinking about it any more. I'm going to get it over with. Today. It won't take us long.'

'Well, OK then.' George picked up the toboggan rope and they began the long walk home. 'Hey,' he said. 'What do you think the time is anyway?'

'That's the weird thing.' Midge puzzled over her thoughts for a moment. 'I'm sure the alarm was set for eleven-thirty. I watched your mum do it. But it wasn't even ten-thirty when it went off.'

'Maybe when the clocks get turned back in the autumn, Dad forgot to do that one.'

Would that make any difference? Midge couldn't work it out. And that was another thing: what was she going to say to Uncle Brian about his nice old alarm clock? That she dropped it in the water and lost it?

'I know what we did forget,' said George, after a while. 'The pillow.'

'Yeah, well. Tough,' said Midge. But then a wave of dizziness hit her again, and she said, 'George, is it OK if I hang onto your arm for a bit? I don't feel very good.'

The Orbis was lying on the floor of the Stick House, still safe in its carrier bag, where Midge had left it. She picked it up, waited for George to prop his toboggan against the wall once more, and the two of them walked in silence over to the farmhouse.

'Oh good. You're back.' They entered the kitchen to find George's mum all packed up and ready to go. Her briefcase was sitting on the kitchen table and she was buttoning up her coat. 'I'm finished,' she said. 'Come on, then, George. I need to be away.'

'What?' said George. 'We don't have to go yet, do we? It's nowhere near lunchtime. You said twelve-thirty.'

'I know, but I've had a call from the office. They've got the auditors in, and they want me to go and look at some figures.' Auntie Pat picked up her briefcase.

'Yeah, but I'm not ready yet. There's some stuff I have to do,' said George. 'With Midge.'

'It'll have to wait then, I'm afraid. Come on. Get your bits together.'

'But I can't . . .' George looked at Midge. 'Couldn't we just have another hour? That's all we need. Just another hour.'

384

'Sorry, no. I have to go.'

'Well can't I stay over for the night, then?'

'George will you come *on*. You've got school to-morrow and there's a dozen things to sort out yet. Now let's get cracking.' Auntie Pat was adamant. She moved around to the back of George and crowded him towards the door. George was furious.

'Well, I wish we hadn't bothered to come back at all now! We should have just stayed out there. And now I'm going to *miss* everything. And it's important! How come nothing I ever have to do is as important as anything anyone else has to do? This *always* happens . . .'

'Yeah, yeah. Just keep moving. Cheerio, Midge.' Auntie Pat looked over her shoulder and rolled her eyes at Midge. 'Have a nice peaceful afternoon,' she said. 'And see you at the weekend, I expect.' She reached across George's hunched shoulders and opened the kitchen door.

'Yeah. Bye, Auntie Pat. Bye, George,' Midge mumbled.

Auntie Pat gave George a gentle shove, and they were gone. Midge could still hear George grumbling all the way down the front path and out to the car.

She was alone.

Midge put her carrier bag on the kitchen table and sat down. The place seemed unusually peaceful, no noise from the builders for once. And the room itself was almost eerily quiet, the low hiss of the Rayburn the only sound.

It was the absence of the clock, Midge realized. The fast friendly tick of the little travel alarm – so much a part of Uncle Brian's kitchen – was no more. It lay silenced for ever at the bottom of the weir, down there in the darkness . . . along with Old Whitey . . . and . . .

Midge shivered. She opened the carrier bag and peeked inside, glad of the plasticky crackle that broke the spell. The Orbis looked so out of place in there, too magical an object for such an everyday setting.

It was a shame that George had been dragged off. She wished that he could have been there too, when she handed this thing over. Soon she would take the bag and trudge up Howard's Hill with it, go to the tunnel and give it to whoever was there to meet her – Maglin, or Tadgemole. Or Pegs. She was desperate to hear what had happened to Pegs, and that was another reason for making this journey today. She couldn't wait any longer. Today was the day, and it had to be done – and at least there was no more danger to worry about.

Midge stood up and began to zip her fleece. But her hands were all shaky, and the zip didn't seem to want to connect. Maybe she'd better sit down again, just until her nerves were calmer. Have a glass of milk or something.

Chapter Twenty-six

Henty led the way through the wicker tunnel, hopping from stone to stone as she moved along the stream, trying to keep her feet dry. Little-Marten splashed along behind her, already too tired and wet to bother about using the stepping stones. He had been surprised to find the tunnel gates open and nobody on lookout duty. Then Henty seemed to hesitate for a moment as she reached the circle of daylight ahead. Little-Marten stumbled sideways in order to avoid bumping into her, and saw that there was somebody on duty after all.

It took him a moment to recognize Ictor, captain of the Old Guard, standing close to the tunnel entrance, bow and arrow at the ready.

'Thee've come back, then.' Ictor's manner was cold, unfriendly. 'Where've 'ee been hiding – in a ditch? I'd not be in your boots, Woodpecker, wet or dry. Not by the time your betters've finished with 'ee.' He lowered his bow.

Little-Marten was still wondering why Ictor had been reduced to the post of tunnel-lookout, but thought it best not to ask insulting questions of one who was armed. All he said was 'Maglin'll be pleased enough to see me, I reckon. I've news for him – and for all here. The Gorji maid be coming. And she've found the Orbis.'

There. That altered the superior expression on Ictor's bearded face.

'The *Gorji* maid?' Ictor's pale grey eyes narrowed, and Little-Marten felt powerful in the knowledge that he carried. Maglin would be equally impressed at this news, and would surely forgive him for deserting his Perch.

'Aye.' Little-Marten pulled himself upright. 'She comes to the forest this very day, she and another. They'm bringing the Orbis, and Maglin shall hear of it directly. I'm away to his pod.'

'No!' Ictor held out an arm, barring Little-Marten's passage, and for a moment it seemed a threatening gesture. But then he said, 'Thee'll not find Maglin in his pod.' His voice grew gentler. 'I were talking with him not a moment since. He be . . . walking the bounds.' Ictor withdrew his arm and pointed away to his left. 'Follow on around. Thee s'll overtake him soon enough.'

'That way?'

'Aye. That way – and thee've no need to fear. If the maid arrives, I s'll keep her safe till Maglin comes. But what did 'ee say, Woodpecker – that she were coming with *another*?'

''Tis another Gorji chi'. A lad that be kin to her, I reckon. He means us no harm.'

'So there be two of 'em?'

Little-Marten shrugged his shoulders. 'Aye.'

Ictor scowled, but said, 'So be it, then. I s'll take care o' both.'

Little-Marten felt vaguely hesitant as he and Henty began to move away, but then Ictor said, 'And thee've done well – the pair of 'ee. But mark 'ee, Woodpecker' – Little-Marten turned – ''twould be best if thee spoke of this to none but Maglin. He'd be angered not to learn of it first. Send him here alone, when thee finds him.'

'Aye.' Little-Marten and Henty set off along the trodden path that bounded East Wood. When they were out of earshot, Henty whispered, 'I thought that one were a captain. What does he do standing tunnel-go?'

'Casn't say,' said Little-Marten. 'Perhaps he've fallen wrong side o' Maglin. He were high captain of the old Queen's Guard. Ictor, he be called, and he were brother . . . to Scurl.'

Little-Marten came to a halt. Brother to Scurl . . .

'What?' said Henty. 'What'll he do then, if he learns that Scurl have died? What if that Gorji maid should tell him?'

Little-Marten shook his head. 'Dunno. All here reckoned Scurl to be dead already. Maybe it wouldn't make no difference to 'un one way or t'other.'

'And maybe it would,' said Henty. 'I didn't like his look, I know that. We'd best hurry.'

They quickened their pace, following the path that bordered East Wood, but saw no sign of Maglin. Little-Marten was still soaked through and shivering with the cold.

'I reckon we've missed him,' he said. 'P'raps he've gone back up to the clearing.'

'Ho – Woodpecker!' A shout from above.

They looked up to see a group of Naiad foragers – four or five youngsters – working the high banks above them. Sorrel picking, by the seem of it. Grinning faces took in Little-Marten's dishevelled state.

'Didst have to swim home, then, Woodpecker? Have 'ee been chasing arter eels?'

'Heh. An eel have been chasing *he*, by the look of 'un.'

Little-Marten ignored their chaff. 'We'm trying to catch up wi' Maglin,' he shouted up. 'Did he come this way?'

'Naw. He've not come by here.' One of the lads popped a sorrel leaf in his mouth and chewed on it. 'We should ha' seen 'un.'

Another said, '*I* saw 'un, though, in Royal Clearing, just afore we come down. He were climbing ladder to Counsel Pod. You be on the wrong path, Woodpecker.'

Little-Marten looked at Henty. It was clear that Ictor had misled them. Now they really were worried.

'We'd best give this up and get to Counsel Pod,' muttered Little-Marten. 'And quick as we might. I don't know what Ictor be at, but he don't mean any good by it that I can see. And I don't like the thought o' Midge meeting up with 'un.'

They left the path and began to make their way up through the woods, taking as direct a route as was possible towards the high clearings. It was a hard climb, and in their weakened state they were soon out of breath. Little-Marten's clothing felt clammy, the heavy damp material chafing against his skin. He was exhausted. As they gained the narrow pathway that opened onto Royal Clearing, he said, 'Hold up. I be about done.' He rested his forearm against a birch sapling, and lowered his head for a moment, to ease the dizziness that overtook him. Henty put her hand on the back of his neck, and the touch of her palm was cool and comforting. 'I s'll be right,' he mumbled. 'And soon as we tells Maglin about the Orbis I'm away to my rest, maid or no maid.' But then he felt Henty's fingers squeeze tighter, as if in fear – or warning. Little-Marten looked up to see a blurry figure emerging from the bushes. He shook his head and blinked. It was the mad hag, Maven-the-Green, appearing before them like some creature from a haunty-dream.

'Orbis?' Her voice was thin and creaky, old as the woods themselves. 'What do 'ee say of the Orbis?' She moved a step towards them, her ivy-wreathed head cocked to one side as though the better to hear.

Little-Marten felt Henty grip his arm tighter yet as she shrank close to him. He had seen enough of Maven to at least be familiar with her wild appearance, but for Henty this was clearly more of a shock.

'N-naught.' Little-Marten tried to keep his voice under control. 'We said naught.'

'Come.' Maven's blackened teeth showed as her mouth opened into a hideous smile. 'Thee knows I, Woodpecker.' She reached into the folds of her trailing green rags as though to draw something from within, but kept her hand hidden for the moment. 'And thee knows enough to answer I straight. Now then. The Orbis. Tell me what 'ee've heard o' it. Bist safe, then? And do it come to the forest?'

Little-Marten remained silent. He kept his attention on Maven's hand, knowing full well what that hand was reaching for, and what it might bring down upon them.

'Aye,' said Henty. Yet again she had taken the situation into her own control. 'It comes to the forest this day – with the Gorji maid. We're away to tell Maglin.'

Little-Marten was shocked that Henty would speak so freely. As he turned towards her his eye caught movement in the nearby hazel thickets, a glimpse of something white. Something there, and then fading away. Gone.

But then Maven was speaking again. 'Thee've seen the Gorji child – talked wi' her?' Her fierce eyes gazed upon Little-Marten. 'Let me hear it from thee, Woodpecker.'

''Tis so,' Little-Marten mumbled. 'She've found the Orbis and shall bring it to East Wood tunnel. She'm not far behind us, I s'd reckon. We've to bring word to Maglin – or to Tadgemole. Don't matter which, so the maid said. Either or t'other to meet her there.'

'Either or t'other . . .' Maven's voice was a croaky whisper. 'Then Maglin shall hear of this d'rectly – but 'tis I that shall tell 'un, not thee. Away then, the pair of 'ee. And leave Maglin to me.'

'But . . .' Little-Marten was lost. ''Tis for we to tell this news . . .'

'And now thee've told it.' Maven began to bring her hand from the depths of her ragged gown.

'Then what should us do?'

'I reckons thee should fly whilst thee still can, Woodpecker, and take this maid to her home. Tell thee tales to the Tinklers instead.'

Little-Marten glanced beyond Maven to where the clearing began to open out. He could see the distant heads of Glim and Raim, standing guard at Maglin's pod – close enough to hear him if he shouted perhaps, but too far away to be of any aid.

'Fly, pretty birds . . , fly away home . . .' Maven drew the blowpipe from her gown, and brought it slowly to her grinning mouth. 'Ssssssss . . .' She was hissing like a snake, her hunched and twisted body weaving from side to side. Henty seemed frozen, unable to move, and Little-Marten had to drag her away. He hauled on her arm as he stumbled backwards along the pathway.

'*Henty!* Move theeself!' At last she seemed to come to life, and the two of them scurried off in the direction that they had come. They turned from the path at the first opportunity, wove themselves deep into the thickets and then looked fearfully back towards the clearing. There was nothing to see. Maven had gone.

Little-Marten wiped his muddy brow. 'She'm mazy as a toad, that 'un. And I thought I were going to have to carry thee to get 'ee to move.'

'She'd have done us no harm, though.' Henty was craning her neck, still trying to see through the thickets.

'Done us no *harm?* She'd kill 'ee soon as look at 'ee,

393

Henty! And've done such a thing more'n once. Tulgi
. . . Benzo . . .'

'No. She meant us no harm – I could tell it. What'll
she do, dost think?'

'Hemmed if I cares. 'Tis what *we* shall do that I be
wondering. Casn't get to Maglin . . . nor the Elders . . .'

'We must go to the caves.' Henty sounded as if she'd
already made up her mind. 'And quick as we can.
Come on.'

'Together?' said Little-Marten. 'And me all stinking
o' mud and river-weed? I hoped to be a sight more
spracked up, afore I spoke to Tadgemole.'

'There be more important things to think of,' said
Henty. 'And I should've brought news to my father
straight away. The Orbis belonged to the cave-dwellers,
and he've a right to know of its coming, but 'tis that
maid I be thinking of. I be feared for her.' She took his
hand and together they began to scramble down the
wooded hillside in the direction of the caves.

Maglin watched the faces of the Elders as they sat
together in Counsel Pod, each warming their hands at
the charcoal burner, their staffs propped upright
against the daubed wicker walls.

'What's the matter with 'ee?' Maglin tried again.
'Have 'ee lost thee tongues? We need strategies, plans
against such a day as the Orbis might return, and all I
get from thee be shrugs and mumbles. Am I to act
alone, without the aid of Counsel? If so, then I'll waste
my time here no longer. I've more to look into than
your ugly faces.'

'Counsel?' Crozer was stung to anger at last. 'When did you ever seek counsel from we? 'Tis the hag that gives 'ee counsel now, and 'tis with she that you waste your time. You be chasing the wind, Maglin, as addle-pated as the old crone herself. And what *strategies* do 'ee bring? Naught but empty talk. Your arm has grown weak, aye, and your thinking with it.' Crozer jabbed a bony finger in Maglin's direction. 'Away with 'ee then, and look to yourself! And we s'll see whose ugly face is still among us come next season . . .'

'Crozer . . . Crozer . . .' Ardel reached forward to grab at Crozer's sleeve.

'Come next *season*? Do 'ee think to threaten me, you old wazzock?' Maglin began to rise from his seat, pushing his fists against the wool-sacked floor.

But then some commotion became audible from outside – loud voices in argument – and a judder of movement shook the pod. Someone was climbing the willow ladder.

'Maglin! Bist in there? Get *back*, dammee . . .'

Maglin, already halfway to his feet, glared at Crozer a moment longer then lunged for the oilskin cloth that covered the entranceway. He swept the stiff material aside, narrowing his eyes against the bright-ness of the daylight. Here was Glim, halfway up the ladder, and Raim at the bottom. Both had left their guard posts to come across to Counsel Pod, and both were now struggling to keep a hold on Maven-the-Green.

'She says she've to see thee,' Raim gasped. His spear was lying some distance away, in the wet grass, and

Maglin could guess how it had got there. Glim too was unarmed.

'Let her be,' said Maglin. 'Glim, jump down and give her passage. Let her *be*, I said!'

Glim balanced on the rungs of the ladder, spread his wings and hopped to the ground. Raim released his hold on Maven, and seemed glad enough to do so, coughing a little as he caught his breath. 'Have her, then,' he spluttered. 'And welcome.'

Maven clutched at her dishevelled rags. She waited until the guards had stepped well away from her, then came forward to rest her skinny green hands on the ladder. 'I must speak with 'ee, Maglin.' She peered up at him from beneath twisted hanks of hair. Maglin regarded her, trying to judge her mood and likely actions. 'Thee'd best come up, then.' He held the oil-cloth aside, and turned to look into the darkness of the pod. Three pairs of startled eyes gazed back at him, like owls in a byre. ''Tis Maven-the-Green,' he said, and the eyes all blinked at the same time.

Up the ladder came Maven, her humped back swaying from side to side. She grasped the rim of the entranceway and paused for a moment. 'The day we've looked for be upon us,' she said to Maglin, 'and this be your time.' She stepped inside.

Maglin glanced down at the guards. 'Pick up your spears and wait here,' he muttered. His gaze swept the clearing, and as he allowed the curtain to fall back into place he saw a pale shadow, disappearing amongst the trees on the far side of the open space. It was barely a glimpse, a brief impression before the wintry world was shut out, but Maglin was sure of what he'd seen: the winged horse . . . threading his way among the hawthorns, carrying something . . .

'What?' he said.

'The Orbis, Maglin. I've word of it.' The dry croak of Maven's voice sounded muffled. Maglin turned from the entranceway, and as his sight grew re-accustomed to the smoky darkness he saw that Maven had her back to him.

'The Orbis? What do 'ee know? Tell me.' Maglin moved into the dim glow cast by the charcoal burner.

'To your hand I said the Orbis would come, and so it now shall, if your hand be quick enough to take it. If not, then 'twill go to another – as maybe it should. Be you its rightful keeper, dost reckon? Then thee'd best get to East Tunnel, maister, and hope to meet that maid before someone else do – for I reckon the Tinklers shall know of this afore long. Now there be a warning for 'ee.'

Maglin waited to hear no more. He swept aside the oilcloth and jumped to the ground.

'Glim! Give me your spear. Go to West Wood and collect any archers you can find – you and Raim both. Bring all to the East Tunnel.'

Glim handed over his spear, but looked doubtful, 'I don't reckon we s'd find any archers in West Wood, Maglin.' He pointed away from Royal Clearing, to where distant sycamores rose above the southerly plantations of the Naiad. 'I spoke wi' Aken at sun-high. His company had poor hunting, and were thinking to try for better luck in South Wood. We'd do better to seek there.'

'Go where thee will, then,' said Maglin. 'But be quick about it. Maven!' He turned back towards Counsel Pod. 'Thee'd best follow I on down to . . .'

Maglin realized that he was talking to himself. Curling wisps of charcoal smoke hung about the entrance to the pod, and the heads of the three Elders peered out at him, but of Maven-the-Green there was no sign.

To the tunnel then, and hope to get there before the Orbis should fall into the hands of the cave-dwellers. Who was on guard there? Ictor. He'd know nothing of such things, nor care.

Ictor . . .

Maglin felt the hair tingle at the back of his neck. *Ictor* was at the tunnel. Ictor, who loathed him, but more importantly was known to loathe the Gorji child who was on her way to the forest . . . who might already be here . . .

What a fool he'd been to place one so dangerous and untrustworthy in the very place where the Orbis was most likely to arrive – and in the path of the child who carried it!

Maglin charged through the trees at the edge of the clearing. As the ground began to drop steeply away he spread his wings, and launched himself into the air.

Little-Marten was horribly aware of his own wretched appearance. He knew that he reeked of river-ooze, and could feel the clag of half-dried mud upon his fingers as he pushed back his hair. Nevertheless he tried to bear himself upright before Tadgemole, and to prepare himself for what would come.

'I wonder you set foot in here.' Tadgemole's look was one of cold contempt, the grim lines of his face set hard and unforgiving in the candle-lit shadows. 'Or dare show yourself to me. Is this what you bring my daughter to, you little ditch-rat? Look at her!' His voice echoed around the stone walls of the inner caves, and down the deserted passageways. 'When did she last eat, or sleep in aught but her own rags? 'Tis plain that you've nothing to offer her but the life of a heathen scare-a-crow. Aye, one of your own. And so I was right. Right to keep you from her, and right to—'

'Father, we've no time for this.' Henty drew herself closer to Little-Marten. 'We've not come to argue, but to bring news of—'

'And as for *you* . . .' Tadgemole reached out and laid a hand on Henty's shoulder. 'Do you not *think*, child, of the pain you cause me? Nor care? Why do you find me awake, dost reckon, whilst all here about me are sleeping? Because I can take no rest. By night and by day I worry, knowing that you are out there amongst the Gorji. And not knowing whether you be dead or alive. Is this what I deserve?'

'But you don't *listen*. I bring news – important news – but you won't listen to me. You never do.'

Tadgemole took his hand from Henty's shoulder, and glanced up. Some slight sound drifted through the tunnels, a distant *tap-tap*. But then it was gone.

'Come, then. Let me hear you out. What could be so important as to bring you back to me, when my own heartache was not enough?'

'The Gorji child . . .' Henty began to speak. 'She's found—'

But then the tapping sound could be heard again, closer now. Henty and Little-Marten turned their heads to listen. Along the dark passages it echoed, coming from the direction of the main cave. *Tap-tap-tap-tap.* A steady rhythm . . . faltering for a moment . . . then steady once more . . .

A tall shadow appeared, thrown along the dimly lit tunnel walls that led to the cavern entrance. Its shape was at first confusing, but then became recognizable. And the sound was now recognizable also – *tap-tap-tap-tap* – delicate hooves upon the hard stone floor. Pegs.

The winged horse came fully into view, pausing beneath the entranceway to look at them.

In his mouth he carried a bundle of some sort . . . oilskin . . . leather straps . . .

'Pegs?' said Tadgemole. 'What's this – why are you here?'

Pegs stepped forward. His gait was slightly awkward, the trace of a limp still visible as he crossed the chamber. He stood before Tadgemole and lowered the bundle to the floor. It was a leather pecking bag.

Pegs raised his head and the cavern was filled with colours, and with sounds that had no echo.

I am here to keep my promise to you, Tadgemole. But listen first to your daughter, and to the Woodpecker. Hear what they have to say.

Chapter Twenty-seven

Halfway up Howard's Hill it occurred to Midge that she had better go and look in the pig-barn. Pegs might be there waiting for her, as he had done before. She had heard nothing of him since that day when she was last here, and so she had no way of knowing how badly he had really been injured. She altered direction. Maybe she wouldn't need to go to the wicker tunnel after all.

Midge walked over to the barn doorway, clutching her carrier bag. She remembered how she had brought such a bag with her on her very first visit to this place. An apple it had held then, and a sandwich. Today she carried the Orbis.

'Pegs?'

Her voice sounded flat and strange in the darkness. There was no hint of warmth, no animal smell, and Midge knew straight away that Pegs was not here. The grey tractor had gone now, its absence making the ramshackle building seem more neglected than ever. She wished that George were here to keep her company. Midge patted her pockets, searching for her mobile. Not there. She must have left it on the kitchen table.

It was a relief to step out into the daylight again. Midge turned away from the pig-barn and began the last part of her climb. She stumbled through the coarse winter grass, making her way up and around the hillside until she came to the gully that would lead her to the tunnel. Here she paused for a few moments, staring up at the bare treetops as she got her breath back and wondering if anyone was watching out for her. She could see no sign of movement.

The ground was far wetter than it had been in the summer, and all churned up by the hooves of cattle, so that the gully opened out to form a muddy delta on the hillside. Midge's Wellington boots kept getting stuck in the ooze. It was a struggle to keep upright. But the bed of the stream grew stonier as it narrowed, and so became easier to walk on. Soon she was able to make better progress, stepping from rock to rock until she reached the barrier of brambles that overhung the tunnel.

Something had changed. The tunnel entrance, usually so well hidden, was now visible behind its trailing curtain of brambles. What had happened to the camouflage – the wicker doors so cleverly woven with briars and grasses as to seem part of the undergrowth? Midge peered closer. The doors had been left open. Why? A dog could easily get in there, thought Midge. Or maybe even a man.

She carefully drew aside the brambles, and crouched down to look along the tunnel. Nobody there, as far as she could see. Just a faint semi-circle of light at the other end. But perhaps she should give the agreed signal in any case.

'Briefly parted, soon united.' Her whisper was deadened by the endless trickling of water, and she tried again, calling out a little louder this time. Still nothing.

Had Little-Marten and Henty not found their way home yet? That was possible. Surely there would've been somebody here to meet her otherwise?

Midge thought about it for a moment. Pegs had warned her not to enter here again, but did she really want to trail all the way home and then have to come back again later? No. She had brought them the Orbis, and she was going to hand it over now. Tadgemole or Maglin would be in there somewhere, and either one of them ought to be very glad to see her. And she had to know whether Pegs was all right.

She shuffled further forward, disentangling herself from the briars that snagged at her clothing before properly beginning to make her way along the tunnel stream. It was horrible in here, even more cramped than she had remembered, and her feet were freezing inside her rubber boots. She had to keep putting her free hand out to steady herself, and the wicker walls were slithery wet, icy drips running down her wrist and into the sleeve of her fleece.

Splash, splash, splash. It was agony trying to walk in such an impossibly low crouch, and Midge had to stop about two thirds of the way along the tunnel for a breather. She didn't recall it being quite this difficult to get through before. Maybe she'd grown since last summer. Come on, then. Keep going. *Splash, splash, splash . . .*

Ohhhh . . . the relief of being able to straighten up. Midge emerged into the daylight, took a few steps more, and stood on the large flat rock that lay in the middle of the stream. She put her hands on her hips as she stretched her back and shoulder muscles.

The cold woods looked even more tangled and gnarled than they had in the summer, with little foliage to soften the stark shapes of the twisted trees. But there was the same damp and earthy smell to the place that she remembered from before, like that of old compost – centuries of rotted-down vegetation and leaf mould. Midge gazed upwards, her eyes searching the forested hillside, the bushes and the rocky crags, and finally the higher belt of sycamores and cedars that marked the boundaries of the clearings. It all seemed very quiet. No signs of life that she could see . . .

'Where be t'other 'un, then?'

Midge nearly stumbled from her perch at the sudden sound. The carrier bag swung wildly as she spun round, her arms flailing in an attempt to keep her balance.

'What?'

A figure was standing near the mouth of the tunnel. A bearded Ickri, armed with a bow and arrow. Midge put her hand up to her chest as she tried to catch her breath. Who was he – a guard?

'Open thee ears, Gorji. I said where be t'other 'un?'

The archer raised the tip of the arrow, not pointing it directly at her, but the threat was there, nevertheless.

'What other . . . who?' Midge was confused – and beginning to feel a sense of danger on top of her initial shock. She didn't much like the look of this one, with his chilly gaze and his sneering voice.

'I were told there was to be two of 'ee. You be one. Now where be t'other?'

What was he talking about? Midge couldn't understand him. But there was something very scary in his manner – something familiar. And there was something going on here that didn't feel right. The archer looked away from her for a moment, leaned sideways to quickly glance into the mouth of the tunnel, then turned back towards her. He was obviously expecting someone else.

'Have 'ee no tongue?'

'Huh? Oh . . .' Midge found herself speaking without thinking, some instinct telling her to just play along with this. 'Oh . . . you mean *him*. Yes. He'll be here soon.' What was she getting herself into? The thought of George came into her head. That had been the original plan – that George would be coming here too. Maybe Little-Marten and Henty had arrived here after all, and had said as much.

'Yes,' she said again. 'He shouldn't be long now. What is it . . . what do you want? I'm supposed to be meeting Maglin. Or Tadgemole. Have you seen them?'

The archer looked at her only briefly. His eyes were cold, like those of a jackdaw, a pale grey ring

405

surrounding the dark pupils. And those eyes were everywhere, constantly watchful – not just of her but of everything around. As though he was nervous.

'Which one of 'ee carries the Orbis?'

'What? Oh, the Orbis. My cous— my friend. The other one. He'll be bringing it.'

'Do 'ee say so? Then what have 'ee got there?' The archer moved away from the tunnel mouth, and took a few paces along the bank of the stream, so that he was directly opposite Midge. 'See . . . I ain't so sure that there be anyone else to come, arter all. No, I reckon thee be all alone, maidy.' He waved the arrow-point at the carrier bag.

'Show me.'

'It's nothing.' Midge was seriously worried now, and already looking for a way out of this. 'It's just some food, that's all. An apple.' The tunnel mouth was unguarded, but she knew that she couldn't hope to escape that way. Too slow. There were bramble bushes lining the bank where the archer stood, and maybe she could have dodged among them if she'd been on that side of the stream. But she wasn't.

'Show me!' The archer raised his bow and Midge automatically stepped backwards, one foot slipping from the rock and into the stony shallows. There was nowhere for her to go. Nowhere at all. She put her hand into the bag, still trying to gain some time.

'See . . .' She took another stumbling pace backwards, and another. 'It's just that I'm not supposed to . . .' Her left foot was on more or less dry land. 'I'm not supposed to let anyone else . . .'

Her only idea was to take the Orbis from the bag and throw it. Maybe if she hurled it straight at this hideous creature's bearded face it would distract him long enough for her to be able to get away. And in any case, that was all that he was really after, wasn't it? The Orbis? Well, let him have it then, and let someone else sort this out.

Midge pretended to fumble in the carrier bag as she made up her mind which way to run. It would have to be the tunnel, after all. There was no other choice.

'Is this what you want?' She drew the Orbis from the bag and held it up for the archer to see. Her fingers closed around the metal frame, getting a proper grip, getting ready to aim . . . but then she saw that he wasn't even looking at it. Not really. A horrible grin had spread across his face.

'Aye,' he said. ''Twill do, now that 'tis here. But that ain't all I wants, maidy. I've other matters to settle with thee . . .'

Maidy. There was something in the way he said that word. A harsh twang to his voice that jolted through her. 'And I've a greeting for thee, whilst we be here.' Slowly and deliberately the archer drew back the bow, his unblinking eye staring at her along the length of the arrow. 'A greeting from my brother. Dost ever think of him? I wonder. His name be Scurl. Aye, ye Gorji brat – Scurl! He that were cast out from here because of thee! Think of him now, maidy. And let it be the last thought thee'll ever have.'

That same cold stare . . . that same sharp-toothed snarl. The terrifying ghost of Scurl was in that look,

407

and Midge felt the blood draining away from her arm, a sickening numbness spreading down through her insides. The Orbis flashed before her as it tumbled from her useless fingers. She was aware of it rolling down to the water's edge, and coming to a halt. But she couldn't shift her gaze. Couldn't take her eyes from—

'Ictor! Let her alone!'

The shout came from high above her – above and behind – but still Midge was locked in her trance as the archer swung the bow away from her and immediately fired into the air.

'Ach!' Midge heard the grunt of pain and the sound broke the spell. She turned to look up, and immediately ducked, throwing her arms out in defence against the shadow that descended upon her, a dark shape that came tumbling from the skies. She glimpsed outstretched wings . . . a spear . . . and was then thrown to the ground, her ears ringing from the force of whatever had struck her.

The weight of her attacker was upon her and she was winded to her stomach. She saw an arrow . . . and then blood. Hers? With a final heave she broke free, gasping for breath, and realized what had hit her. It was Maglin. And the blood wasn't hers, but his. He'd been shot. The arrow was sticking in his leg – a horrible thing to see – and he was lying on his side, try-ing to push himself upright.

'Urrrgh!' Maglin managed to get himself into a sitting position. He reached out, attempting to manoeuvre himself towards the spear that lay on the

ground nearby, but then collapsed again, the breath hissing out of him.

'Ictor!' His voice was a gasp of agony. 'I s'll . . . see thee rot for this . . .'

On the other side of the stream, the archer – Ictor – had already notched another arrow to his bow. Midge rolled over onto her knees, her palms resting on the damp earth. She was dazed and winded, but in any case too shocked to move further. What was *happening* here?

'See me rot?' Ictor calmly raised his bow. 'Thee'll be seeing naught o' me, Maglin. And naught of any other in this world. This be my time, and yours be over. One more arrow, that's all thee'll ever see. And then 'twill be the turn o' this Gorji brat . . .' Ictor swung the bow back towards Midge. 'Though maybe I should do her first . . .'

'Bist mad?' Maglin growled. 'Leave her be.'

'Ha! I shall leave her be, Maglin, don't 'ee fret. And thee also. I shall leave 'ee lying face down, the pair of 'ee. Aye, and all else here shall be lying alongside 'ee afore we'm done.'

'We? I see but one archer, Ictor. You can't kill us all.'

'I've no need. Once this Gorji brat be dealt with, then her kind'll come looking for her soon enough. 'Tis they that'll empty this place for us.'

'What? Thee'd bring all the Gorji down upon us a-purpose?'

'Aye,' said Ictor. 'I would. And let 'em come. Let 'em roast every last one of 'ee on a spit. We s'll be gone. And when the Gorji've left your bones to rot, then we shall return – if we ain't a'ready found a better place. So. First the maid, and then thee . . .'

'Urrrghh . . .' Maglin was struggling to his feet, and at the same time grasping the arrow. '*Grrrrragh!*' He wrenched the thing from his leg and stumbled forward, bending low, trying to get to the spear. Midge saw Ictor shift his stance in order to redirect his aim. The cruel grin on his face said that he knew there was no need for haste. Maglin would never be able to reach the weapon quickly enough to use it. Ictor waited until Maglin's fingers were hovering above the spear before fully drawing back the string.

'Aye – pick 'un up!' he sneered. 'If 'ee can find the strength, thee old sag-a-bones! And let's sithee try and throw it.'

'*We'll* return? Who?' Maglin was breathless with pain. 'Who be with you in this?'

'Ha! Can 'ee not guess? 'Tis Scurl! Aye, my brother Scurl – one that thee'd never thought to see again, eh, Steward? And when all of the Various have been hunted down, and the giants've gone, then this place shall be ours. Mine and Scurl's alone, as we've long planned. And everything here shall be ours . . . the Orbis and the Stone . . . aye . . . the Stone . . .' Ictor raised his eyebrows as though this thought had only just occurred to him. 'And whilst thee and thine lie rotting we s'll live easy. Now curse the day, Maglin, as you ever cast a brother o' mine to the Gorji. I wish he were here now to watch thee die along wi' this meddling snip. No matter. 'Twill cheer him when he hears of it.'

'But Scurl's dead. Just today . . . I saw it happen.'

Midge hadn't meant to say it – the words simply spilled out.

She was crouching on all fours, her eyes locked on Ictor's. She saw those eyes blink, and turn slowly towards her, a look of confusion, disbelief.

'What did 'ee say?' Ictor's twisted mouth spat the words at her.

'Scurl. He's . . . he's drowned. I saw it. He fell off a bridge and into the water. A weir. There was a pike . . . a huge thing. It dragged him . . . it dragged him down under . . .'

Midge stopped talking. She stared beyond Ictor's wild eyes to see a shadow . . . a grey shadow rising up behind the archer, a ghostly creeping form that spread itself like a cape about Ictor's shoulders. But not a cape – a figure, silently appearing from the bushes, hood thrown back to reveal a familiar face. Tadgemole! He was carrying some leather thing in his hand . . . raising it up . . . a sack or a bag . . .

'*Dead?*' Ictor had found his senses. His scream of rage rang through the woodland. '*Yaarrrrgghhh!*' He

411

jabbed the bow towards Midge once more, teeth bared and snarling, arrow drawn back full . . .

'Leave her be, heathen!' Tadgemole stepped to one side, arms raised, and swung the leather sack in a great whirling arc. Ictor had barely time to turn his head as the bag caught him square on the temple – and with such a blow that the sound of shattering bone was as loud as a whip-crack.

The archer's legs buckled instantly beneath him, and he dropped to the ground, toppling forward to lie at full length, face down in the stream. He didn't move.

Maglin had the spear in his hand. Using it as a prop, he hobbled forward to the water's edge. He ignored the body of Ictor, but instead reached down and picked up the Orbis. Only then did he speak.

'Tadgemole.' The sound was a low gasp, a flat acknowledgement of the other's presence, no more.

'Maglin.' Tadgemole's reply was equally cool.

A long silence followed, and Midge was astonished that the two apparently had no more to say to one another. Her own head was spinning with a thousand thoughts and images, and such a whirl of emotions that she hardly knew whether to laugh or cry or scream. There was no way of beginning. But it seemed that this grizzled old pair had already reached the end of all that could be said.

She could bear it no longer. 'What . . . what's going on here? I mean, what's—'

'Dammit then, Tadgemole. I've to thank 'ee.' Maglin interrupted her, spitting the words out as though they cost him his last breath. 'Aye, for I should be dead b' now, if 'tweren't for thee. And this maid too. Though I were the one here first, and took the arrow that were meant for her.'

Tadgemole nodded. 'You were here first,' he said. 'And took the arrow that was meant for her. I see you've also taken something else that was never meant for you . . .'

But then Tadgemole's attention wavered, and he looked away from Maglin. Midge turned and saw archers appearing away to her left – a knot of Ickri hunters, or perhaps guards, hurrying along the bank of the stream. Then a few more, floating down from the hillside.

'Maglin! Bist hurt?'

Midge thought that she recognized the faces of the first couple to arrive.

Maglin waved them away. 'Keep back, Glim. Raim – get behind me.'

'But have he wounded thee?' The guards looked threateningly towards Tadgemole.

'Get back, I say! 'Tis but a scratch. And 'twere Ictor's doing, not the cave-dweller's. Keep away – and keep all others away. Now then . . .' Maglin pointed his spear across the stream towards Tadgemole. 'We shall have this out, thee and I.'

But as he spoke, the bushes behind Tadgemole parted and other cave-dwellers began to appear. Like pale spirits they materialized, silent and serious, to stand on the opposite bank. Some carried staves, and some the implements of their work – hammers and picks. All looked as though they had come prepared for trouble.

Maglin nodded as if in understanding. 'Thee'd already had word o' this, then,' he said to Tadgemole. 'And knew that the maid were coming.'

'As did you. And now it seems that all have learned of it . . .' Tadgemole was watching the hillside, and Midge turned once more to look.

The tangled woods were coming alive with little figures. From among the trees they appeared, in ones and twos at first, and then in larger groups – some walking, some gliding . . . young children . . . mothers with babies . . . Ickri hunters and Naiad field-workers . . .

Midge simply gawped at the sight. It was a medieval painting come to life . . . a film . . . a fête . . . a carnival procession – or a migration. Yes, the little people were like birds or animals, following a common instinct as they moved urgently through the bushes and the undergrowth, the groups converging and all heading in the same direction: towards the tunnel stream. And towards her.

She saw a tiny child stumble and disappear into the rough grass, a mother pausing for a moment, arm out-stretched – and then the infant's head bobbing up again, disorientated, its red cap all askew. More archers circled down from above. A trapper, or a hunter, she noticed, with some half-plucked carcass still in his grasp, the bird hanging upside down, grey wings splayed. A pigeon? Long wooden rakes . . . bundles of withy . . . many of the tribespeople were obviously carrying whatever they'd been occupied with when the word had gone round, so intent were they on getting here as quickly as possible.

The colours . . . the clothing that they wore . . . so perfect, Midge realized, for their surroundings: muted ochres of orange and yellow, washed out browns and greys and olive greens. The colours of winter wood. Only the Ickri stood out, in their flashes of black and white – and even they might be mistaken for magpies at a distance.

And now there were more still, coming along the banks of the stream in single file, another tribe, paler skinned than the Ickri or the Naiad, though not as pale as the cave-dwellers. These must be the Wisp, the night-fishers. They carried pronged spears, simple forked sticks for the most part that had been sharpened into points. One or two had small metal gardening forks, fixed to the ends of homemade poles.

Midge had never realized that there could be so many of them – had simply never thought about the actual numbers that might be living here. But there must have been enough to fill a school playground at least. A hundred? Two hundred? She searched the growing crowd for Little-Marten and Henty, but couldn't spot them anywhere. Nor could she see any sign of Pegs.

It was dizzying to watch them all forming into groups, each to their own kind, huddling into ranks on either side of the stream – crowding together, yet all in silence. Midge was left breathless at the sight.

This was truly another world. Beyond the briars and brambles, the life of humans went on – her life – with its roaring traffic, and airports, and televisions and computers. And school. And here in the middle of it all was this impossible thing happening. It was too much to deal with.

And yet they were just people. That was what she had to keep telling herself. She had stumbled across the border of an unknown country, a foreign land: different people, with different customs. But people, just the same.

That thought helped, and Midge clung to it as she gazed at the wild assembly, the scores of grave little faces that now surrounded her. Ickri, Tinkler, Troggle, Naiad and Wisp – the five tribes of the Various.

And they were so quiet. No baby cried, no child laughed, no archer murmured to his neighbour. An entire population had gathered, yet there was nothing to be heard but the soft chuckle of the stream, and the lone piping of a bird in some distant hedgerow. The gentle sounds of the woodland.

But there was such tension in that silence, such an expectancy, and Midge shrank before the many solemn eyes that were upon her.

'It seems we be mustered, then.' Maglin finally spoke, his voice gruff on the still, wintry air. 'Though I gave no such command. But perhaps 'tis as well that all should hear. Glim – drag that traitor's body out o' my sight. And you, Raim, give him aid.'

Maglin examined the Orbis for a few moments as the guards went about their grisly task, then he held the object up high, turning himself about so that all could see it.

'At last we have it,' he said. 'The Orbis! Look upon it and wonder that it still exists. Aye, and that it should be found – returned here by this Gorji child. We owe her much. To my hand it've come' – Maglin looked at Tadgemole – 'as so it should. For it was my hand that helped guide its return. If there be any that would lay a better claim, then now be the time to speak, and let us have done with all argument.'

Maglin lowered his arm and faced Tadgemole across the narrow stream.

'The Orbis came to you by chance only,' said Tadgemole. 'Aye, and by my mercy. I don't wonder you hide the body of your traitorous guard, Maglin. Does he not serve as a reminder of where you would be if not for me? What if I had let him kill you, as was his purpose, before I brought him down? Whose hand would hold the Orbis then? Mine! And I also played some part in its return, as this Gorji maid would tell thee. But I have another claim. This thing belonged to the cave-dwellers, not the Ickri. It was in our possession, not yours, and it was we who gave it to the maid Celandine, to be taken from here for safe-keeping. And now that it returns, it must return to us. You've no right to it.'

There was a shuffle of movement from the cave-dwellers at this, and a low murmur of agreement. Midge shifted her position slightly, trying to ease the cramp in her legs. She had a horrible feeling that she might be called upon to act as some sort of judge in this conflict, and she didn't relish the idea.

'No *right*?' Maglin's voice was beginning to rise. 'I am Keeper of the Stone! Or have 'ee forgotten? The Touchstone is carried by the Ickri, and the Orbis be only a part of that. It belongs in my Stewardship and should never have been split from the Stone in the first place. Why do 'ee think that the Ickri returned to these woods longseasons ago? To bring together the Stone and Orbis once more. But it was the cave-dwellers who lost the Orbis. Sent it away for "safekeeping" you say? If it wasn't for the foolishness of your kind, we should be gone longseasons since – not starved and trapped among these empty trees. 'Tis you and yours that have brought us to this, Tadgemole! And now thee say I have no *right*? No, the Orbis must be joined with the Stone – where it belongs. And the hand that bears the Stone must now bear both.'

Another murmur arose at the end of Maglin's speech. Midge looked at the faces of those that she could see from her crouching position. Their expressions seemed equally divided: the Ickri and Naiad were approving of what Maglin had said – the Tinklers and Troggles, unsurprisingly, were not. Only the Wisp seemed uncommitted, standing about the shallows of the stream, dibbling in the waters with their pronged spears.

'So.' Tadgemole was speaking again, and Midge returned her attention to him. A grim smile passed across his face, and that did surprise her – never having seen him smile before. 'Possession is all, then.

And is this what you truly believe, Maglin, that . . . what were your words . . . that the hand that bears the Stone must bear the Orbis also?'

'Aye,' said Maglin. 'There can be no division in this.'

'Then we have no argument,' said Tadgemole. He raised the leather bag that he carried, put his hand deep into it . . . and brought out the Touchstone.

It took a few moments to register. There were gasps of disbelief at first, but then a swell of angry voices arose.

'They thieving cave-dwellers have took the Stone!'

'No! 'Tis the Ickri that be the robbers! They've stole the Orbis!'

'Give it back, ye stinking old grey-rag! Give it back – or thee'll take an arrow instead!'

'Not from you we shan't, boss-eyes! You couldn't hit the ground wi' your own foot!'

'Blood, then! Give 'em blood! On the Ickri!'

From both sides of the stream the insults flew, and rocks and arrows looked likely to follow. Midge hunched her shoulders and shrank closer to the earth, bracing herself for outright war.

Maglin was waving his spear at Tadgemole, and shouting . . . but he was calling for peace, not violence.

'Keep them back!' he roared. 'Tadgemole – hold 'em there! Let none attack!'

He turned to his own archers and struck out at the nearest, knocking the arrow from his bow.

'Put down your weapons! Hold, I say! Aken! Glim! Do 'ee not hear? Silence! *Silennnnce!*'

419

Such was the power that Maglin still held that the ruckus gradually subsided, and eventually all weapons and missiles were lowered. Tadgemole too had managed to calm the Tinklers and Troggles, so that the two sides resumed their restless truce, facing each other across the stream with much scowling and muttering.

Maglin leaned heavily on his spear, his head sinking forward, one stubbled cheek resting against the flat blade. He pressed a forearm to his brow, a picture of weariness. His very shoulders were beginning to shake, the effort of bearing himself upright apparently too much for him. But then he threw back his head to give a great shout to the heavens – and it was a shout not of pain but of laughter.

'Ha! Haaaa . . . hah!' The sound was so shocking that those nearest him actually flinched away, half raising their arms in defence. 'We be a match, then, Tadgemole, me and thee! Aye, and each no better nor worse than the other! Neither of us have gained more than we lose. Ha!' Maglin looked about at the astounded Ickri archers, his face split with mirth. 'They that once held the Orbis now hold the Stone, as we that once held the Stone now hold the Orbis.' He chuckled and gave a long sigh. 'Though how such trickery have come about I don't yet see. Well, I look to thee for explanation then, cave-dweller, and we must parley this through. Parley, I say, and not fight. I shall raise no weapon again, where none is raised against me, and there be my vow on it. So let us agree on this much: no more blood. I've none left to spare, and that I do know. Zelma! Bist there?' Maglin searched the crowd. 'Zelma – fetch me a poultice . . . a swab. I be mazed in the head, I reckon. Aye, and must be, to find this to my amusement.'

What had come over him? Maglin, who could always be relied upon to charge headlong at whatever obstacles might stand in his path, now seemed ready to back away from conflict.

As if sensing the amazement about him, Maglin spoke again.

'How else should I act? If 'tweren't for Tadgemole I should be killed already. He've saved me from the treachery of my own kind, when it might have served him better to see me die. What should his reward be – that I attack him in return? No. I shan't do it, and nor shall any under my command.' Maglin looked around at his company in order to emphasize this point. 'We shall settle this by parley. So where do us stand? We have the Stone, and we have the Orbis. We should rejoice in this much. And our task be to find the true way forward. But how? And by whose hand? These two parts must be joined together, 'tis plain enough, but beyond that is beyond my knowledge. All my hope was to bring this day about, and I've looked no further. Perhaps the cave-dwellers can show us more. Come, Tadgemole . . .' Maglin held out the Orbis in his right hand. 'If I give this over to thee, tell me how thee'd put it to use.'

Tadgemole, always so confident in his manner, now looked completely taken aback. And when he spoke there was suspicion in his voice.

'*Give* it to me? And not ask for the Stone in return?'

'I'm become more seasoned of late, Tadgemole, and perhaps a little wiser with season's turning. I have consulted with the Stone many times, and see that here lies a power beyond my own. My heart has altered. I believe that Elysse exists – our true home – and that we might return there if we could only see our path. I believe that the Touchstone would guide us if we had knowledge to put it to such purpose. But I have no such knowledge, and I be willing to step aside for any that do. Keep the Stone, then, and be Keeper of it, and take the Orbis also if 'ee can show 'tis rightfully yourn. I be ready to follow, if thee truly knows the way.' And again Maglin offered the Orbis, holding it out across the shallow waters to Tadgemole.

But Tadgemole made no move to take it. He looked down at the Stone, cradled in his pale hands, and then up again at Maglin.

'Your heart is altered indeed then,' he said, 'if you are ready to give all over to me. And I've no ready words in answer. As with you, so it is with me: I've wished only to bring this day about and have given little thought beyond it. But . . . you say that you have *consulted* with the Stone? What do you mean? You have already learned how it might be used?'

'Aye, but in part only. I cannot say how the Stone and Orbis should work together, or what might betide if they be joined.'

'No more can I.'

'So? But 'tis your kind that've always held a faith in these things, Tadgemole, not mine. I be come

422

to this only lately, and in the sun-wane o' my days.'

'My people do hold faith, Maglin, and I hope we ever shall. Yet faith may not be knowledge. We've no word of such things in our almanacs. We know only that the travelling tribes came from Elysse to the lands of the Gorji, guided by the Touchstone. And that when the Touchstone was split, so we became trapped here. We believed that if Stone and Orbis were brought together again, then on such a day we might return to our home. But now that the day has come . . .'

Tadgemole paused and shook his head. 'No. If you've already worked the Stone, Maglin, then you've more knowledge than I. Perhaps 'tis for the Ickri after all to lead us from this place . . .'

Another moment of hesitation and Tadgemole held out the Touchstone, offering it to Maglin across the quietly trickling stream.

Midge stared at the two of them in wonderment – and with a growing feeling of exasperation. After all the trouble and fuss and danger that she'd been through in order to bring the Orbis to the forest, and now nobody could *give* the thing away! What was the matter with them?

'Why don't you just put it all together and see what happens?' The words simply tumbled out, and every-body turned to look at her. Midge felt stupid then. 'Sorry,' she said. 'I only meant that . . . well . . . it might be an idea, that's all.' She decided to shut up.

Maglin glared at her a little longer before speaking. 'We be thankful to 'ee, maid, for all that thee've done. Aye, more thankful than we could say. But we s'd be more thankful yet if thee'd hold silent till *we've* done. Now, then . . .' He turned to face Tadgemole once more. ''Tis plain to me, Tadgemole, that neither of us see clear ahead, and that each could gain from another's aid. What do 'ee say, then – shall we call ourselves Elders, thee and I, and try to act together in this? I find that there be few Elders around me that I've any faith in – and we be both more of an age for keeping counsel than for cracking heads.'

'Hmf.' Tadgemole gave a grim little snort. 'I'm all for counsel, Maglin, and I'll gladly join with you in that. But whilst I'm still able to crack any head that needs it, then I'll not give up the right.'

'Ha. So be it, then. Until any wiser head comes along, we must put our two together and hope to keep 'em from breaking one on t'other . . .'

But then the two heads in question turned to face upstream, moving simultaneously, as if drawn by some signal. Midge was still coming to terms with the sudden reconciliation of this extraordinary pair, and it took a moment longer for her to catch up. She followed the direction of their gaze.

Something was happening among the Wisp. The fisher tribe, which had been spread out across the shallows, were now stumbling to either side, parting the way. In order to let someone through? Midge peered at the mill of little figures, trying to discover what was going on.

White . . . she caught flashes of white amongst the dividing crowd . . . white hair and wings. It was Pegs! She could see him, picking his way along the centre of the stony stream. He'd not come to any great harm, then. But her relief quickly turned to puzzlement. Because there was something else . . . someone else . . .

Midge rose unsteadily to her feet, aware of the ache in her legs as she looked over the heads of the crowd. Pegs was being ridden. Yes, there was someone on his back – a girl? A figure at any rate, dressed in white. Long silvery hair. Very pale.

The tribespeople had pulled right back. They stood away from the banks of the stream and looked on in silence as the winged horse and his strange rider passed between them, the click of hooves audible on the wet stones. And there was another sound, soft and musical. The chink of bells. Pegs was wearing a bridle, and Midge gave a little gasp as she recognized it. Yes, she'd looked at that bridle so many times that it was like an old friend to her.

But the figure in white was a complete stranger. Who could she be? The eyes of the girl were looking straight at her . . . so dark, they were, for such a pale face . . . and Midge felt self-conscious, a clumsy giant amongst those all around. Her legs didn't seem to want to hold her upright after all. She sank dizzily to her knees again, grateful to be able to rest her fingertips on solid earth.

Was it a girl, though? As Pegs drew closer, Midge wasn't so sure. The figure perched sideways on his back was perhaps not as young as she had first seemed. Her skin was clear and unlined, perfect. But there was something in that perfection that didn't seem very girlish somehow. A kind of tautness that gave away the years. And though her build was slight, it wasn't teenage-skinny. She was too graceful for that, too composed.

The awed silence held as horse and rider approached the flat rock that sat in the middle of the stream.

'Yes, here.'

Only two words, but the low huskiness in the voice told of one who had travelled far beyond childhood. Pegs stepped up onto the rock and turned about, the clink of the bridle bells and the skitter and scrape of his hooves echoing above the constant babble of water. Midge saw for the first time that his strange companion was winged. An Ickri.

'You are safely here then, child. And unharmed. I am glad.'

Midge realized that she was being spoken to, but had to shield her eyes in order to see properly. The winter sun was already low among the trees, dazzling her, so that the face of the Ickri rider was shadowed against wheeling rays of light.

'Er . . . yes. I'm fine.' Midge ducked a little lower. She could see the dark eyes looking at her, extra-ordinarily intense amid the fiery strands of hair. Who *was* this person? She thought she caught the trace of a smile as the head turned away.

They stood in profile now, Pegs and his rider, to face the crowds on either side of the stream. Midge stole a glance at Maglin, and then at Tadgemole. They seemed as mystified as everyone else there.

'Come. Draw closer and look upon me.' The rider had one arm raised, her sleeve falling back to reveal skin paler than that of any cave-dweller.

'Closer. Stand before me. There is nothing to fear.'

She had an air of authority about her, a quiet hypnotic power that seemed to draw the crowd towards her. By ones and twos at first, and then in a general shuffle of movement, the Various tribespeople rearranged themselves, mingling together to form a deep semi-circle around the flat rock, some remaining on dry land, some wading into the shallows. Midge found herself neighboured by Naiad and Ickri alike, all whispering together, and noticed that Maglin and Tadgemole were two of those who stood in the stream, taking up a position side by side and directly in front of the rock platform.

Gradually the muttering subsided and all were quiet once more.

'I hear the whispers, but have not yet heard the sound of my name. Are there none among you that know it?' The husky voice fell upon dead silence.

'Then I will tell you. I am Una, daughter of Avlon.'

More silence. Midge looked about her in order to see what effect this announcement might have, but the expressions on the upturned faces of the little people remained blank. Only Maglin, she noticed, seemed to react. His grey eyebrows met in a frown, and he gave a slight shake of his head.

'Has it been so long then, that all have forgotten me?' The Ickri maiden spoke again. 'And have all forgotten Avlon, my father, King of the Ickri? And how he was slain by Corben, his own brother? Do none know this tale? Come . . . Maglin. You at least have heard of this.'

'How do 'ee know my name?' Maglin growled. 'And where do 'ee come from with this nonsense? Aye, the tale be known well enough among the Ickri.' He raised his voice so that all about could hear. 'Avlon were he who first led our tribe down from the north-lands. He were killed by his brother Corben, who would be King in his stead. And 'tis true, so I've heard, that he had a daughter named Una. But this ain't she! Una were killed also when she were a child. And even if she'd lived she'd be older than I or any Elder here. Now I don't know who you be, maidy, but you ain't seasoned enough to be any daughter of Avlon.'

'Ha. Perhaps I am older than I seem. What do you say, Tadgemole? Or you, Glim? Zelma . . . Aken . . . Zophia? What does Spindra say, or Fletcher Marten? I know every one of you. Do none of you know me?'

'Where do 'ee *come* from, wi' this tricksy talk? We don't know thee!'

Maglin placed the butt of his spear onto the rock, and heaved himself up, so that Pegs had to step aside in order to make way for him. 'But I knows one that might! Find Maven!' he roared. 'Bring Maven to me, and then perhaps we s'll see who this storyteller be!'

'Maven?' The Ickri rider looked down at him. 'Old Maven-the-Green? I doubt she'd have aught to tell you, Maglin, even if you could find her. Maven is dead.'

Chapter Twenty-eight

'*Dead?*' Maglin staggered backwards as though he'd been struck. His mouth sagged open in disbelief.

'Aye, dead and gone. She was shot by an Ickri arrow. I saw it happen.' There was a tinge of sorrow in the low voice of the horsewoman. 'And it should never have been. Maven was a friend to me.'

Maglin seemed lost. He stood with his hand to his brow, staring wide-eyed into the stream below. But then gradually the lines of his mouth hardened, and when at last he spoke his voice broke with anger.

'Who? Who did this? And when did it happen?'

'I never learned who, Maglin, though I always believed it was one called Tuz. An Ickri archer. But it was long ago. Longseasons ago. Before you were born.'

'*What?* What ... *blether* do 'ee talk now? I were speaking wi' Maven this very day!'

'Were you? It heartens me, Maglin, to see you take her death so hard. She would have been glad to know you thought so well of her. Didst truly love her, then?'

'What? Thee durst come here from ... from

nowhere . . . to make a mock o' *me*?' Maglin lunged forward and grabbed hold of Pegs' bridle. It looked as though he would have dragged the Ickri rider from her perch there and then, but she deftly slid down the horse's opposite flank so that Pegs stood as a barrier between the two of them.

'Do 'ee not know me, maister? Thee be blind as a new-born mole, then! But thee surely ain't deaf as well?' The cackle and croak that arose from the other side of the winged horse stopped Maglin in his tracks. His eyes seemed likely to pop – along with all others that were watching.

'What's this? *Maven*?'

'Ssssss . . .'

The figure in white came creeping beneath the horse's neck, her body hunched and twisted, long silver hair hanging over her face. She put a hand into the sleeve of her garment and drew out a strange object – unfamiliar to Midge, at least. It looked like a pipe or a peashooter.

'Do 'ee recognize 'un, maister? Thee should do, then, for it've done 'ee service enough afore this day. Maglin – and all of 'ee here – look upon the poor hag that've walked among 'ee since thee were weans. Do 'ee know me *now*?' The fantastic crouching figure raised the blowpipe to her mouth and started forward, threatening the crowd before her in one sweeping movement. Maven! Those at the front retreated in horror against those behind, so that all were thrown into a bundle of confusion. Maglin dodged sideways, just managing to keep his balance as he stepped back

430

down from the rock and into the shallows once more.

'Aye! And there've been more than one who've come to know the vengeance of Maven-the-Green!' The stooping figure straightened up and swept back her hair to reveal her pale and perfect face once more. 'But . . . I am not Maven, nor ever was. And I shall need this no more.' She tossed the blowpipe away from her. It fell into the stream, tumbling through the stony shallows to be swept from sight. 'I am Una, daughter of Avlon, and rightful Queen of the Ickri. Come. Maglin . . . Tadgemole . . . all. Gather yourselves and listen. Draw closer and hear me out.'

Again she seemed able to exert the power of her will on those before her. The startled crowd, half fearful, half fascinated, recovered some of their dignity and cautiously inched forward. Maglin moved around the rock to stand next to Tadgemole once more, the two of them exchanging a dubious glance, and a shake of their heads.

'Hear my words, and you shall know the truth.' The white-robed figure raised one slim hand, palm outwards, and waited for silence before she began. 'I was a child – no older than this Gorji child here among us – when Maven died. I was there and saw it happen. Such dark and treacherous times. Corben poisoned his own brother, my father, Avlon, and persuaded all that it was I who had done this thing. He and the Ickri Elders sent archers by moonlight to find me and kill me. The archers did find me – or they reckoned to have done – and fired into the darkness. Aye, and when they heard the cry of pain they knew they had hit their mark. But it was Maven who took the arrow that was meant for me, and it was she who died. She fell into a deep pool, and when they later touched her drowned hand they believed it to be mine—'

'What pool?' Maglin interrupted. 'There be no such pools here.'

'It happened in the Far Woods, Maglin, whilst we were still journeying to this place. I could take you there now if you wished, and show you the spot. I'm unlikely to forget it.'

'Hmf. Any of us may tell a tale . . .'

'Then let me tell mine.'

Maglin muttered something to himself, but made no further argument.

'So I was alone, a child with nowhere to go and one who would be hunted down if any knew that I lived. I dared not be seen, yet I could not leave. Nor would I, whilst both my friend and my father lay dead and unavenged. It was then that I took the green mantle of Maven upon myself, and became she.'

'You dressed in her clothes – as a child? And all around believed you were an old crone?' This time it was Tadgemole who spoke, and he too sounded disbelieving.

'It was not so hard, Tadgemole. Maven-the-Green lived alone and was little seen. She was a wise and true spirit of the woods, one who had knowledge of all things, but she was not loved. There were many who feared her witchi ways, and so kept far away from her if they could. Yet my father Avlon took counsel from her, against the counsel of others, and she became a friend to me. She saw that I was like she, one who had the Touch, and she took me into her secrets. From her I learned the calls and cries of beast and bird – aye, and could imitate all. From her also I learned the use of every plant, for good or ill. And from her I learned the history of the Stone, its power and its purpose. Our journey from the north was long. By the time we came to these wetlands I knew all that Maven knew, and when I mantled myself in her rags I was mantled in her spirit also. Her voice stayed in my ear and came easily to my tongue. My wings beneath her robe were very like her own humped back. And when my skin was daubed in green clay, then none saw past it. I was she. Who else would they think me, those that fled at the sight of me and the very sound of my name?'

The pale figure paused and looked closely at Maglin.

'I see into your heart, Steward. And I know that you at least begin to believe me. But what of you, Tadgemole, and all others here? Does my tale not have the strangeness of truth to it?'

Tadgemole thought for a moment, and then cleared his throat. 'When the Ickri first came to these woods,' he said, 'I was but new-born. If your tale is true, then you are even older than I. And yet you appear but a little more seasoned than my own daughter. How can this be?'

'You were new-born, Tadgemole. I remember you, aye, and your brother Loren. And you, Gorji child . . . I met with your kin, Celandine. It was I who helped her to escape the wrath of Corben. I am as old as she. What say you – do I speak the truth?'

433

Midge was in a complete daze, and the question took her by surprise.

'Um . . . yes. I suppose so.' She answered without really thinking and her words sounded hopelessly weak. But what else could she say? She had seen Maven just once, down in the gully on the other side of the brambles, standing like a statue at the water's edge. They had looked at one another. But there was no similarity between that weird and fantastic old creature and the beautiful person she was looking at now. Could they really be one and the same?

'We saw each other once before, you and I.' The Ickri woman spoke again, and Midge had the curious feeling that those dark eyes were able to read her thoughts as clearly as if they had been written across the sky. ''Twas beyond the tunnel. You picked a flower, and showed it to me. Do you remember what it was?'

'Yes . . .' Midge whispered. 'A celandine.'

A celandine. She'd forgotten.

The eyes turned away from her.

'I have lived here among you for all of your lives, and for most of mine. And if I look younger than I am, then I say this: there are many ways of holding the seasons at bay. Some work from without and some from within. The green clays and potions that daubed me have had effect other than disguise. No sun or wind or rain has touched my skin since I was a child. From within also I am protected, by the arts that I learned from Maven. She was far older than any could tell, or would ever believe. As old as the trees, they said, and they spoke truer than they knew, for it was from the very trees that she took her sustenance – leaf and sap and root. From her I gained my knowledge and preserved myself against this day, which I believed would surely come. Speak, Maglin. Ask me now why I waited so long. Is that not the question in your heart?'

'Aye,' said Maglin. 'It is. For once Corben were gone, where was the danger? Why did thee not show theeself?'

'When Corben died his daughter Ba-betts was made Queen. I might have returned then, as Una, to try and claim my right. But I was still reckoned to be evil – one who had poisoned her own father to gain the queen-ship. What would have awaited me? Death. None that lived then would have given me claim over Ba-betts. No, it was better that I remained as Maven, to sow the truth of what had happened, seed by seed. But I also had a greater purpose – to see the Orbis returned, and to find a rightful end to our journey. Better I work alone to bring that day about, to protect those who deserved protection, and to avenge myself on those who deserved no mercy. And there were other reasons . . . but these must wait a little longer. Come, Maglin, raise the Orbis. Show what has come to your hand this day.'

Maglin fumbled in his cloak for the Orbis, and lifted it in his right hand.

'And you, Tadgemole. Raise the Stone, and let all see what you have gained.'

Tadgemole followed Maglin's example, straightening his right arm so that the Stone was held high. The two of them had obeyed as though under a spell.

'Maglin. Who am I?' The husky voice fell almost to a whisper. 'Tell me what you know in your heart.'

'Una.' Maglin answered without hesitation now. 'I believe you be Una, the lost child of Avlon, and rightful Queen of the Ickri.' He bowed his head.

'Then you are with me. And Tadgemole. What say you? Who am I?'

'I also believe you to be who you say you are – Una, daughter of Avlon.' Tadgemole sounded as convinced as Maglin, but perhaps less overawed. At any rate he kept his head up, and added, 'Though as to who should be Queen, King, or Steward of the Ickri, I can't say. Never having had much opinion of any of 'em till now.'

'Ha. A plain answer. Perhaps you will have a better opinion of me than of those that came before.' Una raised her voice to the gathering. 'And so I ask all here now: are there any who still doubt my story? I have lived among you as Maven-the-Green, but truly I am Una, child of Avlon. I, who was once wronged, have returned to claim my right. Do you say that right should be mine?'

'Aye!'

'Aye – she speaks the truth!'

'Make her Queen!'

The crowd were obviously won over, and all lifted their bows, spears, caps or children – whatever they carried – and shouted out their approval. Midge found herself wanting to join in, but wasn't sure how that would be received. Had she earned the right to be anything but a bystander? She began to raise her own hand in support just as Una raised hers for quiet.

'So be it, then. And so it shall be. But . . . there are more important questions to be answered yet.' Una lowered her arms and turned to Tadgemole. 'Would you, Tadgemole, see the Stone and Orbis united and in the hand of one who understands their purpose?'

'I would.'

'Then understand this. The Touchstone is yours. It has come to you as was promised, and none shall try to take it from you. But if you will give it over to me freely, then freedom shall be yours in its stead, and I will show you its true power. What do you say? Can you agree to that?'

'Aye, agreed.'

'And you, Maglin. The Orbis has come to you, as was promised, and is yours to keep if you so wish. But if instead you give it freely to me, then I can show you what you would *truly* wish for. Do you agree likewise to that?'

'Aye. And glad to give it.'

'Come, then, both of you.'

Una stood at the edge of the rock platform. She stretched out her white hands and waited as Maglin and Tadgemole placed the Orbis and Stone one in each palm. Then she raised the two objects high.

'At last we are brought together . . . tribe and tribe . . . hand and hand . . . Stone and Orbis. Without that Maglin and Tadgemole reach agreement, this could never be so. They have made their peace, and it was a peace that needs be made of its own accord. This is why I have waited. I am Ickri, and could never hope to hold Stone and Orbis together whilst other tribes laid claim to either and were so divided. We are divided no more, and at last we may travel on. To Tadgemole and Maglin, then, we must give our thanks. To the Gorji maid also, we give our thanks and praise. Without her courage and her wits we would be lost yet, and I would say more to her on this. But there is one other, to whom I give the most thanks of all. One who watches over me, and aids me in all that I do. One who was sent to me from Elysse itself, and who carries me upon his shoulder as the spirit of one who carried me long ago. Pegs . . . come . . . speak to us.'

The sun had sunk lower yet among the trees, and as Pegs stepped forward he was silhouetted against the light, his mane and tail glowing orange in the late afternoon rays.

All that Una has said is true . . . and now at last the day that we have waited for so long is here.

As the word-colours filled her head, Midge had to take a deep breath. She could never ever get used to this sensation. For all that she tried to tell herself that these were just people, like anyone else, whenever she looked upon Pegs she knew that it wasn't so. Pegs was beyond this earth, and beyond anything else that she had ever seen. He was magical.

When I was first born, to Spindra's herd, I knew that I had walked this world before, but could not say how or when. I knew that I was here to a purpose, but could not tell what that purpose might be.

And when first I saw Una, though she was guised as a crone, I believed that we had met before but could not say where.

The bells on the red leather bridle gave a little jingle as Pegs shook out his mane.

But then when I learned the story of the Touchstone I knew that this too I had heard and seen before. Then I understood my own being and the task that I had been sent to complete.

I am as you see me, a traveller and messenger of Elysse. I am not Avlon, but in me the spirit of Avlon lives again. I must finish the journey that he began, and help his child to bring his people home. In this I have guided Una, but it is she who must bear the Touchstone. And it is she who will lead us from here. Listen to her, then, and do her bidding.

As Pegs stepped back, Midge had to lower her head for a few moments. She wanted to listen, wanted to hear, but the colour-sounds of Pegs' words got jumbled up with her vision and it was hard to focus. And it was too much . . . too much to know . . . too much to try and understand. She blinked and squinted up into the low sunlight as Una spoke once more.

'We are not of this place. Yet we have been here so

long that many have forgotten from whence we came, and what we once were. We were travellers, the great travelling tribes of Elysse, and such were our powers that we could move among the spheres and in and out of our many lives, each life and sphere but a hair's-breadth from the next. For guides we carried Touchstones, the stones of memory, mined and fashioned from the red jasper that seeks always to return from whence it came – Elysse. From there we journeyed, the homelands of our kind, and came to Lys-Gorji, this vale of giants. And here we thought to stay a while before moving on. But then the Touchstone was divided in argument between the Ickri and Naiad, and the tribes parted. The Naiad remained here on the Gorji wetlands and divided into further tribes – cave-dwellers and fishers. It was the cave-dwellers who kept the Orbis, and the memory of our history. The Ickri travelled into the northlands, with the Stone, and longseasons passed. Kings and Elders came and went, and the story of the Touchstone was near forgotten. It was my father, Avlon, who learned what he could of it, and thought to join it with the Orbis once more – if the Orbis could still be found. Avlon brought our tribe south again, and the Stone with him, though it was I as a child who carried it. Now I hold it in my hand again, this same Stone. And in the other I hold the Orbis. Tonight the two shall be joined. Tonight . . .'

Una bowed her head for a moment, as though she were deeply wearied. When she raised it again her face looked paler than ever.

'I must keep them apart a little longer, though I feel such an ache between them that I can scarce hold one from the other. But more time is needed to prepare. Tonight the Stone and Orbis shall be joined, and we may depart this place, any who would go. From Elysse we came and to Elysse we shall return, I and all who will journey with me. Who here has the faith to join me?'

'I!' Maglin immediately raised his hand. He turned round and looked at his company, as if daring them not to follow his example, but there was no need. All had raised their hands – and all about the crowd, amongst Tinklers, Troggles, Ickri, Naiad and Wisp, hands and voices rose as one.

'*I!*'

Una smiled and spoke again.

'Then for those who would truly put their faith in me, here is my bidding – and a test of that faith. Go now to your homes and destroy them. Tear down your pods and your shelters and be joyful. For if you would truly leave, then there will be no returning and you will have no need of these things. Bring all that will burn to Royal Clearing, and build me a circle about the Rowdy-Dow tree – a high wall of willow and wicker that will hold us all within, and with a gap that we might enter. Archers, bring your bows and arrows, fishers your wicker eel-traps, farmers your bean-sticks. And cave-dwellers, bring lavender oil. Bring all that you live by, and heap all upon the pile. Tonight at moon-high we will meet within that circle. There the Stone and Orbis shall be joined together, and we joined with them, hand in hand. We will become travellers once more, free of this world and returned to our own. Now go. Talk one with another and ask if you would truly do this thing, then come to me if you will. But have no fear. For those who have faith, all shall be well. Go . . .'

As the crowd slowly began to break up, Midge caught the whispered snatches of conversation of those passing by her.

'I never heard such talk. What do 'ee think to it all? Do us take food, dost reckon?'

'I be taking a bindle-wrap for certain.'

'What about the horses? Do they come wi' us? I ain't so sure about all this . . .'

Midge wasn't so sure about it either. She was trying to picture exactly what was going to happen, and knew that if it was she who was being asked to take such a leap of faith then she simply couldn't do it. But then she wasn't a traveller.

She watched sadly as the tribespeople began to move away, the archers, fishers and fieldworkers reuniting with their families, tired children being lifted onto shoulders, others being led by the hand. It was like some strange carnival day coming to an end. And it was coming to an end, Midge thought. Everything was coming to an end . . .

'Maglin – Tadgemole . . . stay a while.' Una's voice rose above the general buzz. Midge looked up and saw Una's eye upon her. 'And you, child, come closer. Join us here.'

On the rock? Midge wasn't sure that there was

room. She stood up and walked stiffly over to the rock platform, perched herself sideways upon the edge of it, and sat with her boots in the trickling shallows. She felt cold and shivery, she realized, and suddenly very tired. Too much had happened today. Far too much to take in. But she looked up at Pegs and tried to raise a smile.

'Are you really going?' she said.

Aye. We must.

The soft colours spread outwards inside her head, gentle starbursts of pink and yellow.

'And so I shan't see you again?'

Do you think not? I think that perhaps you will. We each of us have many lives, Midge, so many that truly there is but one life that we are all a part of. We are all one. I am the fly upon my own cheek, and in another life I watch myself through his eye. Wherever we look we see only ourselves. You will see me again, and I you.

But that was too much for Midge, and it was not an answer that brought her any comfort.

'I mean, to speak to.'

We shall see.

'Child, it is time for you to leave. We have much to do.' Una's eyes were level with her own, and now that she was so close Midge could see the age and the wisdom that they held. And she saw that the skin of Una's face was almost transparent. Paper-thin, like her Aunt Celandine's, but taut and unlined. 'Yet before you go, we have to thank you for all that you have done. Give me your hand.'

Una stood beside her, her pale arm outstretched.

Midge reached hesitantly for the tiny hand that was offered, and as their fingers met a little snap of electricity sprang between them. She flinched, but then reached out again and took the delicate hand between her own impossibly clumsy fingers and stubby thumb.

'Ah.' Una's eyes half closed for a moment. 'It is as I knew it would be, and you are truly the kin of she who was here before – Celandine. Like she, you have the Touch.'

'D-do I?'

'You do. And like she you will use it to the good. I will offer you no gifts, child, for you have gifts already. Gifts to be given.'

Midge could feel a warmth spreading through the bones of her hand, the same strange sensation that she had experienced with her Aunt Celandine.

'Tell me about what happened . . .' she said. 'When you met her – Celandine, I mean. She doesn't really remember.'

'She was a child, like you, but one who had suffered much before meeting with our kind. She came here seeking refuge, and hid herself away from her own. But then when the Ickri came she was driven out once more, and in great fear of her life. Corben would have killed her. I helped her to escape, a child myself, and helped to see that the Orbis went with her. I never saw one so frightened or troubled, and perhaps 'tis as well for her that she forgot her time here. But she had great courage, and I see her spirit lives on in you. You will have a happier life than she.'

'Will I?' Midge felt as though she was having her fortune told. She had so many more questions to ask, but knew that there would never be time to hear the answers. Already it was beginning to get dark. She looked at Tadgemole and Maglin, and saw that Maglin now held a swab of some sort to his leg and was wincing as he pressed it against the arrow wound. She should go.

'I'm sorry you were hurt, Maglin,' she said. 'But thank you for what you did . . . saving me from . . .'

''Tis a scratch. And 'twere Tadgemole that got the better of Ictor, not I. Though I've yet to hear how he came by the Stone.'

'It was Pegs that took the Stone, and gave it to Tadgemole,' said Una. 'All our intent was to keep either one of you from getting both the Stone and the Orbis, for then no peace would have ever come. And if I had taken these things for myself, as I might easily have done, then none would have said I had the right to them, or followed me. Such things are to be given, not taken. But you, child, before you go, shall take one thing with you at least, to remember us by. What shall it be?'

'What? Oh . . . nothing. Really. There's nothing . . .' Midge was embarrassed. She looked up at Pegs, so beautiful in the last rays of the sun, and of course immediately saw the one thing that she really *would* like – which made her more uncomfortable than ever.

'Ah. I see into your heart.' Una was smiling at her. 'And how wise you are. Did you not know' – Una moved towards Pegs, and began to unclasp his bridle

– 'that this pretty piece was first made by the Naiad as a parting gift for Celandine? How right then that it should return to you. Here, take it, and keep it safe.'

'*Was* it? No, I never knew . . .' Midge could feel herself going as red as the leather from which the bridle was made. But she took it from Una's hands and said, 'Thank you. I really love it. It's . . . lovely.' The bells jingled softly as she folded the straps. 'Just beautiful.'

'Away then, child. Keep it along with your good heart and don't look back. Pegs will walk you through the tunnel.'

'Yes. I have to . . . have to get back . . .' Midge felt her eyes prickle with tears. She stood up and tucked the folded bridle into the front of her fleece.

'We've much to thank 'ee for then, maid.' Maglin's voice sounded gruff.

'Aye,' said Tadgemole. 'And shan't forget.'

But then Midge remembered something that she had forgotten. She reached into the pocket of her fleece and took out the folded piece of paper that Tadgemole had given her – the drawing of Celandine.

'Here,' she said. 'I meant to give this back . . . but then I . . .'

Tadgemole began to reach for the notepaper, but then shook his head. 'Keep it, maid. A gift from the cave-dwellers . . .'

'Sorry . . . I can't do this . . . I can't . . .' Midge dropped the piece of paper and began to stumble away from the rock, suddenly overwhelmed by all the emotions that the day had brought upon her. It was too much to bear. The bubbling stream was a blur beneath her feet, and the mouth of the tunnel just a vague dark shape ahead. The footsteps of Pegs were following behind her. As she began to duck, she heard Una's voice again.

'Midge . . .' It was the first time that Una had called her by her name. Midge turned, and caught a final glimpse of the three figures standing upon the rock, Una, Maglin and Tadgemole. The little people shimmered through the film of her tears, and wouldn't come into focus. 'Don't look back.' Midge could hear the smile in Una's husky voice. 'You'll have no need.' She managed a nod and a smile in return, but could find no reply.

When they reached the other end of the tunnel Midge had to search through her pockets for some tissue. Pegs stood beside her, looking out across the darkening wetlands.

'I'm sorry . . . I'm sorry . . .' Midge blew her nose and wiped her eyes. 'You haven't even *gone* anywhere yet. I don't know why I'm making such a fuss.'

Parting may not be what parting seems, maid . . .

'Oh . . . don't give me that. Let me give you a hug instead.' This was no time for words of wisdom. Midge crouched down and put her arms about Pegs' neck. She loved the smell of him, the rough warmth of his winter coat upon her face. He leaned into her, and gently rubbed his cheek against hers.

She could have stayed there for ever. But at last she stood up and allowed her hand to run down the length of his neck and mane until her fingers touched his wings. One more time she would experience that extraordinary sensation in her fingertips, the feel of those delicate bones beneath their covering of velvety skin. And then never again.

'Goodbye, Pegs.' She briefly bent down and kissed his mane, then stuffed her hands into her fleece and began to walk down the muddy gully.

Midge . . .

The pink and yellow colours burst in her head. This time she wouldn't look back.

Briefly parted, soon united.

'If you say so, Pegs. I love you.'

Midge thrust her hands deeper into her pockets and kept on going, the farmhouse lights below a blur of dancing stars.

The workmen were just packing up and leaving.

Their white van stood in the yard, engine running, and as Midge wearily climbed the steps onto the flag-stone path, she saw the foreman, Dave, coming out of the front door.

'Ah, there you are.' The man dangled a bunch of keys. 'I was wondering whether I should lock up or not. There didn't seem to be anybody around. Here you go.' He gave Midge the keys.

'Oh thanks. Isn't anybody back yet?'

'No. Don't think so. We'll be off then and, er, see you tomorrow. You OK?'

'Yeah, I'm . . . fine.' Midge took a deep and shaky breath. 'Just been out for a walk, that's all.'

'Sure you're all right? OK. As long as somebody's here. See you, then.'

'Bye.'

Midge was glad that the house was empty. It gave her a chance to sit down for a minute and think. She got herself a glass of milk from the fridge and collapsed onto one of the kitchen chairs. The bridle bells gave a muffled jingle from within her fleece – a reminder of all that had happened to her on this extraordinary day. So many thoughts and pictures crowded her brain that she couldn't begin to put them in any order . . . Scurl and the weir . . . Little-Marten and Henty . . . and George . . . and that awful archer, Ictor. And that was before she'd even properly got into the forest.

She was utterly exhausted, she realized. Numb with fatigue. She stared at her outstretched arm on the kitchen table and wondered whether she could even find the energy to lift the glass of milk. There was something on her sleeve. Midge brought her eyes into focus and saw that it was a hair – very long and silvery, shiny bright beneath the glare of the kitchen lights. She picked at the end of it and gently pulled it away from the material.

Pegs. Of course. It must be from his mane. Midge wound the hair around the forefinger of her left hand and then did the same with her right. It was surprisingly coarse and tough. She tested its strength, tugging her hands apart, feeling the resistance, the slight elasticity as the hair tightened around her fingers. It was tempting to see just how much pressure could be applied before the hair would break, but at the same time she didn't want to spoil it. No, she would keep it safe somewhere. It occurred to her that if she had a few more of the same, she could plait them into a bracelet. Maybe even dye them different colours. But then she remembered that there weren't going to be any more. Because she was never going to see Pegs again . . .

He would be gone, along with the rest of them. Or at least that was their plan. They would all be gone, and she wasn't even going to be there to watch the Stone and Orbis being put together, or to see this miracle happen.

She didn't truly think that it would happen, she realized. Not deep down in her heart. Even after all that she'd seen and heard and been through she still couldn't make herself believe in it. Or perhaps she didn't want to believe it. Perhaps she just wanted to believe that come tomorrow they would all still be there, Pegs and Little-Marten and Henty . . .

Little-Marten and Henty! She hadn't even seen them to say goodbye!

No, they *couldn't* be going. Not yet.

The sound of the phone made her jump so violently that she banged her elbow on the arm of the chair. Midge leaped up and scrabbled among all the papers on the dresser, looking for the receiver.

'Hallo?'

'Oh, hallo. I was wondering if I could speak to – hang on, is that you, Midge? It's Carol Reeve.'

'Oh. Oh, hi, Mrs Reeve. Yes it's me.'

'Midge, I've got your aunt here. She just wanted a word with you, if she could.' Carol's voice lowered.

'She's um . . . well . . . quite tired. But very insistent. I'll hand you over.'

'Thanks,' said Midge. She wound the horsehair into a loop as she waited, tucking the ends over and over.

'Hallo? Is that you, dear?' Aunt Celandine's voice sounded shakier than Midge had remembered it. And weaker.

'Yes. Hallo, Aunt Celandine. How are you?' Midge felt guilty that she hadn't been able to get over to Mount Pleasant for a while.

'Now . . . now, then. Mrs Reeve tells me you found my jewellery casket. Is that right?'

'Yes! It was here all the time – in a barn. And everything was still in it. Everything. And Aunt Celandine, I've given it back. Do you . . . do you know what I'm talking about? I went up to the woods and gave it back to them today. You understand what I mean? You remember?'

'Yes, I do. I understand you perfectly, my dear. And I just wanted to know that you were safe. I was thinking about you, and wondering. I remember everything now, you see. Everything. It's all very clear, and that's a great . . . relief. Thank you. Keep the jewellery casket, Midge. I should like you to have it.'

'Oh, but I was hoping to come across this weekend. I was going to bring it with me, and show it to you. And do you know what else I found? That wicker box thing that you sat on to have your photograph taken! You know – with the bridle? And guess what? *They* had the bridle, and they gave it to me! I've got it right here. I'll bring that across as well, shall I?'

'Well, that would be lovely. Yes, it would be nice to see that again, if there's time.'

'Oh, I've got time. It's just that I need to talk to Uncle Brian about getting a lift.'

'Ah yes. Brian. I remember him as well. Lovely. Well, I must go. I just needed to know that you were safe, and that everything was . . . you know . . . done. Goodbye for now then, Midge.'

'Oh. Goodbye, Aunt Celandine. Hope to see you this weekend, with a bit of luck.'

'Yes. I'll see you again, dear, that's a promise. Byebye.'

Midge heard some vague muttering in the background and then Carol Reeve came on the line.

'Midge? Everything OK? Hope you don't mind me calling, but . . . well. She wanted to talk to you.'

'No, that's fine. Is she all right?'

'Well . . . I think so. As well as can be expected. She certainly seems very peaceful in herself at any rate. So. Shall we see you this weekend then, perhaps?'

'Hope so. Oh – I can hear my mum coming back. I'd better go. Bye, Mrs Reeve.'

'Bye, love. Take care.'

Barry's car was pulling into the stableyard, and Midge still had the bridle tucked into the front of her fleece. She'd be able to think up some story about finding it, given a bit of time, but didn't want to have to deal with it right now. Better get rid of it, then. She ran upstairs to her room, dropped the horsehair loop into the little metal cup at her bedside, and then put the bridle on top of the wicker box, beneath the picture of Aunt Celandine. That's where it would live from now on, she decided. And it would be perfect. Midge stood back and looked at it for a moment. Yes, perfect.

By the time she got back down to the kitchen her mum was just hurrying in through the door.

'Sorry sorry sorry! That all took a lot longer than expected. Poor baby, you must be starving – but listen, we picked up pizza on the way home. Barry's just bringing it in now.'

'Oh. Er . . . good.' Midge watched her mum running around the kitchen, grabbing plates and knives. She wondered how she was ever going to sit down and cope with something as normal as eating pizza after a day like today.

'So, what have you been up to, darling?' Mum rummaged noisily in the drawer of the dresser and took out the pizza wheel.

'Oh . . . just sort of messing about. I feel really tired, though. Shattered, actually.'

She got as far as pulling one of her socks off, but then her energy ran out. Midge perched on the edge of her bed, her hands in her lap, and stared blankly at the photo of Celandine. The red bridle sat on its wicker box, positioned directly beneath the picture that contained those same two objects, so that to Midge's vacant gaze it was like looking down through a hall of mirrors.

All was quiet and still, the only sound in the room the soft whirr of the laptop behind her. Midge allowed herself to just float. No more thoughts, no more think-ing. Just relaxing her vision and floating . . .

Gradually the photograph before her became a collection of blurred shapes and patterns, things with-out meaning, reflected areas of red and grey and sepia. Black and white.

Black and white . . .

The black-and-white shapes were merging into something recognizable. A face. Dark hair . . . pale face . . . deeply shadowed eyes looking at her. Not Celandine's face, but another one, down towards the bottom of the picture. Midge kept her gaze fixed and unfocused, unblinking. The face was that of another child, a ghost-girl, her head entering the picture just where it would be if she was sitting on the wicker box below.

They were a threesome now, three girls together in this silent room. Herself, Celandine – and . . .

. . . Una. The name just came into her head. Midge gazed down through the hall of mirrors and felt her-self part of a repeating pattern. Midge . . . Celandine . . . Una. Midge . . . Celandine . . . Una.

We are all one.

The words of Pegs. We are all one.

Three girls, separated yet connected by one pur-pose. All connected. Sisters . . .

It was too weird, and Midge had to blink. She brought her eyes back into focus and stared hard at the photo. What was it that she could see in there? The black-and-white shapes didn't look anything like a face now, or even part of the picture. They were just

454

reflections, she realized – something mirrored in the glass.

The laptop. Midge turned round to look. It was the magpie, the picture that she used for her screensaver. Somehow those black-and-white patterns had become . . . something else.

Midge shook her head and pulled off her other sock. You could go mental with this stuff. The thought remained with her, though, as she padded into the bathroom to brush her teeth. Sisters . . .

She tried to avoid looking in the mirror.

Chapter Twenty-nine

It was a falling dream, but she was falling upwards. From the underside of the planet she dropped, the fields and the woods spiralling away from her, a revolving map that then became a revolving globe as she entered the deep blue of space. Then she was looking down at the world, but falling upwards . . . her scalp tingling at the rush of it, her back and shoulders cold through the thin white material of her gown.

Very often, in her dreams, she could fly. But not this time. She was definitely falling.

From the left and from the right came two distant figures, speeding towards her. She saw that they were girls – two girls dressed in white – closing in on her until their hands touched . . . sparks of electricity . . . fingers grasping for each other . . . holding on tight. Three of them, skydiving upwards, Celandine, Midge, Una.

'This is the Touch.'
'We are the sisters.'
'Sisters of the Touch.'
But she couldn't see the faces of the other two girls.

And so . . . and so she didn't know which of the three sisters she was. How could she tell?

The revolving planet became smaller and smaller and began to glow red, a spinning orb between the three outstretched pairs of arms. The Stone!

She remembered carrying it. Yes, that dark and endless journey down from the north when she carried the Stone. And she remembered her poor father, dead now, poisoned by his brother. She could see his face, a young man in uniform, far too young to die. But no, that was . . . Freddie. Her brother. And so she must be . . . the one who sat by the fountain. And dropped things into the water. She was the one who found the Orbis, in the wooden casket where she had first put it, and took it to the forest. No, that wasn't right. She was the one who . . . the one . . .

We are all one.

Yes, all one.

Midge . . .

She could hear Pegs. The blue was deepening to absolute darkness, and she was still holding on tight to the other girls' hands. But she could hear him calling her name. And so she must be . . .

Midge . . .

She let go of the hands and sat up in bed. Awake.

'Pegs?'

Her window was open. She didn't remember leaving it like that. No wonder she was so cold. Midge got out of bed to go and have a look.

He was down there, standing on top of the balustrade wall, his coat blue-white in the light of the moon. Looking up at her . . . waiting for her to join him . . .

Midge hauled herself up onto the sill, ducking her head as she stepped through the open window. She balanced herself on the outer ledge, the stone cold beneath her bare feet, and raised her arms towards the moon.

She was about to jump when something occurred to her.

Was she certain she remembered how to do this? She hadn't forgotten, had she? No. You could never forget how to fly.

Midge spread her arms, took a deep breath – a diver's breath – and slowly toppled forward. The ground rushed towards her and for a sickening moment she thought that she'd lost the trick of it after all. But then she was swooping over the balustrade wall . . . past Pegs, and soaring upwards . . . up and up . . .

Yes, she said. I knew I could do it. How silly to think you could ever forget.

It was all in the hand movement. You kept your fingers straight and then tilted them this way and that, as though they were the front end of a toboggan. Then it was possible to swoop and climb and steer from left to right. Air was like water, and flying was just like diving really.

She was speeding above the Field of Thistles and nearing the sheep-gate, flattening her palms in order to gain some lift. But where was Pegs?

He appeared beside her, his wings making a swoosh-ing noise as he beat against the night air. Over the sheep-gate they flew and then onwards and upwards, the grass-tufted slopes of Howard's Hill falling away beneath them. They cleared the rusty roof of the pig-barn, a dark oblong in the moonlight, then the high wall of brambles that surrounded the woods, and so were swooping up through the trees of the Royal Forest itself. Midge could feel herself losing height and momentum. The hillside was too steep. She wasn't going to be able to reach the upper clearings.

The air resisted her now. It began to feel thick and heavy. Midge tried to swim through it, paddling and kicking with her arms and her legs, but it was no good. She sank slowly to the ground, just beyond the circle of trees that bordered the Royal Clearing. Pegs landed on the pathway ahead of her and folded his wings.

'I can't . . . can't get there.' Midge found herself unable to move. She leaned forward and tried to lift her legs, but they wouldn't work. Her flight had drained all energy from her, left her weak and helpless.

Pegs came back, and turned so that he stood beside her. Midge took hold of his mane, winding the silvery hair about her fingers, feeling the coarse textures against her palm.

He was amazingly strong. Midge held on tight, and as Pegs moved forward to take the strain she was able to lift first one leg and then the other. But it was an achingly slow process. Midge felt as though she was being hauled through treacle, and it made her shoulder muscles hurt. She clung on, though, and they progressed step by step until at last they reached the edge of the clearing.

Lavender. The air was laden with it, an over-whelming pungency that caught in Midge's lungs and threatened to choke her breathing. And there was a strange and expectant silence beyond the fringe of bushes that led into the clearing, a feeling that their coming was known to others.

As Pegs hauled her through the parting fronds of foliage, Midge saw in the brightness of the moonlight that Royal Clearing had been transformed. Wicker . . . a great wall of wicker surrounded the Rowdy-Dow tree . . . the wreckage of many pods and shelters, bits of basketwork, all piled high, and strewn with rags, oil-cloth, scraps of clothing . . .

A gap had been left in the circular wall directly in front of her, and within that huge wicker compound Midge could see that the Various were gathered, hundreds of them, all huddled in silence. The crowd had divided, so that a loose pathway had been formed between them, leading to the Rowdy-Dow tree. And at the foot of the Rowdy-Dow tree stood Una, with Maglin and Tadgemole to either side of her. All were looking directly towards the entranceway to the wicker circle, awaiting their arrival, it seemed. Midge tried to pick out Little-Marten and Henty, but could see no sign of them amongst the hundreds of moonlit faces.

Pegs threw himself forward again, and Midge felt herself being dragged towards the gap in the wicker wall. She saw that all eyes were upon her, and felt foolish that she couldn't walk of her own accord.

Una was beckoning her towards the Rowdy-Dow tree, her arm lifted in welcome, but Midge could walk no further. The effort was too much, and in any case she didn't want to come any closer. This was far enough.

'I . . . I can't.'

Midge let go of Pegs' mane, and knew that she was releasing him for ever. She watched him walk between the lines of the Various. He reached the Rowdy-Dow tree and turned to face her. Una swung herself up onto his back, her movements light and easy, like those of a young girl – and from this distance her features were also those of a girl, perfect and unlined. A sister.

Sister . . . the word that had come to her in her dream. Midge felt dizzy, heady with the suffocating fumes of lavender oil. She watched as Una raised the Stone and Orbis, one in either hand.

There was a shuffle of movement as all around linked arms, held hands, hoisted their children up onto their shoulders – each making contact with their neighbours. The pathway between the crowd had closed now, the arena a solid mass of little people. Excited faces looked up at Midge, and small hands reached towards her, ready to draw her into the circle. Midge could do nothing but allow her fingers to be held. She could move neither forward nor back. Nor could she take her eyes from Una.

She saw flickers of light, fiery brands, carried by two of the archers . . . running . . .

Whooomff – a soft explosion of volatile fuel – and flames immediately shot up behind the Rowdy-Dow tree, the crackle and spark of burning wicker loud upon the still night air.

The flames rapidly spread from either side of the tree, raging around the circle at frightening speed, great clouds of white smoke billowing across the arena and rolling down over the heads of the crowd.

'To Elysse!' Una's voice rose above the roar of the fire, a single cry, and Midge saw her pale arms bring together the Stone and Orbis. A jagged streak of blue sprang across the gap between the closing objects, joining metal and jasper in an arc of electricity – and in that moment Midge let go of the hands that held hers. She jolted backwards, away from the gap in the wicker walls, as the flames met before her, and she raised an arm in order to shield her eyes.

'Pegs!' She called out his name but could see nothing beyond the wall of fire. White smoke enveloped her, choking her, the heat of the flames forcing her further back yet. Midge stumbled away from the fire, and saw the shooting sparks that erupted into the heavens, the rising clouds of ash, swirling grey flakes that fluttered like wings . . . yes, like the wings of moths . . . gypsy moths, flying upwards into the night.

She was melting in the heat, rivers of perspiration trickling down her neck and chest. Soon there would be nothing of her. She must get away . . . away from the fire . . .

'*Fire?* What do you mean – fire?'

Midge sat up in bed. She'd heard her mother's voice out on the landing.

'Better come and look.' Uncle Brian, shouting from

462

the top of the stairs. Footsteps, hurrying past her door.

Midge swung her legs out of bed. Her nightie was drenched in perspiration, and she could feel her hair sticking to the back of her neck. She stumbled across to her bedroom door, opened it, and looked out into the corridor.

'What's going on?' She was shaky, barely in control of her movements.

'It's OK, darling. Brian thinks there's a fire.' Mum and Uncle Brian were at the top of the stairs, her mum struggling to pull back the makeshift curtains that covered the little landing window.

'What? Where?' Midge started to walk down the corridor towards them, but had to keep her hand on the wall in order to steady herself. She felt hardly able to stay upright.

Mum and Uncle Brian were both fully dressed. Was it morning then?

'See it?' Uncle Brain was peering through the window, his hands cupped against the glass.

'Well I might if you'd get your great head out of the way.'

Midge stood behind her mum, craning her neck in order to see.

'What fire? Where?' She heard the sounds of her own voice speaking but it felt weird, as though she was listening to herself from miles away.

'Blimey, I think you're right,' Mum said. 'Up there on the hill. What's going on?'

Midge wriggled around her mum and looked out of the window. She could see a faint glow at the top of Howard's Hill, a smudge of orange against the night sky.

It was true, then. All true. She hadn't been dreaming after all.

'What are we going to do, Brian – call the fire brigade?'

'Well, I suppose we should. Though I don't see how it'll help. They're hardly going to be able to get in there with fire hoses and whatnot. And it certainly isn't going to spread. It looks like it's dying away in any case.'

'But I just don't understand. It *can't* be a brush fire. Everything's soaking wet at this time of year.'

'Lads,' said Uncle Brian. 'It'll be lads mucking about.'

Midge said, 'Mum, I don't feel very well. What time is it? Do I have to get up?'

'Get up? We haven't even gone to bed yet. It's only about half-ten. Come on, sweetheart, you're just really tired, I expect.' Her mum put an arm about her shoulders as she walked her back to her bedroom. 'Mind you,' she said. 'You do feel a bit hot – your nightie's really quite damp. Maybe I should get you a couple of paracetamol.'

Chapter Thirty

In the morning she felt dreadful. Her head was all spinny, and her legs and arms ached as though she'd swum the Channel during the night. And her dreams . . . she just couldn't get them out of her mind. Falling through the skies with Celandine and Una . . . and then flying up to the forest with Pegs . . . and then that terrible fire . . . and the moths . . .

Midge padded over to her window and pulled back the curtains. Howard's Hill looked normal enough in the dull grey light of dawn. The woods were still there. No plumes of smoke or charred and blackened trees that she could see.

But they were gone. She knew beyond all doubt that what she had seen in her dreams had really happened. The Various were no more, and she would never see any of them again. How could she get dressed and go toddling off to school after all that she had witnessed? How was she supposed to feel?

Relieved. As Midge looked at her grey-blue eyes in the bathroom mirror, she realized that despite her dizzy head and aching muscles she actually felt as though a huge weight had been lifted from her. The Various had gone, back to wherever it was that they belonged. To Elysse . . . or to another world . . . or another time. But to somewhere other than here. And yes, her first reaction was one of relief.

Her mum was sitting in the kitchen, writing something in a ledger, and there was a boiled egg waiting for her on the table. Usually she just had cereal.

'Thought you could do with a proper breakfast,' Mum said. 'You'll only get a sandwich for lunch today, as it's that steam trip thing. Your money's on the dresser, by the way – don't forget it.'

'OK. Thanks, Mum.' Midge sat down and looked at her boiled egg. Just about the last thing in the world she felt like eating. 'Um . . . what happened last night? Did you call the fire brigade?'

'What?' Her mum glanced up from the ledger, half smiling, half frowning. Even with her glasses on she always managed to look pretty somehow. Midge often wondered why she wasn't better looking herself. It did seem unfair.

'The, er . . . fire, up on Howard's Hill. Did you do anything about it?' Already Midge had the sense that there was something wrong here.

'*Fire*? What fire?' Her mum obviously hadn't a clue what she was talking about, and Midge felt her shoulders go cold.

'We . . . Uncle Brian said there was a fire. I thought he did. We all stood out on the landing and looked at it through the window. Up on the hill.'

'Um . . . sorry, dear. You've lost me completely.

When was all this then?' Mum put down her pen, and the look on her face was quite concerned now.

'It's OK . . . it's OK.' Midge tried to wave the subject away. 'I must have been dreaming, that's all. Just a dream . . .' But now her whole world was somersaulting around her, slipping away from her grasp. 'I had these dreams . . . really weird dreams. But I thought that bit was real, at least. The bit with the fire. Mum . . . Mum, I'm really scared . . .' Midge stared at her boiled egg, convinced that if she blinked it might disappear before her eyes, or that things might start popping out of it . . . ugly things with bows and arrows . . . moths . . .

'Midge – poor sweetheart. What on earth's the matter? Tell me.' Her mum, coming around the kitchen table, crouching beside her, hugging her shoulders.

'Have you been having nightmares? Tell me.'

'Yes . . . nightmares. Really scary dreams . . .' Midge felt the hot tears rolling down her face. 'I don't know any more what's . . . what's *real*. Oh, Mum, I'm so . . . I'm so . . .'

'Hey-hey-hey. Shh, darling. It's OK. Everything's OK. Now *I'll* tell you what's real. You are, and I am – that's what – and nothing else matters. You're my baby and I love you. That's what's real. So.' Mum grabbed a tissue from the box on the dresser beside her. 'Here's what we'll do. First we'll dry your eyes. Such lovely eyes you have, darling – beautiful eyes. Wish they were mine. There. And then we'll take the day off and spend it together. Yes? We'll say blow school, and blow

467

work, and we'll go off somewhere just the two of us, and have a proper day out, and talk. Hm?'

'Oh, Mum. I can't. It'd be really nice, but I just can't. I have to do this trip – and I'm OK really. I just get scared sometimes, that's all.'

'I know, love, I know. And I know what this is all about, deep down – and it's my fault, not yours. We need to be together more. You feel like you're on your own all the time, because I'm so wrapped up in work. And you think that you have to deal with all your problems by yourself. Well, you don't. You're more important to me than any of this other nonsense, and I'd drop it all like a shot if I thought it was affecting you that badly. Look. We'll compromise. Go on your school trip this morning, if you really feel up to it, and then come home at lunchtime. I'll pick you up from the station, and I'll tell your form teacher you've got a dental appointment or something. It won't hurt just this once. What time are you due back into Taunton?'

'About . . . about eleven o'clock, I think.' Midge blew her nose on the tissue. 'It's only like a half-hour train ride or something, there and back.'

'Then it's settled. I'll pick you up at eleven, and we'll take the rest of the day off. Go out and have lunch somewhere – do some of the things we *should* have done together over half-term. OK?'

'Well . . . OK. But you'll have to talk to Miss Oldham. She's *terrible* on kids taking time off for no reason.'

'You let me deal with Miss Oldham. And it's not time off for no reason. It's for a very good reason. I'll phone her and explain, don't you worry. Now are you sure that you want to go in at all?'

'Yeah. I better had.'

'All right. Come on, then. I'll run you down to the bus stop. Just grab a bit of toast to eat in the car, and we'll have proper lunch later on. Together.'

Sam sat next to her on the school coach, and that was a comfort.

'God, I've had a boring half-term,' she said. 'Stuck out in blimmin' Manderville Wick with only the rocks to talk to. I've really missed you.'

'Awww, have you?' said Midge. 'Should have given me a call.'

'Yeah, but I couldn't be zipped. So what about you? Do anything fun?'

Midge thought about it. 'Yeah, I did actually. Went tobogganing with my cousin, George. Laughed so much I thought I'd do myself an injury.'

'What, George Howard? Yeah, I know him – that little nut with the floppy hair.'

'Ha! That's him. The one and only.'

It was good to talk to somebody normal, and they didn't come much more normal than Sam Lewis.

The steam train was really quite beautiful. It was already sitting in the station when the school party arrived on the platform, the engine quietly hissing away to itself. Midge immediately loved everything about it – the cream and brown coaches, with their brass door handles and GWR logos, the friendly smell of steam and coal and oil that hung upon the chilly

March air. And best of all was the engine itself, no awesome monster of the steam age, such as Midge had seen in films, but something rather more modest – a chubby little workhorse with its square tank and rounded dome. It didn't even have a name as far as Midge could see – just a number: 1025. Two bewhiskered men in grubby blue overalls and peaked caps leaned out of the open cab, chatting together. They looked as though they were enjoying themselves. Midge breathed in the atmosphere that surrounded the engine. It smelled like burnt toast. She wrinkled her nose, hovering on the edge of a sneeze.

Sam came up and linked an arm through hers. 'Come on,' she said. 'Let's go and get a decent seat, or we'll be stuck with the dreggos.'

Miss Oldham was standing on the platform shepherding everyone into the carriages.

'Now remember, this will all be part of this term's project on the Victorians. I want completed worksheets handed in to me at the end of the morning . . .'

'Yeah, yeah,' Sam muttered. 'Always with the worksheets. You're never just allowed to *enjoy* anything, are you?'

'. . . and your feet *off* the seats. We've a fifteen-minute stop at Evercreech, before coming back again. There's a shop there, but I want to see no sweet wrappers, no orange peel . . .'

Midge and Sam clambered in through the open doorway, and hustled along the corridors looking for an empty compartment.

'Hey, this is great! Why aren't trains like this now?

470

Look – you get proper luggage racks. And you can open the windows, and everything!'

They found a compartment with only one other person in it – Kerry Hodge. Midge got the impression that Sam would have kept on looking a little longer, but she would have felt guilty if she'd passed by the open door. The snub would have been so obvious.

'Hiya, Kerry. Good half-term?'

'Mm. OK, I shuppose.'

'Budge up then.'

The three of them sat looking out of the window for a moment, but Sam became instantly bored with that.

'Look – they're like hammocks, those luggage racks. You could probably sleep up there. I mean, if it was night-time, and you were like really tired or something.' Sam stood up and grabbed one of the rails, testing its strength. 'I reckon I could get up there.'

'Yeah,' said Midge. 'And you're probably daft enough to try. I can just see the Old'un letting you have a little nap while the rest of us grind away at our worksheets.'

'It'sh dead eashy,' said Kerry. 'I've done mine already.'

'Yeah, well, you would, you Brownie,' said Sam. She sat down again. 'Let's have a look, though.'

Kerry shrugged. 'OK.'

But then there was the sharp *peeep* of a whistle out on the platform, and the carriage jolted forward. Kerry's worksheet was forgotten for the time being as the train pulled out of the station and the world began to roll by.

The three girls sat in silence, lulled by the gentle rocking motion of the compartment and the scrolling landscape outside. It wasn't such a bad way to begin the second half of term.

On the journey back they shared out the sweets and crisps that they'd bought in the little kiosk at Evercreech station.

'It's all very well,' said Sam, her mouth full of Wotsits, 'but it doesn't go on long enough. You can't really soak up all this Victorian shtuff on a train ride that only lasts half an hour each way. I jusht don't feel that I've quite *learned* enough yet – know what I mean? You could do with a whole day of it really. Maybe two.'

'Oi, watch out,' said Kerry. 'You're shpitting bitsh of crishp all over me.'

'What? That's pretty rich, coming from you, you walking hosepipe.'

'Midge Walters? Anybody know which compartment she's in? Oh . . . is she? Thanks.'

Midge could hear her form teacher coming along the corridor, asking her whereabouts. She quickly got out her worksheet, and at least managed to get her name written on it before Miss Oldham put her head into the compartment.

'Ah, there you are. I had a phone call from your mum just before we left this morning, Midge. Told me to remind you about your dental appointment. I gather it should have been during half-term but then had to be rescheduled or something. Perhaps it couldn't be helped, but I'd appreciate it if things could be better organized in future. It is a *bit* much, taking the afternoon off on your first day back. But there. Your mum'll pick you up at eleven from the station – though we'll be on the coach back to school by then. I'll have to ask a porter to keep an eye on you or something.'

'Yes, Miss Oldham. Sorry about that.'

'Well you sneaky old sneak, you,' said Sam, once Miss Oldham had retired. 'I bet you planned that to get an extra half-day.'

'No, I didn't, honest,' said Midge. 'I'd forgotten all about it. Give us a look at your answers then, Kerry, otherwise I'll never get this done.'

There was another school party on the platform as the train pulled back into the station. All girls, and all dressed in blue jackets and berets.

'St Hilda's convent,' muttered Sam as she opened the carriage door. 'Snotty lot.'

'You have to feel a bit sorry for them, really,' said Midge.

'Yeah,' said Kerry. 'Can't be much fun with no wildlife to look at.'

'Wildlife? What're you on about?'

Kerry nodded towards a group of boys from their own class – Carl Polegato and two of his friends. They were already out of the train and passing the time by taking it in turns to punch each other on the shoulder.

'Haha! Yeah, like you said – wildlife.'

'Right! Everybody go out through the exit and line up by the coach. And stay on the pavement!' Miss Oldham's voice, rising above the general hubbub.

'Midge, you'd better come with me. We'll have a quick word at the helpdesk.'

'See you tomorrow then, Midge,' said Sam.

'Yeah, see you. See you, Kerry.'

'Bye.'

The woman at the desk told Miss Oldham it'd be best if Midge stayed on the station. 'If she has a seat just out there on the platform, then I'll be able to keep an eye on her through the window. Go on, love. You'll be fine.'

'OK. Bye, Miss Oldham.'

'Bye, Midge. Now don't go wandering about. Just stay here where this lady can see you and wait till your mum comes, all right? See you tomorrow, then. Ooh – worksheet. Yes, I'll take that. Thank you.'

Away went Miss Oldham, shoulders back, heels clicking briskly on the marbled floor of the lobby. The teacher walk. Was that part of their training? Midge wondered.

There was a chalkboard at the platform entrance, and Midge read it as she passed by. 'Steam Special! Taunton–Evercreech return's. Wed 03 Mar. Ticket's available.' The apostrophes were all wrong.

She heard the guard blow his whistle as she stepped back onto the platform, and then the *thuff . . . thuff-thuff . . . thuff* of the engine. Great clouds of black smoke came shooting out of the funnel. It was a bit messy, she supposed.

Midge watched as the brown-and-cream carriages began to move. Some of the St Hilda's girls were look-ing excitedly out of the windows, just as she and Kerry and Sam had done. Did they have worksheets to complete as well? Probably.

Then she saw a girl in a compartment by herself. A pale and familiar face staring out at her. Cropped hair, dark eyes, some sort of hat. The girl smiled in recognition and raised a hand, her palm very white against the carriage window. She was waving. Goodbye . . . goodbye . . .

Midge raised her own hand automatically and waved in return, but it took her a few moments longer to realize who the girl was.

Celandine . . .

It *was* Celandine. Absolutely and without a doubt. Short cropped hair . . . thin face. Not quite the girl in the photograph that hung in her bedroom – more like the little nurse in that later newspaper clipping. But it was definitely her.

Midge could only stand there and wave, helpless, unable to keep the moment from slipping away. Goodbye . . . goodbye . . .

The chuffs of smoke and steam stumbled over themselves, then fell into a steadier rhythm as the engine gained momentum. Midge kept her eyes fixed on the window, but the angle had changed and she could no longer see the girl. The train was slowly disappearing, curving into a distant belt of trees. *Ba-dum* . . . *ba-dum* . . . *ba-dum* . . . a last rumble of wheels, and the end carriage had rocked out of sight.

Gone. Only the smell of it remained. Burnt toast.

Midge stood in the empty silence, staring down the track. It was a while before it occurred to her to go and sit down.

She was stunned, shocked by the clarity of what she had seen. And some of her earlier fears were coming back to her – the scary feeling that she could no longer tell what was real and what was not. She *wasn't* dreaming, she knew she wasn't. But then that was what she had thought last night. Maybe it was all just her imagination. All of it . . .

Midge sat back on the metal bench and stuffed her hands into her blazer pockets. No. Whatever had happened last night, the Various had been real – George had seen them, and Katie too. She might have had some weird dreams about them, but she hadn't imagined them. This could be different. She might have been mistaken, or she might have just seen a ghost, but she definitely wasn't dreaming.

There was a connection between them. Her and Celandine. And Una. Three girls, linked together across time. And Celandine had somehow seen into the future, seen this person that would be her, Midge, years and years before she'd even been born. She'd known what she would look like, the clothes that she would wear and everything. Seeing someone from the future. That was far more amazing than the other way round, seeing someone from the past, wasn't it?

So when she'd waved at the girl sitting on the train . . . Celandine . . . had she been looking into the past? And had the girl on the train who had waved back to her been looking into the future?

Midge couldn't get her head around it at all. She thought she could remember Aunt Celandine saying something about this, though – seeing her from a train. She'd have to ask.

And then it hit her. There would be no checking back on this story, no comparing of notes. Not any more. Celandine had gone. The smiling face at the carriage window, the last wave . . . goodbye . . . good-bye . . .

Midge felt her lungs collapsing in a huge sigh. She knew. She just knew.

'Yes, we'll see each other again, dear. That's a promise.' Her great-great-aunt's voice.

And Celandine, the child, had kept that promise for her. They had seen each other again, one last time.

The station clock moved on, announcements echoed over the tannoy, people and trains came and went. Midge just sat on the bench and let it all go by, lost in the numbness of her own thoughts. She felt sadness but no overwhelming pain of loss. Nothing had happened that shouldn't have happened. And everything that should have happened had. The Various had gone. And Pegs, and Una. And now Celandine. They'd all moved on, along with the station clock.

'Midge?' Her mum, walking out onto the platform. Smiling, but not smiling quite as she might have been. So she knew too.

'Midge . . . are you OK?' Mum sat next to her on the

477

bench, put her arm about her shoulders. Midge leaned into her. And waited.

'Midge, I've just had a phone call . . . from Mount Pleasant . . . just as I was leaving . . .'

'It's OK, Mum. I know.'

'What?'

'I already know. It's Aunt Celandine, isn't it?'

'Er . . . yes. I'm afraid so. Carol Reeve called . . . but how did you know about it? I thought you weren't supposed to have mobiles at school.'

'No. I saw her. Mum . . . I *saw* her. Aunt Celandine, when she was a little girl. She was on the train – the steam train? I saw her through the window, waving goodbye to me. It was so . . . well, it was so nice really. She was smiling and waving. And I just sort of knew what had happened.'

'My God, Midge . . .' Her mum looked at her, clearly shocked. 'But that's like . . . I don't know . . . it's like clairvoyance or something.'

'She used to see me too. When she was young she saw me lots of times. I never told you that. She said she knew what I'd look like and everything, before she even met me.'

'Whaaat? But Midge . . . that's very *strange*. Are you sure? I had no idea that she was . . . that way.'

'They used to call her Witch, when she was at school. She wasn't a witch, though. Not how they meant it anyway.' Midge snuggled further into her mum's warm winter coat. It was good to be cuddled. 'I think she got happier in the end.'

'Well, that was something that Carol Reeve was very

478

keen that you should know. She said that you'd
brought such a light into that old lady's life. Those
were her actual words, Midge, and it made me very
proud to hear them. Very proud. And a little bit
ashamed for not making more of an effort myself. She
said that she thought that there was a very special
bond between the two of you. Something almost
magical, she thought. And she said that Aunt
Celandine was happy and peaceful at the end, and in
no pain. Maybe they tend to say that whatever the case,
but I got the impression that she really meant it.
Elaine was with her when it happened, so Carol said.
Anyway, it's clear that a lot of her happiness was due to
you, and that's a truly wonderful thing to know. You're
a very lovely girl, and I'm proud of you.'

'Thanks,' Midge whispered. 'I'm proud of you too.'

They sat together in silence for a while, cuddled up
together on the bench, in that warm mother-and-
daughter closeness that always lies waiting to be

rediscovered, no matter how long its absence.

'Come on, then. What do you want to do? Are you still up for lunch, or would you rather go home and just be quiet for a while?'

'Um . . . could we go over to the mall at Almbury Mills and have lunch there?' Midge looked up into her mum's face. 'I don't mean actually go to Mount Pleasant, but just so that we're sort of nearby. I'd like to be close, if I could. Just for a while.'

'That's a very nice idea. We'll do that. And then perhaps we could go and buy some flowers.'

'Yes.'

They got up from the bench and walked out of the station, still with their arms about one another.

Chapter Thirty-one

She'd never flown, and that was one thing that she regretted. Not such a big regret, perhaps, in a lifetime so full of other amazing experiences, but still. It would have been nice to have known what it felt like to be in an aeroplane. To fly.

Miss Howard looked out of the window of her apartment for a few moments before closing her eyes again. Spring. It was already here, so they told her. The crocuses were apparently out, and soon it would be the daffodils. A shame she couldn't see them. But she could barely open her eyes in any case. Everything had become such an effort.

'I'm just going to give these bookshelves the once-over, Miss Howard, and then I'm done. That's unless there's anything else you want.'

Elaine, fussing around as usual. The bookshelves didn't need any 'once-over'.

'Yes. Thank you, Elaine. Would you mind making me some toast before you go?'

'Toast, Miss Howard? It's not long gone breakfast time – not that you've managed to eat anything. But yeah, OK. I don't mind, if that's what you fancy.'

'I do. Thank you.'

Speaking wasn't easy, and she knew that she certainly couldn't cope with eating toast. But she did like the smell of it. Elaine nearly always managed to burn it somehow, and the smell of burnt toast brought back so many memories . . . the kitchen range at Mill Farm . . . her mother, flustered, never able to quite get the hang of the English way of making toast. This very room, of course, was brought back to memory by the smell of fresh bread toasted on an open fire. And railway stations were also in there, curiously. Burnt toast reminded her of railway stations.

Not that her memory needed much prompting now. Thanks to Midge, she could bring to mind whole sequences of events that she thought had been lost to her for ever. Fin, and the little forest people . . . reading to them from Aesop's fables . . . chalking the alphabet on the cave walls. So wonderful that had been, before everything began to go wrong. School, and Freddie, and the Ickri and the Orbis. But it had come right in the end, and nothing else mattered.

It had all come right in the end. All that had needed to be done was done, and it was time to go. She'd better get her bag packed.

'Did you want to hold the fork, Miss Howard?'

No, she didn't want to hold the fork. Not today.

'Not today, thank you, Elaine. I need to get to the railway station.'

'What?'

Her Uncle Josef and her Aunt Sarah were waiting to

walk her down to the station. So kind they had been to her. They understood her in a way that her own mother and father never had. They asked no questions, nor anything of her. They only gave – and what they gave was opportunity, the means to change her life for the better.

She had choices now, and either choice was a good one. She could go to school with Nina, or she could go and work with her uncle at the clinic. How wonderful. How wonderful it was to be a girl, thirteen years old, and with so many good things to look forward to. And how wonderful to feel that she had something to offer in return. Gifts to be given.

It was good to be walking down through the town in the sunshine, her aunt and uncle to either side of her, and she was very happy. Train journeys were still a treat to her, and she was looking forward to this one.

Market days were always cheerful, and Station Road was a bustle of drays and wagons and handcarts, all piled high with boxes of fruit, live chickens, beer barrels, and clothes racks.

'There is something about a railway carriage compartment that clears the mind. Marvellous! Quite magical.'

That was what Uncle Josef said, and it was true. Celandine sat in her compartment and looked out of the window at her aunt and uncle. They stood beneath the station clock, waving to her as the train pulled away. Smiling faces.

And then the girl appeared, there in time to see her off, just as she knew would happen. Midge. A mystery child no more, but one with a name and with gifts of her own. A beautiful girl. Most intelligent, most perceptive.

Her face was alight with sudden recognition, her arm raised in farewell. Goodbye, my dear, goodbye. I'm only sorry that there wasn't more time. Another small regret.

The platform rolled away and disappeared, to be replaced by white fence posts that ticked past the compartment window . . . one . . . two . . . three, four. Too fast now and too many to count. *Ba-dum . . . ba-dum . . . ba-dum.* The rhythm of the wheels, picking up ever greater speed.

And such a speed! The fence posts became a white blur, hedges, telegraph poles, gateways all flashing past. *Barradum . . . barradum . . . barradurrr . . .* the sound of the wheels rose to a crescendo . . . a continuous rumbling roar of metal upon metal . . . faster . . . faster . . .

. . . and then nothing. No sound. The hedges dipped downwards, tilting away from the compartment window, and the open fields became visible, farm buildings and orchards forming themselves into a receding patchwork, a marvellous quilt of browns and greens, all stitched together by rhynes and roads and rivers. A map of the wetlands, far, far below. A map of England. A map of the world.

So this was flying.

The world shrinking into the distance, changing colour . . . purple . . . violet . . . red. Red like a cricket ball . . . red like the Stone . . . red like Goppo's tiny pebble in a game of Blinder. And gone.

Higher and higher, speeding into the blue. So peaceful. A shimmering blue silence, and then nothing at all . . . nothing but the faint aroma of toast . . .

Chapter Thirty-two

The heat of the summer sun streaming through the sitting-room windows was drowsy-making, and so Midge was doubly surprised that it should be Katie, of all people, who suggested they go and have a look at the woods.

'Blimey,' said Midge. 'You *must* be bored.'

'I am.' Katie threw her book across the sofa. 'But that's not the reason. Not really. You were very weird, you know, after Aunt Celandine died, and after all that . . . all that stuff you told me about. And George wasn't much better. Nightmares and everything. I was all for telling Mum and Dad what was going on, but of course I couldn't because then they'd think we'd *all* gone off our heads.' Katie picked absently at the stitching on her trainers as she looked out of the open window. 'I just think it'd be a good thing to do. I heard some-where that if you really want to forget about something you should take it out of its box and have a look at it.'

This didn't sound like her cousin at all, and Midge stared at her in surprise. Perhaps she'd changed. Katie had been reading more lately, Midge had noticed – actual books rather than the usual magazines and TV guides. And she didn't seem to be quite so continually bothered about her appearance.

'It's you, isn't it?' said Midge. 'It's you that wants to forget about it. I thought . . . well, I thought that you never *did* think about it. That's what you told me.'

'Yeah, I know. I was lying. And you're right, it does bother me. Sort of. I feel like I need some . . . proof. Something to make it real, and then that would make it go away. It's like that little cup thing you showed me, you know? You've got something to hold onto to say that it really did happen. So you know you're not crazy. I just remember, that's all. Or I think I do. Then I wonder if it's all some . . . like I'm going to . . . wake up or something.' Katie's fingernail picked rapidly at the seam on her trainers.

'Yeah,' said Midge. 'You're right. That's just what it's like.' She thought about this for a bit. Was it time to face up to what she knew she would have to do in the end – find out whether what she believed had happened was real? To see whether the Various had truly gone? 'OK, then,' she said. 'Let's go and take a look.'

'What – now?'

'Might as well be now. Any idea where George is?'

They found George giving directions to a couple of the weekend guests – a young man and woman, both neatly kitted out in new hiking boots and backpacks.

'You just keep heading that way,' he said. 'And when

you get to the rhyne turn right and carry on till you come to a weir. Cross over the weir, and it's just sort of straight on to Burnham Woods. You can't really miss it. Oh, but watch out for the planks on the weir. They wobble.'

'OK. Thanks a lot,' said the man. He looked at his pocket map, turning it this way and that.

'George.' Katie got his attention and beckoned him over. 'We're going for a walk. Up the hill to the woods. Want to come?'

George looked at her, then at Midge. 'Is she kidding?' he said. It wasn't like Katie to be suggesting anything that involved exercise, and it certainly wasn't like her to be including him in any of her plans.

'No, seriously,' said Midge. 'We were talking. We thought maybe we ought to go and see . . . what's up there. Or, you know, make sure that there's nothing.'

George flicked back his fringe. 'I've been sort of forgetting about it,' he said. 'Or trying to. It goes away in the end – like it did the first time. I think it's better not to think about it. Not to poke your nose in.'

'OK,' said Katie. 'We'll see you later.'

'No, hang on a minute.' Midge wanted George to be there. 'What we were saying was, maybe this *is* the best way of forgetting about it, or putting your mind at rest or whatever. To go and have a look. I bet you anything that they're gone. I know they are, but don't you want to be sure as well?'

George still looked doubtful.

'Come on, you wuss. It'll be fun.' Midge knew she could call George a wuss. He was anything but.

He laughed and said, 'OK, then. But if some little twerp starts shooting at me then I'm off – and you two are on your own.'

They climbed over the gateway into the Field of Thistles.

'Anybody got the time?' said Midge. 'I'm supposed to be going over to Sam Lewis's for tea.'

George pulled something out of his pocket. It was a wristwatch, but it had no strap.

'Two o'clock. Just gone. You've got hours yet.'

'Where'd you get that watch?'

'I told you. That old bloke at Aunt Celandine's funeral. Mr Lickis? He just gave it to me – dunno why. I keep meaning to get a strap for it. Works OK, though.'

'Oh, right.' Midge remembered now. George had said something about it at the time, but she'd been too upset to take much notice. There had been a surprising amount of people at the funeral, and the tiny church at Statton had been almost full. She'd been glad to see that so many had remembered Aunt Celandine – people from the home at Mount Pleasant, of course, but others too. Old patients of hers, a few work colleagues. Girls that Aunt Celandine had trained, ancient themselves now.

And everything had been OK until they brought the coffin into the church. That was what had upset her so much – not just the white-haired old men who carried it down the aisle on their unsteady shoulders, though that was sad enough, but the fact that the coffin was so small. It was tiny, almost like a child's. And it was the image of a child that Midge had pictured in there – Celandine as a girl, the one from the photograph, dressed in her tight frock and lace-up boots, all her lovely hair spread out . . .

She knew that it wasn't so, but it had all been too much for her on top of everything else, and she had burst into tears. Howled and howled.

Afterwards it wasn't so bad. Everyone was very kind to her. Carol Reeve gave her a big hug. And then George had shown her the watch that this Mr Lickis had given him. He'd managed to smear it in butter from the sandwich he was holding, or mayonnaise or something, and it had reminded Midge of the watch in *Alice in Wonderland.*

'Blimey, it's hot,' said George. 'We should have brought something to drink.' They'd reached the sheep-gate, and the steepest part of Howard's Hill still lay ahead of them. The sun blazed down on their bare heads as they trudged on, silent now, saving their breath for the climb. By the time they got to the gully they were all red-faced and panting.

'Phew. I've got a stitch now,' said Katie. 'Great view, though. Do you know, I can't actually think when was the last time I came up here.'

'Probably when you were still small enough for Dad to carry you,' said George.

'Ha! Yeah, probably. Where to now, Midge? Where's this tunnel then?'

Midge had an awful premonition that the tunnel wasn't going to be there – that all they would find would be a solid wall of brambles and that she would be made to look stupid. Or completely insane.

But she said, 'It's at the end of this gully.' She led the way, partly because that was her role, and partly because if this all turned out to be so much nonsense then she wanted to be the first to know of it.

It was still there. The dark mouth of the tunnel could just be seen through the overhanging curtain of brambles, and Midge felt relieved – proud too, in a way. It wasn't every day that you got to show off such an astounding discovery.

'Yipes – is that it?' George bent low and drew aside a few of the brambles. 'It's amazing.'

'God, Midge. And you just went in there all by yourself?' Katie peered into the tunnel.

'Yeah,' said Midge. She still hadn't said very much to either of them about Pegs. She just couldn't somehow. 'Come on. You have to keep your head down or your hair gets all caught up.'

'Yuck! It *stinks* in here.' Halfway along the tunnel Katie was struggling. '*And* it's all slimy. Wish I'd put on some boots.'

The stream had dried to a trickle in the hot summer weather, but the sides really were quite slippery.

'It'll wash off,' said Midge. 'And it's just a few more steps.'

'Good. Because I've nearly had enough already.' Their voices sounded weird in the confined space.

The three of them stood on the large flat rock, and looked about them. For Midge it was both strange and gratifying. Strange because of all that she had witnessed here back in the cold dark days of winter, and gratifying because of George and Katie's open-mouthed amazement.

'It's like . . . it's like a whole other planet or something. I mean, it's so *different* from anywhere else . . . so . . . so . . .' Katie was searching for words.

'Yeah, it's like . . . prehistoric.' George had got closer to the feel of the place. There *was* something ancient about the fallen trees, the swampy smell of dense vegetation, garlicky and musty at the same time.

'I bet we're the first humans in here for hundreds of years,' said Midge. 'You know, actual humans. Well, apart from Aunt Celandine, I suppose.'

'I never even met her. Wish I had now.' Katie sounded regretful. 'I can't imagine . . . well, I just can't imagine that kid in the photo being here as well. So, these *people*. Were they all like the ones we saw at the farm?'

'No. There were different tribes. Some were hunters and some were like farmers. And there were another lot that fished – and then there were the ones who lived in the caves.'

'What caves?'

'I can show you in a bit. I never went in there, though. Come on. I want to see what happened up at the clearings.'

They picked their way up among the winding rocky pathways, ducking beneath the low branches of trees, and eventually reached the fringe of foliage that bordered the smaller clearing. The air was cooler here, and they were glad to stand in the shade of the sycamores, getting their breath back as they looked out upon the sunlit enclosure.

Midge shook her head at the wonder of it.

The Rowdy-Dow tree, once so dead and barkless that its appearance had been white, was now charred and smoke-stained, a great dark stump of a thing, its limbs crow-black against the blue of the summer sky. And around its base was a perfect circle, a ring of fresh grass that had sprung up from the scorched earth, a brighter green than the grass beyond. Like a fairy ring.

So what she had seen, or dreamed that she had seen, had truly happened. The fire had been real. Within that circle the Various had stood, and had brought together the Stone and the Orbis, and had travelled on. They really had gone.

'Is this what you expected?' Katie was staring at her.

'Yes. Pretty much.' Midge tried to keep her voice steady.

'Let's have a closer look then.' George stepped forward into the sunshine.

Midge hung back a little longer. She wasn't sure that she wanted to go poking about among the grass, for fear of what she might find. It would be awful if there were . . . remains or something. She still couldn't grasp what had actually happened in that outlandish ceremony she had witnessed. Or imagined. Because after all, she couldn't *really* have been here. Could she?

'You OK?' said Katie.

'Yeah. I think so.'

There was very little to see. The ashes had been mostly washed away by spring and summer rain, just a few patches of orangey-white stuff still visible here and there. Other areas of the soil were black, and there were scatterings of charcoal amongst the fresh grass. It was surprising how quickly the grass had reappeared. Another season and there would be no evidence left of what had happened here.

But what *had* happened?

'I still don't get it,' said Katie. 'So they were all standing inside this bonfire thing, and then they all just disappeared?'

It did seem ridiculous, put like that.

Midge sighed. 'Well, yeah, basically. That's what I saw. I mean, I dreamed it, but it was like I was really seeing it. I just keep thinking . . . I just keep thinking about this idea of aliens. That's the only thing that makes any sense. I mean, if there are other worlds – and loads of people reckon there are – then maybe . . . you know . . . it's not all flying saucers and UFOs and whatnot.' She was struggling, but she clung onto what she knew. 'They called themselves travellers. That's what they did. Travelled. At least they did before they lost the Orbis. And I *think* they meant travelling through time. Or space. Or other lives. You saw it, didn't you, George – the Orbis?'

'Yeah. Weird or what,' said George. He was kicking around in the grass on the other side of the blackened tree. 'Like an old astronomy thing. All slidey knobs and suns and moons and stuff. Hey, what's this? A relic!' He bent down and picked something up from the grass. It was pronged – the metal part of a small gardening fork.

'Ha! Great find,' said Katie. 'We got what we came for – let's go!'

'No, he's right, though,' said Midge. 'It is a relic. They used things like that for fishing and stuff. Like a spear.'

George brought the fork across to show them. It was encrusted in dried ash, orange with rust.

'What are you going to do with it?' said Katie.

'Clean it up and keep it. Maybe hang it in the tree house. It's my relic.' George stuck the fork in his back pocket.

'Hmf.' Katie sounded unimpressed. Nevertheless she kicked half-heartedly at the grass around her feet, perhaps in search of some relic of her own.

'Let me show you the other clearing,' said Midge. 'Then maybe we should go and look at the caves.'

They walked across to where a gap in the bushes led into the Great Clearing. The short pathway had already become overgrown through lack of use. Soon the bushes would meet and the two areas would become entirely separate.

The pea sticks and beanpoles had all gone now, and the once neatly tended rows of vegetables were a tangled mess, overgrown with weeds and tall grass. You could still see what had once been, though, and Midge said, 'This was like allotments. Beans and potatoes and stuff. Look.' She grabbed hold of a bunch of flower-headed stalks and pulled, not really knowing what to expect. The stalks were fleshy and they crushed easily within her grasp – the immediate aroma giving her a clue as to what she had found. An onion, long gone to seed.

'Want it?' She dangled the sorry object in front of Katie.

Katie laughed. 'Er, no, I don't think so. Come on. Show us these caves.'

As they ducked into the shade of the trees once more, Midge took one last look around the Great Clearing. It was a shame really. All that work gone to waste. She turned to follow George and Katie, but then something caught her attention on the other side of the ruined allotments – dark shadows amongst the stumpy hawthorn bushes. Her heart jumped, and for a moment she thought that they were still here after all. The Various! But it wasn't people that she could see – it was horses. Those funny little horses that they kept, two or three of them, grazing in the distant shade. So they'd left them behind. She opened her mouth to call George and Katie back, but then thought better of it. Leave the poor creatures in peace. Perhaps they'd be discovered someday and per- haps they wouldn't, but she wasn't going to be the one to give them away. And in the meantime at least they'd have plenty to eat. Let them have the run of the place, then, and enjoy themselves whilst they could. They would be her final secret.

'Hang on,' she called. 'You don't know the way!'

It wasn't easy clambering up the bank of loose shale that spewed out in front of the main cave. For every three steps up you were likely to slip back two.

But they managed it, and stood together in the cool entranceway, peering into the gloom.

'I can't see a blimmin'— Whoa! It echoes in here, doesn't it?' George's voice bounced around the cavern. They took a few steps forward and gradually their eyes adjusted to the darkness. The walls to either side of them were now visible, but it was still impossible to see into the depths. How far did it go back? There was an entrance to a kind of little side chamber, and they cautiously felt their way around this, but it was completely empty as far as they could tell. Midge put her hand up to see whether she was able to touch the roof. Her fingertips just reached, and she could feel rough textures . . . bumpy things . . . like barnacle-encrusted rocks at the seaside. But then the thought of bats came into her head, and she quickly withdrew her hand.

'Should have brought a torch,' said George.

They none of them felt like exploring much further without some light to guide them, and so the experience was a bit disappointing.

'Doesn't matter, though,' Katie said. 'We can always come back and have a proper look.'

'Yeah.'

They turned towards the glare of the outside world. Celandine lived here, thought Midge. It just seemed impossible. She ran her fingers along the walls as she followed George and Katie. Smooth flat stone on this particular bit, chalky patterns . . .

'Hang on a minute.' Midge stepped back and looked at the marks on the wall. It wasn't patterns. It was writing.

'Look at this.'

'What?'

Some of the words were still visible, big round letters, written in a child's hand.

'What does that say? *Early one* . . . something . . . *just as the* . . . something . . . *was* . . . *rising*? Does that say "rising"? Is it a poem?' Midge put her head to one side, trying to figure it out from a different angle.

'That word's "maiden",' said George. 'Next line down. Definitely "maiden".'

'Oh, *I* know what it is.' Katie had got it. And to George and Midge's surprise she began to sing, her voice echoing softly around the cave.

'Early one morning, just as the sun was rising,
I heard a maiden sing in the valley below.
"Oh never leave me, oh don't deceive me,
How could you use a poor maiden so?"'

It was lovely. The tune was so pretty, and Katie sang it so beautifully that Midge felt the sudden stab of tears. She didn't trust herself to speak and was glad when George said something first.

'I never heard that before.'

'Yeah, we learned it at playschool. Good old Miss Reade. She misread me, I can tell you. Thought I was her little angel. It's surprising how far being able to sing in tune'll get you. I used to nick her mint imperials and some other poor sap always got the blame.'

Midge burst out laughing and took the opportunity to quickly wipe her eyes. Katie was such a hoot sometimes.

'But this is so . . . fantastic,' she said. 'Don't you see? Celandine wrote this, when she was a girl. She ran away from home – well, from school – and lived here for a while. Right here in these caves. It's just . . .' She couldn't find the words to explain. 'I can't believe it.'

'Yeah, it is pretty amazing.' Katie and Midge stood looking at the chalk writing in awe. Ninety years ago those words had been written, and by a child from another age. Their great-great-aunt.

'Hey . . .' George had found something else. He'd moved further back down the cave and was reaching into a small alcove that had been cut into the opposite wall, a thing that they hadn't noticed before among the deep shadows.

'What's this?' He came back towards them holding a little piece of grey pottery in his hand, a circular dish that had been pinched together on one side to form a spout.

'Is it like an oil lamp or something?' The dish was half full of some waxy substance, and there was a bit of blackened string poking out from the spout. George sniffed at it.

'Oof. It smells perfumy. There you go.' He handed the object to Katie. 'You have it. A relic.'

'What? Can I? Hey, thanks, George. That's really sweet of you. I think it *is* a lamp, you know.'

'Yeah, they had lavender oil, the cave-dwellers,' said Midge. 'I don't know how, quite. I haven't noticed that much lavender about.'

'It's probably just scented with lavender,' said Katie. She sniffed at the lamp. 'Yeah, it's probably tallow.'

'What's tallow?'

'Some sort of animal oil, I think. Or maybe it's whale. Dunno. Anyway, I've got a relic now. Thanks, George.'

'That's OK.'

It was a harmonious moment, a rare enough event in the lives of George and Katie, and perhaps as good a time as any to be thinking of leaving. They slithered down the bank of shale and made their way back towards the tunnel.

'You know what?' said Katie. 'This is all ours. I mean, I know it belongs to Dad and Auntie Chris, but it *will* be ours, won't it? How lucky is that?'

'Yeah, hadn't thought of that,' said Midge.

'I might build a proper tree house here,' said George. 'A really big one – or maybe even a whole adventure trail. Hey – we could start charging people to come in!'

'Nah.' Katie stepped from stone to stone as she headed into the wicker tunnel. 'We see enough of the "guests" as it is. They're not my blimmin' guests.'

Midge was last out of the tunnel, and she pulled at the rickety wicker doors, closing them behind her and rearranging the brambles as best she could. The entrance was better hidden now. No stray country walker would ever know it was there, and soon it would become even more overgrown. She followed George and Katie, climbing up the steep bank of the gully to throw herself down onto the grass beside them. They sat for a while looking out across the hazy expanse of the wetlands. It had been a year now, Midge realized, since she'd first come here. And so much had happened since then that it made her head spin.

From a distance Mill Farm looked pretty much the same as it had last summer – the farmhouse itself and the stables and the cider barn still standing where they had always stood. But how life down there had changed. There was a part of Midge that wished it could all have stayed as when she first saw it: a glorious jumble, the yard and barns piled high with junk, chickens running in and out of the hallway. The Deputation from Rhode Island, she had called them. Then there was the old Wellington boot that lay permanently on the front path with the Favoured One as its occupant, the cider barn that had become the Orphanage, Tojo the Assassin, the Summer Palace . . .

And herself, of course, as mistress of the whole wonderful ramshackle mess – the Mistress of Mill Farm. She smiled to think about it. Things were so different now.

Perhaps the change was for the best. Ever since the guest apartments had opened they'd been pretty well booked up. Mum was happy in her little office, Uncle Brian was happy, pottering about with his napkins and corkscrews. There had been a couple of hints lately that her cousins and Auntie Pat might be moving in, and that would be good. Barry was OK. Sometimes he stayed over, sometimes he didn't. He and Mum didn't appear to be in any rush to go and get married or anything yucky. Although maybe that would be OK too, Midge supposed. Whatever Mum decided to do would be right. Her decisions usually were.

And what they had done today had definitely been right. They'd taken the thing out of its box, and looked at it, and then put it away again and closed the lid. It was still a mystery, something that might never be explained. Something that might be forgotten, or not. But there was nothing in there to be frightened of.

She didn't think she was likely to come up here again, though. Not for a while. And she doubted whether George or Katie would bother. There was no need. Not any more.

'It's good, though, isn't it?' she said. 'I mean, what they've done with the place. My mum, and your mum and dad. It is good.'

Katie tugged at a long stalk of grass, pulling it gently from its sheath so that the soft end was still intact. She put it between her teeth and bit into it, her blue eyes glancing briefly down at the farm buildings below.

'Yeah,' she said. 'It's not bad, I suppose.'

Epilogue

The birds and the beasts had done their grisly work, and there was little enough left of the old Queen now. A few bones lay scattered about the tiny glade, some scraps of stained and rotten material, and of course the ancient wicker Gondla, overgrown with grass and weeds. Such were the remains of Ba-betts.

It was a gruesome sight, but this was the way of the Ickri, to give back sustenance to those creatures that in turn sustained the tribe. And so this was a scene to be witnessed in respect before passing by.

Likewise the hidden world of the cave-dwellers was to be explored and explained: the main forge, cold and silent now, and the meeting hall that contained the almanacs – but also the weaving chamber with its empty loom, the storerooms, the inner depths of the smithies, and finally the morgues. Here were the burial chambers of the Tinklers and Troggles, their rituals revealed and then abandoned for ever.

Together they had looked upon each other's past, and so understood one another the better as they planned their future.

They had decided that they would live neither as Ickri nor Tinkler, but rather as the Naiad and Wisp had done. They would learn to crop the land and fish the waters. They would learn to make their winter charcoal, and to weave the withy and the willow into such traps and pens and shelters as they might need. In this way they would add to the knowledge that they already had, and should they ever have to travel out upon the lands of the Gorji again, then they would be prepared.

But meanwhile they were staying put. The long hazy summer lay ahead of them, and so there was opportunity enough to store both food and knowledge against the far-off days of winter. These were easy times once more for Henty and the Woodpecker, last of the little people.

Journeying was not for them, they had decided. Better the certainty of being together in this world than chance to find themselves apart in another. The Various might travel where they would, but Henty and Little-Marten had travelled quite enough already, and had seen what such excursions might bring. They had made their choice – to remain where they were – and in this they had no regret.

What had they to fear? The Gorji were no great threat that they could see, and had brought them no harm. The long-predicted invasion never came. Henty and Little-Marten had walked and talked amongst giants and had witnessed how they lived. What would such a busy people want with this place? No, the two of them were safer now, they felt, than they had ever been.

The archers had gone, and so the throstles and the coneys would soon multiply. There would be meat, and birds' eggs again in season. With only two mouths to feed they would find more than enough here to live on.

That was if there were only ever to be but two mouths . . .

'Dost reckon we shall have childer?' Little-Marten wondered.

'Childer? If we did, then strange childer they'd be,' said Henty. 'We be of a different feather, you and I, like raven and magpie. What sort of wean would a raven and magpie bring into this world?'

'Casn't say.' Little-Marten laughed. 'A rag-pie, maybe?'

'Aye, a rag-pie. Or a maven.'

'Ha! A maven! It don't sound very likely, do it?'

'No,' said Henty. 'Not very.'

Danger, Magic, Friendship, and Betrayal

THE TOUCHSTONE TRILOGY

A gripping trilogy about 11-year-old Midge and her discovery of the Various, a tribe of fairies whose livelihood and existence are becoming increasingly threatened.

622   www. randomhouse.com/teens

J
AUGARDE   Augarde, Steve
          Winterwood

PEACHTREE

ATLANTA-FULTON COUNTY LIBRARY